Rd

Ⓚ
HIS HOME DESTROYED . . .

The horrors exploded in Little Wolf's brain, slamming against his sense of well-being with the impact of a gunshot. His blood seemed to freeze in his veins, and he shook his head violently, trying to erase the vision from his eyes. Far below, where his cabin had once stood, there was now a charred sore in the green of his valley. The white men had found them!

After a paralyzing moment of despair, he collected himself and forced his mind to work on the signs left for him to follow. He began to cover the area, putting together a picture of what had taken place there. It was not pretty, and the more vivid it became, the more his anger grew. There had been twenty or more riders, all on shod horses. They had burned everything to the ground. With that image flaring in his brain, Little Wolf had not the faintest spark of remembrance that he was born a white man. He was Cheyenne pure and simple, and his war with the white man was rekindled into a raging flame. . . .

D0868888

Medicine Creek

Charles G. West

A SIGNET BOOK

SIGNET
Published by New American Library, a division of
Penguin Putnam Inc., 375 Hudson Street,
New York, New York 10014, U.S.A.
Penguin Books Ltd, 27 Wrights Lane,
London W8 5TZ, England
Penguin Books Australia Ltd,
Ringwood, Victoria, Australia
Penguin Books Canada Ltd, 10 Alcorn Avenue
Toronto, Ontario, Canada M4V 3B2
Penguin Books (N.Z.) Ltd, 182–190 Wairau Road
Auckland 10, New Zealand

Penguin Books Ltd, Registered Offices:
Harmondsworth, Middlesex, England

First published by Signet, an imprint of New American Library,
a division of Penguin Putnam Inc.

First Printing, February 2000
10 9 8 7 6 5 4 3 2 1

Thanks, Ronda Ann

1

"That's him! I swear, Lonnie, that's him, all right! I'll never forget that face. Oh, he ain't all painted up for war like the last time I seen him, but it's him, all right."

The man named Lonnie crawled closer to the edge of the clearing and lay flat on his belly behind a short pine. He pulled his field glasses from his jacket pocket and raised them to his eyes. He said nothing for a long time while he scanned the little valley below them, moving the glasses back and forth, from the simple log cabin to the corral, from the lone tipi near the corral to the rough harness shed, and finally to the tall man working with the spotted horse in the corral. After a second sweep of the valley, he spoke, keeping his eyes trained on the tiny ranch below them.

"Hell, Tolbert, how do you know that's the same man? From way over here, it's hard to say who it is. It could be anybody. At this distance, it could be your own brother."

Tolbert snorted indignantly. "My brother ain't never come at me with no damn tommyhawk. I reckon I can see him good enough to know that man down yonder is that murderin' cutthroat Little Wolf. And he's settin' here pretty as you please, not much more than a hatchet throw from the settlement."

"Hell," Lonnie said, "Little Wolf was a Cheyenne hell-raiser." He stared again through the glasses. "I ain't sure that feller ain't white or, leastways, part white."

"I swear, Lonnie, don't you know nuthin'? That's the thing about it! Little Wolf *is* a white man, raised by the Cheyennes and he's as much a damn Injun as any that ever lifted a scalp." He started to expound on his statement when he suddenly interrupted himself. "Look! Look there! What did I tell you? Whaddaya call them, if they ain't Injuns?" He pointed toward the back of the corral where two Indian women approached from the stream, carrying water bags.

Lonnie was silent for a moment, then said, "Well, them's shore 'nuff Injuns." He lowered the glasses and looked at Tolbert. "You sure about this feller Little Wolf?"

Tolbert's expression was dead serious. "Lonnie, I was there at the Little Horn when Custer's hash was fried. I was in that hellfire river when those devils come down on us like a swarm of hornets, and us just trying to save our hair when Major Reno gave the order to fall back to the bluffs. And that devil Little Wolf, he was right there in the middle of it, only he got caught. I was there myself in that damn coulee when they captured him. I seen him good. It's him, all right. I ain't right about a lot of things, but I'm right about that buck."

Lonnie didn't say anything for a little bit while he thought about what Tolbert was telling him. When he did answer, he spoke slowly, as if just thinking out loud. "Well, I reckon you wouldn't hardly be wrong about something like that. And them are Indian women down there. There's no doubt about that. I can't say if they're Cheyenne or Nez Perce." He paused for a moment as if recalling. "That old Injun we seen driving them horses up the valley was damn shore one of them Nez Perces. That man down yonder may or may not be this Little Wolf you talk about, and

I reckon he probably is. But the fact of the matter is, no Injuns got any business in this valley. I thought we run Chief Joseph and them damn Nez Perces out of here last year. I reckon some of 'em just ain't learned their lesson yet." He crawled back away from the edge of the ridge. "I reckon we better get on back to Medicine Creek and call the Vigilance Committee together."

"Hell, why waste time? Why don't we just work our way down the side of this mountain a little and take care of the problem right now? I can take that 'ere Sharps and knock a hole clean through him if I can git a little closer. It wouldn't have to be too much closer at that. Then we could ride in and run the rest of them poor-devil Injuns outta there. Don't seem to be nobody else down there but women and that one old Nez Perce."

Lonnie gave it a few moments' consideration before deciding. "I reckon we better not. It'd be better if we let the committee decide on it first. Then there won't be any question about it. I mean, about him being a white man. You know, nobody ever thought much about it when that other feller was here, that Peterson feller. He was the only one ever came into town. But he ain't been seen or heard of for months. Reckon where he is?"

"Probably planted around here somewheres. That damn Cheyenne most likely slipped a knife in his gizzard when he wasn't lookin'. I'm tellin' you, Lonnie, white or red, or a little of both, that buck's Cheyenne through and through. We best kill him if we get a good shot at him."

"Dammit, Tolbert, there's a right and wrong way to handle this thing. We'll do well to go on back and tell the others what's what out here. Then we can come back with twenty or thirty men and do the job right. That way, it's the committee doing something about it instead of just you and me bushwhacking somebody."

He paused while he took another hard look at the man far below them in the valley. "Besides, we don't know for shore there ain't no more Injun friends of his'n hanging around somewhere." As if to emphasize his concerns, he had no sooner uttered the words when another man, obviously an Indian and a much younger man than the old Nez Perce, appeared from behind the cabin. "See what I'm telling you?" Lonnie asked. "There ain't no tellin' how many bucks are hiding out around here. We better come back with plenty of help."

The object of Lonnie and Tolbert's last remarks paused at the corner of the cabin to watch the tall, dark-haired man in the corral. He could not help but marvel at the firm yet gentle touch his friend employed in the training of the horse. The horse responded as if anxious to do the man's bidding. Sleeps Standing shook his head and smiled as he recalled the many battles he had fought at Little Wolf's side. What an odd contrast: the patient and gentle nature of the horse trainer, when compared to the fierce and relentless warrior of the past. Standing there watching the friend he had known since they were both small boys, Sleeps Standing paused a moment to consider their present state.

Little Wolf still thought a lot about his old friend, Squint Peterson, although he never mentioned it. Sleeps Standing had only known the huge bearlike scout a short time before he was killed, but he too took an instant liking to the white man. It was too bad Squint was killed, but it was a good death. He died in battle, like any warrior should.

For a time, Sleeps Standing thought that Little Wolf was showing signs of going back to the white man's ways, especially when his white brother and his wife came to live with them in the valley. But Tom and

Ruby Allred had been gone for over a month now, back to the Mussleshell country to help a friend run his cattle ranch. As with Squint, Sleeps Standing held a fondness for Tom, for Tom had saved his life when he had been gravely ill, a soldier's bullet festering in his chest. In spite of this, Sleeps Standing was inwardly glad to see Tom and his wife leave the valley. It seemed that almost instantly afterward, Little Wolf reverted back to the upbringing of his youth as the son of Spotted Pony. Now there were only the six of them left; his wife and her sister; Sore Hand, the old Nez Perce; Little Wolf and Rain Song; and himself. To Sleeps Standing, this was enough. If the white man's world would leave them in peace in this secluded valley, no person could ask for more. He put his idle thoughts aside when Little Wolf opened the corral to let the Appaloosa out to graze with the other horses.

"I think you will make a pet out of that horse. He will soon want to sleep in the cabin with you and Rain Song."

Little Wolf smiled. "He's a good horse, smarter than the others, I think." He looped the hackamore he used to train the spotted stallion with over the top rail of the corral and walked over to the water bag Rain Song had hung on the corner of the cabin. "I think I'll give him the bit tomorrow."

Sleeps Standing watched him while he drank from the bag. Finished, he held it out to his friend. Sleeps Standing shook his head no. "I have been thinking—"

"This could be serious," Little Wolf interrupted, pretending to be concerned.

Sleeps Standing ignored the obvious tease. "Sore Hand told me that he saw his brother's son on the far side of the ridge when he went to bring the horses in. He was riding with three other Nez Perce men. They have been hiding in the mountains ever since the rest of their people left with Chief Joseph."

Little Wolf did not reply but listened with interest. This was not unusual—there were more than a few small pockets of free Nez Perces still hiding out in the mountains, refusing to go to the Lapwai reservation in Idaho territory. He met them frequently himself when hunting high up in the mountains.

"Sore Hand said that his nephew and the others with him were going to go north to King George's land. He said it was no longer safe to stay here. The white men from the settlement found one of their camps last week and they were lucky to escape." Sleeps Standing paused to gauge the effect of his words upon his friend. When there was no immediate response, he prodded Little Wolf. "Do you still think we will be left alone here? That the white men will not try to drive us out as they have with the Nez Perce?"

Little Wolf shrugged. "Why should they bother us? We are peaceful here and have little contact with them. We have been here over two years and none of the white men have even found this valley yet."

Sleeps Standing was not reassured. "The white man will not stop until he has all the land. I think that before long, he will want our valley too. Maybe we should also go to King George's land, before the white men send soldiers here to kill us."

"We have lived here in peace and have traded with the people in the settlement for the things we need. They know us. I think we will be left alone." Little Wolf spoke to salve his friend's worries, but inwardly he had to admit to some doubts himself. It had been the natural thing for him to go back to the Cheyenne ways when Tom left. But with Tom gone, it had become necessary for him to ride into Medicine Creek himself to trade his horses for the staples and supplies that were needed. He didn't like doing it. In fact, it had never been his intention to do it. That was Squint's role in their partnership. After Squint was killed, Tom took it on until he decided it best for him and Ruby to head back to the Musselshell. So, once every three or four months, Little Wolf became a white man again. He pushed his long hair up under one of Squint's old hats, put on some clothes and a coat Tom left him for the purpose, and rode into the settlement to trade. On each trip, he made as few contacts as were absolutely necessary, picking up his supplies and fleeing back to the mountains. No one had ever questioned him about the location of his ranch. Arvin Gilbert at the general merchantile had asked about Squint but Little Wolf did not let on that Squint was dead, telling him instead that Squint went back east with Tom.

He suddenly realized that his thoughts had wandered. Sleeps Standing was still watching him intently, waiting for more reassurance. Little Wolf complied, saying, "No, my friend, the men from the settlement will not bother us. They think there are white men here, breeding horses. Some of them drank whiskey with Squint. Why should they bother us?"

Sleeps Standing did not appear to be convinced, but he would not spend additional thought on it if Little Wolf said they would be fine. "I suppose you are right. It's just that these are troublesome times. The Nez Perces lived in peace with the white men for many, many winters until the white men decided they wanted the Nez Perces' land." He shrugged his shoulders. "I hope they don't decide they want this valley."

Little Wolf did not reply but he knew that what Sleeps Standing said was true. The white men had killed the only mother and father he remembered. They had killed his first wife, Morning Sky, and they had put a price upon his head. After fighting the soldiers at the Little Bighorn, he had decided it was time to quit fighting. So he and Squint and Rain Song had traveled far away from the Bighorn Valley until they came upon this little valley in the heart of the Bitterroots. Little Wolf thought they would be safe here, far away from the soldier forts and the gold miners. But in a year's time, the white men had created a settlement no more than thirty miles from the valley, as the hawk flies. Still, he told himself, that was thirty miles of mountains and narrow valleys, tree-covered ridges and rocky streams. The land was not suitable to farm and, as yet, there had been no evidence of gold in the streams. So why would the white men want to take this valley? There was nothing for them here.

"You put tiresome thoughts in my head," Little Wolf said, laughing. "I'm hungry. I think I'll go see if Rain Song has finished cooking the meat."

Puddin Rooks secured the padlock on the plank door of his storeroom and stuck his head through the open kitchen doorway. "Maggie, I'm going to the committee meeting. Don't know when I'll be back."

"Ain't you gon' eat no supper first?" His wife wiped the sweat from her brow with the skirt of her apron. "I was just fixin' to put it on the table."

"Naw. I'll eat somethin' when I get home. I ain't hungry now, nohow. My stomach's been riled up all afternoon. I might get me somethin' to settle it down at the saloon."

"John Rooks," she scolded, being the only person in town who didn't call her husband Puddin, "you better not go gettin' yourself all likkered up in that saloon!"

"Dammit, Maggie, I told you I have to go to a committee meeting. I ain't goin' to get likkered up. You do beat all! As the mayor of Medicine Creek, it's my responsibility to attend committee meetings and the damn saloon is the only place big enough to hold everyone. You know that."

"I know that it usually takes a gracious plenty likker to run one of those committee meetings. I reckon that's the reason you don't hold 'em in the church."

Puddin just shook his head. "I'll be back when I git back," he said and pulled his head back out of the doorway. After all, he was the mayor, and it was his responsibility to chair the Vigilance Committee meetings, even though he was not the elected head of the committee. That would be Franklin Bowers. Puddin pictured Bowers in his mind, tall and lean as a rake with what seemed to be a permanent scowl on his dark face. Bowers was the logical choice for the committee head. He was the town's sheriff and accustomed to dealing with lawbreakers and ruffians of all description. Consequently, he was well suited to handle the Indian problem. That thought caused Puddin to recall a few years back when he first came to the wide river valley that was now home to more than three hundred souls, all white. Of course, it wasn't always like that.

When he rode in from the California coast back in '68, there was a village of Nez Perces living in the upper valley. The Indians welcomed him and the thirty-odd families that pushed through the mountains along with him. They lived in peace with the Indians for half a dozen years. Puddin had brought a milkcow and two pigs with him. The sow was carrying pigs at the time and it was Puddin's intention to start up a hog farm and slaughterhouse and sell his pork products to the families he felt certain would someday settle the valley. His intuition proved to be reliable, for the little settlement of Medicine Creek soon began to bulge with newcomers. The valley was fertile, with good bottom land along the river, and before long, the white settlers began to crowd the peaceful Nez Perces until they moved their village even farther up the valley, beyond the north pass.

Puddin was a prominent citizen from the beginning due to a healthy demand for the pork he produced. Of special popularity was his liver pudding, a delicacy always in demand by the people of the settlement. He soon established a reputation for the salty dish, hence the nickname "Puddin." When the settlement became big enough to be called a town, it was only proper that Puddin be elected mayor, him being one of the founders.

Puddin was proud of the little town and rightfully so. From a collection of a few families in covered wagons to a bonafide settlement of three hundred souls, Medicine Creek boasted two saloons, a general merchantile store, a barbershop, a livery stable, a jail, and a church. Two years before, the Indians gave them a little trouble, but with the help of General Howard and his troopers, they were driven out of the river valley entirely, leaving the valley open for more development.

These were the thoughts that occupied Puddin Rooks's mind as he stepped up on the plank walk in front of Blanton's, a saloon and official meeting hall of the town council and all other committees.

"Well, here's the mayor now." Henry Blanton sang out from behind the bar as Puddin walked through the door. "You're gittin' behind, Puddin. The rest of the boys has already got two or three drinks up on you."

"Howdy, boys," Puddin greeted the gathering of men standing at the bar. There was a general acknowledgment from the row of drinkers. "Henry, lemme have a shot of that firewater there and a glass of beer." He turned around and leaned up against the bar while he waited for Blanton to pour his drink from a dark brown bottle with no label. He nodded toward Franklin Bowers, who returned the gesture. Then Puddin turned to take the shot glass from Henry Blanton. With one abrupt motion, he tilted his head back and tossed the whiskey down, then quickly chased it with a gulp of beer. With clenched teeth, he skinned the fiery liquid down until it settled to burn a hole in his stomach. "Damn," he said, "that's stuff's bad. I wish I had a barrel of it."

Franklin Bowers sidled over. "I reckon we better get down to business while these fellers are still on their feet."

"Frank's right," Puddin announced. "We better get the meeting started." He nodded toward Lonnie Jacobs. "Lonnie, you and Tolbert called for this meeting. Why don't you go ahead and tell us what's on your mind?"

"Well, I'll tell you what we got on our minds. Me and Tolbert run up on a nest of Injuns back in the mountains, not more than a good day's ride from here." He went on to describe the little horse ranch in the secluded valley and the Indian inhabitants observed there. The initial reaction from the gathering of men was one of irritation, what with the fear of Indian attack having been recently snuffed out. One indignant voice after another complained that there might still be some of the original inhabitants remaining.

"Dammit," Puddin Rooks exclaimed, "when are we gonna see the last of them thieving beggars?" His question was answered in a chorus of disgruntled voices. "Where did they come from? Are they some of that bunch that left with Chief Joseph? Or some of that bunch over at Lapwai?"

Tolbert spoke up. "They ain't neither one. These ain't Nez Perce. They's Cheyenne Dog Soldiers."

This brought a stunned silence over the barroom. "What the hell are you talking about, Tolbert?" Franklin Bowers demanded. "Cheyennes? This far west? How do you know they were Cheyenne?"

Tolbert went on to tell of his identification of the renegade Cheyenne warrior, Little Wolf, so close to their homes and loved ones. "He's a white man, raised by the Injuns," he said. He told them that the army had been led to believe that the notorious outlaw had been

killed while trying to escape from an army guard detail, which reportedly took him back to Fort Lincoln to
be hung.

At once there was a general undercurrent of alarm.
"How many?" Bowers wanted to know. When told
that they had seen only three men and three women,
there was an immediate sense of relief, even some
laughter.

"It ain't just six Injuns," Tolbert warned. "It's Little
Wolf. He ain't just no ordinary Injun."

"Didn't you say he was a white man?" Arvin Gilbert
asked.

"Yeah, I did. But you might say it's more like he
used to be white. For my money, he's a hundert-
percent Cheyenne and the rankest buck of the pack at
that."

Arvin scratched his beard thoughtfully. "Surely you
can't be talking about that wild-looking white feller
that comes in my store, lookin' to trade."

Tolbert shrugged his shoulders. "Hell, I don't know
about that—I reckon it could be. I ain't never seen the
feller you're talking about. But I didn't see no other
white feller out there."

"Well, I'll be . . ." Arvin's voice trailed off. "He never
seemed to be looking for no trouble, sort of a quiet
kind of feller."

"Don't let that fool you," Tolbert quickly replied.
"He'd as soon gut ya as look atcha."

Franklin Bowers held his piece for a few moments
while this latest bit of news circulated the saloon. Bowers didn't like Indians and he had a special dislike for
half-breeds. But at the bottom of his list were white
men who turned Injun. He had heard of the Cheyenne
warrior Little Wolf, but he didn't know until that day
that Little Wolf was really a white man. His hand ab-
sentmindedly fell to rest on the handle of his Colt .45

while he considered the prospect of a Cheyenne renegade living right under his nose.

The noisy discussion continued in the crowded barroom until Puddin Rooks banged on the bar with his empty beer glass. "Let's hold it down for a minute, fellers, so we can decide what we oughta do about this. Franklin, you been kind of quiet. What do you think? You reckon we ought to do anything about it, or has ol' Tolbert and Lonnie got us worked up over nuthin?"

Tolbert started to protest, but Bowers silenced him with a hand raised in check. When he spoke, it was without emotion, masking the deep hatred burning inside him for all things Indian. His voice was soft and deep, almost a monotone. "I'll tell you what I think. I think we've got ourselves a problem that's coming, if it ain't already here. From what Lonnie and Tolbert says, I suspect there ain't but a handful of 'em hiding out up there. But if we don't burn 'em out of there now, pretty soon there's gonna be a whole valley full of their friends and cousins. And then it's gonna be just like the Nez Perces all over again, only this time it's gonna be Cheyennes."

Arvin Gilbert spoke up. "Freighter come through here last week told me ol' Dull Knife's Cheyennes broke out of the reservation down in Oklahoma territory and was trying to head back to the north. Maybe this is some of his bunch, come over our way."

"Naw, I don't think so. You said this feller has been holed up in that little valley for a year or two." He paused to reconsider. "'Course, some of them other Injuns Lonnie and Tolbert seen mighta come from Dull Knife's bunch. That's the very reason we need to get rid of that nest before more of 'em move in."

Morgan Sewell, the town's barber and physician, stood quietly drinking a beer, listening to the discussion. He was confused on one point. "Tolbert, are you sure this feller you saw is Little Wolf? Seems to me I heard that the leaders of that trouble they had down at Fort Robinson was Dull Knife and Little Wolf. But they was both old Injun chiefs. This feller you say is Little Wolf is a young feller, according to what Arvin says, and a white man at that."

"Damn, Morgan, you think there ain't but one Injun named Little Wolf?" Tolbert began to get worked up. "Dammit, I know who I seen, and his name is damn shore Little Wolf. And he's damn shore the son of a bitch I seen at the Little Horn."

Franklin Bowers put his hand on Tolbert's arm to calm him down. "Ain't nobody doubting you, Tolbert. You're right, there's a lot of Injuns with the same name. The Little Wolf we got here is the one we better get rid of. Then there won't be but one of 'em with that name. I ain't worried about the other one." He gave Puddin Rooks a long glance, prompting the mayor to make an official move.

"All right, then. Sheriff, you're saying we ought to form a posse to go clean up this bunch. Is that right?"

"It is," Bowers returned.

"Anybody else have anything to say? Are we all agreed on it?" Puddin paused and looked around the room. No one spoke against the action. "All right. Franklin, how many do you think it'll take?"

"I'll take as many as can ride, but I have to have at least twenty." He paused. "Everybody's welcome but the preacher. Don't even tell him about it. We don't need him getting in the way of our business."

There was no shortage of men willing to ride with the sheriff. They had ridden before to take care of other problems, and more than a few of them were presently farming land that had been home to the Nez Perces before they were driven out. Of the twenty-seven citizens assembled in Blanton's saloon, all but one, Morgan Sewell, were ready and willing to ride. Morgan begged off, saying he had to stay close to home because his wife was about to deliver a third child. Of course Blanton had to remain behind. It wouldn't do for the saloon to be closed.

After an additional hour or so of drinking and discussion, the Vigilance Committee meeting broke up and the members dispersed to their homes to gear up for an early morning departure. Their mission, as seen in their minds, was one critical to protect their homes and families from possible savage invasion.

2

"The elk are moving back up the valleys. I want to hunt while there are so many of them in the mountains."

Rain Song smiled at her husband. "Maybe you can kill a young one that has fattened up on the spring grass." She helped Little Wolf as he gathered his weapons and supplies and packed them on the pack horse tied at the cabin door. "Are you going alone?"

"Yes. Since Lark may have her baby any day now, I think Sleeps Standing would rather stay close by. And I want Sore Hand to take care of the horses."

Rain Song laughed. "Why does Sleeps Standing concern himself? He won't be of any help when the baby comes. What do men know of having babies? When the time comes, White Moon and I will help Lark with the child. Sleeps Standing will most likely be in the way. Why don't you take him with you? He'll go if you ask him to."

"I know. I'm leaving him here for my sake, not Lark's. He is so anxious to have a son, I think he might drive me crazy before we got back."

"He shouldn't worry. I believe it's a son. She's carrying the baby too high to be a girl."

He smiled down at her. *She is probably right*, he thought. *She usually is. How could one so young, and seemingly innocent, know so many things?* He paused a moment to look into her eyes. Dark and mysterious, they seemed to reflect the thoughts of his soul. He wondered if she knew the power she held over him. "Well," he finally said, sighing, "if I don't get started, we may not have any meat for you to cook."

She walked with him to his horse. Sleeps Standing was waiting there, talking to Sore Hand. The old Nez Perce nodded and handed the reins to Little Wolf.

"Where will you hunt?" Sleeps Standing asked.

"I think I'll go up through the north pass and back down to the river on the other side. That was a favorite spot of theirs last spring. If the elk are there, I should be back in three days." He stepped up into the saddle and settled himself, then smiled down at his Cheyenne friend. "Maybe you'll be a father when I get back. Rain Song seems to think it'll be a boy."

A broad smile lit up Sleeps Standing's face. "Lark thinks so, too. She is so big, I think it might be a buffalo."

Little Wolf laughed. "Maybe we can raise buffalo along with the Appaloosas." He started to leave, but paused when Rain Song placed her hand upon his leg. They exchanged meaningful glances, all that was necessary between them. Then she stepped away and he wheeled the spotted horse and started toward the head of the valley.

A little more than half a day after Little Wolf led his pack horse down through the narrow pass that separated two steep mountain ridges, a party of twenty-two heavily armed members of the Vigilance Committee crossed the western slope that guarded his little valley. Of the twenty-six who had originally agreed to ride, four had begged off with various excuses. Franklin Bowers was not concerned. Twenty-two should be more than sufficient to handle the problem, and he preferred to leave behind any who might feel a bit squeamish about the business at hand.

The one man he insisted had to come along was the mayor. Puddin Rooks was of little value in a real fight, but Bowers wanted the mayor's presence to give the mission an official blessing. Everybody was hot to act and ready to shed any amount of blood and plunder while the extermination was taking place, and that's what it was, an extermination. But Bowers knew from experience that, after the deed was done and things cooled down, then people found their religion again and started pointing fingers, looking to disassociate themselves from the slaughter. And the fingers usually pointed at the sheriff. In the end, it always turned out that he was the one who led it, that he was the one who did all the killing, that he was responsible for all of it, no matter if there were a hundred who willingly participated. That's the way it had been in Silver Creek and again in Twin Forks, and the reason he drifted into Medicine Creek. *Well*, he thought, *this time it's the committee that's doing the business and the mayor is here to give it sanction.*

Bowers looked upon himself as an exterminator and he was damn good at his job. He had no patience for people who preached peaceful co-existence with the red man. The Injuns had squatted on the land long enough. It was time they were pushed out of the way of the white man's natural right of progress. Manifest Destiny, they labeled it back east in Washington. Well, he had no use for politicians any more than he did for Indians, but he was right there in bed with them on the issue of Manifest Destiny.

Sam Tolbert appeared on the ridge and waved the party up. He waited in a cluster of pines while Bowers and the rest of the men caught up to him. As soon as Bowers pulled up, Tolbert started talking.

"Just like I said, they're down there all right, pretty

as you please. I left Lonnie and Purcell down the other side of the ridge a piece to keep an eye on 'em."

"How many?" Bowers asked.

"I didn't see but five of 'em, the three women and two men. I didn't see Little Wolf, but that don't mean he ain't around."

"Well, I'd like to get 'em all while we're at it." He turned to Puddin Rooks. "We'll leave the men here while I go back down the ridge with Tolbert. We'll watch 'em for a while and wait to make sure they're all there. When I'm ready, I'll send back for you." Puddin nodded. "And, Puddin, don't let 'em start no damn fires. I don't want to signal the damn Injuns that we're here."

After crouching behind a small boulder for a long while, Bowers pulled his watch out of his vest pocket and stared at it. It was almost four o'clock. "Dammit, we've been settin' here for almost an hour and a half." He looked at Tolbert, who was watching the valley below from behind a twisted pine trunk. "Tolbert, are you sure you saw that white man down there?"

"Shore I'm shore," Tolbert shot back, the irritation plain in his tone.

"Were you sober when you were here?"

"As a damn judge. You ask Lonnie. He saw the son of a bitch too, same as me."

His answer did nothing to ease Bowers's irritation. He wanted the king rat of this little camp of vermin. It was getting late and Bowers was determined to move on the camp before darkness found them still in the steep mountain passes that guarded the little valley. It was already too late to make it back to Medicine Creek that day. He at least wanted to get clear of the mountains before making camp.

"Hell," he finally blurted, "he ain't there. Even a lazy buck wouldn't lay around in the cabin this long. He'd have to come out for something to eat."

Lonnie Jacobs moved over next to him. "Well, whaddya wanna do?"

"What do I wanna do?" Bowers got to his feet. "What I came out here to do. I wanna take a piss and then I'm going down there and burn them lice outta there." He motioned toward Purcell. "Go on back and get the rest of 'em. And tell 'em to keep it quiet. I don't wanna give any of 'em time to run off." He watched as Purcell made his way back up the slope.

"What about Little Wolf?" Tolbert asked. "I thought he was the stud buck we was after."

Bowers thought about it for a few moments before answering. "Well, you're right. He is the one we want, but I reckon when we burn his nest out, he'll most likely hightail it as far away from here as he can. He'll damn sure know we won't tolerate his kind around here. He can haul his ass back down to Fort Robinson with the rest of his Cheyenne trash."

"I don't know . . ." Tolbert started, his voice trailing off. Of the committee, he was the only one who had actually seen Little Wolf before he and Lonnie had stumbled upon the Cheyenne's ranch, and that was at the Little Big Horn, when Little Wolf had been stunned by a bullet and was in captivity. And he had heard many stories about the notorious war chief of the Cheyennes from fellow soldiers who had faced Little Wolf in battle. From what he had heard, Little Wolf was no ordinary fighting man. He glanced up at Bowers to find the sheriff glaring at him. Tolbert shrugged his shoulders and said, "I reckon you're right. He's a mean one. I hope he runs, is all I'm saying."

"If he's got any sense, he'll run," Bowers said. "Now let's get down there and take care of these varmints."

As quietly as possible, the party of citizens moved down the slope, staying in the cover of the pines until coming to a ridge about two-thirds of the way down to the grass of the valley floor. Bowers held up his hand

and halted them. While they watched, the two Indian men got on their ponies and rode out toward the horses grazing at the north end of the valley.

"Wait," Bowers cautioned. "They're going to drive the horses in." This couldn't have made his job any easier if they had put a gun to their heads and pulled the trigger themselves. He quickly split his posse into two groups. "You men follow me. We'll cut them two bucks off before they can get back to the cabin. Lonnie, you and Tolbert take the rest of the men and attack the cabin. And, Lonnie, you men keep a sharp eye. A squaw can shoot a gun, same as a buck."

Sleeps Standing circled his pony around to the northeast, coming in behind the horses grazing in the lush valley grass. Sore Hand rode around to the west and together they started the horses moving back down the valley. As they loped along, heading the herd along the eastern side of the stream, Sore Hand pulled up even with Sleeps Standing.

"That little gray mare doubled back again," Sore Hand yelled. "You keep the horses moving and I'll go after her."

Sleeps Standing nodded and kept driving. This was not unusual. The little mare had an independent way about her and she never wanted to be driven with the rest of the horses. He didn't even glance in Sore Hand's direction as he cut out and galloped across the stream in pursuit of the ornery mare. Only moments later, a movement from the base of the ridge to the east caught his attention. In the next instant, a group of riders appeared, charging hard at him. Before he had time to even wonder at their sudden appearance, the air around him was filled with whistling lead. His first thought was to go to the aid of the women and he kicked his pony hard, trying to make a break for the cabin and his rifle.

As he raced over the valley floor, he could see the riders angling to cut him off. They were white men, though not soldiers, he noticed. His pony splashed into the wide stream and struggled to reach the other side. As he pulled up on the bank, he saw another band of men charging down on the cabin. *Lark!* he thought, his heart pounding like a hammer. At that moment, his pony collapsed under him and he tumbled headfirst in the grass. He tried to scramble to his feet, but the impact of the first bullet between his shoulder blades knocked him down on his stomach. He struggled to his knees amid a hailstorm of bullets from the riders bearing down on him. The posse's fire tore into his body as he sank to the ground again and lay still.

In the tipi next to the cabin, there was total panic. It was not the first time the Indian women had experienced the terror that followed a sudden explosion of rifle fire upon a peaceful valley. Their first impulse was to run. Of the three, only Lark thought of defending them. She picked up Sleeps Standing's rifle and tried to load it as she ran from the tipi, following White Moon and Rain Song. Rain Song yelled for them to make for the cabin where there would be better protection from the riders' bullets, which were now ripping holes through the hide covering of the tipi. Before she could load the first cartridge into the chamber, Lark was hit. She screamed in pain and fell. Moments later, she was dead.

White Moon screamed in agony and ran to her sister. She was struck in the forehead as she attempted to lift Lark in her arms. She collapsed over the body of her sister. The horror of the slaughter taking place before her eyes was like an explosion in Rain Song's mind. She fell back against the cabin wall, the whole valley spinning in her head as consciousness slipped away, leaving her in a numbing black void. She no longer heard the cracking rifles or the wild shouts of the men, nor even her own screaming.

At the north end of the valley, chasing the little mare on the far side of the stream, Sore Hand pulled up hard on the reins when he heard the attack behind him. From behind a screen of willows on the bank, he saw the massacre taking place. It had all happened so quickly there was nothing he could do to help his friends. He saw Sleeps Standing go down as the second group of white men fired at the women. There was no time to get to them. Even if there was, he had no weapons other than his knife and a whip. He slid off his pony and tied him in the willows. When he was certain the pony could not be seen, he worked his way back down the creekbank, getting as close as he dared to the cabin. With eyes wide with the horror of the scene, he tried to see who was responsible for this hatred. *He knew these men!* It had been three years since he had set foot in the settlement the white man called Medicine Creek—three years since the white men drove his people from the river valley. But he remembered a few of the men he now saw.

At the cabin, things were already out of hand. Arvin Gilbert shouted for order. "Cease fire, dammit!" he yelled repeatedly as the blood-crazed posse rode around and around the cabin, shooting at everything in sight, intoxicated by the sound of their own gunfire. Puddin Rooks, caught up in the blood-letting, emptied his pistol into White Moon, his eyes wild with the sight of her broken and bleeding body. Finally, when Bowers rode up, there was some semblance of order restored. Behind him, one of the men dragged the body of Sleeps Standing with a rope tied to one ankle.

"Look here, Bowers," Lonnie Jacobs crowed. "I got me two of 'em with one shot." He rolled Lark's body over to display the ugly black bullet hole in her swollen stomach. "This 'un was about to have pups."

Bowers only grunted in reply as he stepped down
from the saddle and walked over to the cabin. Several
of the men were already inside, searching for anything
of value. There wasn't much; a couple of rifles, some
ammunition. These were immediately carried outside
to be displayed. Bowers emerged from the cabin to see
Lonnie Jacobs bending low over one of the women
who had fallen against the side of the cabin.

"Hey!" Tolbert exclaimed. "This 'un ain't dead!" He
backed away a little as if to get an overall view of the
woman. "Hell, she ain't even been shot."

Bowers walked over and stood looking down at the
unconscious woman, "Fetch me that water bag yonder," he said, and held out his hand. When it was
handed to him, he emptied it over the prone body before him. Rain Song immediately stirred and her eyes
fluttered for a moment before opening wide. What she
saw sent her into a fit of panic. She tried to scramble
up but Bowers harshly knocked her back down with
his foot. She lay still then, terrified, waiting for her execution. Bowers drew a long skinning knife from a
sheath on his belt. With his other hand, he grabbed a
handful of Rain Song's hair and jerked her head back,
the honed blade at her throat.

"Hold on, Bowers!" It was John Schuyler. "Let her
go. There ain't no call for that. We done enough
killin'."

"What the hell's wrong with you, Schuyler? This is
what we come out here for, weren't it?" He pressed the
knife blade against the terrified Indian girl's neck, but
he hesitated.

Arvin Gilbert spoke up. "I think we done what we
come to do and that's run 'em out of here. We burn this
place down and the job'll be done. I think we need to
remember we're all Christian men here and we've got
no call to slaughter this girl. She ain't no threat to us
now."

Bowers held no such notions of Christian kindness. As far as he was concerned, she was no different than the vermin he found in his lard cellar—just another rodent to exterminate. He was of a mind to go ahead and slit her throat, but he sensed a general feeling of guilty compassion taking hold of some of the members of the committee. Reluctantly, he released her and pushed her back against the cabin again. "Well, what the hell do you propose to do about her? Just let her go?"

"I didn't say that, but we can take her over to the agency at Lapwai with the rest of them Injuns. That's where they're supposed to be anyway."

Bowers shrugged his shoulders and got to his feet. "Hell, I don't care." He looked around him at the gathering of citizen vigilantes. "Is that what you all want?" There was a general agreement that this would probably be the Christian thing to do. The one objection came from Lonnie Jacobs, who still wanted to kill the woman. Bowers scanned the faces of the rest of the posse. They all seemed reluctant to continue the slaughter. "All right, then, we'll take her prisoner. Let's burn this place to the ground." He stood back and watched while the rest of the posse set fire to everything that would burn. There was a certain satisfaction Bowers felt in watching the flames licking the sides of the log house. He could not, however, avoid a feeling of disappointment knowing that two of the Indians had escaped. Little Wolf would have been a prize worth catching. The other one, the one Tolbert said was an old Nez Perce, was insignificant. "Some of you boys round up them horses." At least there would be some profit shown for their raid.

The bloodlust had consumed Puddin Rooks, and he too was disappointed that most of the posse favored sparing the girl. It was like a fever had taken hold of him and he craved to see more and more blood flow. While most of the men rounded up the horses, he joined Tolbert and Lonnie in mutilating the bodies of the women while Bowers held a terrified Rain Song, making her watch the atrocities committed. The sight sickened Arvin Gilbert and he turned away.

From a bullberry thicket near the head of the valley, Sore Hand watched the flames leaping into the late afternoon sky and the black column of smoke that curled up toward the mountain tops as he quietly sang his song of mourning.

3

High up on a tree-covered ridge that gave way to a small open meadow still covered with about a half foot of snow, Little Wolf stole silently through the pine-scented forest. He moved with the fluid motions of one who had spent his formative years stalking game like that which he saw below him now. Although they snorted and sniffed the air cautiously, the three elk were unaware of the hunter now within a mere fifty yards of where they were grazing.

Staying downwind of his prey, Little Wolf made his way carefully around a fallen tree to a position where he had a clear field of fire. He paused a moment to admire the animals searching for the new spring grass beneath the snow. The older bull was a magnificent animal, almost regal in the way he pawed and scraped away the snow, lifting his head every now and again to look around, testing the wind. The cow and the younger bull pawed at the snow unconcerned. Rain Song would be pleased with the young bull. In moments like these, Little Wolf was always most in tune with the earth, and he felt a oneness with the elk and the mountains surrounding them. Thoughts of his childhood and his boyhood friend, Black Feather, filled his mind as he remembered the hunts they went on together. He shook his head sadly. Born a white child, he could no longer remember the faces of his white father and mother. It seemed impossible to him to even imagine he could feel the love and respect for them that he felt for Spotted Pony and Buffalo Woman, his adoptive Cheyenne parents.

He had not thought of his Indian parents for some time but they were always tucked away in the recesses of his mind. It was Spotted Pony who had given him the name Little Wolf, when he first came upon the child devouring the still warm liver of the grizzly he had killed. A boy of only ten killing a grizzly was unheard of—and big medicine. Spotted Pony had told him that he had taken the power of the bear and the people of his village had honored him, even at that young age.

That was many battles ago. Black Feather was dead, killed by a soldier's bullet. Dead too were Morning Sky, Spotted Pony, and Buffalo Woman, and more recently his friend Squint Peterson.

He shook himself from his brief fit of melancholy. Why, he wondered, were such thoughts invading his mind? He reminded himself of the joy he knew when he was alone in the mountains or with the loving wife who waited for him back in his little valley. There had been many hard times, but life was good now, and he was thankful for that. He roused himself from his moment of reflection and got back to the business at hand. He was not close enough to the elk for a bow shot, so he laid it aside and pulled his rifle up to his shoulder. The younger bull was large for a spike and would provide plenty of meat for this trip. He raised his rifle and aimed at a spot behind the shoulder, about halfway down the chest, and squeezed the trigger. The bull dropped, shot through the lungs.

Little Wolf watched as the old bull and the cow loped off over the ridge and into the trees. Then he went back up the ridge to get his horses. They were tied no more than two hundred yards away but he wasted no time in retrieving them. Scavengers moved in fast on a fresh kill, and he didn't want to give the eagles or crows or magpies a chance to descend on his meat.

The elk had simply collapsed when shot so it remained in a sitting position with all four legs folded up under it. Little Wolf pushed him over on his side in the snow. The bull was so big that it was a fair struggle to pull his back legs around to point them downhill. He worked quickly to part the skin of the beast's belly. He started by cutting two slits in the hide just large enough to place his fingers. Then, inserting his skinning knife, blade up, he split the length of the bull's belly, holding the hide away from the huge gut with his fingers until he had skinned one side. When the animal's bowels pushed forward, he deftly cut around the sack and gutted it. After he had skinned up to the brisket, he reached inside the rib cage and cut out the organs as best he could. Finished, he crammed snow into the bull's chest cavity to absorb the blood. Then he cleaned it out again and packed fresh snow inside. Though a young bull, the elk was far too large to carry, so he went about quartering the meat, cutting away the portions he wanted. While he worked, he thought about Rain Song and could not help but smile. She would scold him for the way he cut up the animal, wasting too much of the meat. Butchering a kill was women's work and she was very confident of her skills. She was a tiny thing compared to him, but she would let him know in no uncertain terms that she was chief of the tipi.

When he had finished one side, he pulled the hide down once more to protect the meat and, with the help of his horse, turned the elk over on the other side and repeated the procedure.

It was late afternoon by the time he had his meat loaded on his packhorse and covered with the hide. He cleaned his hands in the snow and recited a

Cheyenne prayer of thanks to the spirit of the elk for providing him with food. His hunting finished, he started down the mountain. It would be dark soon and he wanted to get farther down from the high country to make camp. The spring nights were still plenty cool so there was no concern for keeping his meat from going bad, even if he made it all the way down to the valley.

Little Wolf started back to his valley the next morning, after a breakfast of fresh elk, washed down with strong black coffee. It would take him most of the day to make the trek through the mountain passes and over the last high ridge that protected his valley. It was a fresh spring day and, though always alert, Little Wolf was in a carefree frame of mind as he followed the rushing stream through a cut in the pass. He was returning home earlier than he expected. That would please Rain Song. She did not like it when he was away for long periods.

The sun was already resting upon the mountaintops to the west when he climbed the last ridge between him and his little valley. Upon reaching the top, he was immediately aware of a thin gray spiral of smoke drifting lazily up from the valley below him. This caused immediate concern, and he prodded his pony for more speed as he made his way through the trees until he reached an open place from which he could observe his valley.

All the horrors of the past exploded in his brain, slamming against his prior sense of well-being with the impact of a gunshot. His blood seemed to freeze in his veins, and he shook his head violently, trying to shake from his eyes the vision that had caused his heart to stop. Far below, where his cabin had once stood, there was now a charred sore in the green of his valley. At once, he felt his muscles tense as his warrior's instinct alerted his body for battle. The white men had found them!

He drove his pony down the ridge, oblivious to the steepness of the slope and the danger of stumbling. The Appaloosa responded to the challenge. He dropped the packhorse's line and left him to follow on his own. It seemed to take forever, but he reached the bottom of the ridge in only a few minutes and was riding hard toward the still smoking embers of his home. As he rode, bent low over his horse's neck, fleeting thoughts raced through his mind, thoughts that maybe all was not as it appeared. Maybe there had been an accident that started a fire. Maybe Rain Song and the others were all right and the worse that faced him was the need to rebuild. They were thoughts of desperation only, and the closer he got, the more he realized it. For everything was destroyed—the cabin, Sleeps Standing's tipi, even the corral poles had been pulled down and thrown on the fire.

He reined the Appaloosa up hard and dismounted. Frantically, he looked around him for signs of life. There was no one there. He prayed that it meant all had escaped this vicious attack, for the signs told him this was white man's work. As he searched the ground for tracks, he discovered the bloodstains in the grass. His heart sank—there had been a lot of blood. He stood up and scanned the ridges all around the valley, searching for answers from somewhere, momentarily at a loss, afraid to speculate on what had happened to his wife and his friends.

After a paralyzing moment of despair, he collected himself and forced his mind to work on the sign left for him to follow. Putting his grief aside, he began to cover the entire area, putting together a picture of what had taken place there. It was not pretty and, the more vivid it became, the more his anger grew. There had been twenty or more riders, all on shod horses.

They had not only burned everything to the ground, it was plain that they had also ridden around and around the burning cabin, probably celebrating their raid. With that image burning in his brain, Little Wolf had not the faintest spark of remembrance that he was born a white man. He was Cheyenne pure and simple, and his war with the white man was rekindled into a raging inferno.

A movement in the southeastern corner of the valley caught Little Wolf's eye, and he pulled his rifle from the buckskin sleeve on his saddle. Moving quickly to a position behind some smoldering fence rails, he waited and watched while a lone rider approached. A moment more and he recognized the slightly bent profile of Sore Hand. He stood up again and returned his rifle to its sling.

The news Sore Hand brought confirmed his fears. The old Nez Perce explained how he had survived the attack by the white citizens committee from the settlement. He was spared because he had chased the little mare. After Little Wolf reassured him that he felt no anger toward him, knowing there was nothing he could do to stop the massacre, Sore Hand described everything he had seen from behind the thicket across the stream.

"Rain Song!" Little Wolf demanded first.

Before he could fully ask the question he dreaded to have answered, Sore Hand interrupted. "She is not dead. They took her away, but I don't know where they took her."

Although still distressing, the news at least gave Little Wolf some sense of hope. If she lived, he would find her. "The others? I saw a lot of blood."

"Dead," Sore Hand said, his voice so soft it was barely audible. He went on to describe the massacre as he observed it from his position up the stream. He told of the murder of Sleeps Standing and the slaughter of the women. Two of the white men took all three scalps and rode circles around the burning cabin shouting and laughing, firing their pistols in the air. He did not know why Rain Song had been spared, only that they tied her hands and put her on a horse and took her with them. When they had gone, Sore Hand came back and wrapped the bodies in any odd pieces of hide he could find from the remains of the tipi. He took the corpses up on the south ridge and fashioned a rough burial platform for them.

There was nothing left of Little Wolf's peaceful life in the secluded valley where he had come with Squint Peterson two years before. Their plan to raise horses and live apart from the squabbles between white men and red had seemed to hold promise for a while. Little Wolf had leaned toward living as a white man, though only slightly. And there had been a bond between himself and his natural brother, Tom Allred. Now Squint was dead and Tom was gone and Little Wolf was once more a Cheyenne renegade, whether by choice or not. His trail had been plainly marked for him. He had lived in the high mountains before, hunted by the white soldiers. It would be that way again, for he would not rest until he had found Rain Song. After that, the deaths of Sleeps Standing, Lark, and White Moon must be avenged.

"Do you know the men who did this?" Little Wolf asked.

Sore Hand nodded his head. "Yes, I know them. There were four who mutilated the bodies. I have seen them in the town. The sheriff was the leader. The others were the two who live in the shack below the fork of the river, and the little man the others call Pudd."

"Pudd?" Little Wolf repeated it several times, watching Sore Hand's face for a reaction. Sore Hand was not sure. Little Wolf thought for a moment before it dawned upon him. "Puddin?" he asked.

Sore Hand nodded his head vigorously up and down. "Pudd," he repeated.

Little Wolf had heard both Squint Peterson and Tom comment on the town's mayor. He had seen the man himself once when he rode into town to trade some pelts. He prodded Sore Hand to remember anything else about the posse of white men, but the old Nez Perce could not offer much more except to recall that the man wearing a badge seemed to be giving the others orders. *So,* Little Wolf thought, *the mayor and the sheriff.* He did not know the other two Sore Hand named, but to make sure the debt was paid, he vowed to himself to kill two white men for each of his friends who were murdered.

They spent but a short time among the ashes of what had been Squint Peterson's dream before riding toward the south ridge. Sore Hand led him to the burial platforms he had constructed for Sleeps Standing, Lark, and White Moon. They paused there while Little Wolf said a final farewell to his longtime friend. Sore Hand apologized for the rudimentary structures he had built, but Little Wolf assured him that Sleeps Standing would understand. He stood there in silence for a while, thinking of the boy he had known so many years ago. He had hunted with him, played at making war with him when they were just children. When they had grown to manhood he had fought beside him, from the raids with the Sioux on the Bozeman, to the annihilation of Custer at Greasy Grass. He would be missed. He turned to Sore Hand. "Come." They left the slope and started back into the mountains.

Little Wolf knew where he was going. There was a ravine close to a waterfall, high up in the rocks and pines. He had been there often while hunting. This would be where he would make his camp for now in case the white men from the settlement decided to come back with soldiers to look for him. The ravine was protected on three sides, and the entrance would be hard to find for someone who did not know of its existence.

4

Lieutenant Brice Paxton, E Company, 1st Cavalry, walked out of Blanton's Saloon in the little settlement the townsfolk had named Medicine Creek. He paused on the porch to stretch in the midday sun while he waited for his fellow officer, Paul Simmons, to follow. A few moments more and Simmons emerged from the dim interior of the saloon, a beer glass still in his hand. Brice turned to address his friend.

"Damn, Paul, what kind of example are you setting?" Brice began in mock disdain. "Here we restrict the men to one glass of beer and you come out working on your second."

"Rank has its privileges," Simmons replied, a smug smile creasing his lips. He knew Brice was joshing him. Brice was senior in rank, although they were both lieutenants, and Brice was in command on this patrol. But there was never any concern between them as to who gave the orders. In fact, they were the best of friends. There was a certain degree of camaraderie among all the junior officers assigned to Fort Lapwai. Paul suspected it was because of the spartan conditions they all shared at the rather neglected post on Lapwai Creek.

"Sergeant Baskin, get 'em mounted up. I want to get back to the fort before dark."

"Yessir," Baskin replied and went back into the saloon to herd the last few stragglers away from the bar.

There would be some halfhearted protests from one or two of the men who thought the imposed limit of one glass of beer was a mite too strict. But Baskin was quick to remind them that Lieutenant Paxton was probably the only officer who would permit any libation at all on a patrol. Baskin could see no harm in it, since they passed right through Medicine Creek on their return to Lapwai anyway. Why not let the men wash some of the dust out of their throats? It sure made Paxton a popular officer with the men, although Colonel Wheaton would probably have the young lieutenant's hide if he knew about it.

Henry Blanton, always glad to see the soldiers in town, walked out on the porch and leaned against a post to watch the patrol mount up. "You boys come on back when you ain't got your nanny with you," he called out good-naturedly. His remark was met with a chorus of catcalls and mock insults. Henry laughed and nodded to Brice. "Lieutenant."

Brice acknowledged the nod and turned back to his sergeant. "We leaving anybody?"

"No, Sir."

"All right, let's go then."

The column had traveled little more than two miles south of Medicine Creek when they met the returning Vigilance Committee, led by Franklin Bowers. Bowers pulled up before the lieutenant and signaled for the posse to halt.

"Afternoon, Sheriff," Brice said as Bowers came closer. "Looks like you've been out on patrol too." He didn't comment on the sizable string of horses being herded along behind them, most of them Appaloosas, a hearty breed originally developed by the Nez Perces.

Bowers nodded to the two officers. Puddin Rooks pulled up beside the sheriff and started to speak but Bowers cut him off. "You might say that, Lieutenant. We had some trouble from some Injuns but we took

care of it. They've been doing some raiding and other
devilment. Nuthin' to bother the army about." He
flashed a sideways glare at Puddin Rooks to warn him
not to volunteer any details. Puddin understood and
held his tongue. Bowers looked back at Brice. "You
boys goin' back to Lapwai?"

"Yep."

"You could do us a favor. We picked up this here
squaw back in the mountains. We was gonna send her
back to the agency over at Lapwai. If you could take
her off our hands, we'd be obliged."

Brice peered around the sheriff to get a better look at
the Indian woman seated on a horse in the middle of
the line of citizens. "Well," he hesitated, "I guess we
could take her for you." He paused to study the
woman a few moments more. "How did you happen
on her? Was she by herself?"

Puddin started to explain. Again Bowers interrupted him. "Her menfolk wanted to make a fight of it,
but there was too many of us. They was kilt and we
didn't want to leave her up in the mountains by herself, figured she'd be better off on the reservation
where she belongs."

"Sergeant, take charge of the woman." Brice glanced
back at Bowers. "Was it necessary to tie her to the saddle?"

"Yeah. She didn't wanna come." Bowers met Brice's
steady gaze, the hint of a smile parting his lips. He
made no effort to disguise the contempt he felt for any
man, and especially an army officer, who showed any
compassion for an Indian.

Brice chose not to speculate on the actual circum-
stances that led to the woman's capture. Whatever
they were, he felt certain that it was not as simple as
Bowers related. He didn't even want to know why
Bowers had led a posse of twenty or more men up into
the mountains in the first place. He had had very little

contact with Bowers, but what he had seen of him, he didn't like.

After they had left the dust of Medicine Creek behind them, Brice called his chief scout in. He was a Nez Perce named Yellow Hand and had ridden with E Company for over a year. A powerfully built man, Yellow Hand was held in some esteem among the other scouts. Most feared him and Brice had never seen him mingle socially with the other scouts, even the Nez Perces of his own tribe. He did not stay in the tent area with the other Indian scouts when at the fort, preferring to remain aloof, living off by himself. The one exception to his aloofness was a somewhat surly brute named Hump. And Sergeant Baskin said that Yellow Hand only tolerated Hump because they were cousins.

Brice ordered the scout to go back and talk to the woman and find out anything he could. Yellow Hand nodded silently and wheeled his pony around toward the rear of the column. After no more than ten or fifteen minutes had passed, Yellow Hand returned to give his report.

"Woman is Cheyenne," Yellow Hand said.

"Cheyenne? What the hell is she doing this far west?"

"She says her husband is Little Wolf, Cheyenne war chief. She says white men attack them and kill sisters and her sister's husband. They want no war, want to live in peace, but white men kill them anyway."

Brice glanced at Paul Simmons, who was riding at his side. "I figured it was something like that," he said. "Well, we can take her over to the agency."

Yellow Hand started to ride out again but Paul stopped him. "Wait a minute, Brice. You know, I was at Fort Lincoln for two months before I was assigned to the Second. It was a few months after Custer got wiped out at Little Big Horn." Brice waited patiently to

see how Paul's story was connected to the Indian
woman. "They were still talking about a Cheyenne
renegade named Little Wolf. Seems like they had captured him and he had escaped. Only the story I heard
was he had been killed during the escape." He paused
a moment before continuing. "You don't suppose this
Little Wolf could be the same one, do you? Because, if
he is, he's wanted by the army."

"Damn. Could be, I guess." Brice thought about it
for a moment. "But, hell, she said the citizens committee killed them all but her anyway."

Paul shook his head. "She said they killed her sisters
and one of her sisters' husband. She didn't say anything about *her* husband."

"Damn, that's right." He paused, thinking. "But you
said this Little Wolf was killed trying to escape when
they were taking him back to Lincoln. So he's supposed to be dead anyway."

"As far as I know, nobody ever found his body."

This was getting more interesting. Brice turned to
Yellow Hand. "Go on back and talk to her again. Try to
find out if her husband is still alive, and where he is."

Yellow Hand nodded and turned to go. As an afterthought, Paul called after him, "And find out if he's a
white man."

When Yellow Hand came back to report on the results of his second interrogation of the Indian woman,
he told Brice that the woman's name was Rain Song.
She had been reluctant to say more about her husband
after already revealing his identity. He had persisted
but she would not admit that her husband had been
white when he was born. He was Cheyenne, she insisted. And, he added, she was certain he would come
for her.

Captain Hollis Malpas, Company Commander, E
Company, 1st Cavalry, stood before the Adjutant's Of-

fice on the south side of the parade ground. He had been talking to a fellow officer but now he paused to watch his second in command, Lieutenant Brice Paxton, as he entered the fort at the head of his fifteen-man patrol. Malpas walked over to meet Brice. Seeing his commanding officer, Brice dismounted after leaving Paul to dismiss the detail. He told Sergeant Baskin to pick two men to remain to guard the woman. That done, he walked toward Malpas.

"What have you got there?" Malpas asked upon seeing the Indian woman.

Brice related the details of the meeting with the citizens of Medicine Creek and the subsequent discussion with Paul and the Nez Perce scout, Yellow Hand. Malpas was intrigued when told of Lieutenant Simmons's story of the Cheyenne renegade, Little Wolf. He, like Brice, had no personal knowledge of the man, but he felt it important enough to make some inquiries to find if there was any interest in a possible Cheyenne war chief hiding out in this part of the country.

"It might be a good idea to keep the woman here for a while until we find out if there is anything to this story. You and Simmons and I should report this to Colonel Wheaton." He took a few steps closer to the woman standing passively between two troopers. "She looks Cheyenne, all right. Bring her along."

Unlike Brice and Captain Malpas, Colonel Wheaton was very familiar with the notorious Little Wolf. After hearing the story of her capture, he eyed the young Cheyenne girl carefully as if examining a trophy. "Yes, gentlemen, I've heard of this renegade. One of my close friends, an officer I served with for four years, was on General Terry's staff when they rode in relief of Major Reno's battalion at the Little Big Horn." He nodded toward Paul Simmons. "What you say is true, Little Wolf was a white man, raised by the Cheyenne from a small boy. And there was quite a bit of controversy over the details of his escape and subsequent death, a death that was never confirmed. If memory serves me, an otherwise brilliant young cavalry officer was dismissed from the army as a result of his negligence—or possibly his involvement—in the renegade's escape."

"What about the woman?" Malpas asked. "Should we send her on over to the agency?"

The colonel did not answer at once, but gazed steadily at Rain Song while he considered the matter. "No, I think it might be a good idea to hold her here for the time being. If this Little Wolf is the same devil that escaped from Lincoln, then the army would love to get their hands on him." He turned to Brice. "Your scout said she's sure her man is going to come for her?"

"Yes, sir."

"Well, we'll just hold her here for a while and see if he tries to get her. We might just catch us a prize polecat in the bargain."

The decision to hold the Indian woman there at the fort for an indefinite period having been made, the matter of where she was to be held had to be determined. It was agreed that she could not be confined in the Guard House since there were already two male occupants serving time there. The building contained only three cells that opened to the guardroom, and Colonel Wheaton thought it unwise to incarcerate a woman in such close quarters with two men. Someone suggested using one of the small compartments in the laundresses' quarters, but Malpas was quick to remind the colonel that the location of the laundresses' quarters, by the creek, left it too isolated.

Paul Simmons spoke up. "How about the hospital? It's close to the Guard House."

"Do you mean to hold her in the ward? I don't think that's a very good idea."

"Not in the ward. I was thinking of the storeroom they converted to a bathroom behind the dispensary. It really is very seldom used and it has only one door and one small window. I should think a woman, especially an Indian woman, could be very comfortable there. One guard outside the door should be all that's needed."

"That sounds fine to me," Colonel Wheaton said. "Anyone else have any suggestions?"

No one did, so Rain Song was taken to the hospital on the north side of the parade ground and placed in the bathroom. Sergeant Baskin sent a man to the kitchen to find something for her to eat and a bucket was placed in the room for her toilet. He made an attempt to tell her that she was not going to be harmed, but she gave no signs of understanding. Finally he called Yellow Hand in to translate for him. She knew enough Nez Perce to communicate easily with the scout, having learned it from Sore Hand. After listening to Yellow Hand, she nodded understanding to Baskin, but her stoic expression remained. When the men turned to leave the room, she made one quiet statement.

"What did she say?" Baskin asked.

"She say, Little Wolf will come."

Baskin smiled. "I hope he does."

Back at the colonel's office, Wheaton dismissed his junior officers. "Hollis," he addressed Captain Malpas, "send some of your scouts over to the agency and spread it around that we've got Little Wolf's woman here at the fort. If the woman's right, and he comes for her, he's going to be looking for her over there."

Little Wolf knelt to examine the many tracks on the trail south of the settlement of Medicine Creek. There had been no need to track the white men and his stolen horses up to that point. He knew where they were going. But here, where the trail forked off to the west, the posse had met another group of riders. He signaled for Sore Hand to come take a look. He said nothing while the old Nez Perce looked closely at the pattern of hoofprints.

Sore Hand looked up at him. "Soldiers," he stated.

Little Wolf nodded agreement. The heavier army mounts left a distinct pattern and a consistent spread that indicated horses walking in a uniform file. "They met these horses," he said, indicating the prints they had been following. "They stopped to talk." Sore Hand nodded agreement and both men followed the soldiers' trail for a few yards, walking slowly, their eyes glued to the ground. Of special interest to Little Wolf was the single set of unshod prints falling in the center of the soldiers' tracks. It was a clear message to him. "The soldiers took Rain Song with them." Sore Hand agreed.

"They take her to the reservation at Lapwai," Sore Hand said.

Little Wolf straightened up and turned to look in the direction of the settlement. The anger that had torn at his soul was still burning brightly, but he had disciplined himself to rein it in, allowing his mind to operate rationally. Following the trail of the white men who had murdered his friends, he had not allowed himself to form mental pictures of what might be happening to Rain Song. Now, his mind was eased a fraction by the knowledge that Rain Song had been handed over to the soldiers. She would probably not be harmed, but merely taken to the reservation.

In one graceful movement, he jumped on his horse and turned away from Medicine Creek. "We'll go to get Rain Song first. I'll come back to settle with the white men after she is safe."

Holding to a fast walk, Little Wolf and Sore Hand reached the eastern slope of the Lapwai Valley after

riding four hours. They circled around the fort, keeping the ridge between them and the garrison below,
and rode on toward the agency. Sore Hand persuaded
Little Wolf that it would be best if he went in alone. He
knew many of the people on the reservation, and he
would find out where Rain Song was and return with
her. There was no need, he insisted, for Little Wolf to
be seen there. Many of the Nez Perces scouted for the
army and might report Little Wolf's presence there.
Little Wolf reluctantly agreed and waited near the
creek while Sore Hand rode down to the agency.

It was well after dark when Little Wolf saw Sore
Hand's form appear in the brambles near the creek. He
walked to meet his friend, alarmed to see that the old
man was alone.

"She is not there," Sore Hand said as soon as he slid
down from his pony. "I saw Two Kills. He was a friend
of my brother. He said they have been told of Rain
Song, that she was being held in the soldier fort. He
said the soldiers know that she is your wife."

"We'll go to the fort," was all he replied, but Little
Wolf's mind was churning with the realization that the
word was now widespread about his true identity. For
two years, he and Squint Peterson had kept to themselves in the mountains and no one seemed to be even
mildly interested in knowing who they were. Squint
showed up in town occasionally to trade for supplies.
He had a few nodding acquaintances but no one got
close enough to pose questions about who he was, or
where he came from. In this part of the country, it
wasn't anybody's business what your past was. A
good portion of the people who wandered into Medicine Creek were there because they were running
away from something.

But that had all changed overnight for Little Wolf.
No longer could he expect to be left alone as long as he
minded his own business. He was now seen as a threat

to the settlement. Worse than that, the army now knew that the escaped Cheyenne warrior, Little Wolf, was at large in this territory. He was once again the hunted, and Rain Song was the bait they were using to set their trap. He blamed himself for not warning Rain Song of the importance of keeping his name secret. She could not understand the white man's ability to send information over such great distances. In her mind, the Little Bighorn was far away, too far for people here to know him.

As he made his way up the creek, letting his pony walk slowly to avoid stumbling in the dark, his mind turned naturally to his Cheyenne and Arapaho upbringing. His father, an Arapaho warrior married to a Cheyenne woman, lived with his wife's people and trained his adopted son in the Cheyenne tradition. Little Wolf now called on that tradition and silently prayed to Man Above to guide him. After riding for no more than a mile from the creek, he abruptly pulled his horse up to a stop and waited for Sore Hand to come up beside him.

"I've changed my mind, old friend. I will go back up in the mountains tomorrow and talk to the spirits. I will eat nothing so that my mind will be clear. It has been a long while since I made medicine and I think it's a good idea to ready myself for war."

Sore Hand thought this a very wise thing to do. They rode into the hills until they found a suitable place for Sore Hand to camp while Little Wolf went off alone to meditate. The next morning, before the sun rose over the hills, Little Wolf rode out.

Lieutenant Brice Paxton lifted the flap of his tent and stood outside while he watched the familiar rawhide-tough figure of Sergeant Lucas Baskin approaching from across the parade ground. Baskin had an odd way of walking, sort of rolling his feet to the outside with his toes out and his heels in, like a duck. Probably from too many years in the stirrups.

Baskin was a good man, Brice decided, and a first-rate sergeant when it came to whipping a troop into shape. Judging by the direction Baskin came from, Brice guessed he had been to the hospital to check on the woman and was now on his way to report to him. Someone called out across the parade ground as Baskin crossed in front of the infantry barracks and the sergeant responded with something Brice couldn't make out from that distance—some of the constant ribbing that went on between the infantry troops and the cavalry, no doubt. At Lapwai, it was usually good-natured. Due to the overcrowded conditions, the barracks were not sufficient to hold all the troops assigned there, so E Company was billeted in tents pitched to the north of the barracks. Brice and the other officers were also billeted in tents apart from the troopers, in the southwest corner of the parade ground.

"Looking for me, Sergeant?" Brice called out when Baskin approached.

"Yessir. I thought you'd probably wanna know how our guest is doing." When Brice nodded, Baskin continued. "Well, I just come from the hospital. I've checked on her twice already today."

"Well, how's she doing?"

"She just sits in the middle of the room all day, singing some kind of chant or somethin'. I tried to talk to her to see if she was gittin' enough to eat, but I couldn't make no sense outta what she said. I got Yellow Hand to go talk to her again and he said she was all right, that all that singing she was doing was a mourning song. She's grieving for her sisters." He paused to scratch his head, puzzled. "She ain't causing no trouble, though, just making a lot of noise." He paused again. "What if that buck of hers don't come for her? How long are we gonna keep her in that room?"

"I don't know. We'll just have to wait and see what the captain says, I guess."

"I just posted one guard at that door. You think we need to put more than one guard on her?"

"I wouldn't think so. There isn't but one door and the window is too small for anyone to squeeze through. One man ought to be able to handle it during the day. Nothin's gonna happen during the day. Nighttime, that's when we have to be ready. After supper I want you to post guards behind the hospital and on the other side of the guard house. And, Sergeant, they've got to stay out of sight." He thought a moment. "And maybe it would be a good idea to have a couple of men hide out in the stables or the hay yard. He'd most likely come in that way, if he comes."

"Yessir," Baskin replied, nodding his head up and down. He hesitated for a moment as if about to ask something else, but then promptly turned on his heel and retraced his steps.

"Baskin, pick good men. We want to catch this son of a gun."

"Yessir, I will, Sir." *You didn't have to tell me that, Sonny,* he thought to himself as he angled across the parade ground toward the E Company tents.

Baskin picked a dozen men for the special guard detail. He planned to use six on duty at a time and let them alternate on two-hour intervals. A half dozen men should be sufficient to snare one Indian warrior, even if that warrior was Little Wolf. Any more than that would be too conspicuous, making it impossible for them all to hide in the shadows.

The first night passed without incident, the sun rising to find the Indian woman still secure in the small room behind the hospital. As the daylight spread across the gray parade ground, Baskin's special guard detail picked up their gear and headed for the mess tent. Since they were on special detail, they were excused from standing in the reveille formation. Baskin advised them that they would again be on the detail that night. He knew they wouldn't mind because they would be excused from duty during the day.

Inside the eight-by-twelve converted storeroom, Rain Song got up from the pallet she had slept on and moved to the one small window. From it, she looked out on the parade ground with frightened eyes. A bugle was blaring and many soldiers came from the buildings and the tents and formed lines before a tall flagpole. There was a great deal of shouting by some of the soldiers and the bugle blared some more. Then there was more shouting and the soldiers broke from the lines they had formed and most of them ran toward the tents again.

Rain Song did not understand any of it. At first, she thought the soldiers were forming to have a dance, like the warriors of her tribe danced before hunting or going on the warpath. That thought caused her to despair because she feared that they were going out to hunt down Little Wolf. There were so many of them! When the soldiers did not jump on their horses and gallop out right away, she was even more puzzled. It added to her despair when she realized that most of the soldiers would stay here at the fort. How could Little Wolf come for her with so many soldiers there? She should not have told the Nez Perce scout that Little Wolf would come. She feared she had caused them to set a trap for him. Why had she so naively thought she could speak freely to the Nez Perce scout? He was now the army's man.

Her thoughts were interrupted by the sound of the door opening behind her. A soldier with a white apron tied around his waist entered the room with a tin plate of food. He placed it down on the floor and stood looking at her for a few moments, a broad grin on his face. Over his shoulder, Rain Song could see the guard outside the door, peering at her. The man in the apron said something to the guard and they both laughed. She did not understand the words, but she recognized the smug expressions. She turned toward the wall and remained there until she heard the door close again.

"She's a purty little thing, ain't she?" the mess attendant commented to the sentry as he pulled the door closed behind him.

"I guess," the sentry replied, "fer an Injun. I ain't paid much attention to her."

The mess attendant laughed. "Boy, you ain't been out here as long as I have." He started off toward the kitchen, shaking his head and still laughing. "Nossir, you ain't been out here nearly as long as I have."

As soon as the door was closed, Rain Song moved quickly to pick up the plate of food. She seated herself in a corner of the small room, her back pressed tightly against the wall, trying to make herself as small as possible while she hurriedly ate the salt pork and beans. Like a caged animal, she paused frequently to listen to the sounds outside her prison. There were many sounds, all strange to her, and frightening to one who could not understand but an occasional word of the language.

She was left alone for over an hour. No one opened the door to look in on her and she heard no one talking outside. After a little more time had passed, she heard the sentry speaking to someone, but she could not understand the words.

"What are you doing back here, Barnhardt?"

"I gotta pick up the squaw's plate."

Inside the room, Rain Song heard the bolt slide and, moments later, the door swung open. She looked up to see the man wearing the apron standing in the open doorway. He stood there for a long moment, his eyes fixed upon her, a grin spread across his face.

"Did you enjoy your breakfast, sweetie?" Barnhardt cooed, glancing at the empty plate. "Peers like you et ever' last crumb of it. I bet you got a healthy appetite for 'bout every'thin, ain'tcha?"

Rain Song did not understand what was said, but she was frightened by the man's tone. She backed into the corner again and waited for him to leave. But he didn't seem in a hurry to leave the room. After ogling the frightened girl for a few moments longer, he glanced back at the open door. The sentry was facing the other way, unconcerned with what was going on inside. He moved closer to her.

"I bet them bucks had a good time with a purty little thing like you, didn't they? You ever done it with a white man?" He reached out and took her arm.

Rain Song drew back, trying to pull her arm away, but Barnhardt's grip was too strong. The man was filthy and he smelled of sweat and dirty dishwater. She tried to pull back into the corner, but he pressed his body firmly against hers. "No!" she insisted, using one of the few English words she knew.

"Well, you can talk after all, only that ain't the right word. 'Yes' is what you need to be saying." She struggled to separate her body from his. "Take it easy, sweetie. I ain't gonna hurt'cha." He tried to pull her skirt up with his free hand.

"Damn!" Barnhardt cried out in pain as the barrel of Brice Paxton's Army Colt cracked down on his forearm. Not knowing at first what had hit him, he turned to defend himself, his face a mask of unbridled rage. Ready to strike back, he raised his fist as if to deliver a blow, but was immediately subdued when he discovered his attacker was an officer.

"Get your sorry ass out of here and don't come back!"

Brice stepped back to make room for the thoroughly chastised mess attendant, who wasted no time in doing as he was ordered. Barnhardt only glanced up once and was met by the scalding glare of the young lieutenant. If he had any thoughts bordering on insolence, he quickly discarded them. Had it been any of the other officers assigned to Lapwai, a surly cur like Barnhardt might have flashed a brief show of defiance. But Brice Paxton was a solidly built man who had a reputation for enjoying a good brawl, as any of the enlisted men who served under him could testify. This was only one of several reasons he was a favorite among the men of E Company.

Brice followed Barnhardt to the door and watched to make sure he headed back to the kitchen before he turned to address the sentry on duty. "Dammit, Prentice, you're not standing out here just to keep that woman from getting away. You're supposed to keep trash like Barnhardt from bothering her."

Not waiting to hear Prentice's apologies or excuses, Brice turned back to the frightened young Indian woman, still huddled back against the corner of the room. He tried to indicate through his limited knowledge of sign that he was sorry for the incident with the mess attendant. She could not understand what he was trying to say, but from his demeanor, she could see that he meant her no harm. She nodded her head and managed a weak smile for his efforts, knowing that he had acted to defend her. He backed out of the room and closed the door.

After leaving the converted storeroom, Brice went directly to the kitchen. Barnhardt, seeing the lieutenant enter, tried to slide unobtrusively to the rear of the room behind a table stacked high with cooking pots. Brice paid no attention to him, looking instead for the mess sergeant.

"Gentry," he called out upon spotting the sergeant, "I don't want that man going anywhere near the Indian woman again." Without looking in his direction, he pointed to the man slinking behind the kitchen pots. "Send somebody else over there to take her food. And I better not hear about anybody else bothering that poor girl. Do I make myself clear on that?"

"Yessir," Sergeant Gentry answered, his expression unchanged from the stoic countenance that generally graced his round face.

Yellow Hand approached the sentry, who was now standing closer to the storeroom door and looking intensely alert since Lieutenant Paxton's reprimand.

"What do you want, Yellow Hand?"

"Lieutenant Paxton wants me to talk to the woman," the scout replied, his voice without emotion as usual, giving a constant impression of indifference.

Private Prentice stepped aside, permitting the scout to enter, but he was still aware of the lieutenant's reprimand. "All right, but make damn sure you don't bother her none."

Yellow Hand did not reply but glanced nonchalantly at the sentry as he reached for the door latch and entered the room. Prentice stood behind him and made sure the door stayed open before returning to his post.

Rain Song looked up quickly when the door opened. At first alarmed when seeing the doorway filled by a figure in army trousers and boots, she then recognized the dark and sharply defined features of the Nez Perce scout who had talked to her earlier. She lowered her gaze and waited for him to speak.

"The lieutenant asked me to talk to you," Yellow Hand started. "He wants to be sure you understand that the soldiers mean you no harm and he is sorry the man from the kitchen offended you. That soldier will bother you no more."

Rain Song nodded, indicating that she understood. "I know that he is a good man."

Yellow Hand stood silently studying the young Cheyenne woman for a long moment. He could not help but admire the fawnlike eyes that gazed unblinking at him now. She was a handsome woman, worthy of a warrior chief. His thoughts were interrupted by her question.

"Why do the soldiers keep me here in this little room?"

"They hope that your man will try to free you. It is him they want. If you were allowed to go to the agency, it would be too easy for him to come for you there."

Rain Song did not respond at once, her eyes thoughtful and deep, then she said, "Little Wolf will come. All the soldiers cannot stop him."

Yellow Hand shook his head slowly. "There are too many soldiers. If he comes, they will catch him—or kill him. I think he will not come. It would be suicide." He hesitated, his eyes never leaving her face. "I think you should forget about this man and think about your own life. You are young and a fine-looking woman. I would be proud to have you for my wife. I am an important man to the soldiers. You would never have to run and hide in the mountains again if you were the wife of an army scout."

Rain Song lowered her gaze once more as she replied. "I am honored that you want me, but I have given my heart to Little Wolf, and there can only be one man for me."

Yellow Hand persisted. "He will not come. He would be a fool to come, and if he does, he's a dead man. Then you will have no husband."

"He will come because he is Little Wolf," she said, her voice barely above a whisper.

Yellow Hand shrugged and turned to leave. "Think about what I have said. I am an important man to the soldiers."

5

Darkness hung like a heavy blanket over the valley. It was a moonless night, the stars only tiny pinpricks in an otherwise solid black sky. The lone figure kneeling at the edge of the creek had not moved a muscle for almost a quarter of an hour as he watched the routine of the soldier fort. The regular passing of the sentries along the outer fence was backlighted by the few small campfires among the rows of tents.

After watching the sentries for a while to determine the interval between their rounds, Little Wolf rose silently. When the two sentries met and then reversed their directions, he quickly made his way to the fence and lightly dropped to the ground on the other side. He was now in the compound. He wasted no time in finding cover behind a building that appeared to be an office of some kind. To his right, there was another building that appeared to be a storeroom or warehouse. He crawled between the two buildings and lay flat on his stomach. The buildings were far enough apart that he could lie there unseen in the darkness while he studied the camp layout.

Where was she being held? His eyes moved back and forth across the expanse of parade ground before him. He had scaled the fence on the south end of the fort because there was practically no activity on this end of the parade ground. There were many soldiers, but most of them were on the eastern side of the compound, some in buildings and more in tents beyond.

As he lay there watching, he memorized the layout of the buildings and eliminated those that he felt sure Rain Song would not be held in. At the far end of the parade ground were two buildings that might be possibilities. There was not enough light to see them clearly but he could see a flagpole in front of one of them. He would have to make his way around the fort and come in at the north end to check them out.

He started to get up when he heard the door of the building on his left open and a soldier walked out on the porch. After stretching his arms up over his head and turning his neck side to side several times, he unbuttoned his pants and proceeded to urinate off the edge of the porch. Finished, the soldier went back inside. Little Wolf got to his feet and moved to a window at the side of the building. Looking in, he could see the soldier seated at a desk, his feet propped on the corner of it. It was apparent that the man was alone. As he anticipated, Rain Song was not there. He quickly retraced his steps, going over the fence once again, and made his way around to the north end of the fort.

Scouting around the western side of the fort to the northern end, he found the stables and beyond, a hay yard. Before moving down to the fence, he paused and watched for a long while. The pause was worthwhile, for after several minutes had passed with no sound save that of an occasional whinny from one of the horses in the stable, he saw the sudden flare of a match when a sentry lit his pipe. In a moment, all was dark once more. Instead of advancing toward the fence and the buildings inside the parade ground, he worked his way around to the far end of the stables.

Crawling almost to the end of the building, Little Wolf paused again to watch and listen. After a few minutes, he heard a muffled voice. His eyes strained to

locate the source. The first voice was answered by a
second voice, and he was able to pinpoint the source.
They were inside the stable. His mind recalled the
many raids he had led on the forts on the Bozeman
trail, when his Cheyennes had ridden with Red
Cloud's Sioux. From those experiences, he knew that
the soldiers posted sentries around the outside of the
stables, not inside. His instincts immediately cautioned him to be alert.

It did not surprise him that there might be a trap laid
for him. The men at the agency had told Sore Hand
that the soldiers knew he was Little Wolf. The fact that
Rain Song was being held at the fort like a prisoner
was indication enough that they hoped to catch him as
well. Where she was being held was still to be determined, so keeping low and moving without sound, he
climbed through the fence around the hay yard and
made his way to the other side. Pausing frequently to
look and listen, he made his way to the parade ground
fence, moving with the quickness and stealth of a
mountain lion.

Kneeling in the dark, watching the building before
him, Little Wolf glanced toward the parade ground
and the soldiers' tents. Off to his left, in the corner of
the fenced parade ground, there was a small group of
tents, apart from the soldiers. Around the fire in the
center of the tents sat a circle of Indians. *Scouts for the
army*, he thought with contempt, *working for the soldiers
who had driven them off their ancestral lands*. Looking
back toward the building with the tall flagpole before
it, he determined it to be the guard house because he
could see the reflection of firelight on the iron bars
over the windows. *This should be the place*, he thought,
and moved up closer before dropping down on his
belly again.

He lay there for a few moments. Suddenly his eye
caught a slight movement near the corner of the build-

ing and, while he watched, a man moved out of the shadow of the building and made his way, half trotting, across the clearing to the next building. Moments later, the man ran back and disappeared into the shadows behind the guard house. Inching his way even closer, Little Wolf could just make out the whispered exchange between the two soldiers hidden in the shadows.

"Dammit, Spruell, you're gonna get our asses chewed out. The lieutenant said to stay out of sight and you go traipse-assing over to the hospital."

"I had to borrow some tobacco from Purcell. Hell, that damn Injun ain't gonna show his ass around here anyway. In a fort full of soldiers? We're just settin' out here in the dark for nuthin'."

Little Wolf studied the situation for a moment. *They expect me to try to break into the guard house*, he said to himself, *so the soldiers are hidden behind the building.* But there were guards behind the hospital too. *Why are they guarding the back of the hospital?* Little Wolf thought. *Unless that is actually where they are holding Rain Song.* Knowing that he must be certain where Rain Song was being held in order to strike quickly and get away safely, he decided he must wait and watch for his opportunity. He considered the possibility of taking out the sentries one by one until he had eliminated all six, but decided the risk was too great. And it would take too long. *I'll just wait and see what happens*, he thought. *Maybe I'll see a better way.* He withdrew to the corner of the fence.

Every few hours throughout the night, new guards would come to relieve the sentries. Little Wolf watched from the corner of the parade ground. Finally, the deep night began to weaken and the blackness began to bleed into the gray light of dawn. It would be daylight before long. As objects around him began to take on a hazy definition, Little Wolf knew he could stay by the fence no longer. Looking around him he searched for a vantage point that might afford a view of both the hospital and guard house while giving him the cover he needed. He decided on the hay yard next to the stables. Crawling until he had retreated a safe distance from the cover of the fence, Little Wolf got to his feet and made his way toward the hay yard fence. On the opposite corner of the hay yard, he found a shallow gully just deep enough to hide him.

The first slender rays of sunlight spread over the hills, causing a long shadow from the stables to creep across the hay yard. Little Wolf waited. A bugle shattered the quiet remnants of the night and, only minutes later, the fort stirred to life. From his vantage point in the gully, he watched as a lone figure walked from the tents, making straight for the guard house. The figure, a soldier with sergeant's stripes on his arm, approached the sentries at the guard house.

"All right, Spruell," Sergeant Baskin called out, "you men are relieved. Go get some breakfast."

As the Cheyenne warrior watched from the gully, Baskin proceeded to the hospital and then to the stables, relieving all six guards. There was one guard left that Little Wolf had not seen in the darkness. He was posted before a door in the rear of the hospital. The sergeant stopped to talk to this guard for a few minutes, but when the sergeant walked away, the guard remained. Little Wolf knew then where Rain Song was.

Considering the situation that was presented him now, Little Wolf's thoughts were interrupted by another bugle call and the camp came alive in earnest. From buildings and tents, soldiers came on the run and began to form lines in the middle of the parade ground. Little Wolf remembered seeing this procedure before while lying in ambush with Black Feather and Sleeps Standing outside the forts on the Powder River. He knew what was next. They would count heads and then stand at attention while the flag was raised up to the top of the tall pole.

It happened just as he anticipated. While the bugle played once more and the flag was slowly raised, Little Wolf noticed that everyone in the entire camp seemed to be rigidly still, unmoving. Only the small circle of Indian scouts that had now gathered around their campfire ignored the bugle. He noticed something else: The sentry posted at the rear of the hospital had turned to face the flag and was also standing at rigid attention. Little Wolf knew at once that this was the opportunity he was waiting for. He watched intently until the soldiers were told to stand at ease and the sentry turned back toward the door.

How long will it take? he wondered. He could move quickly enough to overpower the guard and break into the room, and he could do it in broad daylight. But was there enough time, while the soldiers were distracted, to rescue Rain Song and make it back to the hay yard before he was seen? It was questionable. If he could somehow get closer to the hospital before the formation started, he could make it. He would have to think hard on a way. Now it was time to make his way back to the hills behind the stables and head for his horse. He would leave now and return when night came again.

Rain Song gazed out the one small window at the fading light of another day of captivity. Soon her little room would be dark and she would wrap herself in the blankets provided for her to protect against the night chill. There was a small stove in one end of the converted storeroom, but there was no wood to burn in it. Yellow Hand had told her that the soldier chief thought it unwise to provide her with the means to start a fire. So he had ordered two blankets to be placed in the room for her use. The officer, the one who had interceded on her behalf when she was accosted by the mess attendant, had brought her two additional blankets.

Now, as she stared at the darkening forms that were the hills beyond the valley, she wondered if Little Wolf was near. He might be hiding now in those very hills she was looking toward from her window. She was alone and afraid in this strange place. But she never doubted that he would come for her, in spite of what Yellow Hand said. All the soldiers in the territory could not keep Little Wolf from coming for her. She remained at the window until she could no longer make out the line of hills on the far side of the creek. Then she went to her pallet in the corner of the room and lay down to sleep.

Before she could close her eyes, there was a gentle knock on the door and, a moment later, it was opened a crack. A voice she recognized as that of Yellow Hand whispered her name softly.

"I am here," she replied. "What do you want?"

He pushed the door open wider. "I wanted to make sure you were all right—that you didn't need anything."

"I need to be set free and allowed to go to Little Wolf," she replied without hesitating.

"Ah, but I cannot do that." He stepped inside the door, straining to make out her features in the darkened room. "Can you see that I have come to make sure you are all right? I am concerned for you. Why do you wait for a dead man?"

She was at once alarmed. "Little Wolf is dead?"

"Not yet, but he will be if he tries to see you. There are soldiers surrounding this building. They wait for him. They will kill him if he comes."

She was relieved and sank back to her pallet. "I am Little Wolf's wife. He will come."

Yellow Hand's patience was wearing thin. "They

will hunt him down and kill him even if he doesn't come. You waste your time waiting for him." Then his voice softened once again. "If you were the wife of an army scout, you could have many nice things, things your Cheyenne renegade could never buy you."

"I am Little Wolf's woman. Now, go away and let me sleep."

Unable to hide his anger and frustration, he stormed out the door. Just before slamming it, he uttered one last thing. "We'll see how you feel when your Little Wolf's scalp is hanging from the flagpole, you foolish woman."

After Yellow Hand left, the sentry peeked in to make sure everything was as it should be. Satisfied, he closed the door again, leaving her to drift off to sleep.

Morning light squeezed through the tiny window and fell across the face of the sleeping woman. She awoke immediately and lay there for a moment, listening for the first bugle call that told the soldiers to get up. Another night had passed and still Little Wolf had not come for her.

A few moments before Rain Song was awakened, a dark, silent form moved quickly cross the parade ground fence and disappeared behind the rows of tents. As the first gray light descended upon the sleeping camp, a drowsy Nez Perce scout emerged from his tent and, after relieving his bladder, went to rekindle the campfire. In a few moments, he was joined by another Indian, who set about making some coffee. Before the bugle blew reveille, a group of six Indian scouts had gathered around the now healthy campfire, talking and waiting for the soldiers to finish with their silly formations and get on with breakfast.

As the first bugle call sounded, no one paid any attention to the tall, lean figure in buckskins that suddenly appeared at the edge of the circle until he seated himself among those gathered there. At once, the talking stopped as the scouts at first looked at the stranger in curiosity. Then it seemed there was a total, heavy silence that descended upon the circle. None of the Nez Perce scouts had ever seen him before, but they all knew instantly that the imposing figure seated among them was none other than the white Cheyenne, Little Wolf.

There was not a word spoken. The fierce eyes of the Cheyenne warrior told them all that needed to be said. There was no thought of crying out the alarm. It was almost as if they were spellbound by a deadly serpent. And yet, the Nez Perces were not frozen by fear of the tall warrior seated across from them, his rifle lying across his thighs. They were moved by his brazen appearance in the fort, one warrior among the many hundred soldiers, fearless and determined, a symbol of what they were once—free and untamed. Not one of them was inclined to sound the alarm on a warrior who had become almost a legend among the Cheyenne and the Sioux, even when Sergeant Baskin walked across the parade ground on his way to relieve the special guard detail around the hospital.

So they sat silently watching the Cheyenne war chief until the bugle blew again, calling the soldiers to the morning formation. Little Wolf's gaze traversed the circle, looking into the eyes of each man. Then, still without a word, he nodded briefly and got to his feet, leaving them to talk among themselves quietly.

Private Edmond Banks turned toward the flagpole and snapped to attention as the bugler announced the raising of the flag. He came to Present Arms moments before the blow to the back of his skull engulfed him in darkness. He was to remember nothing that happened afterward as his unconscious body was dragged back against the wall.

Inside the converted storeroom, Rain Song was startled almost to the point of crying out when the door was kicked open with such force as to almost splinter it. The next instant she was flying into the arms of her husband. He took a moment to lift her gently off her feet and embrace her before springing into action once more.

"Come, Little One," he said softly, and led her out the door. They moved quickly around the hospital building. He lifted her over the fence and, holding her hand tightly, ran toward the stables. Knowing that the sentries were no longer there, he ran through the stables and out the back. A short way up the hill behind, the horses waited, held by Sore Hand. He paused a moment to listen for sounds of pursuit. There were none.

6

"Don't tell me that! Dammit, man, don't tell me that!" Colonel Wheaton sprang up from his desk so violently that he knocked his chair over. Lieutenant Paul Simmons jumped to retrieve the errant chair and replace it while the colonel, ignoring him, stormed around his desk in order to thrust his face inches from that of a totally chastised Captain Malpas. Wheaton's searing glare held Malpas transfixed and unable to reply in his own defense. After what seemed to the younger officers in the room to be an eternity, the colonel spoke again, this time softly and under control. "Captain Malpas, I hope to hell you're not telling me that one lone savage—*one man*—politely walked right into this fort and took the woman, and then walked out unnoticed. Explain that to me, Captain. How could that happen when you were supposedly set up and waiting for him?"

Malpas shifted uncomfortably from one foot to the other, straining to think of an excuse, knowing there was none. He glanced quickly at Lieutenant Paxton for support. Brice, standing to one side with Paul Simmons, would have come to his company commander's aid, but he had nothing to offer either. The fact of the matter was, just as the colonel stated, Little Wolf had simply walked in and took the woman. She had promised that he would. No shots fired, no pursuit mounted, the only casualty being one private with a busted head. Looking back at the colonel, Malpas finally stammered an attempt to excuse his actions. "Sir, I had six men, seven counting the guard on the door, watching that room every night. I . . . we . . ."—he glanced again at Brice Paxton—"never considered the possibility the renegade would walk in in broad daylight with the whole regiment in formation."

"Evidently this savage is smarter than you gave him credit for. He's damn sure as brazen as his reputation contends." At last releasing Malpas from his paralyzing glare, Wheaton moved back to his desk and sat down on the corner of it. He had counted heavily on the capture of the notorious Cheyenne war chief. It would have gone a long way toward a possible reassignment from the lonely post on Lapwai Creek. It was even more distasteful to learn that the infamous Little Wolf had been living practically under his nose, for two years—while everyone assumed him dead. "Dammit!" he uttered under his breath. Then looking up at Malpas again, he ordered, "Well, mister, you lost him. Dammit, you find him!" He got to his feet again. "I want that son of a bitch, Malpas. Do I make myself clear?"

"Yessir," Malpas stammered, his face still a bright crimson from the dressing down he had just received.

Brice Paxton, seeing that his captain was at a loss for words at the moment, stepped forward to assist. "Sir, on Captain Malpas's orders, B Troop has already been advised to draw ammunition and rations and be ready to ride. We've sent for Yellow Hand. He's the best scout we've got. If anyone can trail the renegade, he can."

Wheaton turned his flint-like gaze upon the younger officer. "I want that son of a bitch," he reiterated, his voice a low growl.

*   *   *

Yellow Hand bent low to the ground, studying the faint hoofprints in the pine needles. After a moment, he stood up and looked toward the south. Then he turned back to Captain Malpas. "One other wait here with horses—one with horseshoes, two no shoes. Go up behind hill. That way." He pointed south.

Malpas nodded, then looked at Brice. "Looks like he stole a horse too."

"Looks like," Brice agreed.

"Let's get after them," Malpas said and signaled the troop forward.

Yellow Hand hopped up on his horse and moved out ahead of the column. No man among them was more anxious to overtake Little Wolf than he. On any given day, he harbored a certain amount of contempt for what he considered the incompetence of the captain. This morning he was silently angry at the total incompetence of the guard detail that was supposed to set a trap for the Cheyenne renegade. He had counted upon the success of the trap and the imprisonment of Little Wolf, maybe even his execution, to clear the way to Rain Song's heart. He had been struck by the beauty of the Cheyenne girl and was confident that he could soon make her forget Little Wolf. Now, she was bound to see her husband in an even more favorable light since he had defied the might of the army and had come to rescue her. Now Yellow Hand could no longer depend upon the soldiers to eliminate his competitor. He was determined to track him down and, when the opportunity appeared, he intended to kill Little Wolf before the soldiers had a chance to capture him. If Little Wolf was dead, there would no longer be any reason for Rain Song to reject him.

The trail skirted around the western side of the fort. Once it turned east again and came back to the creek, south of the fort, the troop was forced to sit and wait while Yellow Hand scouted the banks with two other

Nez Perce scouts. The sun was already high above the hills when one of the scouts finally found the trail that exited from the creek. Yellow Hand followed it, closely examining it as he did, for a distance of almost a mile before going back to report to Malpas.

"Little Wolf left creek maybe half mile," he said, pointing toward the south. "Head that way." He indicated a circle back toward the northeast.

They took up the trail again, moving as rapidly as possible when the trail was easy to distinguish, slowing sometimes to a temporary halt when Yellow Hand had to search for prints. All the while, Brice could feel the urgency that spurred Malpas on. He understood the colonel's irritation over the failure of their attempt to trap Little Wolf. But he had to admit, he himself had given no consideration to the notion there was any possibility the renegade would walk in right in the middle of the morning formation. Adding to his bewilderment was the fact that the renegade was not noticed by anyone. There were at least a half dozen Nez Perce scouts sitting around a campfire no more than forty yards from the hospital. Surely one would think that one of them might have noticed a stranger walking right by them.

Well, he thought, *there's a pretty good chance we'll catch him. Yellow Hand in particular seems determined to track him down.* Brice could not remember seeing Yellow Hand work so relentlessly and carefully over a trail before.

It was not to be as easy as Brice had hoped. Nightfall found them skirting the mountains at a point approximately eight or ten miles east of the little settlement of Medicine Creek. While Yellow Hand and his scouts were still able to follow the trail, it had become increasingly harder, slowing their progress. Captain Malpas finally called a halt to the day's march and ordered the troop to encamp near the banks of a shallow stream. They would take up the trail again at first light.

Little Wolf made his way down from the rock ledge where he had gone to watch their backtrail. As he approached the pine thicket near the stream where he had made their camp, Rain Song rose from beside the small fire and hurried to meet him. She hugged him tightly around his waist, the top of her head no higher than his shoulder. There had been little time for embraces during the ride from Lapwai and she was anxious now to feel the lean, muscular body of her husband. She felt a need to assure herself that he had really come for her and was not a phantom image in her mind. Yellow Hand had insisted that the soldiers would kill Little Wolf, and while she did not believe it could happen, still there had been small worrisome fears that crept into her mind at night. Now she wanted to touch him to make sure he was always there.

She looked up into his face. "I have cooked some meat for you." She shifted her balance toward the old Nez Perce seated by the fire, chewing on a strip of roasted meat. "Come, before Sore Hand eats it all up," she teased. She took his hand and led him to the fire.

"There is no hurry," Sore Hand said. "My teeth are so old they hurt when I chew this meat. It would take me two days to eat all this."

Little Wolf laughed and sat down beside the old man. "You should have killed a young deer instead of this old buck."

"I would have, if we had had the time. We're lucky to have this old buck." He paused to pull the strip of venison from his mouth and examine it, turning it from one side to the other. Then he put it back in his mouth and began to gnaw it again. "It wouldn't make any difference if he was a fawn. These old teeth are worn out. I lost another one yesterday." He pulled his lip up to show them the gap.

"I am only teasing, my friend. We are grateful for the meat." He paused for a moment. "You have done well. I could not have rescued Rain Song without you." He laid a hand on Sore Hand's shoulder and patted it.

Sore Hand only grunted in reply. He appreciated the sentiment behind the remark, but he knew Little Wolf could have rescued Rain Song without his help. He paused in his chewing. "Do you think the soldiers are still following us?"

"I don't know. We'll see tomorrow. If they are still following, we'll lead them up into the mountains. We have to lose them before we go to our camp by the waterfall." He didn't reveal his feeling inside that the soldiers would continue to dog them until they caught him and killed him. He knew there was no amnesty for him. He was a Cheyenne warrior and he would be hunted like Dull Knife and Two Moon, and like the Sioux chiefs, Sitting Bull and Crazy Horse. The soldiers would not be content until all the free Indians were either on the reservation or dead.

"He is good," Little Wolf remarked to Sore Hand as they watched the column of troopers making their way along the bottom of a deep ravine some six or seven miles behind them. "The one scout, out in front of the other two, he is the one who stays on our trail."

"I think it is the one called Yellow Hand," Rain Song said. "He said he was the head scout for the soldiers."

Little Wolf turned to look at his wife. "Yellow Hand, huh? He is the one who talked for the soldiers?" She answered with a nod. "Well, this Yellow Hand might become a problem for us. He is good." He got to his feet. "Come, we'll go down the other side of the mountain to the river and see if we can take him for a swim. Then I think we'll be able to go to our camp."

*   *   *

Yellow Hand sat on his haunches, stirring the ashes of a campfire by the river. He turned to look at the officers as they rode up to him. "This is where they camped last night," he said without emotion. "Trail leads that way." He pointed.

Brice glanced at Hollis Malpas, waiting for a signal to march. Malpas seemed hesitant, as if unsure whether to continue or not. After a moment, Brice prompted him. "The colonel will be fit to be tied if we don't bring this man back."

Malpas gave him a quick look, nodded, then gave the order, "All right, Yellow Hand. Lead out and we'll follow."

For the balance of the morning, the troop worked slowly up the mountain and down into a small valley, trying to stay on a trail that became more and more difficult to follow. Finally, at the head of a ravine, the trail seemed to disappear, leaving the line of troopers facing a sheer rock wall. Malpas called a halt for the noon meal while Yellow Hand and the other two Nez Perce scouts combed the sides of the ravine in an effort to find a track.

Paul Simmons helped himself to a cup of coffee, poured from the pot Sergeant Baskin had simmering over a small fire. He ambled over and sat down on a rock beside Brice Paxton, then watched with some amusement as Yellow Hand and his two associates inched their way along the steep sides of the ravine. "Looks like our scout has met his match," he said between sips of the hot black liquid.

Brice grunted. "Yeah, looks like. I've got a feeling this Little Wolf is no ordinary Indian."

"It seems plain as day to me. He rode up here until he came to this rock wall. Then he just flapped his arms and flew over the mountain."

Brice laughed. "Maybe, but I doubt it."

At first baffled, Yellow Hand became furious after two hours had passed, still without any indication that Little Wolf had ridden beyond that point at the base of the rock. He considered himself second to no man in following a trail. Three horses could not have simply vanished. He examined the face of the wall, looking for some hidden passage. There was none. His Nez Perce scouts were already admitting defeat and doing little more than poking around aimlessly, waiting for Yellow Hand to give up. As the afternoon wore on, Captain Malpas grew impatient and, expressing concern about being caught in the narrow ravine by darkness, made the decision to pull back to the base of the ravine and make camp by a small stream. This, he felt, made more sense than riding around in the mountains, hoping to stumble upon a trail. His lieutenants agreed, having no better suggestions of their own. So they went into camp while the scouts continued to comb the ravine.

B Troop spent the next morning languishing by the busy little stream at the head of the ravine. The troopers were content to lounge on the grassy banks while their horses grazed. Captain Malpas, however, wallowed in an agitated state. After noontime came and there was still no progress on the part of his scouts, he ordered Baskin to organize the men into scouting parties of four men each to help the Nez Perces. This, Brice recognized, was done not so much to find the elusive sign. Rather, it was because of Malpas's irritation at seeing the men idle for so long.

Malpas's decision to keep his men occupied was not well received by Yellow Hand, who saw the order as simply one more impediment to his search. His initial thought proved to be accurate as the sides of the ravine soon became covered with tracks, making a difficult job impossible. The frustration he felt began to eat a hole in his stomach and it was bitterly galling for him to have to finally accept defeat. Had he known that he had missed the most critical sign before entering the ravine, he would have been doubly furious.

Little Wolf had not led the three horses into the ravine. Leaving the stream where the soldiers were now camped, he had carefully led the horses out of the water onto a shale outcropping. Changing horses with Rain Song, he told Sore Hand to lead Rain Song up the ridge beside the ravine. Then he rode the shod horse into the ravine, being careful to pick his way along the bottom so as not to leave more than a few prints. When he came to the boxed-in portion of the ravine, he led the horse back the way he had come until clear of the ravine. To complete his deception, he retraced his steps on foot, carefully covering any tracks that revealed his return trip, leaving only a couple of clear prints that indicated a trail into the ravine. Satisfied that he had done his work well, he then followed Rain Song and Sore Hand up over the top of the ridge.

Admitting that the Cheyenne had stymied them, Malpas gave the order to return to the fort. He could see no prospect of success in riding haphazardly around in the mountains when every hour meant the renegade was farther and farther away. One of Yellow Hand's Nez Perce scouts paused to look at a distinct print where a horse had slipped on the bank of the stream. Since it was that of a shod horse, he assumed that it was made by one of the troopers. The fact that it was pointed toward the ridge seemed to hold no significance for him. He jumped on the back of his pony and galloped off to rejoin the head of the column.

High up the mountainside, beyond the ridge, Little Wolf sat watching the actions of the soldiers below him as they searched for his trail. From that distance, he could not make out the features of the Nez Perce called Yellow Hand, but he could see the dogged determination of the scout as he combed the ravine for sign. He seemed much more dedicated than his two brothers. Little Wolf wondered if there was a reason. He would have to question Rain Song further on the matter. When the soldiers finally mounted up and filed out of the ravine, Little Wolf got up and made his way back over the crest of the hill. "We can go now. The soldiers have given up," he announced to Rain Song and Sore Hand. *At least for now*, he thought to himself. *They will be back.*

7

Puddin Rooks was not especially happy with his
share of the spoils. There were enough horses captured from Little Wolf for each man who rode with the
posse to get one. This was fair pay to ride against the
Cheyenne, and Puddin had no quarrel with that. What
bothered Puddin was the three horses left over. Bowers had laid claim to two of them, claiming he had a
right to them because he led the raid. Puddin might
even have stood for that. But the other horse, a fine-
looking Appaloosa about fourteen hands high, somehow wound up on Sam Tolbert's string. Puddin was
the mayor, and he had expected to be treated fairly
and awarded spoils according to his rank.

When the posse had returned to Medicine Creek
after the raid, Rooks had to go home to attend to some
business. He didn't have time even to attend the cele-
bration at Blanton's Saloon, so he assumed Franklin
Bowers would watch out for his interests when the
horses were divided up. He was on his way to see
Bowers now.

It was past suppertime so he didn't expect to find
the sheriff at the jail. He went directly to Blanton's instead, where he was certain he would find the raw-
boned Bowers having his evening drink. Bowers was
there all right, his chair tilted back against the wall, a
shot glass in one hand and a cigar in the other.

Puddin acknowledged the scattered howdies from

several of his fellow townsfolk as he made his way to the back of the saloon and Bowers's table. He pulled a chair back and sat down facing the sheriff. "Bowers, we need to talk a little bit about somethin'."

Bowers gazed coldly into Puddin's eyes for several seconds without saying a word. Then, just before Puddin started to repeat his words, he acknowledged the mayor's presence. "Evening, Mayor." He flicked the ashes from his cigar on the floor and took a long drag. "What are you all lathered up about?"

"It's them horses, Bowers. I don't think we did a fair split on 'em."

Bowers was not concerned. "Why? You got a horse, didn't you? Same as everybody else."

"Well, no. I mean, yeah, I got a horse. That ain't the point. What I'm sayin' is, there was three horses left over after everybody got one. You took two of 'em, and I say that's fine. You're the sheriff, you led the posse. But I'm the mayor, dammit. How come Sam Tolbert got the other horse? It shoulda been mine."

"Hell, Puddin, I don't know." In fact, he didn't care. "He just did. I 'spect he figured it belonged to him because he's the one found the damn Injuns in the first place. That seems fair enough to me."

Puddin sat looking at Bowers for a few moments. It was not the response he was looking for. "I don't suppose you'd consider parting with one of yours."

Bowers just grinned. After he tossed the shot of whiskey back, he wiped his mouth with the back of his hand. "Reckon not. I figure I put my life on the line for this little town for damn little pay. I earned them horses." He could see that Puddin was not at all happy with his lack of compassion, but he also knew Puddin Rooks didn't have sand enough to do anything about it—not with him, at least. "If you don't think Tolbert shoulda got the extra horse, you can talk to him about it."

"Maybe I'll do that," Puddin replied weakly. "Have you seen him in town today?"

"Nope. I guess he's out at that little patch of weeds him and Lonnie call a ranch."

The two men sat in silence for a few minutes before Puddin got to his feet, mumbling something about needing to do something for Maggie. Bowers watched him as he made his way back toward the front door, stopping to exchange a few words with first one man and then another. *Came in here all ready to demand one of my horses, the little turd. He can't ride worth a shit anyway,* Bowers thought.

It was dark when Puddin left Blanton's. There had been rain the day before and Medicine Creek's main street consisted of a rank mush made of equal parts mud and horse droppings. Puddin had to shield his eyes from the glare of the bright lamps streaming through Blanton's windows as he carefully stepped off the wooden steps and made his way along the street. "Damn!" he muttered as what appeared to be solid footing turned out to be a nasty puddle, and he hastily stepped back and went around it. He made his way past Arvin Gilbert's General Merchantile, the windows dark now, and rounded the corner of the building.

Puddin didn't see the shadowed form standing in the alley between the general store and Morgan Sewell's barber shop until he was no more than ten feet from him. Puddin glanced up, startled. "Whoa, mister. I dang near ran into you." When there was no response, Puddin stopped in his tracks and squinted his eyes, straining to make out who it was. When he realized what he was actually looking at, he simply froze with fear. There before him in that dark place, he stood face to face with death in the form of a Cheyenne warrior, his bow fully drawn, the arrow aimed point-blank at his heart. The silence roared in Puddin

Rooks's ears and the terror that paralyzed his whole body left him too numb to react, except for a step backward in response to the blow to his chest. He looked down in horror at the arrow shaft buried deep in his lungs. Dropping to his knees, he began to whimper as he felt his life draining from his body.

Unmoving after releasing the fatal arrow, Little Wolf watched, stone-faced and without emotion, as the first of his friends' murderers slowly sank to the ground, gasping feebly for breath. Watching the whimpering little man, Little Wolf could not help but recall the scene as Sore Hand had described it—and he wondered if Puddin was feeling the same horror that White Moon and Lark had felt as he carved them up.

After a few moments, the Cheyenne warrior, moving without haste, walked over and slit the dying man's throat. Then he took his scalp. Before he left, Little Wolf ripped Puddin's shirt away and, with his knife, carved one solitary mark above the arrow shaft. He made no attempt to extract his arrow. He wanted those who found the man to know it was Cheyenne.

Henry Blanton was the first to realize that Puddin Rooks might be a victim of foul play. After eleven o'clock came and went and Puddin still had not returned home, Maggie became worried and sent their fourteen-year-old boy to the saloon to fetch his father. It had been several hours since Puddin had said his good-nights and started for home. Since home was no more than a twenty-minute walk, Blanton saw the need for concern. He questioned the few hangers-on at the bar, as well as the five still playing poker at the back table. No one had seen Puddin since he left earlier in the evening. Blanton sent the boy to get Sheriff Bowers.

Bowers was just retiring for the night, but he pulled his boots back on and accompanied the boy back to

Blanton's. With a lantern and several of the men at the
saloon, they retraced the path Puddin would have
taken to return home. It didn't take long to discover
the body of the late Puddin Rooks. His boy had passed
within ten feet of the body, failing to see it in the dark
alleyway.

The murder of Puddin Rooks was a discomforting
event for the people of Medicine Creek. It had been
some time now since the threat of Indian trouble had
disappeared. Now, right in the middle of town, their
mayor was brutally slain, and by all indications it was
the work of Indians. More than one of Medicine
Creek's citizens had already been by the sheriff's office
to express their concern, much to Franklin Bowers's irritation.

Sam Tolbert and his partner, Lonnie Jacobs, were
among those who came into town upon hearing the
news. After stopping by Morgan Sewell's barbershop
to view the body, they went to the jail to talk with the
sheriff.

"Morgan said Puddin had an arrow in his chest,"
Tolbert said. "What kind of arrow was it? Nez Perce?"

Bowers shrugged. "Hell, I don't know, maybe. I
don't know one arrow from another."

"I might," Tolbert said. "When I was in the army, I
rode against enough Sioux, Arapaho, and Cheyenne to
know one of them when I seen it."

Bowers reached behind him and pulled the arrow
from under the table. "Here it is."

Tolbert took the arrow and studied it for only a moment before announcing, "Cheyenne." He glanced up
at Bowers.

Bowers's expression did not change. "I figured it
might be." There was no comment from any of the
three for a few moments. None was necessary, as they
were all thinking the same thing.

Finally Lonnie put it into words. "We shouldn't have killed them people."

"We should have killed 'em *all*," Bowers quickly corrected him. "We should have stayed there and killed that son of a bitch when he came back."

"I figured he'd run," Lonnie said, glancing nervously over his shoulder even as he said it.

Bowers was unmoved. "Well, I expect he might, now that he's had his revenge. But I tell you this, I hope to hell he ain't. Ain't nobody coming in my town and murdering somebody and living to tell about it.

The sheriff's confident bluster served to reassure Lonnie somewhat. "Yeah, I expect he ain't fool enough to hang around here after what he done to poor ol' Puddin. I guess he went after Puddin because he was the mayor." He shook his head and added, "Poor ol' Puddin."

"Just the same," Tolbert cautioned, "it wouldn't hurt to keep a sharp eye out. This ain't no ordinary Injun."

"They're all ordinary Injuns," Bowers said, his face a twisted mask of contempt.

On a tree-covered ridge south of the little valley where he had built his home, Little Wolf made his way up through the pines to the platforms Sore Hand had constructed. He tied Puddin Rooks's scalp to the platform at Sleeps Standing's feet. "This is just the beginning, my brother. You will be avenged, I promise you that." He stood for a few minutes, listening to the moaning of the wind in the pines. It seemed to be mourning the loss of his childhood friend. After a time, he leaped upon his pony's back and headed for his camp by the waterfall. There was work to be done, but first he must rest. He had ridden through most of the night and he was tired.

*　　*　　*

Franklin Bowers emerged from the darkened stable into the dusky light of twilight. He carried his rifle cradled across his arms. Pausing to look to his right and left before proceeding, he then turned toward Blanton's. It had been some time since he had made regular patrols around the little town, but he deemed it prudent for the time being, what with Puddin Rooks's demise two days before. This Little Wolf fellow was more than likely long gone from this territory, but Injuns were sometimes unpredictable, especially those who were born white. It wouldn't hurt to keep a closer watch over the town.

Ike Friese's stables were at the far end of the town and Bowers had felt a desire to check on his three new horses. Otherwise, he would not have included the stables on his walking patrol. Indian ponies or not, he had to admire the unusual spotted breed. Ike promised to have his boy start breaking them the next day, and Bowers intended to spend some time watching the process. Everything seemed peaceful enough in Medicine Creek as he expected, although there seemed to be a lot more of the town's citizens wearing their guns these days. *Whole town's scared of one damn Injun*, he thought to himself.

The regulars had thinned out for supper when Bowers stepped through the doorway at Blanton's. Henry Blanton was polishing some dust off the mirror behind his bar. When he caught Bowers's reflection in the glass, he turned around and greeted the sheriff.

"Howdy, Sheriff. Want your usual?"

"I reckon," Bowers replied, propping his rifle against the end of the bar.

"Looks like you're toting a little more artillery tonight."

Bowers grunted, then replied, "I reckon. It's mostly for show, so the townsfolk will think they ain't gonna get scalped in their beds."

Arvin Gilbert, standing at the end of the bar, slid his glass down to their end to join in the conversation. "Looks like folks has got Injuns on their mind again, Sheriff." When Bowers's only reply was a grunt, Arvin waited a moment, then began again. "I'd say it was a right nice service we had for ol' Puddin yesterday." Blanton solemnly nodded his agreement. Bowers's expression remained unchanged. "Anybody say what Maggie plans to do now?" Again there was no response from Bowers. "It's a real shame, I swear it is." No one spoke for several minutes. Bowers finished his drink, picked up his rifle, and started to leave. Then Arvin blurted out the one thing that was really on his mind. "I swear, Sheriff, a lot of the folks coming in my store the last couple of days have been kinda concerned about this dang Injun attack."

Bowers stopped and cocked his head around to look Arvin straight in the eye. "Is that so? But you ain't concerned yourself, are you, Arvin?"

Knowing the sheriff had a hair-trigger temper, Arvin was hesitant to confront Bowers with what worried him. But he felt he should say something about it. "No, 'course not, Sheriff. I'm just passing on some of the things people have been saying. Thought you'd want to know."

"What have they been saying, Arvin?" Bowers was already showing signs of getting testy.

"Well, they say they're wondering why you don't go out after the killer instead of just planting ol' Puddin in the ground and letting that be the end of it." When Bowers's look of impatience immediately turned into a menacing glare, Arvin hastily reminded him, "Now it ain't me talking. I'm just telling you what I hear."

Bowers didn't like for anyone to tell him how to do his job. The truth of the matter was nobody hated Indians more than he did, and his first reaction was to hunt the savage down and skin him alive. The morn-

ing after Puddin Rooks was killed, he scoured the alley
between those buildings but could find no evidence
that an Injun had even been there, let alone in what direction he headed afterward. He liked to think he was
a practical man, and his practical side told him that he
didn't have a fart's chance in a windstorm of finding
Little Wolf. Another thing his practical side told him
was that there was the possibility the savage might be
waiting for someone to follow so he could bushwhack
'em. At any rate, the son of a bitch was long gone by
now. These thoughts he kept to himself. To Arvin, he
said sarcastically, "Maybe I'm just settin' around waiting for him to come get another one so I can catch him
when he does." He turned and walked out the door,
leaving Arvin and Blanton to speculate on his comment

Bowers paused to relight his cigar as he looked up
and down the muddy street of the mostly darkened
town. *All buttoned up for the night,* he thought. Walking
past Arvin Gilbert's general store, he drew his lip up in
a snarl at the thought of the gutless little man. The
town was full of men like Arvin Gilbert, and they all
expected him to tuck their little asses into bed every
night and protect them from the boogie man. And they
expected him to do it for damn little pay. That reminded him of his conversation with Puddin Rooks
the night he was killed. The greedy little bastard, sug-
gesting that he should get one of his horses. *Well,* he
thought, *His Honor, the late Mayor Rooks, is more than
likely riding a bony mustang bareback through the streets of
hell just about now.*

The jail was dark since there were no occupants in
the cells on this night. Bowers stepped inside and
struck a match to light his way to the lamp on the desk.
Once the lamp was lit, he turned the wick down a bit
and replaced the chimney, leaving his rifle lying on top
of his desk. He turned toward the cell doors. "Jesus!"

he blurted and stumbled backward when he was confronted with the terrifying spectre before him. The tall,
sinewy bulk of a Cheyenne warrior in full war paint
stood poised, bow drawn fully, the arrow aimed at
Bowers's stomach.

In spite of his terror, Bowers tried to react. He
looked furtively at the rifle, now out of his reach, and
then reached for the pistol on his side. No more than
three seconds elapsed from the time he turned to face
Little Wolf, to the instant his hand rested on the handle
of his .44. It was one second too long. The jolt of the
arrow slamming into his belly caused Bowers to let go
of the pistol before it had even cleared the holster.

Bowers gasped, his face twisted in pain as he stumbled backward until he crashed against the front door.
He stood there for a long moment before his legs became weak and he slowly slid down the door to a sitting position on the floor. The stoic expression of his
executioner never changed as he methodically
notched a second arrow and unhurriedly drew his
bow. Watching in horror, Bowers put his hands up before his face, trying to protect himself. He screamed in
agony when the solid thump of the arrow in his chest
drove him back against the door again.

The dying man struggled to pull his pistol again, his
hand weak and slow as the arrows in his body burned
his insides like hot pokers. Little Wolf did not seem
concerned as Bowers managed to pull the weapon
from his holster. The warrior calmly stood over the
sheriff and placed his foot over Bowers's wrist, pin-
ning it to the floor. Bowers struggled, but had no
strength to free his hand. As Bowers strained to get
loose, he squeezed the trigger, causing the pistol to discharge. Little Wolf kicked the weapon from his hand.
The loud discharge of the pistol did not seem to cause
any sense of urgency on the part of the fierce avenger.
Unhurriedly, he ripped Bowers's shirt open and

carved two long marks on the dying man's chest. Bowers only whimpered when he felt the knife rip into his flesh. Little Wolf did not bother to cut his throat before taking Bowers's scalp. When it was done, he stepped to the door and listened.

The only thing that saved Ike Friese's life that night was his immediate panic at the sight of the body. Ike, on his way to Blanton's Saloon for a little drink before calling it a night, was almost in front of the jail when he was startled by a gunshot from inside. He hesitated at first, not knowing whether it was something he should investigate or not. Franklin Bowers was a hard man to figure out. The gunshot might have meant a pistol had accidentally gone off; a prisoner might have tried to escape and Bowers shot him; or Bowers might have been in one of his ornery streaks and simply decided to shoot at a cockroach. Ike considered it for a few moments before deciding he had best find out if anything was wrong.

He tried to open the door but something was blocking it. Exerting more force, he pushed it open a few inches and called Bowers's name. There was no answer. He put his shoulder to the door and forced it open far enough to stick his head through. He immediately discovered the object that was blocking the door.

The blood almost froze in Ike's veins when he glanced down at the ghastly remains of Franklin Bowers. Ike's eyes were wide with horror as he looked away from the two arrow shafts to see the last flickering spark of life in Bowers's eyes. Though he was too far gone to speak, the sheriff's eyes seemed to be trying to convey something. And then he was gone. Ike was completely unnerved. He backed out of the door in terror, stumbling and almost falling over the hitching rail. As soon as he regained his balance, he was off at a run to the saloon, yelling at the top of his voice.

In the shock of discovering the body, Ike didn't see the tall figure standing calmly in a darkened corner of the room by the cell door, his rifle raised and aimed at the horrified stable owner. As Ike ran to spread the news, Little Wolf paused to take the sheriff's rifle and some ammunition from the cabinet behind the desk. He took one last, unhurried look at the man who had led the massacre in his valley, and then slipped silently out the door, disappearing into the night.

8

Colonel Frank Wheaton, 2nd U.S. Infantry, Commanding Officer, Fort Lapwai, Idaho territory, glanced up from his desk when his aide knocked and stuck his head in. "Sir, there's a group of citizens from Medicine Creek that want to see you."

"Oh? What about?"

"Indian trouble," was the answer.

Arvin Gilbert, Morgan Sewell, and Ike Friese filed into the room and stood before the colonel's desk. Three other men had ridden over from the settlement with them, but they decided to wait outside. It was obvious to Wheaton, even before anyone spoke, that the three civilians were extremely concerned about something. He glanced from one to the other, noting that all three seemed to be wearing similar grave expressions. He turned back to Arvin Gilbert when it appeared that he was to be the spokesman.

Arvin explained the reason for their visit, relating the two recent murders in the little settlement. Not only had the savage renegade brazenly walked into town and killed two people, he had taken the lives of the two most prominent men in the settlement, the sheriff and the mayor. The purpose of their visit, Arvin explained, was to seek protection. They had no law officer and the people were frightened. This savage was evidently hell-bent on killing the whole town one by one, and they needed the army's protection.

Upon hearing all the details, Colonel Wheaton was concerned, but he also held a stronger feeling—one of irritation. According to the citizens committee before him, there was little doubt the murders were the work of Little Wolf—the same Little Wolf he had sought to trap unsuccessfully. It was inconceivable, he thought, that one man could so brazenly go wherever and do whatever he pleased. Wheaton was irritated, and more than that, angry that the cavalry unit under Captain Malpas had been unable to track the renegade down, although there had been ongoing patrols, and Malpas had let his Nez Perce scout Yellow Hand range on his own. Wheaton had pushed the problem from the forefront of his mind. Now the savage was becoming more of a problem than ever before.

After assuring the committee from Medicine Creek that the army would indeed come to their assistance, Wheaton sent for Malpas and Lieutenant Paxton. He promised Arvin Gilbert that he would send a company of infantry to bivouac near the town while cavalry patrols scoured the hills in an effort to find the renegade's camp. Satisfied they were going to get the protection they requested, the men of Medicine Creek headed back to their homes.

Brice Paxton stood by silently while Colonel Wheaton expressed his disappointment with Captain Malpas's failure to capture Little Wolf. Malpas openly cringed at the criticism, no doubt enhanced by the fact that the colonel was infantry and had no affection for cavalry officers in the first place.

"I want you to find that savage, Captain, and I mean right *now*." His eyes drilled holes through the captain's forehead. "Is that understood?" Before Malpas could answer, Wheaton went on. "Do you have any clue where to look for him?"

"Well, we think he's got a camp somewhere in the mountains east of the settlement, but that's a lot of wild territory, and he's only one man. It's not like we're trying to locate a whole band of Indians. He may not stay in one place. We're doing all we can, Sir. Yellow Hand is searching on his own, camping in the mountains himself. All we can do is cover the territory section by section and hope to flush him out."

"Very well, Malpas. Get on with it then." He signaled an end to the meeting. As Malpas and Brice started toward the door, Wheaton added, "And, Captain, don't take any chances with the murdering savage. When you find him, shoot him."

"Yessir."

Brice looked sharply at Malpas and then back at the colonel. "Begging your pardon, Sir, but aren't we to attempt to capture him first?"

Wheaton jerked his head up to look at the young lieutenant. "Son, I'm not aware that I stammered. I don't intend to waste any effort on a rabid dog that goes around killing innocent people."

Brice felt he had to comment. "With all due respect, Sir, shouldn't some thought be given the fact that a band of those innocent people went up there and burned this man out, killed his people, and abducted his wife?"

Colonel Wheaton was not without compassion, but his practical side told him that Little Wolf would be tried and then hanged regardless. So why waste time if he was to be killed anyway? The Indian's plight was a sad one, but Wheaton also believed strongly in the Manifest Destiny of the white man. It was only natural that the Indian would resist the white tide that was overrunning territory that he thought was his. The Indian's time was over. He had roamed over the land long enough. Now he must give way so the country could become civilized. He could understand young Paxton's concern, but he could not side with the savage. To Brice, he simply said, "I believe my orders are clear."

Brice didn't move for a moment, then he snapped to attention and replied curtly, "Yes, Sir."

Outside, Malpas turned to Brice and said, "Get the whole damn company ready to march in the morning. We'll go up in those hills and comb every ridge and valley for that bastard." He thought for a moment. "Maybe we can find Yellow Hand while we're at it."

"How many rations?"

"Fifteen days."

Yellow Hand slid down from his pony's back and made his way up through the pines. He stopped short of a small clearing and peered at the burial platforms, one of them slightly higher up in the trees than the other two. Undecided as whether to go around them or not, he continued to stare at the bodies wrapped in hides. They were all recent burials.

He decided to have a closer look, although there was nothing unusual about them except that they seemed to be quite barren of symbols and ornaments, and the hides that were used to wrap the bodies were burned in places, the edges singed. As he led his horse to pass within several feet of the platforms, something caught his eye and he stopped to look more closely. There, tied to the higher platform, were two scalps, both freshly taken by the look of them, one of them no more than two days before.

He immediately looked all around him to make sure he was not being watched. He walked closer and, when his pony shied away, he jerked hard on the reins, forcing the animal to follow. He was not anxious to remain in the company of the dead himself, but he wanted to take a closer look at the scalps. They were white men's. He could not say for certain, but his instincts told him that these scalps were the work of the

Cheyenne warrior. He must be extra cautious now. Little Wolf might be close.

Backing away from the burial platform, he carefully made his way around and up above the site until he found what he was searching for. A hoofprint, no more than a day old. Another few minutes' scouting turned up a second print. He stood up and peered in the direction the prints pointed. They led across the ridge to the east. Yellow Hand's pulse quickened. It was the first trail he had struck since losing the original one, when he had followed Little Wolf from the fort. Still on foot, he followed the line toward the top of a second, higher ridge, stopping often to look around him before starting again to follow the tracks.

At the top of the second ridge, he paused to check his backtrail before climbing out on a rock overhang to look out across the valley beyond. A rare moment of sadness washed over him as the thought came to him that this country was once the country of his people, the Nez Perce. This wild and beautiful land, these untamed mountains that stood up against the clouds— how could the white man claim they were now his? The land belongs to no one. The land is the land.

He shook his head as if to clear it of useless musings. It would do no good to dwell on such thoughts. The day of the Nez Perce had passed. He, Yellow Hand, was fortunate to be held in high esteem by the soldiers. The few moments of melancholy passed as quickly as they had come, and once more he became intent on his search for Little Wolf. For, when he found him, Rain Song would be there also. When he had slain the Cheyenne warrior, the woman would come to him. She would be foolish not to. His medicine was strong with the soldiers. She would be the wife of an important man.

* * *

No more than eight or nine miles from the burial platforms, as the hawk flies, a surging mountain stream forced its way through the rocks. It gathered strength as it tumbled past the tree line, speeding recklessly toward a narrow gorge, where it plunged some two hundred feet below into a deep green pool. The sides of the gorge were steep, hiding the clear pool from even a short distance so that very few human beings had discovered the place. Little Wolf had found it quite by accident one year before while following a wounded mule deer.

Now, Rain Song sat working at an elk hide by the side of the pool. She glanced up frequently at Little Wolf and Sore Hand as they sat before the fire talking. Since she was still in mourning for her sisters, her hair was not braided, but loose and wild about her face. The scars on her breast and arms, stark evidence of her mourning, were almost healed, and she waited for Little Wolf to tell her that she had mourned enough.

She paused in her work and sat gazing at her husband. *This is a good place*, she thought. *Why can't we forget about the white men at the settlement and just live here as we are now*? She feared for her husband's safety. He seemed overly reckless in his passion to avenge the death of his friend and her sisters. Maybe, if he would stay here, the soldiers would forget about him in time and they could remain here, free and away from the rest of the world. He must have felt her warm gaze, for he glanced in her direction. Meeting her eyes, he got to his feet and walked over to the edge of the water.

"Little One, I think you have been in mourning long enough."

His remark brought a wide smile to her face. *Good*, she thought. *I will oil and braid my hair and make myself pretty. Then maybe he will not be so anxious to leave us again to track down the white murderers*.

He reached down and laid his hand on her hair. His

touch was affectionate, but when she looked up into his eyes, she saw that his thoughts were far away. Rain Song knew where his mind was, and she feared that his obsession might cost him his life. Looking down at her, he spoke at last.

"I must go now. I have rested enough. The elk should be enough food until I return. Sore Hand will look after you."

"Why must you go again?" she pleaded. "You have killed two of the white men. Isn't that enough? Sleeps Standing's spirit must feel avenged. He wouldn't want you to risk your life anymore."

He looked at her with patient eyes. "You don't understand. It goes deeper than the mere killing of two white men. It is the whole settlement that is guilty of this crime. The town should be killed for the evil they have done."

Rain Song looked alarmed. "You are intent on killing everyone in the town?"

He shook his head, still patient. "No, but I will kill the leaders of the town. Then the town will die on its own. Already I have killed the mayor and the sheriff. There are others that were leaders in the attack on our home. I know who two of them are. I have seen them while I watched the town. They do a lot of boasting and they ride two of my horses. They must pay."

"Please stay here with me. You have taken the town's leaders. That should be enough."

"No. I made a promise to Sleeps Standing that I would take two lives for each of our lost ones. I must finish what I have started. Then we will leave this place and find somewhere to live in peace." Looking into her big dark eyes, his heart could not help but melt a little. He reached down, taking her by the elbows, and lifted her to her feet. "Maybe you are right. I'll rid the earth of these last two vermin and then I'll consider it done. I vowed to kill six of them, but after these two, the rest of the men are toothless dogs, shop-keepers, and clerks anyway. These four are the leaders of the murderers."

Rain Song knew it was useless to plead further. He had made up his mind. At least she could be happy to know there would be no more killing after this last mission. She walked with him to his horse and stood with him while he checked his weapons and ammunition. When he was ready, he took her into his arms and embraced her. Then, after a few words to Sore Hand, he was gone.

Lonnie Jacobs sat down on a three-legged wooden stool outside the door of the log cabin he shared with Sam Tolbert. He reached in his pocket and pulled out a square plug of chewing tobacco. Eying it carefully, he took a few moments to pick off the pocket lint that had accumulated on it before cutting off a chew with his pocketknife. A half-empty bottle of Henry Blanton's cheapest rye whiskey sat beside him on the ground. It was still a good three hours before the sun would set beyond the hills on the western side of the valley. Although there was plenty of daylight left, Lonnie and Tolbert were not fond of working long hours on their little cattle ranch. To them, drinking was a full-time job and it didn't leave much time for working a ranch. That was a truth easily verified by anyone taking a casual look at the place.

Working up his chaw until he was ready to spit, Lonnie watched with a bored expression while his partner walked over from the corral. "You know somethin', Tolbert, I'm damn shore sick of settin' around this little valley. I'm thinkin' 'bout moving into town."

Tolbert had heard this talk on more than one afternoon. "Is that so?" he replied. "And do what?" He reached for the whiskey bottle beside Lonnie.

"Well, seems to me the town is needin' a new sheriff, and that's right up my alley."

"The hell you say," Tolbert snorted.

Lonnie propelled a long brown stream that landed a good six feet distant in the dust. He wiped his mouth with the back of his hand, and the hand on his trouser leg. "'Pears to me Franklin Bowers had hisself a nice little deal going before he cashed in. I don't see no sense in letting some other damn gunman come in and take it."

Tolbert looked hard at Lonnie for a few moments. "You're serious, ain't you?" He scratched his chin whiskers thoughtfully. "You know, that wouldn't be a bad deal at that. Why, hell, we could run that town."

"We? Who said anything about we?"

Tolbert handed him the bottle, smiling as he did. "We're partners, ain't we? You'd need a deputy."

Lonnie grinned. "Yeah, I would."

They sat and considered the possibility for the better part of an hour. Lonnie on the stool, Tolbert on the ground beside him, the bottle passed between them. After a while, a thought occurred to Lonnie. "You know, Tolbert, we'd best get over to the stable and put our rope on Bowers's horses before Ike claims 'em. He's got three of them Appaloosas and a right nice bay and them horses might as well belong to us."

Tolbert was quick to agree. "We'd best ride in there in the morning and let folks know how things are gonna be from now on. There might be some objections to us taking over the sheriffing."

Lonnie snorted. "Who's gonna stop us? Morgan Sewell? Arvin Gilbert? Hell, there ain't one in the bunch with any sand." He was about to say more when Tolbert interrupted him.

"Now, who the hell's that?" he said, squinting his eyes as he looked into the setting sun, which appeared now to almost sit on the mountaintops.

The two had become so engrossed in their plans to take over the town of Medicine Creek that they were not aware they had a visitor until he was already at the corner of the corral. Lonnie shielded his eyes with his hand. The glare of the sun framed the outline of a rider but it was almost impossible to make out his features until he walked his pony right up to the cabin.

Lonnie got up from the stool and took a few steps to the side to get the sun out of his eyes. Tolbert didn't budge from his position leaning against the cabin. "Mister, you must be lost," Lonnie said. He took a few more steps to the side, looking hard at their visitor. The man was a stranger to him. Tall, sitting straight in the saddle, he wore buckskin trousers and a coat that looked a size too small. His hair was dark and long, worn Indian style, flowing out from under a flat-crowned, wide-brimmed hat. The man's clothes didn't seem to fit him, a fact that didn't strike Lonnie as being odd. Very few men were well tailored in this part of the mountains. It was the stranger's expression that struck Lonnie. It was cold and hard, like the rugged mountains behind him. Lonnie noticed that he had a Winchester resting across his thighs. It made him wish that his own rifle was not leaning against the wall inside the door of the cabin.

"Somethin' we can do for you?" Lonnie asked, a hint of irritation in his tone, seeing as how the stranger had still not uttered a word.

The stranger stared, unblinking, for a few moments before he finally spoke. "Those horses," he said with a nod of his head toward the corral, his eyes never leaving Lonnie's.

Lonnie misunderstood. "Them horses? What? You wanna buy a horse?" He glanced at the Appaloosas, then back at the stranger. "I got a blue roan I might be willing to sell. But you ain't got enough money to buy them Appaloosas." He glanced over at Tolbert and gave him a wink. "Then, again, maybe you have. How much money you got?"

The granitelike face never showed any emotion. "I'm going to take the horses. I'm not going to buy them."

This brought a thin smile to Lonnie's face. "Well now, is that a fact? Mister, you're about the dumbest horse thief I've ever run into. Me and ol' Tolbert there, we're pretty easygoing, but we ain't in the habit of giving good horseflesh to every saddletramp that rides by." The smile suddenly disappeared. "Is this somebody's idea of a joke? Who the hell are you, anyway?"

"I'm the owner of those horses."

There followed a deathly silence as it dawned on the two partners who the dark stranger was. For a full minute, there was no sound. Lonnie was frozen by the stranger's piercing stare. Tolbert, until that moment, had been unable to identify the warrior he had last seen at the Little Big Horn because of the sun in his eyes. Then, realizing that he was soon to be participating in his own death ceremony, Tolbert lunged for the door of the cabin. Before he made it to his feet, he was cut down by Little Wolf's rifle. Tolbert fell heavily back against the cabin, shot through the lung.

Lonnie was unable to move. His bowels were in the grip of fear's icy hand. He wanted to run, but he could not. He dropped to his knees, his legs no longer able to support him. The bullet that he dreaded still did not come. All was quiet again, the silence even more pronounced after the sudden roar of the rifle. Now there was only the soft choking gurgle coming from Tolbert's throat as he tried desperately to breathe. Lonnie's chin dropped to his chest as huge tears began to fill his eyes.

Slowly, Little Wolf dismounted and walked up to the broken man. Sickened by the sight of the cowardly murderer of his people, he grabbed a handful of Lonnie's hair and jerked his head back so he could look directly into his eyes. Lonnie screamed, then started sobbing. "I didn't have no part in it, I swear. I didn't kill them women! I wasn't even there!"

Little Wolf lifted him by the hair until he was halfway up. Lonnie whimpered thinly, then suddenly grunted as he was doubled over by the force of the knife that sank deep into his stomach. Little Wolf withdrew the blade and stepped back to let the man fall at his feet. Feeling no need to hurry while the two white men lay mortally wounded, Little Wolf went back to his horse and took his bow from the loop of rawhide behind the saddle. He drew one arrow from his quiver for each man, a calling card to let the people of Medicine Creek know these men had paid for the senseless murders of Sleeps Standing, Lark, and White Moon. Tolbert, lying against the side of the cabin, was already dead, and did not move when the arrow smashed his breastbone and buried itself deep inside his chest. Little Wolf notched the other arrow and turned back to Lonnie. Lonnie was still alive but was no longer whimpering, his vocal cords paralyzed by terror and pain. His eyes were wide, almost bulging from the shock of facing certain death. Fueled by his passion for revenge on those who had slaughtered his longtime friends, Little Wolf was reluctant to end the white man's torment. He stood staring down at the wounded man with eyes that burned with a cold flame. Finally, he drew the bowstring back and released the arrow that hastened Lonnie Jacobs's departure. To complete the execution, he ripped each man's shirt open and, with his knife, carved three long slashes on one man's chest and four on the other.

When it was done, Little Wolf stood silently looking around him. As before, when he dispatched the sheriff and the mayor, the killing did nothing to ease the anguish and sense of loss he felt. He decided then that

Rain Song was right. There was no purpose in taking
more lives. There had been enough slaughter. These
would be the last two scalps to adorn Sleeps Standing's burial platform. He would go back for Rain Song
and Sore Hand and go farther south, deeper into the
Bitterroots, and try once again to make a new start. Relieved to be done with the business, he lowered the
corral poles and led the Appaloosas out. With his
horses once again in his possession, Little Wolf struck
out across the valley toward the mountains and the
camp by the waterfall.

Captain Hollis Malpas held up his hand to halt the
column of troopers behind him. "What is it, Charlie?"

The half-breed scout, Charlie Rain Cloud, pulled up
from a gallop and wheeled his horse alongside the
captain. "Dead men!" he blurted.

"Dead men? Where?"

"In the valley, two white men laying dead by a little
cabin."

Brice Paxton pulled up beside them. "That cabin
would be Tolbert and Jacobs's place. That's the only
cabin I know of in that valley."

Malpas nodded and said, "More of that devil's
work, I expect." He prepared to signal the troop to
move out.

"Ain't no hurry," Charlie Rain Cloud said, "he's
done and gone."

E Company filed into the little valley and, under orders from Malpas, split up to circle the cabin in the
event their quarry might still be lurking about. When
it was determined that there was no one else around,
Malpas dismounted the troops while Charlie looked
around for sign.

Sergeant Baskin walked up beside Brice, who was
standing over the body of Sam Tolbert. He stared at
the bodies of the two partners for a few moments be-

fore commenting. "Cheyenne arrows. Looks like it's our man, all right. This'un was killed with a rifle. Looks like our renegade just wasted an arrow."

"He wants us to know who did it. It's all about revenge. These two were part of that posse we met over at Medicine Creek." He looked down at the scalpless corpses. Noticing their mutilated chests, Brice suddenly realized the significance of the slashes. "Number three and number four. I wonder how many he figures to kill." He didn't voice it, but the thought occurred to him that the two men probably got what they deserved.

After Charlie Rain Cloud had scouted the area and concluded that Little Wolf had left there at least a day before, Malpas decided to search the mountains east of the settlement of Medicine Creek. According to Charlie, this was the country Yellow Hand was scouting and Malpas figured the Nez Perce scout had a better idea where to find Little Wolf than anyone else. He decided to divide the company into three patrols, headed by each of the three officers. The company remained intact until they crossed the river. On the far side, Paul Simmons, along with twenty men, broke off and pushed directly east. Brice also with twenty, continued north, working his way toward the east to follow a narrow valley that led into the mountains. Malpas, with the balance of the company, followed the river, planning to veer off to the east before reaching Medicine Creek. He kept the half-breed scout with him, while Paul and Brice each took three of the remaining six Nez Perces as scouts.

Before leaving the river, Malpas instructed his two lieutenants, "Scout out any trails you come across. It's pretty hard going in some places in these mountains and he will more than likely stick to the trails. We'll rendezvous back here in three days. And, gentlemen, watch yourselves."

*   *   *

After climbing steadily through a seemingly endless band of lodgepole pines that ringed the line of mountain ridges, Yellow Hand stopped dead in his tracks and looked hard through the trees. A movement on the other side of them had caught his eye. He tied his horse to a limb and continued on foot. For the last half hour or so, he had heard the sound of rushing water and yet he had not found a stream. Now the sound was close. Moving cautiously, he made his way through the tall pines, so thick he had to weave his way through them. He climbed higher up toward the crest of the ridge. There it was again! A movement, a glimpse of something or someone darting along the ridge above him. He hurried to gain the top of the ridge. Crawling the last few yards to the crest, he peered over the spine of the ridge in time to see the fleeting image of a man just as he disappeared into a thicket below.

Yellow Hand's heart beat against his breastbone. *I have found him!* The sound of the rushing water was now louder than ever and he strained to see the source through the trees. Working his way quickly down to the thicket where he had last seen the man, he dropped to his knees and searched the brush before him with his eyes, his rifle ready. He could see no sign of the man, but now he discovered the waterfall that sent water crashing down the face of the cliff. A moment later, the man appeared again. He emerged from the thick forest and walked across a small clearing toward a pool at the bottom of the waterfall. There, sitting by the edge of the pool, he saw her. *Rain Song!*

Yellow Hand's heart was pounding now. He looked back at the man. It was not Little Wolf. He was an old man, a Nez Perce he remembered having seen on occasion at the reservation at Lapwai. *Bad luck,* he thought, disappointed that Little Wolf was not there.

Too bad for you, old man, but you must die. I can't be bothered with taking you back to Lapwai.

Although dissatisfied to find that the man he sought to kill was not there, Yellow Hand was still pleased with himself that he had found the woman. He would take her with him and then see if Little Wolf dared to track them down. As long as he had the woman, he no longer had to search through these mountains. He would let Little Wolf come to him, and then he would kill him. Unable to keep a smile from his face, he rose to his feet and went back to retrieve his horse.

Rain Song took a large rock and pounded down a stake that had loosened as the drying elk hide pulled against it. Satisfied that it was now secure, she sat back on her heels and gazed out across the rocky stream toward the waterfall. A busy water ouzel caught her eye. The tiny bird had built his nest of moss close by the water's edge and was constantly darting in and out of the rushing water, searching for his supper. *This is a good place*, she thought. *When Little Wolf returns, I will beg him to let us stay here and make our home.* The thought of her husband caused a warm trembling inside her breast, and she smiled when she pictured in her mind the tall, graceful warrior who loved her. At almost the same time, she heard Sore Hand call out that someone was coming.

She quickly got to her feet and looked toward the ridge behind her. There was a rider making his way through the pines. At first she thought Little Wolf had returned and her heart began to race with excitement. She started running to meet him, but halfway across the grassy bottom, she stopped. The rider had emerged from the thicket, and it was not Little Wolf. She could see that it was not a soldier, but another Indian. She was not alarmed, since it was not a white man approaching, but she remained still, watching the rider as he reached the bottom of the hill and rode toward them.

When approximately within fifty yards, the stranger brought his rifle up to his shoulder. At the same moment the rifle cracked, she realized the man was Yellow Hand. She heard herself scream as she saw the bullet rip into Sore Hand's chest and the old Nez Perce was knocked over backward. Frozen by the horror she had just witnessed, she stood stone still for a few moments before gathering her senses enough to turn and run back toward the waterfall. Yellow Hand galloped after her.

He easily overtook her before she had covered half the distance to the water. With his rawhide whip, he trapped the running girl's ankles, causing her to trip and stumble to the ground. Yellow Hand was off his horse and upon her in a flash. She fought like a young mountain lion, straining and struggling against the superior strength of the Nez Perce scout. But soon it was over. She lay exhausted and helpless under him.

When he was certain she had no strength to break away, he relaxed his grip on her wrists a little. "Do not fight. I have no desire to hurt you."

"Then let me go!" she spat back at him.

"No, I will never let you go. I have come to do you a great honor. You will be my wife now."

"Ha!" she laughed defiantly. "I will never be your wife." She struggled against his grip. "You talk of honor. You are a murderer. You killed Sore Hand, a member of your own tribe. He has done nothing to anger you."

"He was in my way. Besides, he was an old man. He would have died soon, anyway."

His comment made her furious and she once again summoned strength to struggle against her imprisonment. He squeezed down hard on her wrists, merely smiling at her futile struggles. "I am a patient man.

You will see that it is the best thing for you to be my wife. I can give you many things your Cheyenne dog cannot. I am the number one scout at the fort. You will be proud to be my woman."

"I would die first. I would rather mate with a coyote than go to your tipi."

He smiled. "We will see. As I said, I am a patient man, but don't think I will not punish you if you disobey me. Now, get up." He got off of her and pulled her to her feet. She attempted to kick him between his legs, but he avoided her foot and gave her a hard slap for her trouble.

Refusing to cry out, she stared defiantly into his eyes. "You are a dead man," she hissed. "Little Wolf will find you and kill you."

He laughed, showing his contempt for the Cheyenne warrior. "He is a dead man if he tries to follow us. He had better pray that the soldiers get him before I do. His death will be slow and painful if I catch him."

Yellow Hand knew it was unreasonable, but still he had hoped the woman would realize Little Wolf had no future and she would come willingly. There was no uncertainty about her feelings, however. She had already made them quite apparent. So he felt he had no choice but to bind her hands and feet to her pony to prevent her from escaping. He felt that, in time, she would eventually weaken in her defiance and become a proper wife to him. But if she didn't, he would keep her tied to a stake, if that's what it took. His passion for this woman was strong, and he could not abide the thought of another man having her.

Rain Song sat silently on her pony while Yellow Hand tied Sore Hand's horse on a line behind his. She looked at the body of the old Nez Perce who had lived with her and Little Wolf ever since they first came to the Bitterroot country. His body looked small and frail, lying in the lush grass of the streambanks. When Yellow Hand had finished tying off the spare horse and had climbed up on his own, she spoke.

"Aren't you at least going to bury him? He is a Nez Perce, like you, one of your own people."

"I don't have time to waste on that old man. The buzzards and the coyotes will perform his burial ceremony for him." He kicked his horse hard and led them off down the narrow ravine.

Brice Paxton reined up and raised his hand to bring the patrol to a halt. Sergeant Baskin pulled up beside him. "What is it, Sir?"

Brice pointed toward a low ridge off to their left where one of the Nez Perce scouts had just appeared, riding on a course that would intercept the column. "Looks like he might have found something."

Brice ordered the patrol to resume the march at a walk to meet the scout. In a few minutes, the scout was within shouting distance and Brice called out, "Yellow Hand!" and pointed back toward the top of the ridge. He rode to meet the column. When the scout had closed the distance between them, he told Brice that he had found Yellow Hand and that Yellow Hand had discovered the Cheyenne's camp.

Brice led the column at a full gallop, following the scout back toward the ridge. Near the top, they found the other two Nez Perces talking to Yellow Hand. Yellow Hand walked his pony to meet the lieutenant when he saw the column making its way up to him.

"Is it true?" Brice wanted to know. "Did you find Little Wolf's camp?" Yellow Hand nodded. "Is he there?"

"Not there," Yellow Hand replied. "Old man," he struggled to put his words into English, "old man there, fight. I kill him."

Brice was confused. "Old man? Little Wolf was not there? Was the woman there?"

Yellow Hand shook his head. "No woman there."

"Well, how the hell do you know it was Little Wolf's camp?"

Yellow Hand's expression remained unchanged. He solemnly nodded his head up and down and said, "It Little Wolf's camp. Old man friend of Little Wolf."

Brice looked at Sergeant Baskin. "I don't know, Sergeant. Whaddaya think?"

Baskin shrugged. "I don't know either. Yellow Hand's the best we got. He's probably right, and if he is, maybe we can set up a little welcoming party for Little Wolf when he comes back."

Brice was mildly surprised when Yellow Hand balked at leading the column to the Cheyenne's camp. Instead, he gave the Nez Perce scouts detailed directions so they could find the camp. He insisted that Colonel Wheaton gave him specific orders to continue scouting for the renegade on his own. This made no sense to Brice. If he was certain the camp was Little Wolf's, then it figured that was the place to catch him and the woman. Brice was not alone in questioning Yellow Hand's reasoning. One of the other Nez Perce scouts seemed to be arguing the point with him as well. In the end, Yellow Hand remained stoically intent on going off on his own, saying that Little Wolf may or may not return to the camp. If he didn't, Yellow Hand might strike his trail somewhere else. He insisted that he needed only one man to ride with him, pointing to the scout known simply as Hump, the cousin of Yellow Hand.

"Well, go on then," Brice said. "Are you sure these two scouts can find the camp?"

"They find," was Yellow Hand's curt reply before leaping upon his pony's back and riding off across the ridge. Hump, ever somber and expressionless, wheeled his pony and galloped after him.

Brice stood for a moment watching the departing scouts. "What the hell was that all about? You think ol' Yellow Hand might be a little afraid of meeting up with this Cheyenne?"

Baskin shook his head. "Naw, I doubt it, not Yellow Hand. He's just got a briar up his butt about something. Who knows?"

It was not a briar on Yellow Hand's mind, but a Cheyenne flower, securely tied to a tree in a wooded canyon some three miles distant from where the column now stood. He was intent upon having the woman, and he feared that if the lieutenant knew she was a captive, he would order Yellow Hand to give her up.

Rain Song pulled against the rawhide as hard as she could. She strained until blood ran down her arms from the cuts caused by the tough thongs around her wrists. Still she struggled until the rawhide became slippery with her blood. It was no use. Yellow Hand had done his work well. She could not free herself. Frustrated and exhausted, she lay back against the rough bark of the pine. It had been hours since the Nez Perce scout had tied her to the tree and ridden off to intercept the soldiers. The sun was well past its high point and sinking closer to the mountaintops.

She had had nothing to eat or drink since she had been abducted, but her thoughts were not of food or water. Her soul called out for Little Wolf. He must come, for she feared Yellow Hand meant to carry her far away. In her despair, huge tears began to form in her dark eyes, slowly welling over until they were pushed down her cheeks, leaving long streaks in the dusty film that had covered her face.

Suddenly he was there. Walking his pony through the curtain of pines, Yellow Hand pulled up before her.

Behind him, another man followed. Yellow Hand sat looking at her for a moment before dismounting to stand over her. She stared defiantly at him, refusing to cower before him. He reached for the canteen on his saddlehorn.

"Drink."

She did not refuse, and drank eagerly from the canteen held to her lips. He let her drink until she pulled away and leaned back against the tree again. He replaced the canteen and knelt beside her, his face close to hers.

"I'm sorry I had to leave you tied, but it was necessary to save you from the soldiers." His eyes searched hers for some sign of gratitude. There was none. "You won't have to worry or be afraid anymore. I'll take care of you. You will be my wife. The soldiers won't harm you if you are my wife."

"Little Wolf will come for me. He'll kill you for what you have done."

"Ha! Little Wolf is dead!" He rocked back on his heels, his face displaying the disdain he held for the Cheyenne warrior.

Her eyes opened wide, shocked by his blunt retort. "Little Wolf is dead?" she almost screamed. "I don't believe you. Little Wolf is not dead!"

Yellow Hand smiled, then nodded solemnly. "He is dead," he lied. It was not really untrue, he told himself, for there was little doubt that the Cheyenne renegade soon would be. He, Yellow Hand, had found Little Wolf's camp and the Cheyenne warrior was sure to come back for his woman. When he did, he would find Lieutenant Paxton waiting for him with twenty soldiers. It was best now if she thought he was already dead, for the sooner she would accept it, the sooner she would turn to Yellow Hand to care for her. He glanced at Hump, who was now seated on a dead log, watching the confrontation but seemingly disinterested in what was being said. It was of no concern to him what Yellow Hand did with this woman.

Yellow Hand took her hands in his and examined her bloody wrists. "You have hurt yourself. That was foolish. You will soon learn that you are my woman now." He attempted to embrace her but she pulled away from him as far as her bonds allowed.

"Do not touch me! I am Little Wolf's wife!"

"Not anymore!" he shot back, his patience strained, his attempted gentle approach having failed. "The Cheyenne dog is dead. The sooner you accept that, the better off you'll be." He took her by her shoulders and shook her violently. "You are *my* wife now!"

Still glaring defiantly, she said nothing then. After a moment, she lowered her head and cried silent tears. He watched her carefully for a few minutes, thinking it best to let her exhaust her defiance. After a while, when she had remained calm and quiet, he decided she was at last resigned to her fate. Taking his scalping knife, he cut the thongs from her feet. When she made no effort to move, he cut her wrists free as well. Then he took a couple of steps back and stood watching her.

She sat there for a long time before she moved. Then she began rubbing her ankles where the thongs had bound her. Watching Yellow Hand cautiously, she slowly rose to her feet, her legs stiff and sore from the position she had been forced to sit in for hours. When she had regained the feeling in her limbs, she looked into his eyes and softly spoke. "You must let me go now, for I will never be your wife. I love Little Wolf. I can be wife to no other."

Yellow Hand almost cried out his frustration with the woman. He almost wished he had not come to desire her so. But he knew he must have her. So, if she must be broken like a wild horse, then he would break her. He was obsessed with her now, and the fact that she continued to reject him frustrated him to the point of humiliation. He stepped up to her and slapped her hard across the face. She was knocked backward a step by the blow, but uttered not a sound. This infuriated him even more. He glared at her, his eyes like burning coals, and raised his hand to strike her again. She thrust her face forward to receive the blow, unyielding in her defiance. He hesitated but slapped her again, though not as hard as before. He growled in his anguish.

"Let me go," she said, her voice low and soft.

"You will be my wife."

"No," she replied.

In response, he took the rawhide thongs and looped one end around one of her wrists. With the other end, he tied her to his own wrist. He then bound one of her ankles to one of his own. "We will sleep together as husband and wife. This way we will be married."

She struggled at first but soon realized he was too powerful to resist. When he had tied them together, she stood passively for a moment. Mistaking her calm for resignation to her fate, he reached for her. When she reacted, it was so sudden he was taken by surprise. Moving as quickly as a serpent strikes, she reached under his arm and grasped the long scalping knife in his belt. His first thought was to protect himself so he jumped backward, throwing his free hand up to defend against the attack. To his surprise, she did not strike out at him. Instead, she thrust the knife deep into her own body with a force that sank it almost to the handle.

The blow caused her to gasp in pain. Then, her words straining through her pain, she uttered, "You will sleep with a corpse. I go to join Little Wolf."

Yellow Hand was horrified. Rain Song's frail body slumped and, even though she weighed little more than one hundred pounds, the dead weight was enough to cause him to stumble. He was barely able to maintain his balance as the mortally wounded girl sank to the ground.

Stunned by her desperate and final act of resistance, Yellow Hand could only stare in shocked confusion, unable at first to believe his eyes. Forced by the rawhide thongs to stand in a stooped position, he had to withdraw his knife from the wounded girl's body in order to free himself. One last involuntary gasp from Rain Song's lips was the only sound she made when the blade was withdrawn. Then she lay still. Shock, followed by astonishment, and finally anger tore through Yellow Hand's brain. He grimaced as he sawed the bonds that held him to the girl. When he was free, he stood over her body, unable to look away from her. Suddenly his humiliation and rage became overwhelming, and he roared out in anger. He did not interpret Rain Song's ultimate sacrifice as testimony to her love for her husband. To him, it was a stark insult to his prestige as a warrior and a leading member of his tribe. As relentlessly as he had pursued her before, he now viewed her body with disgust. In a fit of anger, he took the still-bloody knife and prepared to slash her throat. Hump, also stunned by the girl's impulsive actions, now blurted out the words that saved her life. "She's not dead." It was enough to stay the executioner's hand, as Yellow Hand harnessed his anger long enough to see for himself.

Perhaps if Little Wolf had not taken the time to take the scalps of the two white men to Sleeps Standing's burial platform, he would have been in his camp when Yellow Hand struck. Now, as he made his way down through the pines, he became immediately alert. Sensing something wrong, he stopped at the edge of the thicket and scanned the clearing by the waterfall. There was no sign of Rain Song or Sore Hand. The horses were nowhere in sight. It was unusual that both

Rain Song and Sore Hand would be away from the camp at the same time.

Aware now of the pounding of his heart, he searched the narrow ravine with his eyes, his anguish mounting with every second that passed. Moving slowly and quietly across the clearing, he was almost to the edge of the water when he discovered Sore Hand's body, lying at the base of a twisted laurel near the edge of the clearing.

Moving quickly then, his rifle ready, his eyes darting constantly from left to right, he went to his old friend's side. Thinking him dead, he bent low over him and placed a comforting hand upon the old Nez Perce's shoulder. Sore Hand's eyelids fluttered and then opened. Little Wolf sat back, surprised. The old man was still alive, although barely.

"Little Wolf?" The question was feeble and barely audible.

"Yes, I'm here, old friend." He waited only a moment, then asked, "Rain Song, where is she?"

"Gone," he gasped, straining to make the words. "The army scout, Yellow Hand . . . took her . . ."

Before Little Wolf could ask more, the old man's eyes fluttered again, then opened wide as if staring into death's cold face. His final breath escaped in a long sigh, and then he was gone.

Little Wolf, suddenly weary, sat down beside the old man. Sore Hand had evidently been mortally wounded for hours, but the old Nez Perce had clung desperately to life, determined to stay alive until Little Wolf found him so he could tell him that this was Yellow Hand's work. Gazing into the faithful old man's face, he silently thanked him, then gently closed Sore Hand's eyes. "Sleep, my friend," he whispered.

Though anxious to go after Rain Song, Little Wolf remained long enough to bury his old friend. He knew it was important to the old man to have his body returned to Mother Earth so that his spirit could roam freely in the land of the dead. He felt it was the least he could do for one who had been so true a friend to him and Rain Song. At least Yellow Hand had not scalped the old man.

When Sore Hand's body was safely interred beneath the branches of a tall pine, Little Wolf started out after Yellow Hand. The trail was not hard to follow. He suspected that Rain Song had made every effort to mark it whenever she could, judging by the occasional broken branch. His senses alive and ever searching, he hurried after them, watching the trail before him for a possible ambush. Yellow Hand was cunning. He had watched the Nez Perce scout when the soldiers searched for him after he had rescued Rain Song from the fort. He might be clever enough to lead him into a trap.

After leaving his camp by the waterfall, Yellow Hand had doubled back toward the river, seeming to head in a general direction that would take him back to the fort on Lapwai Creek. But before reaching the river, the trail abruptly turned again into the mountains, leading up into a stand of pines that covered most of a low ridge. She had been here—he was certain of it. The pieces of cut rawhide, some with blood on them, along with the tracks around the tree, told him she had been tied there. There were other tracks that told him there were two who held her captive. There was a struggle, evidenced by a great deal of blood on the ground. Devastated, he sat back on his heels and tried to form a picture in his mind of the events that had happened there. She had been carried away. Someone was badly wounded. Was it her? She might be dead, but then why would they take her body with them? Perhaps to display, hoping to entice him to come after her.

Under the crushing weight of his despair, he gave

no thought to his own safety. He didn't care if a bullet found him at that moment for, without her, his soul was already dead. In his mind, he could see her, alone and crying out for him, and he wanted to slash his own body in his grief.

After a few minutes, he forced his mind back to concentrate on the task before him now. He would find her, whether she was dead or living. These two, Yellow Hand and his accomplice, must pay for what they had done, even if it took the rest of his life. Following the trail left by the four horses, Little Wolf set out again, a warrior with only one thought: revenge.

9

"Hell, we're just wasting our time here, Sergeant." Brice stood up and walked out into the open. "It's pretty damn obvious the renegade isn't coming back to this camp."

Sergeant Baskin got up from the shallow rifle pit he had fashioned behind a small tree. He dusted himself off and walked out to join the lieutenant. "Yessir, I'd have to agree with you. We got here too late to catch him. Looks to me like Yellow Hand must have found this camp a lot sooner than he let on when he met the column yesterday. I wonder what the hell he was doing all that time."

"Who knows?" Brice answered. He was a little irritated that the company's best scout had apparently waited for some time after finding Little Wolf's camp before reporting to him. Long enough, he noted, for the Cheyenne to bury whoever's body was in the grave and leave. He looked all around the clearing by the waterfall then shook his head, disgusted. "We'd best get going, I guess. Maybe we can catch up with him. We'll follow the trail the scouts picked up leading off down the ravine."

Baskin nodded and, walking out into the center of the clearing where he knew he could be seen from the rocks above the waterfall, he signaled the pickets. Brice waited while the rest of his patrol were called in from their ambush positions and the horses were brought up. When they were mounted, he signaled the two Nez Perce scouts out in front.

There were tracks from several horses leading out of the ravine and across the narrow valley. The scouts seemed to think that the fresher tracks indicated that one rider, Little Wolf it was assumed, had trailed someone else from the valley. They followed the trail for most of the afternoon until Brice called a halt to make camp for the night. At daybreak the following morning, they were mounted and back on the trail. Before the sun had made a decent showing, they came upon the pine grove where Rain Song had been wounded.

Brice studied the dried blood on the pine needles while the two Indian scouts searched the area carefully, trying to piece together enough fragments of information to determine what had taken place there. After scouting the thicket and small clearing, they could only speculate what had happened. Someone had been bound to the tree. There had been a struggle of some kind, resulting in bloodshed. Both scouts agreed that one of the ponies was the red sorrel Yellow Hand rode—the horse was distinguishable by a slot in his front left hoof.

Brice turned to Sergeant Baskin. "So this is where he ran off to instead of leading the column to Little Wolf's camp. Didn't you tell me Yellow Hand was sniffing around that little Cheyenne girl?" It didn't take much more than a moment's thought before the picture became crystal clear. He glanced up at Baskin. "What would you say the odds were that the person tied to this tree was that little Cheyenne girl?"

"I'd say they were pretty good. He could have found the woman in Little Wolf's camp and run off with her."

Further speculation prompted them to come up with a pretty complete notion as to who they were now trailing. The tracks leading away from the thicket told them that Little Wolf was tracking Yellow Hand, although it appeared Yellow Hand had a fair start on the Cheyenne. The trail led them farther up the side of a long mountain ridge and then descended into a wide ring of timber. The tall lodgepole pines were growing so close together that the column had to enter the timber single file. Even then, it was difficult to get the horses through in some places. The trees towered up to the sky, shutting out the sunlight, and the trail soon became impossible to follow. The pine needles on the floor of the forest were so thick that tracks disappeared. The scouts halted and confessed that they were unable to pick up the trail again. Brice ordered the column to rest while the two Nez Perces scouted in vain for some sign of the horses they had followed since the day before.

"Whaddaya wanna do, Lieutenant?" Sergeant Baskin stood ready to order the patrol out again. "Push on?"

Brice didn't answer for a moment as he considered what they had found there. "No," he finally said. "You can tell 'em to mount, but we're going back to the river to hook up with the rest of the company, if we can find a way out of this damn timber."

Baskin was surprised. "You ain't gonna keep after him?"

"No, unless you can follow a trail with no tracks. We're running out of our supplies anyway. We were supposed to rendezvous with the captain this morning."

"What about Yellow Hand?"

Brice looked Baskin in the eye and stated, "Frankly, it would serve the bastard right if Little Wolf catches him. From what I've seen here today, I hope he does." There was no question in Brice's mind that the white man turned Cheyenne would have to be brought to

justice for the murders of four citizens of Medicine
Creek. But, in his own mind, he could not say that he
blamed Little Wolf for taking the action he did. If the
so-called Vigilance Committee of the settlement had
left the man alone in the first place, there would have
been no killings. Who could blame the man? They had
killed his family and burned him out, and sought to
kill him too. *If it were me*, Brice thought, *I might have
done the same as he.*

When Brice's patrol approached the designated rendezvous point by the river, they found the rest of the
company already waiting for them. Leaving Sergeant
Baskin to see to the watering of the horses, Brice reported to Captain Malpas. He found the captain seated
in the shade of a willow tree by the water. Paul Simmons was also there, and the two officers were talking
to the scout, Yellow Hand. The fact that the scout was
back with the company was surprising to Brice. He
had somehow expected him to still be up in the mountains, either trying to catch Little Wolf, or elude him.
Yellow Hand's cousin, Hump, was nowhere to be
seen.

Paul was the first to spot his friend when he walked
up. "Well, Lieutenant Paxton, I see you didn't have
any better luck than the rest of us." He flashed his
usual warm smile. "I'm glad you finally showed up. I
was afraid we were going to have to search for you."

"Paul," Brice simply returned. He was more interested in what Yellow Hand had to say. After he made
an informal report to the captain, Brice turned to question the Nez Perce scout. "How about you, Yellow
Hand? What kind of luck did you have?"

"No find," he said in his broken English, his face devoid of expression.

"What about the woman Rain Song? Did you find
her?"

Yellow Hand studied the young lieutenant's face for a few moments before answering. He sensed a hint of suspicion in Brice's tone. When Brice repeated the question, Yellow Hand chose his words carefully. "No woman. Maybe woman dead. I think maybe Cheyenne kill her."

"I hardly think so," Brice was quick to reply. "Where's Hump? I don't see him here."

Yellow Hand shrugged. "Hump sick, have to go home. I don't know."

Turning to Malpas, Brice related the events of the previous day. "When the fugitive failed to show up at his camp, we trailed him to the mountainside where we found signs of some little set-to. Judging by the tracks that led away from there, my scouts were pretty sure there was a lone rider that followed after whoever was there in the first place. I figure that rider was Little Wolf." He kept his gaze fixed on Yellow Hand to see his reaction. There was only a flicker in Yellow Hand's eye, but it was enough to tell Brice what he suspected all along. Although he hid it well, Brice was certain the news that Little Wolf had trailed him caused Yellow Hand concern. "I'm guessing that person he was trailing was you, Yellow Hand, and I figure you had the girl with you. What I'm not sure of is what happened to her."

Malpas and Paul appeared confused. Malpas looked sharply at his scout. "What? You didn't say anything about finding the Cheyenne girl."

Yellow Hand shrugged as if unconcerned. "Woman dead. She not matter."

"Did you kill her?" This from Brice.

Yellow Hand turned to stare at the young lieutenant, his eyes squinted and surly. "No. Like I say, woman dead. I don't find her." With that, he abruptly got to his feet and said, "I go now."

While the three officers watched the back of the departing scout, Captain Malpas spoke. "Paxton, if you could enlighten me on what that was all about, I'd appreciate it."

Brice gave a more detailed report on what he had seen on his patrol, including his suspicions that Yellow Hand had abducted the Indian girl from Little Wolf's camp and taken her away and killed her. Probably because she wouldn't consent to being his wife, he added. When he learned from Paul Simmons that the Indian had come into camp with an extra horse, he was even more convinced that Yellow Hand had been up to the devilment he suspected.

Malpas found Brice's comments interesting but, without harboring the compassion for the woman that his lieutenant obviously did, he shrugged it off. "Well, what does it matter? She's just an Indian. As far as that goes, you didn't find her body." Brice and Paul exchanged quick glances but neither commented.

Yellow Hand walked off by himself to think about what he had just heard—that Little Wolf had trailed him from the camp by the waterfall. The thing that bothered him most was that he had not been aware of it. The fact that the white Cheyenne had not overtaken him before he was back in the soldier camp was not sufficient enough to ease the discomfort of knowing he was being stalked. It was a good thing that he sent Hump back to the reservation at Lapwai with the wounded girl. Hump was skilled in the ability to cover his trail. The Cheyenne would most likely follow Yellow Hand anyway, thinking he had the woman with him.

Yellow Hand prided himself in his prowess as a warrior and he considered himself the best scout the army employed. But he had never been hunted before. He was always the one who tracked someone for the soldiers. Even when Chief Joseph's people left the val-

ley and made an attempt to flee to Canada, Yellow
Hand had scouted for the army, feeling no allegiance
to those Nez Perces who followed Joseph. He told
himself that he feared no man. Yet this strange dis-
placed white Cheyenne made him feel uneasy. He decided it best to remain in the company of many
soldiers for a while until the renegade was caught, or
he tired of trying to seek his revenge.

The man who caused such serious thoughts in the
mind of the Nez Perce scout knelt on one knee, watching the company of cavalry from a knoll some two
hundred yards distant. The floor of the pine forest was
so thick with needles that it had been impossible to follow Yellow Hand's trail. He had been forced to scout
the trails below the band of lodgepoles until he picked
it up again. Because of this, Little Wolf had lost valuable time in overtaking the Nez Perce scout.

When Yellow Hand's trail led to the gathering of soldiers by the river, Little Wolf knew he would have to
wait and watch for an opportunity. Working his way
down closer to a smaller knoll where he could get an
unobstructed view of the entire camp, he scanned the
bivouac from side to side. He saw Yellow Hand, but
there was no indication that his wife was captive in the
soldier camp. He tried not to think about what this
might mean, that Yellow Hand had killed her. The
very thought twisted his guts into icy knots.

He remained there on the knoll all night and followed the soldiers for a few miles the next morning,
until he was sure that Rain Song was not with them
and that the soldiers were returning to Fort Lapwai.
There was little doubt in his mind now that Rain Song
was dead. And the man who had killed her was riding
back to the fort, surrounded by soldiers. *There will be
another time*, he told himself and turned away, riding
back to a gulch below his camp by the waterfall. There,

he rounded up the three horses he had left to graze when he went after Yellow Hand. He would move them to a new place where he could make his camp, high up in the mountains. The soldiers would most likely continue to search for him, but probably in the valleys and foothills.

He felt alone in the world now. The only person, friend or kin, left to him was his brother, Tom Allred. And even the memory of his brother was fading. It was his preference at this time to be alone with the mountains and streams. If Rain Song could not be at his side, then he preferred no one. He was as much at home in the mountains as the eagles and hawks, and it was there that he would dwell with the memory of his wife.

With his horses on a string behind him, he made his way up through the lodgepoles, following an old elk trail until he emerged high up on a rocky divide. Riding parallel to the summit when the climb was too steep, he led his horses over steep bluffs of shell rock and sand that threatened to slide out from under him with every step. He pushed on, looking for a place that offered grass and water. High above the timber, there were only occasional patches of bear grass, a tough, sour grass that a horse would eat only if starving.

This was new territory to him. He had not traveled into this part of the Bitterroots, toward the Idaho country. As the afternoon sun sank closer to the hilltops, it began to look like he would have to make a dry camp that night. Just as he was about to resign himself to this, he came to a gulch that led down into the trees. Following it, he was surprised to find a side gulch that led to a small meadow with good grass for the horses, and a busy stream coursing through it. This was what he had hoped to find. This was where he would make his camp .

Little Wolf did not leave his new camp for two days.

In the custom of his adopted people, he slashed his
chest in his anguish over the death of Rain Song. He
did not eat and only drank sparingly of the cool mountain stream. As all Cheyennes knew, death was a part
of living. There had always been war between the different tribes. Since the westward invasion of the white
man, this truth was even more pronounced, and since
his boyhood, death was a constant trail companion.
Little Wolf accepted this, but Rain Song's violent death
was almost more than he could bear.

He looked at his horses. They were well fed and
rested after two days in this secluded mountain
meadow. It was then that he first felt his own need for
nourishment and he decided it was time to take to the
warpath once more. He would mourn for Rain Song
no more.

Although he had some dried venison still left in his
saddle pack, he decided that he needed some fresh
meat to restore his strength. He saddled one of the
horses, and leading another to pack his meat, rode
down through the band of lodgepoles, following the
stream to the lower slopes. Before even reaching the
high grass of the lower hills, he came upon an elk cow
feeding in a clump of buck brush. He interpreted this
as a good sign, and that the medicine he had made
during the past two days was strong. After killing it,
he skinned and quartered the cow and packed the
meat on the extra horse. With part of the hide, he fashioned a crude bag to hold the head and hoofs. He hung
the bag in a tree so that other elk and deer would know
that he had not wasted his kill and would look favor-
ably on his hunting in the future.

After another day at his new camp, fed and rested,
he was ready to fulfill his promise to Rain Song and
Sore Hand. The slashes on his chest were already scab-
bing over and were now only a minor irritation. He felt
the strength that had carried him through the many

battles with the soldiers in the Black Hills and on the Powder, the Rosebud, and the Greasy Grass. He cleaned and readied his weapons and painted his face as he had when he and Sleeps Standing had plunged into the mayhem that was Little Big Horn. This time, however, he was not riding against the soldiers. This time, he rode against one man only—Yellow Hand. Even in this time of sorrow and vengeance, Little Wolf had no thoughts of vengeance toward more white men. He felt that he had punished the guilty ones for the raid on his ranch in the valley. Yellow Hand was the only target on his mind. If others got in the way, then it would be their misfortune.

In final preparation, he tied two eagle feathers in his long dark hair. One of them was badly singed and he was careful to avoid stripping the tattered plume with the rough rawhide cord. The feathers were among the few things he had salvaged from his burnt-out cabin after the Vigilance Committee had paid their call. They had originally been presented to him by the great Lakota spiritual leader, Sitting Bull, and he always wore them in battle. He turned the horses loose, knowing they would not stray from the lush grass of his campsite. It was time. He would not wait for Yellow Hand to look for him.

10

For the second time in the last two miles, Rain Song slid from her horse's back and fell to the ground, re-opening the ragged wound in her side. Hump had pushed the horses relentlessly in an effort to put distance between them and Little Wolf, and finally Rain Song became too weak to hang on. The sullen Nez Perce rode on for thirty yards before realizing the horse he was leading was riderless. When he looked back and saw Rain Song's frail body lying in the trail behind him, he became angry. He yanked his pony's head around so forcefully that the animal screamed in pain.

Galloping back to the wounded girl, he expressed his anger with his whip, slashing her legs and buttocks with the stinging rawhide. When this attack did not provoke response, he paused and sat staring down at her, wondering but not really caring if she was dead. After a moment, she groaned and struggled to get up, but her efforts were in vain. She was too weak to rise.

Hump climbed down from his pony and squatted by her side, his dull, expressionless eyes fixed upon the wounded girl while he speculated on her chances of survival. Yellow Hand had instructed him to take the girl to his uncle's lodge on the reservation where she could be cared for until she recovered from her wound. Looking at the half-delirious young woman, he wondered if it was worth it. It would be much easier to leave her here to die. Still, Yellow Hand was a dangerous man when angered. He stood up and looked back the way they had come. There was no sign of anyone following. He was certain the white Cheyenne had not picked up his trail.

"Get up," he said and prodded her with his foot. She only groaned and rolled over on her back, revealing a blood-soaked buckskin dress. He stared, dumbfounded, not certain if the woman would live or die. Hump was a dull-witted brute and was uncomfortable with the prospect of having to make a decision. But he feared Yellow Hand's wrath, so he decided he would deliver the girl to his uncle, even if she was a corpse by the time they arrived. He cut down two young trees and fashioned a travois to carry Rain Song the rest of the way to the reservation.

It was well after dark when Hump rode into the circle of lodges, leading a horse and travois. The injured woman on the travois had not made a sound during the last three hours, so Hump was not sure if she was alive or dead. At this point, he was unconcerned. He had delivered the woman to the tipi of his uncle. Consequently, in his mind, he had done Yellow Hand's bidding and had nothing to fear from his cousin.

Inside the tipi, seated at the back of the lodge as was befitting the head of the family, Two Horses paused to listen. He was sure he heard a horse approaching. Moments later he heard his name called. His wife, Broken Wing, pulled the entrance flap back far enough to peep outside.

"It's Hump," she said, dropping the flap again while she looked back at her husband. "He has something on a travois." She noted the strained look of irritation on Two Horses's face. Hump was not a favorite nephew, a feeling shared by Broken Wing. He was a powerfully built young man, but was somewhat simpleminded and Two Horses tolerated him only because he was his

brother's son. Two Horses sighed wearily and got up
from the fire. He flashed a tired grimace toward his
wife as he lifted the flap and went outside.

Hump raised his hand in greeting, then gestured toward the travois behind him. "Yellow Hand told me to
bring her to you to take care of her wound. He will
come for her in a few days."

Seeing this was the only explanation the surly
Hump was to offer, Two Horses grunted a reply and
walked over to the travois. There he discovered, to his
astonishment, a half-dead Indian woman, barely able
to open her eyes. He looked back at Hump for some
further explanation. The scout's face was without expression. Two Horses turned back to the woman on
the travois. In the darkness outside the tipi it was still
obvious that the black stains covering the front of her
dress were blood. He called for Broken Wing to come
outside.

Broken Wing, upon examining the injured girl, immediately took charge. She instructed Two Horses and
Hump to carry Rain Song into the tipi, admonishing
the clumsy Hump to be gentle. "She is not a deer carcass," she scolded as she held the entrance flap aside
for them.

While Broken Wing tended to the wounded girl,
Two Horses and Hump went outside where Two
Horses questioned his nephew about their unexpected
visitor. After Hump told him of the events that had
brought Rain Song to his lodge, Two Horses reluctantly agreed to look after the girl until Yellow Hand
came for her. Hump remembered the one thing that
Yellow Hand had stressed—that neither the Indian
Agent nor the soldiers must know about the girl. Satisfied that he had completed his assignment, Hump
left, planning to return to Captain Malpas's company
of troopers in the morning.

Broken Wing was concerned but not overly stressed

to learn the identity of their guest. It would not be possible to keep her presence secret in the small circle of lodges. But the white agent never came to their village, so it was unlikely he would ever find out. Like Hump, Yellow Hand had never been a favorite of hers. They, like many of the Nez Perce warriors, had chosen to turn from the old ways of their fathers and ride as scouts with the soldiers at the fort. Unlike Hump, Yellow Hand enjoyed a reputation of skill and cunning that gave him power among the soldiers and, consequently, created a sense of fear in the reservation of Nez Perces. In spite of her disapproval of her husband's two nephews, she did not hesitate to administer to the wounds of this unfortunate young woman who had landed in her lap.

"She is Cheyenne," Two Horses stated as he watched his wife working to close the ragged wound in the woman's side. "She is the Cheyenne woman the soldiers held captive in the fort, the one the white Cheyenne warrior snatched from the soldiers."

Broken Wing nodded, then asked, "Is her husband dead?"

"Hump was not sure, but he is certain that he will soon be. The soldiers have found two of his camps and Yellow Hand is leading them on his trail."

Broken Wing smiled knowingly. "So Yellow Hand has decided to take the woman for himself." She paused to look into the woman's face. "I can see why he wants her. She is a pretty thing." She sent her husband outside while she stripped Rain Song's dress away and covered her with a soft robe. Rain Song's eyelids fluttered rapidly as if awakening from a deep sleep. Broken Wing laid a cool hand on her brow. "Don't be afraid. You are safe now."

"Damned if I'm not getting tired of these useless patrols. An entire Indian village could hide in these hills and we couldn't find them. If that renegade's got any sense at all, he's so far away from this territory by now that we're just wasting time and rations."

Brice grinned at his complaining friend. In his opinion, Paul Simmons was the least likely candidate to wind up in a cavalry regiment. Paul didn't like horses and, for the most part, they didn't like him. It seemed that even the most gentle of mounts would be tempted to take a nip at him, somehow sensing his dislike for them. Consequently, he had gone to a great deal of expense of time and his personal finances to find the one mount that held no grudge toward him. She was a fine-looking animal, a chestnut mare with white stockings named Daisy, and his greatest fear was that Daisy might be shot out from under him.

Paul's dislike for horses was not the only thing that made him out of place in a cavalry unit. He despised long expeditions in the field which, lately, were constant. Ever since Colonel Wheaton had been thoroughly chastised by his superiors for letting the Cheyenne renegade slip through his fingers, the company had been ordered out on one patrol after another.

"Paul, how the hell did you end up in the First Cavalry anyway?"

"Damned if I know," Paul shot back. "Because I was near the bottom of my class at The Point, I guess. I had my mind set on a desk job in Washington."

Brice laughed. "Well, maybe you'll get there yet." He liked Paul even though the two had very little in common. Contrary to Paul's dislike for the field, Brice thrived on it. He enjoyed being out in the hills away from the routine of the fort. Garrison life in general was boring to him, and life at Lapwai was even more intolerable. The fact that the fort was originally built to accommodate no more than two companies made it vastly overcrowded, with Companies E and H sharing space with the 2nd Infantry Regiment. There were

only two small duplexes provided for the officers'
quarters, which made it necessary for E Company's officers to live in tents in the Southwest corner of the parade ground. As far as Brice was concerned, life was
better in the field, even if the rations were somewhat
lacking.

Paul was about to complain further when Brice silenced him with a raised hand. Both officers looked up
ahead to where Yellow Hand sat on his pony, signal-
ing. "He may have found something," Brice said and
spurred his horse into a canter.

The patrol had been following an old Indian hunting trail for the better part of the morning, leading up
through a dense stand of pines. The lodgepoles on either side of the trail were thick, seemingly impenetrable, with the floor of the forest as much as a foot deep
in pinestraw. There had been no particular reason to
follow this trail, aside from the simple fact that it had
not been searched before.

When the column caught up to Yellow Hand, Brice
saw that the trail had finally emerged from the dark
forest of pines only to descend again across a rocky
ridge toward a narrow gulch. As soon as Brice had
pulled up beside him, Yellow Hand got off his pony
and led it a few yards up the trail. Brice dismounted
and followed.

"Here," Yellow Hand grunted, pointing to hoofprints in the soft sand and shell rock. He got up and
walked a few yards farther, where he pointed to a pile
of droppings. Picking up some of the manure, he held
it out for Brice to see. "Fresh, maybe two hours."

Declining to take the sample, Brice nodded and said,
"I'll take your word for it. Do you think it's Little
Wolf?"

Yellow Hand shrugged. "Don't know. Could be."

"Well, let's follow it and see who it is."

Yellow Hand nodded and climbed back in the saddle. The tracks he had found left the trail and led higher up in the rocky bluffs above them. Brice could hear a few low remarks in the ranks behind him, questioning the wisdom in continuing to climb up the steep mountain. He ignored them. Before long, the trail became so steep that it was difficult for the horses to climb without sliding in the shifting gravel. The soldiers had to sidle along the slope to prevent the horses from going over backward and taking an unfortunate rider on a wild tumble a quarter of a mile down to the trees below. Brice now began to question his wisdom in leading the column along a route so treacherous. He glanced up at the summit of the mountain, several hundred feet above them. Glancing back at Yellow Hand in front, he could see that the scout's Indian pony was having no easier time of it than the heavier army mounts.

From his position high above the single line of blue shirts inching their way across the slope, Little Wolf sat passively watching the troopers laboring to traverse the precarious terrain. He had purposely left a trail they could not possibly miss, and now he waited patiently for the Nez Perce scout to pass a point directly below his position. When Yellow Hand reached that point and entered a narrow gulch, Little Wolf rose to one knee and prepared to go into action.

Brice Paxton glanced nervously at the trees below. *This is crazy*, he thought. Up ahead some forty or fifty yards, he could see that Yellow Hand appeared to have reached more solid ground. Encouraged, he called back to Paul Simmons, "If you can stay in the saddle for a few minutes more, it looks like there's solid footing ahead."

"The question is, can I stay in the saddle a few more minutes?" Paul answered. He hesitated when Daisy sank over her fetlocks in the loose sand and shell rock. "I hope to hell we don't have to go back this way."

No sooner had the words left his lips when the mountain above them erupted in a massive rock slide. Started by a single boulder the size of a washtub, it gathered loose shale and boulders, building as it came crashing down the steep slope, catching larger boulders in its path until, within seconds, it appeared the entire mountain was sliding away. Horses screamed and reared back. Men cried out in alarm, fighting to remain in the saddle. In the wink of an eye, the column of cavalry was plunged into chaos as horses got sideways on the slope, trying to turn around on the narrow trail. First one, then another trooper parted company with his mount and was sent sliding and tumbling down the mountainside, clutching desperately at scrubby pines as they were swept past them.

Brice, at the head of the column, barely escaped being whisked down the mountainside by the slide that passed before him like a tidal wave of earth, boulders, and shell rock. He managed to hold his horse steady, backing him up to a wider place in the trail before turning around. Paul Simmons was in front of him now, struggling desperately with his mount.

"Hold her back, Paul! Don't let her try to run! Hold her back!" Glancing back over his shoulder, Brice could now see that the slide was not spreading toward them. They were safe where they were, if they could calm the horses. "We're all right here. It's behind us," he called out to the troopers still struggling to control their terrified mounts. "Take it real slow."

Looking down below him, he counted four horses and riders scattered in various places along the steep slope. Only one horse had tumbled all the way down to the edge of the lodgepoles. Its rider was making his way down to recover his mount, sliding on all fours to keep from building momentum. The horse, however, appeared to have broken its neck because it lay still, not moving, its head bent at a peculiar angle. *It was pure luck none of the men were killed*, Brice thought.

He ordered the men to start inching their way back down the trail toward the pine forest. Even though the slide had ended, the trail before them was buried, cutting them off from Yellow Hand, who was stranded on the other side. *He'll have to find his own way down*, Brice mused.

Yellow Hand, watching the sudden slide from the safety of the gulch, sensed there was a reason why he was spared but was now unable to get back to the column. He looked quickly around him. All was quiet ahead. He looked back at the wall of dirt and rock that now blocked his way back to the column. Something told him that the rock slide was no accident. His eyes darted nervously back and forth across the rocks above, straining to catch a glimpse of anything moving. Seeing nothing, he had no choice but to continue on, following the gulch, hoping it would lead to a way down the mountain.

Behind him, on the other side of the rock slide, he heard Lieutenant Paxton calling out to him, telling him that they would wait for him at the base of the mountain where they had camped the night before. Yellow Hand heard it, but the message held no importance for him at that moment. His one concern now was Little Wolf. The Cheyenne had cut him off from the soldiers for one purpose only, and Yellow Hand's senses were alive now as he tried to pinpoint the likely spot where Little Wolf might be lying in ambush.

He dismounted. Holding his pony's bridle, he moved cautiously down the rocky gulch, walking close to the wall of rock on one side, and using his horse to shield his other side. As he moved farther along the narrow rock corridor, he could no longer hear the sounds of the troopers behind him. It became as quiet as death, with no sound now except the low moan of the wind sweeping through the boulders above. Yellow Hand would admit no fear of any mortal, yet he had an uneasy feeling that left a metallic taste in his mouth. At every step, he expected the rifle shot that was bound to ring out at him from somewhere. Why did it not come? He felt a rivulet of sweat trace its way from his armpit down his side. He stopped and stared hard at the trail behind him. Where was the Cheyenne dog? The cautious, uneasy feeling became anger, and his face twisted with rage as he frantically searched the cliff's above for sign.

Rounding a sharp turn in the stone corridor, Yellow Hand discovered that the gulch spread out into a shallow ravine with scrub pines along the sides. He stopped and looked it over carefully, his gaze darting from tree to tree. It was the way down he had hoped for—the decline, though not gentle, was not too steep to ride his pony down without fear of going head over heels. Looking down toward the bottom of the ravine, it appeared there was a clearing in the trees. He looked all around him again, above and below. He could see no place that offered real concealment for anyone waiting in ambush. Could his senses have given him the wrong message? Maybe the rock slide was nothing more than a natural slide after all. Yellow Hand was almost disappointed. *Maybe I won't get the chance to kill the Cheyenne dog today*, he thought.

He climbed up into the saddle and sat there for a long moment. He was convinced then that there had been no danger of attack. If Little Wolf was lying in wait for him, this would have been the moment, when he was sitting on his mount, exposed to anyone in the rocks above. There was still no sound save that of the wind. He prodded his pony and started down the ravine toward the clearing.

Although the slope was not dangerously steep, still Yellow Hand had to hold his pony back in an effort to keep from building too much momentum. His pony, nimble though he was, almost stumbled several times as he planted his front legs stiffly before him in the loose gravel, his rump high behind him. Yellow Hand almost lay on his back at times in order to remain in the saddle.

At last, the slope leveled off enough to enable him to sit more easily in the saddle. The pony, upon feeling solid ground beneath his hoofs once more, broke into an easy run, almost a full gallop. Yellow Hand did not hold him back as he made for the cover of the trees and the clearing behind. Free of the burning anticipation of the bullet he felt was certain to come minutes before, Yellow Hand nevertheless deemed it prudent to seek the safety of the tall pines. He did not like the feeling he'd had while exposed on the slope above, a feeling that a rifle's sights were trained on his back. He was anxious to remove himself from that position and once again take on the role of the stalker. He would wait to pick up the renegade's trail again.

The rawhide rope was all but invisible against the background of pine needles on the floor of the forest. Not more than two feet off the ground, tied firmly between two stout pines, it was impossible to see by a rider riding recklessly into the shade of the trees. Yellow Hand's first thought, when he was suddenly hurled into midair, was that his pony had been shot out from under him. In the confusion of that split second, it did not register in his mind that he had heard no gunfire. He was more concerned with trying to break his fall so as to minimize his injuries. He landed hard, rolling to lessen the impact. As soon as he could recover his senses enough, Yellow Hand scrambled to his feet, still dazed by his fall. Looking into the lodgepole forest, he blinked his eyes to adjust to the darkness of the shade. Suddenly his whole body stiffened. *There he was!* Standing before him, his feet planted

wide, coolly watching the efforts of the confused Nez
Perce scout to gather his senses. In the midday darkness of the lodgepole shade, he appeared as a demon,
naked from the waist up, his face painted with red and
white stripes leading from his nose across his cheeks.
He stood squarely, seemingly as tall as the pines
around him. For the first time in his life, Yellow Hand
experienced raw, undiluted terror.

His senses clear now, sobered by the spectre before
him, he glanced around to determine his chances for
survival. His pony, having recovered from his stumble, was now several yards down the trail, past the
menacing figure planted before him. Yellow Hand's
rifle was still in the saddle boot. There was a pistol in
his belt, but the rifle leveled at his midsection acted as
the deterrent that kept him from reaching for it. There
was no place for him to run. A bullet would find him
before he took a step in any direction. After a few frantic thoughts, he resigned himself to his execution and
began to mumble a low death chant.

"Shut up!" Little Wolf spat in the Nez Perce tongue.
"Stop your cowardly whining, killer of women and
old men. It is not time to sing your death song yet."

Mistaking Little Wolf's intention, Yellow Hand was
not surprised that his captor meant to torture him,
killing him slowly. "I am a warrior. I deserve to die
with dignity," he blurted.

"Do not talk to me of dignity. You have the dignity
of a coyote." He motioned with his rifle. "Take the pistol from your belt and throw it to me." He anticipated
the thoughts running through the doomed man's
mind. "Take it out with your left hand, slowly. If you
try to use it, I promise you your death will take many
days." When Yellow Hand drew the pistol and tossed
it at Little Wolf's feet, Little Wolf reached down and
picked it up. He opened the cylinder and ejected the
bullets, then tossed the gun aside. "Now the knife."

When he had relieved him of all his weapons, Little
Wolf said, "We will now see if you are a warrior, as you
claim."

A bewildered Yellow Hand looked on, astonished,
as Little Wolf ejected the shells in his own rifle and
tossed it aside. He then took his own knife and threw
it into the trees where he had thrown Yellow Hand's. It
was plain to him then what was to occur and it left his
mind in a state of confusion. He had a chance to save
his life, but there was a feeling deep inside his soul
that told him he did not want to fight this painted
demon before him. He stood motionless, watching Little Wolf as he stepped closer to him.

Little Wolf knew that he could have easily killed the
scout as he stood there defenseless, cutting him to
pieces with his rifle. But that would not have satisfied
the burning hatred he had for this man. In his grief for
his wife and the rage he harbored for the man who
killed her, he knew that he would not be content with
ending the murderer's life with a bullet. That would
be far too merciful. He had to kill him with his bare
hands, rip the life from him, as Yellow Hand had torn
Rain Song away.

Yellow Hand geared himself to fight for his life,
moving a few steps to his right and then waiting for
Little Wolf to approach. Little Wolf closed then, his
body tensed and ready to spring, like a mountain lion
preparing to kill. Yellow Hand made the fatal mistake
of looking into the Cheyenne's eyes. They were cold,
unblinking, measuring, and Yellow Hand felt his body
shudder. He had seen his own death in Little Wolf's
deep dark eyes.

In the next instant, Yellow Hand bolted, making a
desperate dash for the trees where Little Wolf had
thrown the knives. Little Wolf was on him instantly,
overtaking the terrified man before he had cleared the
narrow trail, sending him sprawling with one blow be-

tween his shoulder blades. Like a cat, Little Wolf showed no mercy in his attack. Yellow Hand tried to roll away from him, but Little Wolf was on top of him in a heartbeat, his hand clamped on the helpless man's throat with the force of a puma's jaws. Slowly, he clamped tighter and tighter. Yellow Hand flailed at his tormentor, trying to break his grip. Little Wolf ignored the blows, clamping down tighter and tighter on Yellow Hand's throat until the Nez Perce could hear the crunching of his own windpipe as it collapsed under the fierce pressure. Consumed by the fury within him, Little Wolf clamped down harder and harder until the object of his terrible vengeance ceased to struggle. Even then, he did not release his death grip on Yellow Hand's throat, staring trancelike at the bulging eyes that looked up at him but no longer saw.

After what seemed a long time, he sat back on his heels, still staring at the body of the Nez Perce scout. The storm that had raged inside him was at last stilled and he sat there on the ground, exhausted. Vengeance was not to be a balm for his tormented soul, however. At that moment, he missed Rain Song more than ever.

The late afternoon melted into dusk and still there was no sign of Yellow Hand. Brice told Sergeant Baskin to have the men make camp there by the stream since it would soon be dark. They would wait until morning for the scout to show up. Paul strode up from the stream where he had been washing away some of the grime that had covered him when the rock slide sent clouds of dust swirling around the troopers. He stood there listening as Brice gave Baskin his orders. When the sergeant walked away, Paul sat down against a willow and stretched his legs out before him.

"I swear, Brice. Do my legs look like they're trying to bow a little? I've got to get transferred out of this damn cavalry."

Brice laughed. "You know, they do look like they're beginning to curve a little." He couldn't resist teasing his friend a bit, although Paul's legs were as straight as the day he was assigned to the 1st Cavalry.

"Damn. If I don't get my desk job, I'll end up bow-legged as hell. I'll be like Baskin there. He's so damn bowlegged he can take a dump standing up and he won't even get any on his boots."

"I wouldn't worry about it, Paul. You'll get your ass shot before that happens."

"You really know how to cheer a person up, don't you?" Turning serious for a moment, he asked, "What do you suppose happened to Yellow Hand?"

"I was wondering myself. He might still be trying to find a way down that mountain, and might have had to cross over to the other side to find a way down. If he doesn't turn up by morning, I suppose we'll have to go looking for him." It riled Brice that he was bound to look for Yellow Hand. He had never cared much for the aloof Indian scout before the incident with the Cheyenne woman. Since then, he had developed a rather strong dislike for him. But he couldn't very well order the troop back, leaving Yellow Hand to fend for himself. That wouldn't set a very good example for the rest of the Nez Perce scouts.

Night passed and morning came bright and clear with a chill on the air. Still there was no sign of Yellow Hand. Now Brice feared the scout was in trouble. He called Paul and Sergeant Baskin over to discuss the best direction to start searching in. They decided it would be pointless to retrace their tracks of the day before. They would still be unable to pass the rock slide. Having that avenue closed to them, Brice decided to skirt the base of the mountain in hopes of finding a way up that would bring them past the slide and intercept the trail beyond that point.

It took them all morning, probing the mountainside

for a way up. But each time they climbed through the ring of lodgepole forest that circled the mountain, they were met with slopes so steep and shifting that they would have to turn back and try in another spot. Finally one of the troopers riding out ahead reported that he had found what looked like a trail through the pines and, from below, there looked to be a ridge high up above it that might be passable. This seemed to offer some possibility, so Brice ordered the column forward.

The patrol weaved its way through the forest, following the game trail in single file. They had almost come to the upper edge of the thick stand of lodgepoles when the point man returned to meet the column, pushing his horse as fast as he could manage in the dense timber.

"Lieutenant!" he called out as he reined up sharply beside Brice. He took a moment to quiet his horse before reporting his find. "I found him. It ain't pretty."

The patrol followed the trooper up the trail to a small clearing less than a hundred yards from the upper treeline. The clearing had no doubt been caused by a fire some years before, because there were singed tree trunks scattered throughout the clearing, nearly covered now by knee-high bushes. Brice didn't see it at first until the trooper pointed toward the right side of the trail. There, from the limb of a stunted pine, hung the body of Yellow Hand. The scout's killer had used Yellow Hand's whip to tie his ankles and hang him upside down. The scalplock had been taken, the skin around the crown of his head hanging jagged and loose from the scalping knife.

"Damn," was all Brice could manage at first. He dismounted to examine the body up close. Baskin moved up beside him. Paul remained in the saddle, seeing all he wanted without need for closer inspection. "Damn," Brice repeated. He noted the dried blood that had formed from rips in the dead man's throat and the small droplets of blood on the ground under his head. "Not much blood," he said.

"Nossir," Baskin replied. "Looks to me like that devil crushed his windpipe, and damn near broke his neck." Looking around the body at the trampled bushes, he said, "Looks like there was a helluva tussle."

"Looks like," Brice answered. He moved around behind the body. "What do you make of this, Sergeant?"

Baskin stepped over beside Brice and looked at the ripped shirt of the late Nez Perce scout. It revealed areas of torn flesh on the dead man's back and shoulders. He studied the wounds for a moment before answering. "Buzzards, or magpies maybe. If I had to guess, I'd say he's been here since yesterday afternoon. Hanging here in these trees, ain't nuthin' found him but the birds. It mighta been another day before the walking critters found him."

"Damn," Brice muttered again. "Cut him down from there." He stepped back as Baskin motioned for the first two troopers in line to dismount. "Let's get him in the ground and then we'll push on. Maybe we can pick up his trail."

"Yessir," Baskin mumbled. The lieutenant knew as well as he did that their chances of following Little Wolf's trail were the same as following a piss trail up the river. It was Brice's notion that it would be fitting to bury Yellow Hand among the thick lodgepoles. The sergeant, having done his share of digging during his years in the army, persuaded him that it would be best to bury the Indian in the rocks above the treeline. "We'd be trying to dig through pine roots for the rest of the day," he explained. So several of the troopers set to it and carved out a shallow grave a few yards above the trail at the head of a massive boulder. After Yellow

Hand was laid to rest, they piled rocks on top to keep predators away.

They made an attempt to pick up Little Wolf's trail, knowing they could not expect much success. It was easy enough at first, for the tracks were obvious, leading up away from the trees. Above them, the peaks of the mountains stood high against the deep azure of the sky, their snowy crowns glistening in the afternoon rays of the sun. Breathtaking yet foreboding, they seemed to defy invasion by mortal man. *The horse ain't been made that can scale those cliffs*, Brice thought, knowing the man they trailed would, out of necessity, have to descend pretty soon. Still, the trail led upward until they came to a vast field of solid rock. That was where the trail ended. Not surprised, Brice ordered the column to turn back.

Halfway back to Lapwai, the patrol met Hump, who was on his way to rejoin the column. As stoic as ever, Hump showed little emotion when told of his cousin's death at the hands of the Cheyenne renegade. Brice was amazed by the sullen scout's reaction to the details of Yellow Hand's demise. If he could have read the thoughts the news generated in the brute's limited brain cells, he would have understood Hump's lack of grief. The scout's first reaction was to realize that the woman, Rain Song, was now his property, and perhaps Yellow Hand's position as chief Indian scout as well. His eyes immediately shifted toward Charlie Rain Cloud, who would be his major competition for the job. No, there would be no mourning for Yellow Hand in Hump's tipi.

Colonel Wheaton reluctantly cut back on the daily patrols searching for the renegade Cheyenne warrior when, day after day, his officers reported back with no contact and no trail to follow. Their Indian scouts could only shrug their shoulders and explain that they

could not follow where there was no trail. On the last
several patrols he had led, Brice noticed an increasing
tendency to hang back on the part of the Nez Perce
scouts. They seemed reluctant to venture far afield,
preferring to work in closer to the column of cavalry.
The scouts also tended to give up on a trail early on,
arguing that it was not Little Wolf's trail but only that
of a harmless hunter. It became clear to him that the Indian scouts had come to believe Little Wolf was perhaps more than a mortal man. Finally, Charlie Rain
Cloud confirmed his suspicions.

"This white Cheyenne, many people think he talks
with the spirits. He has many kills, but all revenge. All
who have tried to catch him are killed. Yellow Hand
was killed, Yellow Hand was a mighty warrior. All the
scouts at the fort feared Yellow Hand. Little Wolf killed
him. People are saying maybe it is best to leave the
white Cheyenne alone and let him go his own way."

It soon became apparent to Colonel Wheaton that
the morale as well as the effectiveness of his Indian
scouts had become decidedly diluted, due to the existence of one man. He would have been inclined to
clean the slate himself and declare the renegade gone
from the territory except for one thing: General Sher-
man was adamant in his demand for the Cheyenne's
capture and hanging. He continued to apply pressure
on Wheaton for results, and threatened to send General Howard back to do the job. Wheaton knew that it
was no more than that—a threat. The one-armed general's reputation had grown to heroic proportions
since he had chased Chief Joseph's band of Nez Perce
from the Wallawa Valley. Still, the pressure from his
superiors was intense enough to warrant Wheaton's
decision to invoke more desperate means. Sergeant
Baskin first learned of the colonel's desperate move
from the regimental sergeant major, and he passed it
along to lieutenants Paxton and Simmons.

Brice and Paul stood talking near the infantry barracks when Sergeant Baskin came out of the commis-
sary storehouse, heading toward the kitchen. When he
spotted the two officers, Baskin veered toward them.

"Well, Sir," he started, addressing Brice, "looks like
our job's been give away. The colonel's sent for Tobin."

Brice raised his eyebrows, mildly curious. "Who's
Tobin?"

"Folks used to say he was the best scout around
these parts. Used to ride for General Howard till they
had a falling out over something to do with the way
the general was chasing Chief Joseph. Folks say he's
part Injun."

Paul snorted an amused snicker. "Is that so? Which
part?"

Baskin glanced at him soberly. "The part that ain't
panther, according to what I hear."

"Well, I guess he'll be welcome." This from Brice.
"We could damn sure use some help."

"Maybe," Baskin said. "But, from what I've heard,
Tobin ain't any too welcome anywhere he shows up."

"Why is that?"

Baskin shrugged. "This is just what I've been told,
mind you. The man's got a bone-deep mean streak.
He's supposed to be a helluva tracker, but he don't
usually come back with prisoners. Seems they most all
get shot trying to escape—least that's his side of it.
And that ain't all they say. Sergeant Becker in H Company says he killed a whore over in Lewisburg. Everybody knew it was him what done it, only they couldn't
prove it."

11

It had been over six months since he had had any contact with the U.S. Army, and by his own choice, at that. For that matter, everything Tobin did was by his own choice. And it had been his own choice to quit his job scouting for General Howard when the general decided he was going to chase Chief Joseph over the Lolo Trail to Canada. He thought the army was wrong in chasing after that band of Nez Perce Indians. Not that Tobin had any great compassion for the Nez Perce. To the contrary, he wasn't particularly fond of them. It was just that he thought if the damn fool Injuns wanted to go to Canada, then let 'em go the hell on to Canada. He told General Howard this and the general responded, in so many words, that it wasn't Tobin's business to make decisions. His job was to do as he was told. Well, that kind of attitude never did set well with Tobin, so he told the general to find him another scout to lead his little tea party.

For that reason, he was somewhat surprised when a Kutenai runner approached the Blackfoot camp where he was living, looking for him. He didn't expect to work for the army again. For that matter, he didn't expect the army would even be able to find him. He had lived with Kills Two Elks's band of Blackfeet for the past several months and, since spring, they had been on the move between the mountains and the buffalo country to the east. Blackfoot was the only tribe Tobin

had any use for, owing to the fact his mother was a
Blackfoot—and even so, he really didn't care much for
living with his mother's people for any length of time.

The Kutenai runner found him at the right moment,
for he was getting tired of the Blackfoot camp. He
might still have ignored the call for help but he was in
need of some spending money, as well as ammunition
for his weapons and some staples. He could live off
wild meat as well as the next man, but he had a strong
hankering for some beef, even maybe a little salt pork
to flavor his beans.

So, when the Kutenai told him that he had been sent
to find him and give him a message from Colonel
Wheaton at Fort Lapwai, Tobin decided to accept the
employment. According to Wheaton's message, he
was needed to track down one renegade Cheyenne
after an entire regiment failed to accomplish it. "Well,
that there's my specialty," Tobin snorted as he read the
letter, "tracking down varmints." The messenger offered to lead Tobin back but Tobin told him to go on
ahead, he could find his own way to Lapwai. He preferred to travel alone. The truth of the matter was
Tobin didn't care for Kutenai any more than he did
Nez Perce.

Kills Two Elks tried to persuade Tobin to stay with
his band because most of the other Indians feared the
huge half-breed with the bushy black whiskers, and he
felt Tobin's presence in his camp gave him a measure
of prestige among his people. Tobin was well aware of
this, but he didn't give a damn about the chief's respect. He was ready to go to work again. And so it was
that he found himself on the trail leading into the Lapwai Valley a few minutes before sunset one early summer day.

*   *   *

Sergeant Baskin glanced up from his guard roster, his roll call having just been completed. It was the second time in three weeks that he had caught sergeant of the guard and he was about to post the guard for the night. The sheer bulk of the rider approaching from the north end of the parade ground had caught his eye and he paused to look at the man. He knew Tobin by reputation only, and had never seen him. But he knew immediately that the imposing figure riding the buckskin horse could be no other.

Walking his horse unhurriedly through the rapidly lengthening shadows from the hills to the west of the fort, Tobin rode right through the middle of Baskin's guard formation and pulled his horse up short before the astonished sergeant.

"Where can I find Colonel Wheaton?" Tobin asked, his voice gruff and harsh.

Amazed by the big man's sand, Baskin didn't answer at once, but stared wide-eyed at the bulk of man before him. The buckskin he rode was a light tan, almost yellow in fact, with a black mane and tail. The horse, with its wide chest and blocky body, was built to carry the load settled solidly upon his back. He stamped nervously at the flies buzzing around his hoofs.

When Baskin didn't answer right away, Tobin's face darkened, showing his annoyance. "You hard of hearing, sonny?"

Baskin bristled. "No, I ain't. The colonel's at his quarters, I reckon." He turned and pointed to a house on the other side of the creek. "Yonder. Now I'll ask you to get that damn horse outta the middle of my formation."

Tobin stared back at the sergeant for a moment, his face devoid of expression. Then he glanced at the line of soldiers behind him, standing at attention. Unimpressed with the sergeant or his formation, he unhurriedly turned the buckskin in the direction pointed out to him and slowly walked toward the creek.

Baskin watched him for a few moments before turning back to the business of inspecting the guard. At almost the same time, the sun dropped behind the hills, plunging the parade ground into heavy shadows. Baskin couldn't help but note that, with the coming of this strange man, a darkness had settled over the land.

The next day, immediately after the morning formation, Brice Paxton was summoned to Colonel Wheaton's office. When he arrived, he found Captain Malpas and Paul Simmons already there. Seated on a stool, looking like a trained bear in a circus, was the imposing bulk of the man known only as Tobin. Brice had heard that the man was in camp, and there was no mistaking this bearlike brute for anyone else. Tobin sat on the tiny stool, looking directly at no one, his eyes staring into the distance at some faraway place that only he could see.

Wheaton started introductions around the room. As each man was introduced to the scout, Tobin shifted his gaze to each one for an instant, with but a flick of his eyes, before resuming his faraway vigil. Brice was fascinated by the trancelike indifference the scout showed to the officers there. Colonel Wheaton went on to bring Tobin up to date on all that had occurred in regard to the white Cheyenne called Little Wolf. He told him about the citizens of Medicine Creek who had been murdered, and the death of the renegade's wife and friends. He ended up his briefing with the gruesome account of the death of his best scout, Yellow Hand.

Tobin listened with no change of expression and without comment. The other officers offered any additional information they felt was crucial. When there was no more to say, the four officers waited for the scout to acknowledge their briefing. Still in his strange

trance, Tobin made no response for a long moment.
Brice began to believe the man was asleep, but then the
great bear roused himself.

"So you killed this buck's wife, did you?"

They all nodded. Colonel Wheaton answered. "Yes,
we believe the Indian woman was killed, although her
body was never found."

The faintest hint of a smile creased Tobin's rough
features. "And that kinda riled him a little."

"I guess you could say that," Brice responded,
"judging by what he did to Yellow Hand."

"Ha!" Tobin snorted. Although that was his only
comment at the moment, his mind was already working on the hunt. It sounded like this buck was not
going to be a simple chase and kill. This white-man-
turned-Injun gave signs of being a little more crafty
than the average renegade. Nothing could have
pleased Tobin more. He admired a man who gave him
a run for his money. It made the killing part more sat-
isfying. And kill him he would. Of course, his instructions were to capture the man and bring him in so the
army could say some words over him and then hang
him. But that would all change when he met up face to
face with a warrior like this Little Wolf.

Colonel Wheaton interrupted the huge man's
thoughts. "Let me know how we can help you in tracking this renegade down. You will, of course, be in the
pay of the U.S. Army for as long as it takes to get him."

"And supplies and ammunition," Tobin inserted.

"And supplies and ammunition, of course. Fresh
mounts too, and I suppose you'll need to take along a
couple of the Nez Perce scouts, maybe more, whatever
you think you need."

Tobin cocked his head, the faint smile reappeared.
"Nez Perce scouts?" He rubbed his chin whiskers as if
thinking on it. "Have them Injun scouts caught this
feller yet?"

Wheaton was confused. "Well, no, of course not."

"Then what the hell do I want 'em fer?"

Brice and Paul exchanged glances. Wheaton was at a loss for a moment, then said, "Suit yourself. When will you start?"

"In the morning. I'll pick up my supplies and ammunition. I don't need no other horses. That there buckskin is all I need. If he gives out on me, I reckon I'll just carry him."

No one laughed. It was unclear whether the brute of a man was joking with them. One could not tell from the expression on his face. One thing for sure, after their first meeting with the fabled tracker, not one of the officers would have bet against his being able to carry a horse on his back.

"Jesus," Paul Simmons exclaimed after Tobin had left the adjutant's office. "That was the damnest thing I've ever seen. I almost feel sorry for Little Wolf."

Brice laughed. "Tobin's a wild one, all right. I think Baskin might have been wrong about him. I think he's more like ninety percent panther."

Sergeant Baskin walked up in time to hear his lieutenant's remark. He had been waiting outside, more than a little interested in hearing the results of the conference. "Panther or grizzly, I reckon it's a toss-up." He moved into the conversation, not waiting for an invitation. "Like I told you, I've heard some things about that cuss. Word has it he ain't never come back empty-handed, and they're usually belly-down across the saddle at that. If you can believe what you hear about him, the man can track a cat across a marble floor, and he's a fair shot with a rifle or an Injun bow."

Paul shook his head, laughing. "Now I really feel sorry for that poor damn Cheyenne. It doesn't seem fair. Maybe we should send a couple of Nez Perce scouts out to help Little Wolf."

*   *   *

Henry Blanton had his back to the door, drying some shot glasses he had just swished around a few times in the pan of water kept behind the bar for that purpose. He thought the sun must have gone behind a cloud until he turned around to discover his doorway filled with the biggest man he had ever seen.

"Damn." The word seemed to drop out of his mouth on its own. He recovered to invite the man into his establishment and ask his pleasure. When the reply was whiskey, he immediately pulled a bottle from under the counter and filled the glass he had just polished. "Best in the house," Blanton announced, having decided it wasn't worth the risk to push some of the cheap stuff on the stranger.

Tobin tossed the drink down in one gulp, seemingly oblivious to the fiery trail it etched down his throat. He smacked his lips a couple of times, savoring the last glow of the flame. Wiping his mouth with the back of his hand and leaning on the counter, he ignored several pairs of eyeballs staring at him from the tables behind. Blanton held the bottle up, questioning. Tobin motioned and the glass was refilled.

"You'd be Blanton, would you?"

"I'm Henry Blanton. This here's my saloon." Looking beyond the huge man's shoulder to the men playing cards at a table, Blanton was met with more than one worried look. That triggered a sense of anxious concern on his part as the same thought occurred to him that had obviously struck his patrons. He stepped back a step and took another look at the stranger. Medicine Creek had been without a sheriff for some time now since Franklin Bowers was killed. It had not occurred to him until that moment that maybe their little town was plump and ripe for the picking by some desperado. And he had never seen a scarier-looking man than the bearlike brute standing before him now.

Tobin licked his lips and tossed the second drink

down. After he had savored it, as he had done with the first, he laid an intimidating eye on the saloon keeper. Blanton froze. "The army's hired me to find that there rogue Cheyenne what's been cutting ever'one to pieces around here. Who can tell me what happened?"

There was an almost audible sigh of relief from the saloon patrons. The room, deathly quiet seconds before, now returned to noisy conversation as the card players realized their lives were not in immediate danger. One of the players rose from his chair and moved to the bar to address the stranger.

"I'm Arvin Gilbert. I'm the mayor of our little settlement. I'd be glad to tell you what I can about the murders." He offered his hand, which Tobin ignored. After an awkward interval, Arvin dropped his arm and continued. "I have to say, Mister, you gave us a start for a minute there."

"Why is that?" Tobin asked, not really interested.

"Why, because you look . . ." Arvin realized what he was about to say and stumbled over his words. "That is, what I meant was . . ." He turned to Blanton for help but Blanton turned mute at that point. "You know, we don't get many strangers come through here and . . ." he trailed off.

The expression of boredom never left Tobin's face. "You mean you thought I was going to rob you? You're saying I look like an outlaw?"

"No, Sir!" Arvin blurted. "I didn't mean that at all."

"You think I look more like a parson, then?"

"Yessir . . . Well, nossir. I don't know what I think. I think you look fine."

"Shit," Tobin grunted, finished with amusing himself for the moment. He was well aware of the effect his appearance had on most people. He enjoyed it, watching the fear in other men's faces when he locked eyeballs with them, seeing them sweat. Having had his small portion of self gratification, he got down to the business at hand. He wanted to know as much about the murders as he could find out. He wanted to know the man he was hunting, how he operated, how he thought. If he could get inside Little Wolf's mind, he could know where to look for him. "Well, I ain't meaning no harm to nobody here," he finally said.

Tobin spent over two hours in Medicine Creek. Arvin Gilbert described how they had found the former mayor, Puddin Rooks, dead in the alleyway, his throat cut, an arrow buried in his gut. He told him about Franklin Bowers, murdered in his own jail; Tolbert and Lonnie lying in front of their cabin, scalped. After an hour, Morgan Sewell drifted in for a drink and helped fill in any details Arvin left out. When he'd finally had one more drink of Blanton's finest, this one paid for by Arvin, and nodded his farewells, Tobin felt he knew a great deal more about Little Wolf. His enthusiasm for the kill was growing with each hour that passed.

Tobin stepped down from the saddle. Leaving the buckskin to graze on the grass by the stream, he walked over to examine the pile of burnt timbers and ashes that were once a cabin. *Burnt him out*, Tobin thought, and he pictured in his mind the scene that must have taken place. Twenty or more vigilantes, according to what Arvin Gilbert had told him. It must have been a hot little party, with plenty of blood. Nothing like killing a couple of women to stoke the courage of a mob of storekeepers and farmers. He had an idea that if this Injun, Little Wolf, had been home at the time, things might have been a little different. He stood up and looked all around him. *Right nice little valley*, he thought. *Good place to start a little ranch.* When he climbed back in the saddle and started out toward the south end of the valley, it was clear to him that the man he hunted was probably as peaceful as any rancher before the good folk of Medicine Creek paid a call.

According to what he had been told at Lapwai, the bodies of the two women and the one man were not found when cavalry patrols scouted the valley. He felt a curiosity to find the bodies, knowing they had been buried somewhere. *Cheyenne,* he thought, *most likely he'd wanna build a platform for 'em, instead of putting 'em in the ground—and he'd wanna hide 'em from the white mob.* As he crossed the valley floor at a walk, he studied the slopes that converged on the south end. Thick with pine and spruce, a line of foothills led to the higher peaks. "If it was me," he said, "I'd wanna set 'em up on the leeward side of one of them hills."

He spent most of the rest of that afternoon searching for sign that might give him a trail to follow. There was an abundance of sign for game, both large and small, but nothing that hinted that a horse might have passed that way. It had been too long, he concluded. Tobin decided to give up the search and go on to the camp by the waterfall. The scouts at Lapwai had given him pretty good directions to that camp as well as to the mountainside where they had found Yellow Hand's body. He turned the buckskin back down the mountain when, quite by accident, he stumbled upon the gravesite he had been seeking.

The buckskin was not at all comfortable with the three bodies on the makeshift scaffolds, and he balked when Tobin spurred him closer. Tobin, however, was not burdened with the superstitions of his Indian mother, and he felt respect for damn little in a world where he feared no man, living or dead. To satisfy his callous curiosity, he dismounted and proceeded to climb up to the platforms.

He found that he was not the first intruder to desecrate the grave. Scavengers had found the bodies, magpies probably, and had picked away at the rotting

flesh exposed by a rip in the hide wraps. He only
sought to verify the bodies as the victims of the vigilantes, and he was satisfied on that count within minutes.

Descending from the tree, he discovered four scalps
tied to the lower end of one of the poles. *Four white
scalps,* he thought, *payment on account.* As he rode
down the slope, he felt more and more confident that
he was getting inside the mind of his man. The
thought caused his heartbeat to quicken with the excitement of the hunt, and he unconsciously rested his
hand on the stock of his rifle.

The following day, Tobin spent little time at the
mountain camp by the waterfall. He saw the begin-
nings of a permanent home the Cheyenne had started
for himself and his wife, and the grave beneath the
branches of the tall pine. Tobin knew his man now. He
felt the fury of the Cheyenne warrior as he raced after
Yellow Hand. The sensation fueled the excitement in
Tobin's mind. This was a man worth tracking down, a
warrior of strength and cunning. This would be a kill
equal to a grizzly or a mountain lion.

He spent several hours studying the trail leading
from the site of Yellow Hand's execution. His senses
honed and receptive, he combed through the multi-
tude of tracks left around the tree where the body was
hung. The cavalry patrol had effectively obliterated all
sign that might help to follow Little Wolf. Still, due to
the ruggedness of the mountainside, there were only
two directions open to the Cheyenne, and he rejected
the one that led back down through the lodgepoles. He
knew his man would make his way along the slope,
above the treeline.

Tobin had not ridden far before finding what he was
looking for—distinct evidence of sliding hoofprints
where Little Wolf's horse had struggled to cross an
area of loose gravel and sand. Tobin smiled to himself,

knowing he and the Cheyenne were of a like mind. Two more hours of slow, hazardous travel brought him to a rocky divide. Crossing over, he came to a deep ravine that led down toward the trees. Following it down, he soon came to a tiny meadow, dissected by a rushing stream that originated in the snow-capped peaks above. This was where Little Wolf had camped, and for more than one night, according to the sign— long enough to hunt and prepare food.

"This is where you're making up your mind," Tobin said softly. "What are you gonna do? What direction are you going in?"

Tobin was confident that Little Wolf had satisfied his lust for revenge. Now he was probably making a decision as to what to do with the rest of his life. He had to be fairly sure that the army could not have followed him this far, so he had to figure he was in the clear. Tobin smiled to himself when he thought about it. It would make his job a little easier.

He spent the rest of the day scouting the Cheyenne's former camp. From the sign he pieced together, he concluded Little Wolf had four or five horses. He could see where they had fed on the meadow grass. He was looking for a trail out of the clearing where the tracks of all the horses led in the same direction, rather than random comings and goings. This would tell him which way he had headed when he didn't intend to return. He had it figured that the renegade would strike out across the mountains, maybe on the Lolo Trail, headed for the safety of Canada. There were a great many Indians living wild in the mountains, like the Nez Perces. Flatheads, and the Kutenai, and the army knew they couldn't flush them all out. Furthermore, Little Wolf was a marked man. Being a white Cheyenne, specifically wanted by the U.S. Army, Little Wolf would most probably flee to Canada out of the army's jurisdiction.

After searching the secluded mountain meadow for almost an hour, Tobin finally found the trail he was looking for. It confirmed his gut feelings about the man he tracked. Little Wolf was indeed headed northeast. It was Tobin's guess that his man would cross over the Bitterroots, through the valley of the Flathead, then across to the eastern slopes of the Rockies. It was going to be hard for a man driving four horses to cover his trail the whole way.

Tobin pushed the buckskin hard. From the tracks leading up through an old game trail, he concluded that Little Wolf had no more than a day's start on him. He could make that up in two days if he kept the buckskin hard after him. After one day's travel, it appeared that Little Wolf had intercepted an Indian trail leading through the mountains toward the valley of the Flathead. Tobin slept very little, starting out each morning at first light and pushing on until dark. Tobin knew he was gaining on his prey as he came upon each of Little Wolf's campsites, but the Cheyenne was making better time than he had anticipated.

It was not until several days later that he came down the slopes and struck the Flathead River. He followed the trail along a deep gorge with the waters of the river rushing and crashing against huge boulders on the steep sides of the gorge. The trail was little more than a narrow footpath in some places. He could well imagine the difficulty involved in driving four horses through.

As Tobin pushed his horse even harder, the buckskin began to show signs of fatigue. Leaving the river, the trail led through a broad valley, lush with grass and thistle, and early summer blooms of flowers. The fragrance of the blossoms was lost on the single-minded scout, so intent was he on cutting the distance between himself and Little Wolf. He whipped his horse mercilessly when the weary animal tried to pause to graze on the sweet thistle. Although feeling no sympathy for the horse, Tobin knew that he would have to stop soon or he would be on foot. He cursed the buckskin for his weakness.

Emerging from a low hill covered with pine and larch, he came upon a small grassy clearing where several springs converged to form a sizable stream. Tobin pulled up short. There, in the meadow below him, were four horses grazing on the sweet spring grass. Tobin could not suppress the smile that formed on his grizzled face. He knew Little Wolf had to stop to let his horses feed sometime, especially after the difficult travel through the heavy forests of the mountains.

He tied his horse in the trees and, with his rifle ready, made his way down to a willow thicket where he could get a closer look at the camp. Other than the blackened spot where a campfire had recently burned, there was no evidence of his prey. Figuring Little Wolf was most likely hunting in the foothills beyond, Tobin settled himself to wait for the Cheyenne's return. In one sense, he was reluctant to see the chase ended. Maybe he had overestimated Little Wolf. Part of him had hoped the white Cheyenne would provide more of a challenge than the simple drygulching he now planned. He did not hear the silent tread of the moccasins behind him, and was unaware of the warrior's presence until he felt the cold hard barrel of a rifle press against his skull.

The blood seemed to freeze in his veins. He was stunned to find he had been outfoxed by the man he tracked. Tobin was not accustomed to being outfoxed by any man. He let his rifle drop to the ground immediately and raised his hands. "Hold on," Tobin sputtered. "Hold on! I don't mean you no harm."

Little Wolf took a couple of steps back. "Turn around. Stand up." He watched as Tobin slowly turned and rose to his feet, his arms still raised above his head. Little Wolf examined the huge man silently for a few moments, then asked, "Why are you following me?" If the man was an army scout, it was not evident to the warrior.

In the few moments Tobin paused to formulate a story, he assessed the man standing before him now with a rifle pointed at his gut. They had told him that Little Wolf was a white man, but dressed in buckskins, he could have passed for either Indian or mountain man. Tobin had not been prepared for the physical appearance of the man. He was taller than he had expected, straight and sinewy. Tobin re-evaluated his foe. "Why, neighbor, I weren't following you a'tall." He endeavored to effect an innocent expression. "I was just fixing to camp here myself and rest my horse up some. I didn't know nobody knew about this spot but me. When I saw them horses, why, I didn't know but what they was wild. But I see they's yourn." He paused to gauge the effect of his words on the menacing figure before him. Since he was still alive at that point, he felt somewhat encouraged that the Cheyenne was uncertain about him. The one thing Tobin counted on was that Little Wolf was not a bloodthirsty murderer at heart, out to kill every white man who crossed his path, and would kill only if given a reason.

Little Wolf lowered the rifle slightly, though not taking it off Tobin completely, ready to use it in an instant if necessary. "You can go," he stated simply.

Tobin didn't require extra time to decide whether the warrior facing him would empty the rifle into his gut if he made one false move. Holding the smile on his face, he moved very slowly. The Cheyenne watched intently as Tobin reached down to retrieve his rifle.

"I'll tell you what, mister. I'm right glad I run into you." Tobin made a big show of taking his rifle by the barrel and propping it on his shoulder, completely unthreatening. "One man alone in this territory ain't the best thing in the world." He paused for a response from Little Wolf. There was none. "Maybe we could share a camp for the night. I shore could use the company. I ain't had nobody to talk to in a month of wandering around in the mountains, looking for elk. It's getting nigh on to sundown and my poor ol' horse is plumb wore out. When you get right down to it, I could use a night's sleep without one eye open for a change. Whaddaya say? A little company for just one night?"

Little Wolf took a long look at the stranger, making no attempt to hide his skepticism. Could the huge white man be telling the truth? Was he only an innocent hunter? His horse back in the trees had been ridden hard. The man brought no packhorse to carry meat back. Finally Little Wolf said, "I camp alone."

Tobin effected a genuine look of dismay on his grizzled features. Putting on his best version of a worried man, he pleaded. "Look here, mister. I shore would appreciate it if you'd let me share your camp. Truth of it is, I got me a little place about twelve miles back yonder in the mountains and it's gittin' too close to dark to make it back tonight. And I ain't much at finding my way through these mountains in the dark. I'll be on my way at sunup."

Little Wolf was not completely convinced even though the man did appear to be sincere. There were very few white men that he trusted but this huge man reminded him of the one white man he had trusted more than any other—Squint Peterson. Like Squint, this man was big, almost half as wide as he was tall. There was really no reason to suspect that anyone this far away from Lapwai would know the army was chasing him. He finally decided he would allow the man to camp with him, but he would keep a sharp eye on him anyway.

Tobin could put on a front as well as any man, and he performed brilliantly for Little Wolf, seeming to be a simple soul with no thought save a good meal and some friendly conversation. Little Wolf had met men like that before who spent long lonely months in the mountains, starved for human companionship. Tobin appeared to be openly impressed when Little Wolf led his horse down to the campfire, a fresh blacktail deer carcass across the saddle. Tobin talked the entire time Little Wolf silently cut the meat and placed strips of flesh on the fire to roast.

For his part, Tobin was patient. He had put on a convincing performance and he was content to wait for his chance. Little Wolf never seemed to take his eye off of his guest, even when Tobin went up to fetch his horse. Tobin credited the Cheyenne's caution as a natural habit. Had Little Wolf not been so physically intimidating, Tobin would have made a bolder move. As it was, he thought it more prudent to wait until the Cheyenne relaxed his guard. In the meantime, he could enjoy a good supper and take his ease by the fire.

As darkness filled the little valley, Tobin got up to stretch and said he was tuckered out. He spread his blankets out away from the fire where he could be out of the firelight. Little Wolf made his bed on the opposite side of the fire, and the two men turned in. Both pretended to sleep, each keeping an eye on the other.

The night deepened as the flames from the fire died away, leaving glowing red coals that eventually faded to gray-white ashes. Tobin blinked away the sleep that continued to threaten him. He could not afford to sleep that night. If he waited until morning, he might not get another opportunity to surprise the ever watchful Cheyenne. Along toward dawn, he heard an owl call in the distance and the faint murmur of a nightbird rustling in its nest. He forced himself to wait a little while longer, listening for any sound from the dark shadows on the other side of the long-dead fire. There was nothing. Beneath his blanket, he cocked the hammer back on his .45 Peacemaker. Moving surprisingly silently for a man so big, he slowly rose to his feet. Still there was no sound from the other side of the clearing. As Tobin stood there, the first faint rays of light crept over the hills. It would soon be light enough to see. Being careful not to step on any branches that had fallen from the firewood, he moved patiently, step by step, his pistol ready for any sudden reaction from the sleeping man in the shadows. It was not yet light enough to make out distinct shapes and forms, especially under the lower limbs of the pine where Little Wolf had made his bed. Tobin hesitated for an instant. He had a desire to see the expression on the Cheyenne's face just before he pulled the trigger, but decided against it. The Cheyenne was too dangerous to give even a split second's warning. But, it was necessary to get close enough to make out the sleeping man's form in the darkness. Carefully placing one foot after the other until he was sure he must be over Little Wolf's body, he reached out and slowly pulled the lower pine bough aside. *There was no one there!*

His immediate thought was that he had been ambushed. The blood froze in his veins when he heard a slight movement in the tree behind him. His reaction was automatic—he whirled around, dropping to his knee, firing at the same time. There was nothing there except his own empty bedroll and the silent pines. Something caught his eye, and he turned, ready to shoot again. It was a squirrel, scurrying to safety. Furious, his nerves stretched taut, he sent two bullets after the fleeing rodent. The act of frustration did nothing to soothe his anger, for he knew the renegade had bested him. Little Wolf was gone, having slipped away during the night. Then another sobering thought struck

him, and he ran down into the meadow to find, much
to his relief, his buckskin busily grazing alone. The
other horses were gone.

Over three miles away, making his way up along the
lower slopes that framed the valley, Little Wolf
stopped and listened. There had been three shots, the
sound partially muffled by the hills. *So*, he thought, *I
was right not to trust that man.* He was still uncertain
whether the man was specifically after him or if he
was just intent on killing him for his horses. He was
sorry then that he had not taken the hulking man's
horse too, but there had been the possibility that he
was telling him the truth. Little Wolf nudged his horse
and continued toward the mountain pass that had
brought him through these same mountains many
moons before when he and Squint had first come to
this country. Perhaps he had seen the last of the big
man on the buckskin horse, perhaps not. He would
watch his backtrail carefully.

Back in the clearing, Tobin was stunned. *How in hell*,
he wondered, *could the Cheyenne steal out of camp and
lead five horses away without making a sound?* He must
have dozed off sometime during the night, but he
could have sworn that he didn't. Then he got mad. Little Wolf had made a fool of him. Tobin counted no man
a better tracker, no man a more skilled hunter, and no
man cunning enough to outsmart him. He hurried to
saddle the buckskin, not pausing to eat any breakfast.

12

After two days, when it appeared that Broken Wing's patient was not going to make it, Rain Song suddenly began to recover from the severe wound in her side. On the third day, her fever cooled, and she was able to take some nourishment in the form of a thin soup made from prairie turnips and seasoned with some bits of rabbit meat. Although her first three days in the Nez Perce camp were a blur in her mind, she came to recognize the smiling face of Broken Wing, and was conscious of the occasional stern countenance of Two Horses peering down at her.

Broken Wing had done her work well, and before a week had passed, Rain Song was able to sit up by the fire outside the lodge. Her benefactors questioned her extensively, curious about her people and how she happened to be so far from the land of her tribe. Rain Song, reluctant at first to talk of her husband, was eventually worn down by Broken Wing's insistent questioning, and the Nez Perce woman soon came to know Rain Song's story. Still burdened with the grief of Little Wolf's reported death, she held no desire to live without him at her side. But her natural sense of survival dictated a fight for her life as long as Yellow Hand was absent. Broken Wing said nothing to her about her husband's fearsome nephew, but she overheard Two Horses telling his wife that the girl was Yel-

low Hand's property and there was nothing he could
do to change that.

As yet another day passed with no sign of the feared
Nez Perce scout, Rain Song and Broken Wing began to
talk more and more. Two Horses's wife soon developed a genuine feeling of compassion for the
wounded girl, especially when she learned exactly
how Rain Song had come to be stabbed. As she felt
herself growing stronger each day, Rain Song decided
she must escape before Yellow Hand returned to get
her. She had no notion as to where she could run. She
only knew that she must flee from the reservation village. In her desperation, she also knew that she had to
confide in someone, and she sensed that she could
trust Broken Wing. It was obvious that Yellow Hand
was not held in high regard by Two Horses and Broken Wing. And, while Two Horses hesitated to risk
Yellow Hand's anger, Broken Wing did not. Counting
on this, Rain Song told Broken Wing of her plans to escape.

"He will surely come after you," Broken Wing
warned.

"I know, but I will die before I go with him. My only
chance is to run."

Broken Wing studied the young girl's face for a moment, thinking hard on what she was about to say.
"Very well. If you are sure. I will help you. I know of
someone who may help you escape, but I will have to
go to talk to them first." She got up to leave. "Say nothing of this to my husband. He is a good man, but he
fears Yellow Hand."

Broken Wing was gone for almost an hour. When
she returned, she met Rain Song's anxious stare with a
smile. "They will help you. There is a man here,
Wounded Bear. He and his sons have decided to leave
the reservation and make their way to King George's
land to the north. With their women and children,

there will be this many." She held up all ten fingers twice. "They say you are welcome to join them."

Rain Song's spirits soared. It was the first sign of cheer Broken Wing had seen in her new friend. The Cheyenne girl took Broken Wing's hands in hers and spoke, almost in a whisper. "Why don't you and Two Horses come too? This is no place to live."

Broken Wing smiled but shook her head sadly. "Two Horses would not go. He did not choose to go with Chief Joseph and the rest of our people when they made their brave march to the buffalo country. He says it is useless to resist the white soldiers. They are too many. I miss the old ways, but I must stay with my husband."

Rain Song was disappointed that Broken Wing would stay, but her heart was light with anticipation of her escape. However, her elation was shattered later that afternoon when Yellow Hand's surly cousin Hump rode into the circle of tipis. Rain Song and Broken Wing quickly slipped into the tipi to avoid catching the brute's eye. Sighting Two Horses talking in a group of men, Hump rode directly toward him and dismounted. A few minutes after, Two Horses came to the tipi to tell the women the news.

"Yellow Hand is dead!" He paused a moment for the news to fully register. "The white Cheyenne killed him." He looked into Rain Song's eyes, which were wide open in disbelief.

"Little Wolf?" Rain Song gasped. Her eyes even wider, she looked at Broken Wing and then back at Two Horses. "Little Wolf killed him? Then . . ." She could not finish. Her throat choked with emotion, she simply stared at Broken Wing for a long moment. Finally, when her emotions were under control again, she said, "They told me he was dead!"

Two Horses shook his head. "He is not dead. The

soldiers still search for him, and they have sent for a special tracker to hunt him down."

Before Rain Song could speak again, the flap of the tipi was suddenly thrown aside and Hump pushed into the lodge, startling everyone. He stood in the center of the lodge, staring down at Rain Song, a triumphant sneer etched into the usually thoughtless countenance. "You are my woman now. Get on your feet!"

Broken Wing quickly stepped between him and Rain Song. "She cannot go with you. She is not well yet." Taking her cue from her friend, Rain Song sank back upon the buffalo robe she was seated on. "She will not be strong enough for several days."

Hump was undecided. He looked at his uncle, only to meet a blank stare. He returned his gaze to the Cheyenne woman. "She looks well enough to me. I will take her now."

Broken Wing was adamant. "No. She is too weak to go with you. She cannot cook or work. Wait a few days and she will be strong enough."

Confusion was written on Hump's face. He wanted the woman now, but he didn't relish the thought that he might have to care for her until she was well enough to do his bidding. He stood there saying nothing for what seemed an eternity to Rain Song. Finally he turned back to Broken Wing. "Make her well. I must return to the soldier fort now, but I will be back for her in three days' time. She is my woman now." Turning his attention back to Rain Song, he glared down at her. "You are my woman!" He made a gesture to reach for her but Broken Wing intercepted his arm and turned him toward the entrance.

"You go now. She must rest." The simple brute allowed her to lead him outside. "You must be hungry. Sit down here by the fire and I will get you some food before you go."

Inside the tipi, Rain Song sat terrified. Moments earlier, she had been elated to hear that her husband was not dead, only to have her hopes dashed to the depths of despair by the ugly savage, Hump. She lay down on the robe, pulling it up around her, afraid to move while Broken Wing and Two Horses played host to their unwelcome guest outside. When he stuck his head inside the entrance for one more look at his prize before leaving, she pretended to be asleep, not moving until Broken Wing came in to tell her he was gone.

Rain Song was immediately up on her feet. "Little Wolf is not dead!" she exclaimed, walking frantically back and forth, oblivious now to the soreness in her side. "Why does he not come for me?"

Broken Wing put her arm around Rain Song's shoulders, seeking to calm her. "He thinks you are dead. That's why he doesn't come for you. Hump said the soldiers think Yellow Hand killed you. That's the reason he brought you here, to hide you from the soldiers. Yellow Hand was afraid the soldiers would make him give you to them."

"I must find Little Wolf! He thinks I am dead! Little Wolf . . ." The words trailed off as a picture formed in her mind of her husband, hunted by the soldiers and thinking her dead, disappearing into the mountains where she could never find him. She could not bear the thought. "I must get away from here!" Frantic, she realized, "I don't know where to look for him!"

Broken Wing did her best to calm the stricken girl. "The soldiers think he is heading for King George's country. Wounded Bear is going there with four lodges of his family. You can still travel with them, and maybe Little Wolf will be there."

Rain Song struggled with her dilemma. She didn't know what she should do. She was sure that if Little Wolf was truly alive, he must surely think she was dead. Otherwise he would have come for her already.

She could not stay in the village, hoping he would come. Hump would be back for her in a few days. There was little choice, she decided. She must leave here with Wounded Bear and hope to find her husband in the land to the north.

"You sent for me, Sir?"

Brice Paxton put aside the army Colt he had been cleaning. "Yeah, Baskin." It registered in his mind that the sergeant did not salute when he reported. Not that Brice cared—Baskin never saluted unless reporting to the colonel. Brice supposed Baskin figured his years of service added up to equal status with any lieutenant. It rankled Paul Simmons a little, but Brice laughed about it. "Get the troop ready to ride on an extended detail. Draw rations and grain for twenty days."

"What's up?"

"A band of about twenty or so left the reservation. The agent thinks they're trying to head to Canada. We've got to go after them and bring 'em back."

"Who are they? I mean, men, women, who?"

"The colonel said it was ol' Wounded Bear and most of his family. Probably only about six or seven men. The rest are women and children."

Baskin scratched his chin whiskers. "That don't sound like it oughta take twenty days."

"I hope it doesn't. But they've got a full day's start on us. We didn't find out about it until today and the agent said he figures they've been gone since sometime yesterday."

"Light marching orders?"

Brice paused to consider. "Yeah, except they can carry cooking utensils. One blanket and a hundred rounds of ammunition per man. No tents. Hell, the weather is warm enough to sleep outside."

Baskin nodded after each item called out. "How many Injun scouts we taking?"

"Take Charlie Rain Cloud. Let him pick two others." Brice started to leave but Brice stopped him. "Tell him I don't want that damn Hump. I can't depend on that moody brute. He's dumber 'n a stump."

Baskin nodded and said, "I don't think he's in camp anyway. I saw him riding out earlier this morning."

It was a little past noon when the column of twenty-eight regulars, headed by Brice Paxton, filed out of the fenced area of Fort Lapwai and struck out for the Nez Perce reservation. Brice planned to bivouac near the village that night and start early the next morning on Wounded Bear's trail.

There had been no rain for a week, so it was a dry and dusty column of troopers that made camp that night across the shallow creek from the gathering of Indian lodges. It was still light enough to see, so Brice and Sergeant Baskin, along with Charlie Rain Cloud, rode over to the circle of tipis to question the Indians. Two Horses and Broken Wing were among a small gathering that stood silently watching the soldiers approach. Brice noticed that Broken Wing's lip was bruised and swollen. Upon coming closer, he could see that it also had been bleeding. He knew Two Horses to be a kind man and didn't think him likely to be a wife beater. Aside from that, he knew Broken Wing too and, if Two Horses beat her, she would probably have shoved a knife between his ribs. He raised his hand in greeting. Two Horses nodded in recognition. Broken Wing made no reply.

"What happened to you?" Brice asked in sign and laid his finger on his lip.

Broken Wing flushed, embarrassed. Then, with the hint of a spark in her tone, she answered, "Hump."

"Hump?" He looked quickly beyond the group of Indians, half expecting to spot the surly Nez Perce scout. But he was nowhere to be seen. He told Charlie

Rain Cloud to ask Two Horses what happened. While Charlie talked to Two Horses and his wife, Brice walked over to where Baskin was standing, looking at a wide open space in the line of tipis. There were four worn-out circles where Wounded Bear's lodges had stood. As they were speculating on how long it had been since the lodges were taken down, Charlie rejoined them.

"Hump was here today but he's gone after Wounded Bear already."

Brice was startled by this bit of information. "Gone after him? You mean he's running too?"

Charlie went on to explain that the Cheyenne woman had been in the camp, recovering from a severe wound. It was Yellow Hand's doing but, with Yellow Hand's death, Hump figured the woman belonged to him. He had gone to overtake them and get the woman back.

"That lying son of a bitch," Brice said, thinking of Yellow Hand. "He snatched the woman and hid her out here somewhere after all." He pictured the frightened little Cheyenne woman as he had last seen her, locked in the room behind the hospital, her only crime the fact that she was an Indian. And now these two Indian scouts were passing her around like she was a piece of property. She deserved better than that—any woman did. Brice shook his head slowly as if to clear the picture from his mind, turned to Sergeant Baskin, and said, "Too late to do anything else tonight. We'll pull out at sunup."

Approximately twenty miles north of the cavalry bivouac, Wounded Bear had made camp near the banks of a deep stream still swollen with runoff from the mountains above. The valley they were passing through was split at the north end by a river that forked a few hundred yards above his chosen campsite. Wounded Bear saw to his horses while the women started their cookfires. He turned to see his eldest daughter's husband approaching, a short, blocky man named Blue Otter.

"We have not gotten far since leaving the reservation," Blue Otter started. "If we don't make better time, the soldiers will be after us before we get to the land of the Salish."

Wounded Bear nodded solemnly to the younger man. "I know. But we don't have horses for everyone so we must do the best we can. I think it will be several days before the soldiers know we are gone. If the spirits are with us, we may cross over the mountains before they catch us."

Blue Otter did not always agree with his father-in-law on matters pertaining to their escape to Canada. "I know you have said we will hold to the western fork of the river and find a new way through the mountains, and that is a good plan. But I wonder if it wouldn't be quicker to take the east fork and strike the old trail to the buffalo country."

Wounded Bear patiently reiterated his reasoning to his young son-in-law. "I think what you say is true. That way might be quicker. But it would be quicker for the soldiers too. That way is an old trail, and they would expect us to go the way hunters have always gone. If we take the west fork, we may be able to lose them in the mountains."

Blue Otter nodded his head in understanding. "You are probably right."

Blue Otter said nothing more, but Wounded Bear knew the brash young warrior still questioned the wisdom of the older man's decision. Like most young men, Blue Otter was in favor of taking the quickest route, no matter the dangers. As it turned out, the decision would be made for them.

Rain Song, strong enough now to help Wounded Bear's wife prepare the food, was busily making a corn

paste to fry over the fire when Wounded Bear returned
from the horses. She waited for the old man to situate
himself before the fire before she spoke.

"I am much stronger today. I think tomorrow I will
be able to walk with the other women." Rain Song
knew the horse she doubled on with Wounded Bear's
wife was poor and almost broken down. If she continued to ride, the animal would not make it through the
mountains with the two of them.

By his expression, she could tell her words were
good news to the old chief. But he only nodded and
said, "We shall see what the new day brings." Hers was
not the only horse that was in bad shape. It had been a
hard winter. The grass was lush now in the early days
of summer, but the horses had not had time to fatten up
from winter because of the poor quality of the grass on
the reservation. Wounded Bear knew they were not in
any condition to make a run for it and that was another
reason for not choosing to take a trail familiar to the
soldiers. He needed time to rest the horses. He might
have chosen to wait until later in the summer to make
their escape, but all the people at the reservation were
ready to leave then. For that reason, the soldiers were
much more alert to the possibility of their flight.

The old man's thoughts were interrupted by a shout
from one of the warriors. Someone was coming. He
immediately got to his feet and looked around to see
where he had laid his old Henry rifle. Finding it
propped up against a willow, he grabbed it and ran to
the edge of the stream. In the fading light, he could just
make out a single rider, approaching at a gallop across
the grassy floor of the valley. Upon seeing the people
gathering at the streambank, the rider called out when
still a hundred yards away, and they recognized the
greeting as Nez Perce. It was not until the rider
splashed through the stream and bounded up the
bank that Wounded Bear recognized Hump.

He was immediately alarmed. The presence of Hump could only mean bad news of one kind or another. Hump was on the payroll of the army as a scout. Was a column of soldiers close behind? Or was he here because of the Cheyenne woman? Hump did not make him wait long before declaring the purpose of his visit.

"Where is the woman?" he demanded, stepping down from the saddle even before his horse had fully halted. When no one spoke, he lashed out at a young man standing closest to him with his whip, laying a raw welt across the unfortunate man's neck. The young man recoiled from the stinging blow and gathered himself to retaliate. Hump quickly leveled his rifle at the young man's stomach and gestured for the man to come at him.

"No!" Wounded Bear shouted and stepped between the two. He knew the savage Hump would not hesitate to kill the young man, and Wounded Bear needed every man he had. With anger blazing in his eyes, he turned to his nephew. "Why do you come here, making war on your own people? Have you no honor? Have the soldiers made you their camp dog, as they did Yellow Hand?"

Hump ignored his chastising. "Where is the woman? She belongs to me." A movement beyond the campfire caught his eye and he turned in time to see a woman disappear into the darkness, running toward the horses grazing close by. Without hesitation, he leaped on his horse and charged after her.

Rain Song ran for her life. Her only chance was to reach the horses and escape in the dark. Ignoring the sharp pain that stabbed her side with each step she took, she strained as hard as her body would permit. Almost immediately, she heard the thunder of hooves bearing down upon her, louder and louder until they seemed to be almost on top of her. The closest horse in the grazing herd was still a long twenty yards away.

She felt the impact of Hump's horse as he slammed into her. Like a boulder, the solid blow from the horse's chest sent her rolling head over heels in the knee-high grass. Before she could recover her senses, Hump dismounted and was on top of her.

"You are *my* woman," he hissed and laid his whip upon her bare legs a dozen times, leaving bloody welts each time it kissed her flesh. Subdued, and too hurt and frightened to fight back, she tried to cover her head with her arms and submitted to the beating.

When he had exhausted some of his anger, he reached down and grabbed a handful of her dress and pulled her up on her feet. He pulled a length of rawhide rope from his saddle pack and bound her hands together. Then he threw her up on his horse as easily as lifting a sack of flour, and led the animal back through the silent gathering of people. The thought of putting a bullet into the brutish scout entered the minds of more than one of the braves there, but none dared. Hump was feared as much as Yellow Hand had been. Of the handful of men there, only old Wounded Bear dared to speak out against him.

"Why don't you leave her alone? The woman does not want to go with you." Hump turned to face him, an angry scowl on his face. Wounded Bear was not intimidated. "She already has a husband. Leave her with us and go back to your soldier friends."

The muscles in Hump's arm tensed. He thought about giving Wounded Bear a taste of his whip, but he restrained himself. "This is none of your affair," he said, his voice threatening. "She is a Cheyenne, a slave. She belongs to me. I will kill any man who stands in my way." His rifle in one hand, he pulled himself up behind Rain Song and kicked his horse hard, disappearing into the night.

Wounded Bear was truly sorry to see the Cheyenne woman carried off by this savage bully. Had he been younger, he might have defied Hump, but he didn't blame the young men in his band for not resisting. After all, Rain Song was a captured Cheyenne. Maybe Hump did have some justification in his claim of ownership. Anyway, it was over and done. The brute had what he wanted. Wounded Bear had more important things to occupy his mind at the moment. Blue Otter was right—it was imperative that they make better time on the trail tomorrow.

Brice had his men in the saddle before sunup. There was a great deal of grumbling among the troopers, but Brice intended to overtake the runaways before they had an opportunity to cross the mountains into the Flathead Valley. He drove the men hard, keeping them in the saddle all day, stopping only at dark to rest the horses. The trail was easy enough to follow so they were able to make forty miles that day. When camp was made that night on the west fork of the river, he sent Charlie Rain Cloud on ahead to scout the next morning's trail for a few miles. When Charlie returned, he reported that he had seen cookfires in the bluffs, no more than four or five miles ahead.

"We caught 'em," Sergeant Baskin announced, upon hearing Charlie's report. "I didn't figure we'd need twenty days' rations to catch up with this bunch."

"We haven't got 'em back to the reservation yet," Brice responded. "What does the trail look like up ahead, Charlie?"

The scout shrugged his shoulders. "Not bad. They follow river pretty close."

Already knowing what his lieutenant was considering, Baskin said, "There's gonna be a moon tonight, almost a full moon."

Brice nodded. "Looks like a perfect evening for a night march. Sergeant, let the men have fires tonight but keep 'em small. After the horses are rested for a

few hours, we'll move up to within a mile or two of
their camp and hit 'em in the morning."

A light mist rose from the river and Quill shivered in
the chilly morning air that settled in the narrow valley.
She tapped her fingers impatiently while she waited
for the water bag to fill. Looking back at the camp, she
realized that she was the first to rise. This pleased her.
She liked to be awake and cooking Blue Otter's breakfast before the other women crawled out from their
warm blankets. Blue Otter would brag about his hard-
working wife.

Her water bag filled, she climbed up the steep bank
and started toward her cookfire, which was already
blazing with the limbs she placed on the coals only
minutes before. She paused to listen. A soft thundering
sound came to her from across the river. *The horses are
running,* she thought, *someone is stealing the horses!* She
ran to the edge of the bluff and looked beyond to the
grassy meadow. The horses were not running—they
were still there where the men had left them to graze
the night before. As she looked at them, first one and
then another, they pitched their heads up and whin-
nied, aware of the presence of strange horses.

Quill dropped her water bag and screamed out in
alarm, for she realized then what the thundering hoofs
were. At almost the same moment she screamed, the
first shots rang out. As she ran to alert the others, she
saw the first line of cavalry plunging across the river,
their horses struggling to climb the steep bank.

Brice, at the head of his charging troopers, had given
the order to shoot for effect only. His intention was to
surprise the Indians and demoralize them with a sudden show of force, without killing anyone if possible.
His job was to bring them back to the reservation, and
his plan might have been successful but for the un-
foreseen steepness of the river banks. As his horse

struggled and pawed to gain the top of the bank, he saw other horses sliding backward and falling on both sides of him, dumping their riders into the chilly water. The troopers behind, seeing their comrades tumbling, thought their horses were brought down by rifle fire from the Indian camp. Consequently, they returned fire, no longer shooting into the air but aiming at the fleeing figures now running to the safety of the bluffs behind them.

Brice, fighting hard to keep his horse from sliding into the water, managed to gain the far bank along with a handful of his men. He was forced to lose valuable time and waste the element of surprise while he waited for the rest of the column to ford the river. During that period of perhaps ten minutes, not one shot was fired by the Indian camp as they ran for cover. By the time at least half of Brice's patrol had regrouped, the Nez Perces were safely positioned in the gullies and cuts in the bluffs, and were now returning fire.

Sergeant Baskin pulled up beside Brice. He was soaked to the skin from a dunking in the river. "You want to charge and run 'em out of there?" The sergeant had let his anger override his common sense.

"Shit no," Brice responded, "I don't need to lose half the men charging those bluffs." It was bad enough that his original plan had been bungled. Now he was in a skirmish.

Baskin was still hot. He would rather have been shot than take a bath and he was eager to make someone pay for it. "Well, what the hell do you aim to do?" When Brice cocked his head around and locked a cold eye on him, he added, "Sir."

"We don't have much choice." Standing up in the stirrups, he yelled, "Dismount! Send the horses back out of range along the riverbank." He then had Baskin set up a perimeter fronting the gullies to keep the renegades pinned down in the bluffs. As the handlers col-

lected the mounts and led them out of the line of fire,
the rest of the men scurried about, finding cover anywhere they could, some scratching out hasty rifle pits
in the sand. Brice deployed eight of his troopers between the hostiles and their horses.

From early morning until just before noon, the
troopers kept a steady rain of gunfire on the Indian positions. Brice figured the renegades could not repel
them if he ordered a charge, but he knew he would
take casualties if he did. And he still wanted to avoid
killing any Indians if he could. He counted on the half
dozen or so rifles among the Indians running out of
ammunition before long, forcing them to finally surrender. So Brice kept them pinned down and waited
for the inevitable.

In the gullies, things were not going well for
Wounded Bear's band. The old chief had caught a bullet in his side during the flight into the bluffs. One of
the younger men had been killed trying to get to the
pony herd, leaving only five of them to defend their
families. Although the wound pained him badly,
Wounded Bear fired his rifle until the old Henry
jammed with dirt in the magazine and he was forced
to lie back and let the others shoot what little ammunition they had left.

It soon became apparent that they could hold out no
longer. The sun was almost in the middle of the sky
and pretty soon the soldiers would realize there had
been no shots fired at them for some time. Wounded
Bear counciled his young warriors to save a few bullets to use only if the soldiers charged. "We are finished. We have women and children to think about. I
think we must surrender."

Blue Otter alone protested the decision. "I will not
go back to the reservation. I will die first!"

Wounded Bear understood his son-in-law's anguish, but he had concern for his daughters and his

grandson. "It is not for me to say what another man must do. If I were younger, I might feel as you do. But how will you escape? We are cut off from our horses. The soldiers will surely kill you if you try to run."

Blue Otter had been looking for an escape route from the moment he pulled his family into the deep gully. He discovered a likely exit from the trap they found themselves in when he spotted another gully, separated from the one they were in by no more than three feet of clay bank. The second gully ran perpendicular to theirs and led down to the river. While he fired his rifle at the soldiers, Blue Otter told his son to pick away at the dirt between the two gullies with his knife.

Everything fell silent. The soldiers had stopped firing. They sensed an order was soon to come to attack the Indians' position, since there had been no return fire from the Nez Perces for fully a half hour. Blue Otter knew there was no time left. "I speak for only myself and my family. We can crawl through this hole and follow the gully down to the river. If others want to come, I welcome them, but I and my family will certainly go."

"How will you get to your horses? The soldiers will kill you."

"We will go on foot. I would sooner walk to Canada than go back to that reservation of slow death."

None among the others chose to slip out of the trap with Blue Otter. He waited as long as he thought prudent before gathering what belongings he had been able to salvage when the soldiers attacked. Wounded Bear embraced his daughters and grandson and then bid them a solemn farewell. Tears streamed down his daughters' faces as they dutifully followed Blue Otter through the opening fashioned by his son. Wounded Bear watched them until they could no longer be seen from his place at the head of the chasm. Then he crawled back to the lower end of the gully to watch the soldiers' position. There was no indication that the troops had seen Blue Otter escape.

Back near the banks of the river, Brice signaled for Sergeant Baskin. When Baskin made his way over to the lieutenant's position, he dropped down on a knee, still keeping a wary eye on the bluffs. Brice looked at his watch. "It's been over thirty minutes now with nothing from those gullies. I think we've waited long enough. Let's go get 'em outta there."

"Wait!" Baskin blurted and Brice turned back toward the bluffs to find a white cloth waving on a rifle barrel protruding from one of the gullies. "Looks like this little picnic is over."

Once the Indian ponies were rounded up, and the wounded and dead were loaded on travois, the troop started back to Lapwai with four good hours of daylight left. Wounded Bear, mortally injured, had made his last attempt to regain the life of freedom he had been born into. The wound in his side eventually became infected and he was to die within two weeks of his return to the reservation. Back in a willow thicket by the river, Blue Otter, his wife, her sister, and his son hid until the column was out of sight. They then crossed the river and started making their way toward the mountains on foot.

13

"What the hell?" Tobin roared and pulled back hard on the reins. What he saw didn't make sense. Little Wolf had run north just as Tobin figured he would, following the valley, heading toward Canada. Now, for no apparent reason, the white Cheyenne had turned back dead west, following an old hunting trail that led up into the mountains. This caused Tobin some measure of irritation. He thought he had figured out his man, knew what he was thinking, and he had him heading straight for Canada as fast as he could get there.

"Hell," he blurted, "he's heading into Kutenai territory." Tobin didn't like it when his prey didn't run true to form. He paused to think it over for a few minutes while he scrutinized the trail plainly left by the four horses. *Maybe he's just trying to throw me off*, he considered. Then another thought struck his mind. *"Maybe this ol' boy has still got a taste for blood and he's thinking about taking a few more scalps from his good friends in Medicine Creek before he leaves the country.* Maybe Little Wolf was more bloodthirsty than he had figured him to be. The longer Tobin followed the trail up through the spruce and pines, the more the idea appealed to him. He felt he was back inside Little Wolf's head again. "That musta been one purty little Injun gal," he said.

Although Tobin never hesitated to follow a hunch,

he still kept a sharp eye to make sure Little Wolf was not intent on doubling back and heading north again. As slick as this renegade was, Tobin did not discount the possibility that the Cheyenne was waiting to ambush him.

The trail was steep in places as it climbed higher into the trees, sometimes blocked by fallen timber, deadfalls that necessitated a detour. But the tracks always came back to the trail. Hours passed with no long departure from the trail leading to the west.

It was almost sunset when the tracks split off from the trail and led off through a thick forest of lodgepole pines, with trees so close together that Tobin marveled how a man could lead four horses through it. *Uh-oh*, he thought and smiled to himself. *He's trying to lose me now.* Though there were still a couple of hours of daylight left, it would soon be black as night in the pines. So Tobin decided it best to make camp where he was and wait for daylight to follow Little Wolf's trail. The Cheyenne was slick—it wouldn't do to give him any advantage.

Morning came. Tobin knew he was losing ground by having to wait for the sun to filter a little light through the tall pines, but he had little choice. Even when he decided it was as light as it was likely to get, the floor of the forest was still cloaked in a dark veil. Tobin was not discouraged. He was confident that no man was his equal when it came to tracking. At times he found it necessary to dismount and proceed cautiously on foot as he searched for disturbed patches in the deep floor of pine needles.

After hours of dogged tracking, he emerged from the trees on a downslope. Out in the open, the trail led down through a grassy bottom to a small stream where it appeared the Cheyenne had stopped to let his horses feed on the knee-high grass. The water ran deep and swift, and there was beaver sign everywhere among the clumps of willow. Tobin gnawed on a piece of buffalo jerky while his horse drank from the stream. He studied the trail leading off up the stream, paralleling the coursing water. Tobin glanced ahead, toward the mountain where the stream originated, thinking, *After holding to the west for more than a day, he's turned back north.* Again Tobin smiled. *This is where he figures to throw me off. Wants me to think he's heading for Canada after all.*

The trail was easy to follow until the stream narrowed as it carved its way through broad areas of shale and rock, approaching the treeline. The buckskin began to labor as the incline became more severe, but Tobin pushed him onward. "If that damn renegade can drive four horses up here, you better damn shore make it," he scolded.

"Here it is," he stated at the place he expected to find, where the trail he had been following vanished. *Now we'll see who's the best,* he thought as he dismounted and began a careful examination of the rocky ground. He covered the area, working in a wide circle until he found what he was looking for. It was barely noticeable, a handful of disturbed gravel and a small hoofmark on a rock. "East," he noted softly, and he paused to look off in that direction, a path that would lead back to the valley of the Flathead. "You son of a bitch, I know you! You ain't going back to that valley."

Leading the buckskin, he worked slowly along the rocky ledge until he found the sign he knew had to be there: two clear prints in a patch of bear grass. *I don't care how damn good you be, four horses is gonna leave sign somewhere,* he thought to himself. He stood up and looked around him, satisfied that he was always a step ahead of the man he followed. "Yessir, Mr. Little Wolf, you're about as slick as any I've chased. But you ain't got no notion of heading north like them tracks say."

Farther up, he found more sign that led through the trees until he reached another outcropping of rock where the trail disappeared again. Undeterred, he turned west once more, knowing where his man was going. *You got careless now*, he thought. *You ain't figuring on nobody staying on your trail this long.* It was as he figured. Little Wolf, thinking he had surely thrown Tobin off his track, had not been as careful when he led his horses out toward the west again. It was then that Tobin was certain Little Wolf was intent on returning to raid the citizens of Medicine Creek.

Just as Tobin expected, Little Wolf doubled back until he struck the old hunting trail he had originally started on, toward the country of the Kutenai. The tracks were not easy to follow in some places, but he was always able to pick up some sign farther along on the trail. That is, until he eventually realized there had been no sign for the last mile or so. He found himself staring into a wide valley with a long narrow lake and absolutely no sign that a man with four horses had passed that way. Dumbfounded, he realized that he didn't know for certain where Little Wolf was.

"That son of a bitch," he mumbled, almost stunned by the knowledge that he may have been outfoxed again. It was especially galling to Tobin to accept the fact that he was reduced to guessing on the direction Little Wolf had taken. He had been so cocksure of his man. Now he was more determined than ever to add this trophy scalp to his string. Without a trail to follow, Tobin had no choice but to follow his hunch and strike out for the settlement of Medicine Creek.

From a ridge on the north side of the mountain, Little Wolf sat, an interested observer of the befuddled man on the buckskin pony in the valley below him. The huge man was an excellent tracker and Little Wolf had attempted to lose him if possible. But he also decided that if his ruse to lead him off to the west didn't work, he had no choice but to kill him. He had figured the big man correctly, knowing that if he made it too easy to follow him, Tobin would become suspicious. Content now that he was free of the man, Little Wolf climbed on his horse and started out north to Canada once more.

Blue Otter, strong in his resolve to live as a free man in the old ways of his father and grandfather, was beginning to question the wisdom in that decision. Perhaps he should have returned to Lapwai with Wounded Bear. His wife, Quill, and her sister were near exhaustion, their feet sore and bleeding from two days straight of walking along the rocky ledges and down through an endless line of waterless gulches. He had chosen to travel the high country where the soldiers' horses could not follow. But he had paid a price for it in the toll the journey had taken on the women and child. He himself was sore and heavy of limb.

At last, they crossed over the last ridge that separated them from a wide valley where they might rest. Although their throats were parched from thirst, they stopped near the summit of the ridge to catch their breath before descending through the belt of pines and spruce that girded the mountain. It would take at least an hour to make their way down the mountain to the meadow below, but at the end of that hour there would be water and a place to rest in the willow thickets, and maybe even time to hunt, for they had not eaten since the day before.

Little Wolf remained still as stone. His bow raised, the arrow sighted on a young black-tailed deer, he drew the bowstring back slowly, paused a fraction of a second, then released it. The arrow flew straight to its mark, close behind the animal's front leg, sinking deep in its ribcage. The young buck was staggered by the impact of the missile, but righted himself in a moment and managed to take three great bounds before crashing to the ground. He struggled to regain his feet, taking several more faltering steps before falling for the final time. Little Wolf was upon him quickly and ended the animal's misery with his knife.

He gutted and bled the deer. Then, carrying the carcass on his shoulders, he made his way back to the trees where his horse was tied. After loading the deer on his horse, Little Wolf started back to his camp, holding to the slope and the cover of the trees. He was about to emerge from the pines and go down to the stream when he pulled his horse up suddenly. Had he not been vigilant by habit, he might have missed the flicker of movement in a willow clump near the water's edge.

Little Wolf immediately slid off his pony and tied the animal to a tree limb. Making his way down to the edge of the meadow, he positioned himself behind a fallen tree where he could watch the willow thicket. His eyes had not deceived him. He could now see that there were three women, or two women and a child perhaps, hiding deep in the willows. He glanced quickly around the valley. There were no horses. Little wonder he had not seen them before. Two women and a child on foot was strange indeed. Where were their men? They were Indians—of that he was certain. But what could they be doing out here in the mountains, many days' travel from any village? He decided to watch them for a while.

He had not waited long before he saw a solitary Indian man, loping slowly across the upper end of the little valley on foot. He carried a rifle and a small animal over his shoulder. From a distance, it appeared to be a rabbit or possibly a marmot. But Little Wolf was sure of one thing—the man had not had much luck with his hunting. Little Wolf had not heard a rifle shot, so he concluded the man was just as reluctant to an-

nounce his presence in the valley as he was. *He probably killed the animal with a stone*, he thought.

Little Wolf continued to watch the little group as the
man entered the thicket. The excited reception the man
received from the women told Little Wolf that the people were evidently short of food. It was apparent they
were in a desperate state, probably escaping a reservation. If they were intent on running to Canada as he
was, it was going to be a long, hard way on foot.

Quill got to her feet and took the rabbit from her
husband. Her sister fed more limbs to the fire to bring
it to a flame. Blue Otter shook his head as if to apolo-
gize although he said nothing.

"It will be all right," Quill reassured him. "It will be
enough to give us strength. And tomorrow, maybe you
will find something bigger."

Blue Otter nodded solemnly. "We need food. Tomorrow I may have to go up in the hills and take a
chance on shooting the gun."

As the sun settled behind the hills to the west, and
the valley gradually cloaked itself in shadows, the
three adults lay about the tiny fire, watching the child
suck the last bit of nourishment from the bones of the
rabbit. Blue Otter's heart was sad, but he resolved to
make a better day of it tomorrow. Quill sat staring into
the glowing coals and wondered about the fate of her
father and mother, who had been taken back to Lapwai by the soldiers. Then her thoughts returned to her
own plight and the ordeal facing her sister and herself.
King George's land was a strange and faraway place.
She wondered if they would make it. In the land of the
Salish now, they had to journey through Blackfoot and
Pend d'Oreille country. Would they find hospitable
people there? Or would they be killed, or turned over
to the soldiers?

Thinking her husband had made a noise, she looked

up from the fire. She gasped uncontrollably, her heart in her throat. A man was standing there at the edge of the firelight, seeming as tall as the willow behind him and as wide as a grizzly. Hearing her gasp, Blue Otter turned to see what had caused her terror. He sprang to his hands and knees and attempted to scramble to his rifle, which was leaning against a tree trunk. The towering spectre stopped him with no more than a casual motion with the rifle in his hand. Blue Otter knew there was no chance.

"Have no fear," Little Wolf said. "I have come as a friend." He stepped into the circle of light and they could now see that what had appeared to be the huge shoulders of a monster was, in fact, the carcass of a deer draped across his shoulders. Little Wolf let the animal drop to the ground.

As the two women set immediately into the butchering, Blue Otter stood up to welcome their benefactor. After expressing his gratitude for the deer, he told their visitor that they were Nez Perce and were trying to make their way to Canada. He looked up at the stranger towering a head taller than he, and did not have to wait for Little Wolf to introduce himself. "You are the white Cheyenne."

"My name is Little Wolf. I am Cheyenne."

They sat beside the fire and talked while the meat roasted over the flames. When Little Wolf heard Blue Otter's recounting of their journey, he scarcely could believe his ears. Blue Otter told him of the Cheyenne woman Hump had brought to Wounded Bear's tipi, how Broken Wing had taken care of her wounds. He then told of her flight from Lapwai with Wounded Bear's family, thinking Little Wolf was dead.

"I thought she was dead too," Little Wolf interrupted.

Blue Otter nodded understanding. "She was sure that must have been the reason you did not come for her." He went on to tell of the abduction of Rain Song by the evil Hump. Then he told of the attack by the soldiers and their subsequent escape. "It has been hard. As you can see, we are weak and hungry. And there is still a long way to go."

"Rain Song, where is she now?" He tried to remain calm but the tremble in his voice revealed his apprehension.

"I cannot be sure, but Hump often lives on the reservation. He and Yellow Hand never stayed at the fort with the other scouts."

Little Wolf's first impulse, upon hearing that Rain Song was alive, was to leap on his pony's back right then and find her. He knew he could not, however. He would have to wait until morning light. He stayed to eat with them, then got up to leave. "I must leave and prepare to go after this man Hump. I'll be back in the morning before I go."

"Good," Blue Otter responded. "We will finish the deer in the morning."

At first light the following morning, Little Wolf appeared as suddenly as he had the night before. This time he was leading four horses. "I must go after my wife now. I wish you well on your journey to King George's land. You have a long way ahead of you, too far to walk. I'll leave you these four horses. I won't need even a packhorse. They are a strong breed, as you well know. They will carry you to your freedom." In an effort to stem an overwhelming flow of gratitude from the destitute Nez Perces, he insisted that five horses would only slow him down now that he must travel fast.

Blue Otter thanked him profusely anyway, knowing that the white Cheyenne may have saved their lives. He recognized one of the horses, but did not comment. It was Yellow Hand's pony. They parted company then, the Nez Perces to the north toward Canada, the Cheyenne back the way he had come to find Hump.

14

Tobin grumbled to himself as he prodded the weary buckskin along. He had been in a black mood ever since realizing that the man he hunted could be anywhere between here and the Divide. He continued on this old Salish trail because his instincts told him the Cheyenne was heading back to Medicine Creek. The buckskin stumbled and Tobin lashed out at him, laying his whip across the exhausted horse's rump. Even a man with Tobin's scarcity of compassion had to relent eventually and let his horse rest, if only to prevent being set afoot. So, reluctantly, he made his camp for the night.

There still being a full hour of daylight left, he climbed up to the crest of the ridge before him to take a look at the country that lay ahead. From this higher vantage point, he could see the narrow ribbon through the trees ahead that indicated the trail he intended to follow in the morning. He turned and peered intently at the trail behind him, then to the east and west. There was nothing in any direction that might indicate there was another living soul within miles of where he stood. He grunted his displeasure and turned to retrace his steps to his camp below. That was when he saw it. It was no more than a gray wisp, a single, slender smoky thread, drifting up to be caught in the evening breeze. He locked his gaze on the slender ribbon, staring intently at it until he was sure of what he saw. There could be little doubt it was a small camp-fire, one a man would make if he didn't want to attract attention.

A wide smile, more nearly resembling a grimace, spread across Tobin's grizzled features, certain his in-stincts had been right. He remained staring at the thin line of smoke for a few minutes, judging the distance. Two miles at the most, he calculated. He glanced back at his weary horse, pulling at the grass around the cot-tonwoods. "Damn!" he uttered, for he knew he would be pushing a dead horse if he tried to ride him now. He looked back at the smoke. "Hell, I can walk two miles."

Making his way back down the hill as quickly as he could, he was already thinking of the pleasure it would bring him to pay Little Wolf a little visit that night. "Thought you was pretty slick," he mumbled, the smile still etched across his hairy face. Tobin fig-ured he could cover the distance between them before dark if he didn't tarry. From habit, he checked his rifle and pistol. Then, leading his horse, he set out on foot.

Rain Song lay on her side, her legs drawn up under her protectively. Her legs were not bound but her hands were tied, each one to a separate sapling so that they were about a foot apart. He had gone to hunt, but she made no effort to free herself. She knew it was use-less. She had strained against her bonds as soon as he left, but to no avail. Now she lay exhausted from the effort, knowing what was sure to come when Hump returned.

Thanks to Broken Wing's efforts to convince the dull-witted brute that Rain Song was still too weak from her wound to be of any use to him, Hump per-mitted her to rest for a couple of days, content to ap-pease his lust with an occasional crude groping of her body. Although she endeavored to feign illness, he, even with his slow mind, would be put off no longer. The thought of a union with the hulking savage was enough to send her mind reeling. But, knowing she was helpless to prevent it, she tried to strengthen her resolve to withstand his abuse. She was determined to live through whatever happened, for now she knew that Little Wolf was still alive. She heard a horse approaching and a tear slowly seeped from her eye and traced a path down her cheek.

Hump threw the carcass of a small deer on the ground and dismounted. He dragged it over and held it up for her to see. "You see, no one is a better hunter than me. I will also be a better husband than your white Cheyenne." He pulled the carcass back by the fire. "I will butcher the meat. Then you will cook it. After we eat, we will make love."

The thought sent a cold shiver the length of Rain Song's spine, but she tried not to show her fear. "I am still too weak. I would not be good for you. It would be better to wait."

"No!" Hump roared. "I am tired of waiting. I think you are lying to me. I think you are not weak anymore. First, I will have food, then I will have you." He hacked away angrily at the deer carcass, cutting off strips of flesh to be roasted over the fire. Hump was slow of wit but he would be fooled no longer. He had lived alone for so long, due to his inability to convince any woman to live with him, that he naturally prepared the meat himself. He placed it on branches to hold over the fire, forgetting that he had just told the woman she would cook it. As he worked, he glanced often at the woman lying helpless before him. From the lust in his eyes, there was no disguising the thoughts that dwelled in his simple mind. Rain Song swallowed hard to choke back a sob. She tried not to think of Little Wolf because she was ashamed for him to know what was about to happen to her.

He sat watching her while the meat cooked. His mind was of a single thought beyond filling his stomach. He had waited for her since Yellow Hand's death and now he would have her. She answered his stare with only fleeting, fearful glances. The horror he saw in her eyes only served to heighten his pleasure and increase his desire for her. He was somewhat puzzled when her eyes seemed to fix on him and grew wide with alarm. Confused, he realized too late that she was staring at something behind him. He turned to stare into the barrel of a Winchester rifle. A split second later, part of his brain was spattered on the feet of the woman tied to the sapling behind him.

Rain Song screamed, certain the next bullet would come her way. There was no second shot, however, as the hulking man dressed in animal skins calmly dragged Hump's body closer to the fire and turned him face down. Without speaking, he sat down on Hump's body and pulled a strip of the roasting meat from the fire. After he had eaten most of the skewered meat, he glanced at Rain Song, seeming to notice her for the first time.

"Well, little missy, it don't appear to me you was too anxious to mate with your boyfriend here." He laughed, enjoying his joke. "Can't say the same for him, though. He was so busy lookin' at you, he didn't have no time to pay attention to the likes of me." He laughed again, a deep, hollow laugh. "I reckon that cost him."

Rain Song was terrified. She had dreaded the abuse she was bound to receive at the hands of Hump. But this new menace made her blood run cold. His dark eyes, set back behind heavy scowling brows, seemed to dissect her with their steady gaze. The huge man looked her over from head to toe. She could almost feel his touch as he examined every inch of her without ever leaving his seat on Hump's corpse. There was an aura of death about him, and she feared she would not see another sunrise.

Finished with his supper at last, he wiped the grease from his hands, using his shirt for a towel. Releasing a loud belch that sounded like the bawling of a buffalo calf calling for his mama, he swung one leg around so that he straddled Hump's body. From that position, he calmly drew a long skinning knife from his belt. Taking a handful of the dead Nez Perce's hair, he yanked his head up and neatly scalped him. Rain Song looked away.

Tobin laughed. The scalping done, he got to his feet and walked around the fire to stand directly over the terrified woman. "Now lemme see," he started, stroking his chin whiskers as if thinking on it real hard. "I reckon I can guess who you might be. You ain't who I expected, though, when I seen your smoke back yonder." He bent down to get a closer look. She tried to draw away from him. "You ain't Nez Perce, that's fer damn shore." He smiled, pleased with himself. "Cheyenne, ain'tcha?" The look in her eyes told him he had guessed correctly. "You ain't dead after all. No ma'am, I wasn't expectin' you—the varmint I was looking to find was your husband. But finding you might just make my job a whole bunch easier."

He reached down and grabbed her ankle with one huge paw. With the other hand, he flipped her skirt up to her waist. She kicked at his hand with her free leg but he caught it in his hand and held her fast by both ankles, her skirt still above her waist. She cursed and spit at him. He ignored her venom while he looked her over as callously as if examining a horse. "Yeah, I figured you to be a pretty little thing, to make a man go to all that trouble just to get you back."

Much to her immediate relief, he released her and moved back by the fire. Looking around at Hump's sack of supplies, he asked, "You got any coffee?" She did not answer. "Damn, I ain't had no coffee in a week." Finding nothing that interested him in Hump's parfleche, he threw it aside and sat down by the fire, this time on the ground. Rain Song could not help but recall a time when a bear rummaged through her father's camp, poking at everything, strewing things about. "Now, little lady, let's you and me get acquainted. I'm figuring you to be Cheyenne. Is that right?" She did not answer. "And I'm thinkin' your man is that white man that calls hisself Little Wolf." Again she did not answer. She didn't have to—her eyes answered for her at the mention of her husband's name. Tobin smiled and slowly nodded his head. "I figured as much." He knew he now had something Little Wolf wanted more than his freedom, and he would have to come to him to get her. Things couldn't have worked out much better for Tobin.

At last Rain Song spoke. "Untie me."

"Untie you? Hell, why would I do that?"

"I have to relieve myself."

"Well, go ahead and relieve yourself. You don't have to be untied for that."

Rain Song was shocked. "I can't do it here."

"Shore you can. Just scoot over to one side and squirt, and then scoot back over. You got room."

She said nothing more about it, determined to hold it until he had gone to sleep. It proved to be an extremely uncomfortable evening for Rain Song before her huge captor decided to turn in for the night. Frightened to think what plans he might have for her before going to sleep, she trembled when he at last got up from the fire and dragged Hump's scalped corpse into the brush. After checking her bonds to make sure she wouldn't bother him during the night, he rolled out his blankets and was soon snoring.

As the darkness deepened, the flames in the campfire died away, leaving a bed of glowing red coals.

Other than the snoring of the hulking man, the night was quiet with no sounds but the calling of a night bird and the soft crying of a forlorn Cheyenne girl. Rain Song was too frightened to sleep, even had the aching in her arms relented. What would her fate be when morning came? Would she ever see her beloved Little Wolf again? This was an evil man who had captured her. She feared her death would be slow and painful.

She would have been relieved of one of her worries if she'd had any way of knowing the strange man sleeping by the fire. Tobin would not hesitate to frighten her, and he would have killed her if he had no use for her. But she was very useful to him—she was the bait he would use to set the trap for Little Wolf. As for the danger of rape, there was none. Tobin was not interested in her body at this point. Though she was fair enough, the problem was Tobin's. He did not pursue sexual favors with women because of a profound fear of failure. This was possibly the only fear the man had, a fear of rendering himself vulnerable to ridicule. The last time he had entertained thoughts of a sexual nature was six years before with a prostitute in Lewisburg. He had failed to perform, most probably due to the tremendous quantity of whiskey he had consumed immediately prior to the liaison, and the woman laughed at him. Tobin was mortified. The woman was found dead the next morning, her throat slit from ear to ear.

Tobin knew what he was going to do. He needed a place to hold his captive, a secure place where she would not have to be under his constant watch. There was just such a place available: The little settlement of Medicine Creek had an empty jail. He might as well put it to some use. Before setting out for Medicine Creek the next morning, however, Tobin planned to effect an understanding with his prisoner so as to make the trip less bother.

Rain Song had finally fallen asleep a little before daybreak from sheer exhaustion. It seemed her eyes had been closed for little more than a few minutes when she was rudely rousted from her sleep. Groggy with fatigue and lack of sleep, her mind was in a state of utter confusion, and when she managed to shake the cobwebs from her brain, she became panic stricken. The monster who had invaded the night before was now standing over her, leering down at her, a twisted smile his only expression.

"It's time for you to pay for your passage to Medicine Creek," he said. Before she could react, he grabbed her ankles as he had done the night before, one in each hand, and spread her legs apart. She was helpless in his powerful grasp, no matter how she screamed and struggled. Her efforts seemed to amuse him and his grin spread wider across his hairy face. The sheer terror in her eyes told him she was getting the message he intended to send. Clamping a leg under each of his arms, leaving his hands free to explore, he grasped her thighs and slowly advanced his hands under her skirt. All the while, Tobin kept his eyes locked on hers, measuring the terror he instilled. He made no move to stop her screaming, sliding his huge body closer in between her legs. She struggled to stop him from coming any closer, but her pelvis felt as if it were about to split apart. She could do nothing to prevent what was about to happen. She felt her head reeling, close to losing consciousness.

He leaned over her until his face was almost touching hers. The dank, sweaty smell of him assaulted her nostrils. His grimy whiskers brushed against her cheek. He held her in that position for a long moment and then he spoke. "How do you like it, missy? I guarantee you it'll be more fun for me than it is fer you."

He let her think about that for a few moments more, then added, "Maybe you and me can have a little understanding." He pulled away from her a little. The terror he saw in her eyes pleased him. "Maybe we don't have to do this. If you don't give me no trouble, I'll leave you alone. How 'bout it? But if you give me even a pinch of trouble . . ." He didn't finish, but she understood fully.

"No trouble!" she screamed, her voice trembling with fear. "No trouble!"

He backed off, still holding her ankles. "All right," he warned, "but you just remember what I said. One pinch of trouble, and I'll split you up the backbone so fast you'll wish you was dead."

She believed him. Weak from her terrifying experience, she lay back, limp and drained. Right then she determined that she would still run if the opportunity arose. But she would make no attempt unless her chances of escape were extremely good. This creature would hunt her down. Of that she was certain.

Satisfied that he had thoroughly put the fear of the devil into the young woman's heart, Tobin cut her hands loose and let her eat. He sat on his horse outside a thicket of serviceberry bushes, and waited while she performed her toilet. When she was finished, he put her on Hump's horse and started toward Medicine Creek. Before they rode out, he gave her one more bit of instruction.

"Can you ride pretty fast?" She wasn't quite sure how to answer the question. He didn't expect a reply. "Well," he continued, "I don't reckon you can outrun a bullet from this here Winchester. So don't forget, I'm right behind you." She got the message.

He let her lead and he followed, since all she had to do was stick to the trail traveled by countless hunting parties through the valleys.

The journey to Medicine Creek took two full days of

riding. During that time, there was no attempt by Rain
Song to escape. In return, there was no repeat of the
brutal treatment suffered at the hand of her grim captor. Although Tobin had no intention to have sexual
knowledge of the woman at present, he could still not
help but let his mind imagine the pleasure she might
be capable of giving a man. He had seen enough of her
body to know that she might have the power to arouse
his reluctant passions. But he needed her alive, and he
knew if he failed to perform, he'd kill her. He'd have
to—he would not be able to tolerate the humiliation.

Tobin permitted her to ride unfettered during the
day, tying her up at night while he slept. On the morning of the third day, they left the Indian trail, crossed
over a ridge thick with spruce and pine, and emerged
from the trees to see the rough buildings of Medicine
Creek.

Ike Freise scurried up the muddy street to the general store. Holding the door open while he remained
on the wooden walkway, he yelled to Arvin Gilbert.
"Look yonder at what's coming!"

Arvin dropped a half-eaten pickle back in the jar
and, wiping his hands on his apron, joined Ike on the
walkway. Squinting against the morning sun, he followed Ike's pointing finger, looking toward the north
end of the valley. "Who is it?" he asked, unable to
identify the two riders approaching the town.

"Well, less I'm mistaken, it's that big ol' tracker the
army hired to go after that damn Injun." He glanced at
Arvin, who was still squinting to make out the riders.
"They ain't many men around that size. And it looks
like he may have found his man."

The two men watched the approaching riders until
they were within a couple hundred yards of Ike's stable on the north end of town. "No," Arvin said, "that
ain't the renegade. That looks more like a squaw." He
turned to call back inside the store. "Lester, watch the

store. I'll be back in a minute." He and Ike started up
the street toward the stable.

They stood in front of the stable and waited for
Tobin to approach. As he reached the beginning of the
muddy sea of ruts that served as Medicine Creek's
main street, the two men got a better look at his prisoner.

"Why, that's that little Injun woman, the one we
brung in from that Cheyenne's place."

"Damned if it ain't," Ike replied.

Nothing more was said until the massive scout on
the buckskin horse reached the stable. They had assumed he would put his horses up right away but he
went right on by, now leading the horse the woman
rode. "Morning, gents," was all he said as he walked
by. Like schoolboys following a circus wagon, they
walked along beside Tobin, staring at the woman and
waiting for an explanation. Tobin reined up in front of
the jail and dismounted. He motioned for Rain Song to
do the same.

Arvin Gilbert stepped up on the tiny porch. "We
ain't got a sheriff yet. The jail's empty."

"I figured," Tobin replied. He pulled his rifle and
bedroll from his horse and motioned for Rain Song to
open the door. It was locked. Unfazed, Tobin turned
his gaze on Arvin. "If I recollect, you're the mayor of
this little swamp, ain'tcha?"

"Yessir," Arvin replied at once, "I'm the mayor."

"Well, Mayor, I aim to use this here jail for a spell. If
you ain't got a key to open that door, I reckon I'll have
to kick it in."

Arvin glanced at Ike, then back at the imposing bulk
of Tobin. He knew that, as mayor, it should be his decision as to whether or not someone could simply con-
fiscate a public building. It didn't seem right for Tobin
to come into their town and do what he damn well
pleased without so much as a by your leave. He briefly

considered informing Tobin that he would take it up with the town council—until he looked into the cold depth of the huge man's eyes. There was violence there that lay just beneath the surface, promising to explode if given the slightest provocation. "I've got the key," Arvin said, moments before Tobin got set to kick the door in.

He unlocked the door with a key from a ring holding a dozen others and stepped back to permit the Indian woman entry. Before he could replace the ring of keys, Tobin clamped his wrist in his huge hand and, with the other, opened the ring and took the key off. "I'll need to keep this," he said, a smile creeping across his face.

Arvin froze. He wanted to protest, but he did not have the courage. He looked to Ike Frieze for support but Ike had already backed away to give the big man room. Finally, he mumbled that he guessed it was all right to use the jail temporarily. Tobin's smug expression told him that he had expected as much.

"I've got to get back to the store," Arvin muttered and turned to leave the tracker and his captive.

Ike turned also and was at Arvin's elbow as they walked back toward the south end of the street. When he figured they were out of earshot, he glanced back nervously before speaking. "Damn, Arvin, that devil's figuring on doing damn near what he pleases."

Arvin, like Ike, had had the same thought after their confrontation with Tobin. Medicine Creek was vulnerable to being run over roughshod by men like Tobin. It was too promising a settlement to be endangered by the possibility of a corrupt sheriff. Franklin Bowers had been domineering, but he did submit to the general wishes of the town council. On first appearances, Tobin appeared to do as he pleased. This could be disastrous for the settlement of Medicine Creek.

"I don't like the look of this," Arvin said as they approached Blanton's Saloon. "Maybe we ought to call a meeting of the council and discuss it."

Ike agreed. "Maybe we ought to. You know, I don't cotton much to him keeping that squaw in there anyway, just inviting that damn crazy Injun to come in here and shoot the place up." In front of Blanton's now, he suggested, "Let's go in and talk to Henry."

Henry Blanton was sufficiently concerned about the potential problem when told of the recent occupants of the jail. "You're right, Arvin, we need to have a meeting right away. I'll send my boy to fetch Morgan and Mr. Norsworthy."

Within thirty minutes, the nucleus of the town council was assembled in the back of Blanton's Saloon. The last to arrive was the Reverend Norsworthy, who loathed the practice of meeting in a saloon but put aside his principles for the purpose of conducting community business. When everyone but Rev. Norsworthy had a beer in front of them, Arvin called the meeting to order and related the news he and Ike had learned a short time before. To a man, they all agreed that Arvin's assessment of the situation was most likely accurate and it was absolutely a necessity to set things right with their uninvited guest.

"Somebody needs to put the fear of God—excuse me, Reverend—in him before he thinks he can just ride in here and take over the town." Having said it, Ike sat back down quickly before somebody suggested he might be the one for the job.

There were nods of agreement all around. Morgan Sewell spoke up. "I reckon it would be the mayor's job to notify him."

Arvin was afraid he was going to hear a suggestion like that. He was quick to respond. "I don't think that devil can be persuaded by one man. It would be far more effective if he sees the whole town is behind this." He looked around the table, discouraged by the lack of commitment he read in their faces. "Listen, maybe we're jumping to conclusions here. Let's speak to the man. We might be reading him wrong." He still saw doubt in their faces. "Why don't we just invite him to come up here and talk to us? We might be making a mountain out of a molehill."

"What if he won't come?" Morgan asked.

"Well, instead of asking him to come up here, we could all go down to the jail." Arvin looked around the table for agreement.

"I don't know," Morgan said. "Hell, you're the mayor, Arvin. Just go on down there and tell him how things are."

Reverend Norsworthy, having held his piece until that moment, spoke up. "Arvin's right. We should all go down to the jail in a show of support. Surely we can reason with this man. He can't be as uncivilized as you paint him."

"I don't know," Morgan repeated, shaking his head.

There followed two more beers' worth of discussion but, in the end, they reluctantly agreed that all five of them would march down to the jail and inform this impudent bully that they ran the town of Medicine Creek, and any actions he took would only be with their approval.

While the Medicine Creek town council was meeting in the saloon, Tobin was inspecting his new lodgings. Rain Song was locked in one of the two cells, and Tobin had stowed his possibles in the other. Before locking Rain Song up, he tested the bars on the small window of the cell and was confident that a horse and rope couldn't budge the inch-thick iron bars. When he was satisfied that all was to his liking, he locked the front door and took the horses down to Ike's stable. Duly intimidated by the frightening countenance of the imposing figure, Ike's eldest son respectfully stabled the horses in the first stall and fed them some grain. He didn't question it when Tobin told him his credit was good.

Tobin smiled to himself when he left the stable and saw the committee waiting for him outside the locked door of the jail. *Well, well,* he thought, *here's the good citizens of Medicine Creek, coming to lay down the law.* The thought amused him. He took his time getting back to the jail.

"Well now," he said when he was within earshot of the nervous group. "This is more like it, an official welcoming committee."

Arvin Gilbert flashed a nervous smile in an attempt to seem casual. "Mr. Tobin, as mayor of Medicine Creek, it's my duty to speak for the town council." Tobin's smug grin did little to lesson Arvin's discomfort in the role of town spokesman, but he continued. "The thing is, I don't—the committee, that is—don't know if it's proper to let someone take over the jail without getting approval from the council." He paused but Tobin made no response beyond a widening of his self-satisfied grin. Arvin got the distinct impression that what he was saying appeared to be amusing to the rough tracker. When Tobin still made no reply, Arvin began to sputter. "Well, ah . . . well, I guess we'd like to know what your intentions are. I mean, that's our jail, a public building, and we need to know what you aim to do in there."

"Oh, you do, do you?" Tobin replied, still apparently amused.

Reverend Norsworthy spoke up then, from his position safely behind Arvin and Henry Blanton. "The fact is, Mr. Tobin, a man simply cannot ride into town and decide to take over the jailhouse. We won't stand for it."

Norsworthy's fellow council members all took a step backward upon hearing the preacher's blunt statement. Arvin quickly tried to soften the reverend's words. "We're just saying we need to talk about—"

"I hear what you're saying," Tobin interrupted. The smile faded from his face and his eyes seemed to harden and go stone-cold. Tobin had sized up the situation in the little settlement the first time he rode in, and knew then that the town was wide open for the first wild gunman who happened by. A collection of storekeepers and barbers, no sheriff, no backbone—he knew he could use the town any way he saw fit to suit his purposes. And his purpose at this time was to set a trap for one renegade Cheyenne. Always finding it more proficient to operate from a position of intimidation, he laid out his own rules for the council.

"Now I'm gonna tell you gentlemen how things is gonna be around here until I'm done with what I come for. I'm taking over the jail to hold that little Injun woman until her buck comes after her. I don't expect no interference from any of you good citizens. The reason I'm taking it over is that I don't see nobody in this town that can stop me." He paused, shifting his piercing gaze on each man in succession. "Unless one of you gentlemen want to object right now." He dropped his hand to rest on the handle of his pistol. "No? I didn't figure. Well, there's five of you and only one of me." He took a step backward to give himself some room. "That 'pears to me to be about the right odds. We can settle this thing right now."

To a man, the committee froze. Not one among them had the nerve to stand up to the ominous hulk before them. It was painfully clear to the town council that what some had feared might happen after the death of Franklin Bowers had come to pass. Even if Bowers was still here, he could not have stood up to this fearsome maverick. For a long moment no one spoke. The men of Medicine Creek stood immobile in shocked silence. The imposing figure stared unblinking at Arvin

Gilbert, a slight smile returning to split his dingy whiskers. Finally, Reverend Norsworthy broke the silence.

"There's no need to threaten violence, Mr. Tobin. We're all civilized men here. At least I certainly hope we are. We're not looking for any trouble. We just wanted to talk this over."

Tobin relaxed. His lips parted in a wide grin, exposing a row of dingy brown teeth. "Why now, that's more like it. I knew you gents wasn't lookin' for any trouble. And as long as nobody gits in my way, there won't be any." Again Tobin let his gaze fix on each man individually for a few seconds. "I'm a fair man. I'll tell you what I'll do. Since you ain't got one, I'll fill in for your sheriff for a while. Then, if some drunken saddletramp steps over the line, why I'd be more than pleased to bust his skull for ya. How's that for being neighborly?"

This seemed to animate the frozen committee once more, triggering a great deal of nodding and gestures of agreement. Moments before there had been a wolf at the door. Now the wolf had offered not to eat them. Arvin Gilbert was the first to reply.

"Well, that does change things a mite at that. I mean, with you offering to act as sheriff, it's only fittin' you use the jail." He looked around at his fellow councilmen and received nods of approval. There was an almost audible sigh of relief for the salvation of their dignity.

"Good, then." Tobin almost looked genial. "Now I take it this here meeting is over." He started to enter the jail, then paused. "As part of my pay, I'll take my meals in the saloon, and you can feed my prisoner. Two meals a day ought to be enough for her. I'll need three, sometimes more if I'm real hungry." He stood there a moment longer to see if there were any objections. There were none.

The committee abruptly turned on their heels and made for the saloon, no one saying a word until they had passed the barbershop and were practically at the door of the saloon. Only then did Blanton feel safe to object.

"Well I don't know about the rest of you, but I feel like we just got buffaloed."

Arvin shook his head slowly. "Henry, I'd say we're lucky he didn't decide to shoot up the whole town."

"Lucky?" Henry blurted. "Maybe you feel lucky. But I'm the one's got to feed that big son of a bitch. How about that? And I'm expecting the town to pay for that. I ain't gonna take him to raise."

"I reckon we'll handle it the same as when Bowers held a prisoner. It won't be all your expense." He shot an accusing look at Blanton. "Although you could damn sure afford it. You make more money than anybody else in town."

Things were different around the little settlement in the valley now that the jail was occupied by the strange visitor and his Indian prisoner. There was a sinister cloud that seemed to hover over the entire town, entirely due to the presence of this one man. While Tobin made no outward attempts to intimidate the citizens of Medicine Creek, they were intimidated just the same. It was akin to living in a cave with a rattlesnake. You knew if you riled the snake he would surely strike. So it was best to avoid the snake if possible. Consequently, Tobin went his own way in peace, almost in a vacuum, because most of what he saw of the people of Medicine Creek was the back of their britches as they darted around corners whenever he walked the street. This was the kind of fear and respect Tobin appreciated. He knew the town was his for the taking and he began to give that notion serious thought. First, however, was the business with Little Wolf.

Tobin's prisoner sat alone in a corner of her cell for most of every day. She was provided a bucket for her toilet and twice a day a boy from the saloon brought her a plate of food. True to his word, Tobin did not bother her. In fact, he barely spoke to her. Even when checking on her, which he did several times during the day and sometimes at night, he rarely spoke. It was as if he was merely checking the bait in his trap to make sure it had not spoiled. Rain Song feared this man. She found herself torn between hoping Little Wolf found her and praying that he didn't. She feared what might happen if Little Wolf fell victim to this great bear that held her captive. She never doubted her husband's strength and cunning, and no one ever questioned Little Wolf's courage. But this man Tobin was not like any other man she had ever seen. He was not only ruthless, he was powerful and possessed a cunning in his own right, like the gray wolf and the coyote. As much as her soul ached for Little Wolf, she feared for his safety. Maybe it was best he never found out she was alive, and was on his way to Canada and safety.

15

It had taken only a few days of searching before Little Wolf found the last encampment site of Wounded Bear's band. He studied signs that told of the standoff that took place between the Nez Perces and the soldiers. It was more difficult to find the trail he was intent on discovering—that of a single horse carrying double. Amid all the tracks left behind by the Indian ponies and the cavalry, it seemed impossible to distinguish between them and tracks that might have been left by Hump's pony. Still he searched doggedly, examining every possible sign. Discouraged, he sat down to think the situation over. Then he remembered—Blue Otter had told him that Hump had come to take Rain Song away when they had camped the night before the soldiers caught up with them. He leaped on his pony and galloped back, along the obvious trail the Nez Perces had taken.

The trail led him to another grassy valley and a wide stream. The blackened circles in the grass told him this was where Wounded Bear had camped. As before, he started searching for the single set of tracks that would show him the trail Hump had taken after leaving with Rain Song. After considering and rejecting the various comings and goings of single sets of prints, he decided on a trail of prints in the soft sand of the creek bank. The tracks were deep, indicating a heavier than usual load. If they had been leading toward the camp, instead of away from it, he might have rejected them as those of a hunter carrying a deer. His instincts told him these were the tracks he sought.

Within a mile of the next campsite, circling buzzards led him to Hump's body. The huge, grotesque birds were making short work of the army scout's carcass, and Little Wolf had to chase them away with his whip in order to take a look for himself. There was just enough left for him to make a guess that this was the remains of the Indian Blue Otter had called Hump.

He looked from the body to two small saplings where two lengths of rawhide lay, evidence that someone had cut them. Rain Song had been tied there. He had to choke back the emotion that threatened to overflow when his mind formed the picture of his wife lying there. He forced himself to keep his mind on the business of tracking. He backed away from Hump's carcass and let the buzzards finish their meal.

At least he was confident Rain Song was still alive. But someone else had killed Hump and taken her. The bear-sized tracker who had followed him came to mind at once. When Little Wolf last saw him, he was headed in the general direction that could have led him to this spot. So now he would be trailing two horses. He stood up and peered out across the meadow toward the mountains as if hoping to see Rain Song. The trail led out down the valley toward the south. *Medicine Creek,* he thought.

Little Wolf rode across a valley floor that danced in the morning breezes rushing through the mountain pass. Tall yellow blossoms waved like golden spears, reaching as high as his pony's chest and parting before the two horses as they loped along. It appeared that the trail led toward a sheer rock wall at the end of the valley, with no outlet. Still, the trail did not waver. Little Wolf decided the man he followed knew where he was going. It was not the trail of a man who was unfa-

miliar with the country, wavering in around the rocky
bluffs, searching for a way through the mountains. As
he suspected, when he was practically boxed in by the
bluffs' stone walls, he discovered a forceful stream that
raced through a narrow corridor of solid rock, leading
off to the west. If he had not been following a trail
across the grassy valley, there was doubt that he
would have ever discovered the stream.

Little Wolf reined up for a few moments, studying
the narrow passage. The tracks led into the water. He
looked to each side of the passage. The walls were
solid rock and extended up more than a hundred feet
before tapering away to form ledges thick with pine
and spruce. It was barely wide enough to allow a horse
to pass. He hesitated but a moment more, then nudged
his pony gently with his heels and entered the water.

The sides of the stone passage were damp and cold,
having seldom seen the sun. The water seemed to
gather intensity as it was forced through the narrow
confines, causing it to roar like a waterfall and send up
clouds of fine mist that engulfed his horses. He looked
up at the thin ribbon of blue sky, a hundred feet above
him, and the thought occurred to him that a man
would be helpless against ambush in this place. There
was no room to turn around and go back. Several
times his horse nearly stumbled on the slippery rocky
stream bottom, causing his packhorse to run up on
him. Little Wolf wondered if perhaps he had been
fooled and might be riding into a trap. No, he told
himself, the horses he followed had come this way so
there had to be a way out.

After about a hundred yards, the passage began to
open up and pretty soon he saw sunlight ahead. Moments later, he emerged from a wide ravine into broad
daylight. He paused to look back the way he had
come, at the narrow crack through the base of the
mountain, then up at the crest high above. The man

knew where he was going—it would have taken the best part of the day to work up and over the mountain. It served to trigger a warning in Little Wolf's mind. He was obviously in territory the big tracker knew well.

Thoughts of an ambush disappeared when he found the trail again, leading from the water. The man he followed made no effort to disguise his tracks, leaving a plain trail across a short flat and up the gentle slope of a foothill. Down the far side of the hill, the tracks intercepted a frequently used trail that led through the mountains to Medicine Creek. There was little doubt where the big man was taking Rain Song. He nudged his pony to pick up the pace. Medicine Creek was no more than a day's ride away.

"What's all the fuss about?" Arvin Gilbert wanted to know as he walked up to the bar in Blanton's Saloon. He was looking toward the back of the saloon, where several men seemed to be arguing.

Henry Blanton shook his head impatiently. "Johnny Blevins," was all he offered, knowing that was explanation enough for Arvin. Johnny was as friendly and reasonable a man as you'd want when he was sober, which was most of the time. A hard-working man trying to scratch a living out of the soil, Johnny let the hard times get the best of him from time to time. When that happened, he usually rode into Medicine Creek to drown his troubles in Blanton's cheapest whiskey. Sometimes he got a little bit rowdy, and Franklin Bowers would lock him up and let him sleep it off. Johnny was always remorseful the next day and made his apologies before riding back to his farm.

Arvin and Henry ignored the loud bursts of conversation from the back table while Arvin had his evening drink before going home to supper. As it usually did in recent days, the conversation worked its way around to the new resident in the town jail.

"How long do you suppose we're gonna have that damn grizzly laying around the jail, gittin' fat on my grub?"

Arvin shrugged. "I don't know. It don't look like he's accomplishing a helluva lot, does it?" He took a sip from the glass of whiskey in his hand. "Of course, you know you can go down there and politely tell him to move on."

"Did I say I was tired of livin'?" Blanton snorted. "Seriously, Arvin, he's running up a helluva bill. I ain't never knowed a man could eat that much. We're gonna have to do something about him. I sure don't want him taking root around here."

Arvin was about to reply when the voices at the back table raised to a shouting match. "Looks like Johnny's getting riled up again." He had no sooner said it when both men were suddenly startled by a gunshot. "Damn!" Arvin yelled and both men jumped.

Henry ducked behind the bar. When no more shots followed, he slowly raised his eyes high enough to see over the bar. Johnny was standing, though not on steady legs, his pistol in his hand. Henry glanced up at the new hole in his ceiling. "Dammit, Johnny, put that damn gun away before you kill somebody!"

Johnny turned toward Blanton, straining to focus his whiskey-glazed eyes. "I'm just tryin to have a little drink and play some cards. And I ain't gonna stand for nobody dealing offen the bottom of the deck." He cast an accusing eye at Bert Thompson.

Henry knew Bert wouldn't cheat anybody. He didn't have enough skill to deal from the bottom anyway. "I reckon you've had about enough to drink, Johnny. Why don't you just go on home now?"

"I'll go home when I'm damn good and ready," Johnny replied harshly, and for emphasis, shot another hole in the ceiling.

"Dammit, Johnny!" Blanton shouted. He was not especially enthusiastic about taking further action. Blanton didn't care to force the issue even though he was sure Johnny would never do any real harm. Still, a drunk with a gun in his hand was always dangerous. He turned to give Arvin an exasperated look.

"Hell," Arvin suggested. "Why don't we let that big side of beef earn his keep. He said he'd act as temporary sheriff." He grinned and added, "Maybe Johnny'll shoot him." That seemed like a good idea to Blanton. He sent his boy down to the jail to fetch Tobin.

Tobin was not pleased to be disturbed. It was after seven o'clock and he generally liked to bed down at that hour. He started to tell Blanton's boy to tell his daddy to go to hell, but changed his mind and decided to take care of the trouble. He found Henry and Arvin waiting for him on the walk in front of the saloon.

"Much obliged, Mr. Tobin. It ain't much, really. It's just Johnny Blevins. He's had too much to drink. He don't mean no harm. Bowers used to let him sleep it off in the jail."

Tobin met Blanton's remarks with a bored stare. Without saying a word, he brushed past the two men and pushed through the swinging doors. Inside, he paused only a moment to look the situation over. His rifle in his hand, his smoldering gaze came to fix on Johnny Blevins, who was still standing at the table. Although he still had his pistol in his hand, it was hanging down, pointed at the floor, and he appeared to have calmed down quite a bit. Tobin moved deliberately to the back table and confronted Johnny.

"Drop that damn pistol," Tobin demanded.

Johnny looked at the giant man as if only then discovering his presence. The puzzled look on Johnny's face was evidence that he was too drunk to know he was still holding a gun. Tobin didn't give second warnings. Faster than anyone there could believe a

man that size could move, he brought his rifle barrel
down on Johnny's forearm with so much force, the
bone was clearly heard to snap. The gun clattered on
the plank floor. Johnny screamed and clutched his broken arm, completely sobered by the pain. Unable to
comprehend what was happening, he made no move
to defend himself. Tobin didn't give him the chance to
surrender. While Johnny was bent over in agony, his
right arm dangling limp and useless, Tobin smashed
the rifle barrel up against the side of Johnny's head,
laying open a long gash. Johnny went down in a heap.
He had barely hit the floor when the toe of Tobin's
boot landed squarely against his ribs, rolling him over
against a table leg. Johnny expelled a loud, painful
grunt as the wind was knocked from his lungs. Unable
to defend himself, he tried to crawl under the table to
escape his attacker. With one hand, Tobin flipped the
table over and sent it crashing against the wall. With
the other hand, he set in with the rifle, raining one
powerful blow after another upon the back and head
of the helpless man. Johnny tried to cover his head
with his arms but soon the relentless beating rendered
him unconscious and he went limp on the floor, no
longer responding to each heavy blow of Tobin's rifle.
Still Tobin hammered away at the unresisting lump of
flesh. It appeared he was intent upon breaking every
bone in the unfortunate man's body. At last he
stopped, long after Johnny was reduced to nothing
more than a bloody pile on the barroom floor.

The barroom was filled with a stunned silence. Not
a man moved—no one dared, afraid the terrifying
brute might turn his wrath upon him. The horror of
the terrible beating was etched on each man's face as
they stood silently staring in disbelief at the broken
body of Johnny Blevins. Tobin turned to face the patrons of the saloon. Arvin was shocked to see there
was no longer any trace of fury reflected in the giant

man's face. Quite the opposite, Tobin's eyes were clear and his features calm. The man was as cool as a cucumber, and it frightened Arvin even more.

After studying the faces of the collection of Medicine Creek citizens who had just received an honest introduction to the man known simply as Tobin, the brute spoke. Calmly, in a measured voice, he issued a clear warning. "I said I'd take care of these little set-tos for you, but I don't like to be bothered when I'm fixin' to go to bed."

Henry Blanton was the first of the townsmen to find his voice. "Johnny didn't mean no harm. Bowers just locked him up and let him sleep it off."

Tobin cocked his head and fixed Blanton with a cold stare. He held it for a long moment before speaking. "There ain't no need to lock him up now, is there?" He glanced back at his victim, still unmoving on the floor. "I reckon it'll be a while before this bastard decides to raise another ruckus." He reached down and ripped off a large square from Johnny's shirt and cleaned the blood from his rifle. That done, he started for the door. The gathering parted before him. As he reached the door, he said, "Reckon he'll need some doctoring. Suit yourself on that. All the same to me whether he lives or dies."

They waited until his footsteps could no longer be heard on the boardwalk, and then they all moved at the same time. "Is he dead?" someone asked as they crowded around the victim.

"Somebody go get Morgan," Arvin said.

When Morgan Sewell arrived, he was stunned to see the broken man he had been summoned to treat. "My God! What happened to him?" When told of the cause of Johnny's injuries by several of the men, he was aghast. "This is worse than Edgar Rawlins when he got mauled by that grizzly—and Edgar died."

"Can you patch him up?" Blanton asked.

"Hell, I don't know. First, I reckon we better see if he's even alive." He bent down on one knee and attempted to straighten Johnny out. After a few minutes of gentle prodding and poking, he put his ear to Johnny's chest and listened. "Well, I don't know how, but he's still breathing. I can put a splint on that arm. The rest of it will just have to be up to the good Lord."

When Morgan had done all he could for Johnny, a couple of his friends put him in a wagon and took him home. No one was overly optimistic about his recovery. Time would tell. Arvin stood talking to Morgan and Blanton as they watched the wagon roll out of sight.

"I tell you what, I can see a lot more of that kind of thing happening around here." It was Blanton who voiced the thought that was running through the minds of all three men.

Arvin agreed. "I'm afraid you're right, Henry. We're gonna have to do something, but I don't know what. We might as well have a grizzly living down there in that jail."

"I reckon the Vigilance Committee will have to do something about him. Run him out, like we done with the Injuns."

"I don't know, Morgan," Arvin responded. "I don't think this will be that simple." He didn't voice it, but Arvin wasn't sure there were enough men in Medicine Creek to take on this grizzly. "Might be we're jumpin' the gun a little. You know, he might be just making an example outta poor ol' Johnny so everybody else will stay in line."

Little Wolf could hear the rumble of a wagon and the voices of two or more men long before they drove into sight. It was a bright moonlit night so he guided his horses up off the trail into a patch of fir trees. Little Wolf sat in the saddle and waited for the wagon to pass below him. When it was abreast of his position in the trees, he could clearly see them in the bright moonlight. Two men rode in the seat of an open farm wagon. There appeared to be another man lying in the bed of the wagon, either drunk or wounded, he couldn't tell for sure. He had no interest in these men—he was merely intent on avoiding them. When they had driven out of sight, he guided his horse back down and continued to follow the trail leading to Medicine Creek.

16

The full moon had drifted downward and would soon be behind the high mountain to the south and west of Medicine Creek. Little Wolf sat on a ridge north of the settlement, looking at the dark buildings, trying to remember the layout of the town. He had been to the town a half dozen times before the two nights when he came in to kill the mayor and the sheriff. But on those occasions, before all the trouble started, he went only to the general store on the south end of town to trade with the proprietor, Gilbert. Always, as soon as his trading was completed, he retraced his steps back into the mountains. Now he must familiarize himself with the various buildings in order to determine where Rain Song was being held.

He got to his feet and led his horses down the ridge to a closer position, feeling secure in the knowledge that it was too dark to be concerned with being seen. He reminded himself that he was not even sure Rain Song was here. The big scout may have taken her to some other place. But, one thing for certain, he brought her through Medicine Creek. Whether he stopped here or not would be Little Wolf's task to find out.

The town was quiet. Even the saloon in the middle of town was closed. He would come back in the morning and set up a vigilance, watching the town until, sooner or later, he would see something or somebody who might indicate where Rain Song was being held. There being nothing more he could do that night, he got on his pony and, leading his packhorse, rode off into the low hills behind him to make his camp.

Rain Song lay still on the straw pallet provided for her bed. It was late, but she was not asleep. Someone had come for Tobin earlier in the evening, and he had gone with them for a while. When he came back, he said nothing to her and went straight to bed. She tried to sleep but could not. Her mind was filled with thoughts of Little Wolf and Canada, thoughts that settled heavily on her heart, causing her to weep silent tears. Several hours passed and still she did not sleep. The moon made its way to a position over the pines behind the jail and shone its light through the tiny window of her cell. She got up from her pallet and, on tiptoes, tried to look out the window. The town was silent now, the only sound was the mournful song of a lonely night bird. It was like the call Little Wolf used to make in order to signal her when he was near. Suddenly, she felt a sense of calmness. She could not explain why. It was almost as if he actually were near. Maybe it was the golden light of the full moon that painted the cold bars of her prison. Maybe it was the assuring sound of the night bird's call. She couldn't say, but her mind was eased of some of its sadness. She returned to her bed and finally drifted off to sleep.

When the sun's first rays found their way over the hills to the east of the little town, Little Wolf was already in position on the eastern slope. From the narrow gulch he had selected, he could observe the entire length of the one street through the town. Content now to wait until the citizens of Medicine Creek began to rouse themselves to the business of the day, he chewed on a strip of dried elk meat. It wasn't long before the first early risers began to appear to open the few commercial establishments that lined the muddy thoroughfare.

A squat little man appeared in the open door of the stable at the north end of the street. He stood there for a few minutes, scratching his belly and looking around as if appraising the new day. Little Wolf watched him for only a few moments before shifting his gaze to the postmaster fumbling with a ring of keys, eventually yielding the one that opened the front door. Further down toward the south end of town, he recognized the one man he knew, Arvin Gilbert, sweeping the board walkway in front of the general store. Though only weeks had passed, it seemed like many months since Little Wolf had walked into the store to trade for supplies. Dressed as much like a white man as possible in his brother's coat, with his long dark hair stuffed up under a hat, he had made his trade as quietly and as rapidly as he could. Now he sat looking at the little storekeeper, the bitter bile of contempt rising in his spleen as he pictured the once friendly merchant riding down amid the bloodthirsty posse to murder Sleeps Standing and his women. Little Wolf had exacted his revenge on four of that posse and, after Rain Song had pleaded with him, he had been content to let those four be the end of it. Now he wished he had killed every man who rode down on his valley that day.

From his position on the hill east of the town, he could not see the front of the saloon, as it faced west. So he did not notice the young boy carrying a tin plate of food until he emerged from the cover of the saloon and crossed the street, angling toward the jail where Little Wolf had waited to settle his score with the late Sheriff Bowers.

He watched as the young man stepped up from the street, stopping to stomp some of the mud from his boots before rapping on the door of the jail. Little Wolf knew the plate was probably for a prisoner. Medicine Creek must have gotten a new sheriff. The door opened, but Little Wolf could not see who was inside. The boy entered and reappeared seconds later with an empty plate. He returned to the saloon. Within a quarter of an hour, the door of the jail opened again, and Little Wolf's spine stiffened. He had found what he was seeking. The man was so huge, his shoulders so wide, that he had to turn slightly on an angle when he passed through the door. There was no mistaking him, even at that distance. It was the big tracker that had trailed him. Now he knew who the prisoner was. He had found Rain Song.

Having come up on one knee when he first sighted Tobin, Little Wolf settled back on his heels and watched, fighting the impulse to jump on his pony and charge down on the little town. *No,* he counciled himself silently, *I must be patient and see how difficult my task will be.* He watched Tobin pull the heavy door shut and fix a padlock on it. Then the huge man made his way across the street to the saloon.

He wondered how securely the jail was locked, but was unable to determine at that distance. He would have to get a closer look at the building. This was not possible in the bright light of day. He entertained thoughts of attacking the saloon and killing the tracker, but only for a moment. He was confident he could kill the big man, and maybe several others. But there was a very good chance someone else in the saloon might shoot him. And that would do no good for Rain Song. No, he must find a way to get to Rain Song without anyone seeing him. He must wait until nightfall and then make his way down to the jail. The river flowed barely fifty or so yards behind the buildings on the west side of the street. It would be best to approach the rear of the jail from the river. That decided, he settled back to watch the little town.

In a short while, Little Wolf saw Tobin leave the saloon and return to the jail. It was apparent the man was staying close to his prisoner, and Little Wolf realized that the wild-looking tracker was waiting for him, hoping he would attempt to rescue Rain Song. There would be no element of surprise. The man had baited a trap and was content to sit on it, knowing Little Wolf had to come for his wife. While this fact prompted Little Wolf to be more cautious, it had no bearing on his determination to free Rain Song. He waited for nightfall.

Hours later the gentle breeze was chilly on the Cheyenne's wet shoulders, although the river water had felt warm when he crossed. Oblivious to the chill, he crouched low in the darkness, his eyes shifting back and forth, making sure he was alone behind the buildings. It was no more than a hundred feet from the spot where he now stood that he had killed Puddin Rooks. He did not think of that now as he watched the rear of the jail. There had been a light in the building for only a short time after sundown. It was out now. Little Wolf pictured the man waiting inside for him. Was he sleeping? Or waiting—alert and ready? He thought back to what had happened while he watched the building all day. The tracker had come out of the jail a total of three times, to get his meals Little Wolf assumed. The rest of the day he did not show himself. It was even more curious that not one soul had gone near the jail all day either, except the boy who brought food. In some instances, he observed some men crossing to the opposite side of the street when passing the jail. The whole town seemed intent on avoiding the man completely.

Like the night before, there was an almost full moon shining down on the peaceful settlement between the

river and the hills. From the riverbank, Little Wolf
made his way carefully through the low bushes that
ringed the shallow crossing to a stand of trees some
twenty yards from the rear of the building. From the
many hoofprints he had seen in the sandy riverbank,
Little Wolf figured that the ford was used by most
folks who rode from the homesteads on that side of the
river. He had avoided the narrow footbridge that
crossed the water a dozen or so yards downstream,
seeing no need to chance an encounter with one of the
local citizens on his way home from the saloon. It had
been on that same path, leading to the footbridge, that
he had settled with Puddin Rooks. On this night, his
only intention was to confirm his suspicion that Rain
Song was being held in the jail.

Rain Song lay awake on her straw pallet. There was
no sound outside her cell door. Tobin had been asleep
for hours, but she had been unable to sleep and had
tossed and turned since first closing her eyes. The days
were long this time of year, and Tobin often went to his
cot while there was still light outside. She always
waited for the sound of his heavy snoring before she
performed her toilet. The huge brute was true to his
word—he never laid a hand on her. But he was not
above leering at her on the few occasions he had
caught her washing herself, or using her bucket.

Nighttime was the only time she felt at peace, even
though her respite was of short duration, lasting only
until the sun came up again. So it was often she lay
awake on nights like this, her thoughts going out to
her husband and praying that he might somehow find
her. And then she would think of the savage brute
asleep in the next room and feel guilty for wishing Little Wolf would come.

She did not realize she had been crying until she felt
the tear drops on her arm as she lay on her side,
cradling her head. From outside her tiny window, she

heard the lonely call of a night bird—probably the same one she had heard the night before. He was pining for his mate. She listened as it called again. But there was no answer from his mate. *Sad*, she thought, *he is alone like I.* Still the forlorn little male called out, although his calls were in vain.

After a few minutes, his persistence puzzled Rain Song and she suddenly sat up, listening now with added concentration. There it was again. Fully alert now, she got quickly to her feet and pulled herself up to the window. Knowing in her heart that it was nothing more than a melancholy bird, she still strained to lift herself high enough to see out, unable to explain the tingle of excitement that coursed through her body. She peered out at the moonlit patch of bare ground behind the jail. There was nothing.

It's a bird, she thought, *nothing more,* and started to lower herself back down to the floor. But she hesitated—there was a movement in the shadows under the trees across the narrow clearing. Had she really seen something? Or were her eyes simply playing tricks on her in the middle of the night? She stared hard at the spot where she thought she had seen movement. Again, she thought she saw something move in the shadows. Then she felt her heart quicken as if it would burst from her bosom. *He was there!* As she watched, scarcely believing her eyes, he rose to his feet. Standing tall and straight, it could be no other, even though she could not see his face. It was Little Wolf, but spirit or man, she could not be sure. She feared her grief had been so intense that her eyes were seeing a phantom image of her husband.

Although her arms were trembling from the strain of supporting her body, she refused to drop to the floor, continuing to stare at the figure under the trees. In the next instant she forgot the pain in her arms. The figure suddenly stepped to the edge of the shadows, the moonlight falling on his face. It was no phantom. "Little Wolf!" she gasped. At almost the same instant, the still night air was ripped apart by the explosion of a rifle.

Rain Song screamed. The shot seemed to come from directly behind her. Little Wolf fell backward, rolling over and over, disappearing into the shadows. His sharp senses had detected the barrel of the rifle a split second before he saw the muzzle flash. It came from the other small cell window next to Rain Song's. Had it not been for the glint of moonlight on the metal of the rifle barrel, Tobin's bullet might have found its mark. As it was, the lead was embedded in a tree trunk and the massive tracker cursed his luck, unsure if he had hit flesh or not.

"Little Wolf!" Rain Song called out, her voice almost a scream. "Little Wolf!" But there was no answer from the shadowy trees on the other side of the little clearing. Tears filled her eyes as she began to lose her grip on the iron bars of the window. She had seen him fall, but she could not be sure if he had been hit or not.

"Git away from there!" In her anxiety, she had not heard the rattle of the key when Tobin opened her cell. He grabbed her roughly by the neck and pulled her away from the window, shoving her out of his way and onto the floor behind him. He upended the bucket in the corner and stood on it in an effort to sight his rifle out the window, hoping to get a better angle to shoot from. It was no use—the shadows were too dark. He emptied his rifle into the clump of trees anyway, hoping for a lucky shot. He stood there for a few moments, listening. There was nothing but utter silence. "Damn!" he swore and stepped down from his makeshift stool.

During the few seconds while Tobin fired into the trees, Rain Song lay stunned in the corner of her cell. Her wits about her now, she scrambled to her feet and ran through the open door from her cell. Tobin saw her run but made no move to chase her. Instead he casually walked to the front of the jail where Rain Song was frantically trying to open the heavy door. He stood and watched her frustrated attempts to escape for a moment before telling her she could yank on that lock all week and still wouldn't be able to break it.

Rain Song shrieked in agony and turned to attack the smirking giant, flying at him with flailing arms. Her frustrated assault seemed to amuse him and he stood solidly before her like a stout oak, absorbing her harmless blows on his massive chest. When he tired of the game, he flattened her with one quick backhand. It was enough to calm her venom, and she sat on the floor, quietly whimpering.

"Why, if I didn't know no better, I'd think you didn't appreciate my hospitality—wantin' to run off with the first buck that come along." He laughed at his own humor. "I had a suspicion that husband of yourn would be showin' up pretty soon. I mighta put some lead in his tail, can't say for sure. Reckon we'll have to wait for daylight to find out." He reached down and pulled the stricken woman to her feet and gave her a shove, the force of which drove her back into her cell. "'Course I could go outside and find out right now, I reckon. But I know you don't want me to git shot." He laughed again, thoroughly enjoying her dismay.

When Rain Song sank down on her straw pallet, still silently sobbing, Tobin stood there and studied the tiny window above her head. After a moment, he turned and went into the front room of the jail. He returned with a flat stool. After breaking the legs off, he took the flat board seat and jammed it up into the window, blocking it completely. "Now, ain't that better? Now you can sleep without no nightbirds bothering you." This brought forth another throaty chuckle as he locked her door once more and retired to his cell.

There was no more sleep that night for either of them. She could hear him moving around all through the night, checking the door and window. She knew he was watching for Little Wolf. She had been puzzled at first when Tobin did not rush outside in an attempt to catch her husband before he could escape to the river. As she thought more on it during the sleepless night, it became apparent to her why he did not. He thought he might have hit Little Wolf, but he wasn't sure, and wounded or not, Little Wolf was far too dangerous out in the open. On the other hand, the jail was built like a little fortress, with boards of solid pine four inches thick. The only windows were the ones in each cell, and one more over the front door, and they were no larger than a large baking sheet. Tobin knew the building was impenetrable. He could simply stay put and be safe from attack. Little Wolf would have to burn him out, and he knew he couldn't risk that with his wife inside. So he could afford to wait until sunup when he could see anyone lying in ambush.

Dawn came, and Tobin studied the trees behind the building for a long time until he was certain there was no one there. Only then did he leave the building to investigate the area behind it. With rifle in hand, he scanned the expanse between the buildings and the river. When he was sure Little Wolf was no longer there, he turned his attention to the tracks around the trees and in the clearing. He smiled when he sighted a small string of blood droplets near the largest of the pines. There wasn't much. He might have easily missed them, drying on the pine needles, had he not been scouting the ground so thoroughly. "By God, I nicked him," he muttered, pleased that he had drawn first blood. "Well, the game's on now. He knows where she is. It's up to him to come and get her."

Back inside again, he propped his rifle against the wall and lit a fire in the small stove. When Blanton's

boy came with Rain Song's breakfast, he would send
him to the river to fetch water for coffee. He was not
concerned about Little Wolf now that the sun was up.
There was no cover close enough to town to afford
concealment for anyone with a notion to take a shot at
him. This didn't mean he wouldn't keep a sharp eye
anytime he left the jail, though.

As for his prisoner, she remained huddled in a corner of the cell, her head down, pining for her man, he
figured. She didn't even look up when he informed
her that he had caught Little Wolf with at least one
shot. She still did not respond when Blanton's boy
brought her breakfast. Tobin sent the boy to the river
for water. He usually had him empty Rain Song's toilet bucket as well, a chore the boy despised but was
too afraid of the sinister tracker to refuse. On this
morning, the contents of the bucket were on the floor,
since Tobin had upended it to use as a stool the night
before. Tobin stood staring at the Indian girl for a few
moments before leaving to walk down the street to
Blanton's for his own breakfast. She did not move
from her position in the corner. He knew that as soon
as he locked the front door and left, she would wash
herself and eat her breakfast, and no doubt clean up
the mess he had made on her floor.

Blanton looked up from the table when Tobin
walked in. He took another sip from the coffee cup in
his hand, saying nothing as he watched the huge man
pull out a chair and settle himself heavily. As always
during this daily routine, Blanton's face wore an expression of extreme irritation. He may not have been
aware of the obvious display of his feelings, but it did
not go unnoticed by Tobin. It was a source of mild
amusement for Blanton's unwelcome guest—it always
pleased Tobin to irritate people.

"Where the hell's my breakfast?" Tobin growled.

Blanton did not answer him, but got up and walked

to the back door. Opening it, he called out, "Frances, he's here—wants his breakfast." Blanton, along with his wife and son, lived in a small house behind the saloon, no more than ten or twelve steps from the back door of the barroom. He came back and sat down at the table again. "She'll bring it," was all he said to Tobin.

"I'll have some of that coffee," Tobin said and studied the saloon keeper as he reluctantly, but obediently, got up to get it. *He's getting a little too sassy*, Tobin thought, *I might have to put a little fear of the devil in him.* It had been a few days since Tobin had damn near beaten Johnny Blevins to death, and the big scout suspected Blanton was getting too secure in his relationship with him, just because he was feeding him. Tobin decided he didn't feel like expending the energy to soften Blanton's head up a little. Maybe tomorrow.

"What was all the shooting last night?" Blanton asked as he watched Tobin gulp down his breakfast.

Tobin looked up from his plate and hesitated a second. "Varmint," he said and returned his attention to his food.

"Varmint?" Blanton grunted. "Shore sounded like a heap of shooting. What kind of varmint was it?"

Tobin paused again, gravy dripping from his whiskers. "The kind that ain't none of your business." He glared at Blanton.

Blanton blanched. "I was just making conversation," he stammered.

"Well, don't. When I feel like making conversation, I'll let you know."

Blanton stood inside the saloon door and watched as Tobin stepped off the walkway and headed back toward the jail. He halfway wished he had the guts to take his shotgun and shoot the huge scout in the back. He had a feeling Medicine Creek was not going to be rid of Tobin after he caught that Cheyenne renegade. Hearing a footstep on the walk behind him, he turned to see Arvin Gilbert approaching. Blanton smirked. He knew it wouldn't be long before the rats scurried out of their holes now that the cat was gone. No doubt Ike Frieze would also be along any minute now, as soon as Tobin was inside and Ike could safely pass the jail without having to confront the brute.

"Morning, Henry," Arvin greeted the saloon keeper. "What was all the shooting about last night? Did Tobin say?"

Blanton held the door for Arvin. "No, he didn't say."

"Did you ask him about it?"

"I asked him—said it wasn't none of my damn business."

Arvin looked worried. "There were an awful lot of shots, seven or eight at least. He was damn sure shooting at something."

"I wouldn't be surprised if that damn Injun mighta showed up." Blanton poured a cup of coffee for Arvin. "You know, I don't feel any too stout about that crazy son of a bitch using our town for a trap. A lot of innocent folks could get hurt before he catches that Cheyenne."

Arvin nodded solemnly. "We should have held off until that damn Injun came back to his shack. We shoulda killed them all. That was a big mistake. I'm blaming Bowers for that."

Blanton only snorted in reply. Arvin could blame Bowers if he wanted to, but Bowers wasn't the only one who had been reluctant to sit around in the hills that day, waiting for the white Cheyenne to show up. The blood was up that day and most of the posse was eager to burn the rat's nest and get on back to the comfort of their own hearths. If Arvin wanted to dwell on what they should have done, as far as Blanton was concerned, they should have just left the Injuns to hell alone. Then they wouldn't be in this mess.

Arvin was dead right about one thing, though—Medicine Creek was just beginning to get a taste of the trouble coming their way from Mister Tobin, who was getting more demanding and sullen with each passing day.

17

Little Wolf knelt down on a flat rock that jutted out into the swiftly running stream. Cupping the cool water in his hand, he washed the dried blood from the long crease in his left shoulder. Tobin's bullet had cut a shallow trench in his skin. There was no real damage, as the injury was little more than a deep scratch. He had been lucky to catch the glint of moonlight on the rifle barrel in time to avoid taking the shot in his chest. The bullet wound was nothing when compared to the pain in his heart, knowing that he had been so close to Rain Song and unable to rescue her. He would have returned fire had the big scout not moved to the window Rain Song had called from. Little Wolf could not risk firing into the window for fear of hitting his wife.

The night was not a complete loss. He now knew for sure that Rain Song was being held in the jail. He had wanted to try to talk to her—it had been so long since he last saw her. He wanted to tell her that he would come for her, that she mustn't give up hope. But the big tracker was more alert than he had anticipated. No matter, she knew he was there, and she had to know that as long as he drew breath, he would come to her, even if it meant he had to kill the entire town.

When he finished cleaning his wound, he moved back away from the stream into the trees and sat down to decide on a plan. The jail was too fortified to break into. Tobin was obviously staying put inside his fortress, knowing Little Wolf could not very well storm the building. That would be suicidal. He had to draw the huge man outside. He thought hard on it. His fighting would have to be done at night. He could not be sure how much support the big tracker had from the town, so he couldn't expose himself to some storekeeper's rifle fire. After a minute of thought, he decided that since the town had burned him out, it was only fitting that he return the favor.

Arvin Gilbert knew something was amiss as soon as he walked in the front door that morning. He went at once to the back door where his fears were confirmed. The door was closed, but it was not locked as he had left it. The bottom panel had been kicked in and the intruder had reached in and lifted the bar. He had been robbed!

He walked quickly back to the front and stood in the middle of the store, looking around him. Some things were out of place, but there was no sign of wanton pillaging. The safe in the corner of his stockroom had not been disturbed, a fact that distressed him momentarily. Did someone know that he only kept a token amount of money in the safe? Hurriedly, he crossed over to the back counter. He crawled under the counter and lifted the floorboard. Brushing aside the straw and sawdust that covered the square iron box, he breathed a sigh of relief. It was still there! Just to make sure, he took a key from his watch pocket and opened the lock. Nothing was amiss. What was the thief after, if not the money?

Returning to the front of the store, he began a careful inspection of his shelves. At first he was ready to conclude that nothing had been taken, but soon he began to discover the loss of first one thing, then another. After canvassing the entire store, he could say for certain what his losses were; a five-gallon can of

kerosene, a block of salt pork, two boxes of rifle car-
tridges, and as near as he could figure, part of a bolt of
cotton cloth. Later that morning, when he went down
to the saloon, he puzzled over his robbery with Henry
Blanton.

"Whaddaya make of that?" Arvin asked his friend.

Henry scratched his head thoughtfully. "It is a mite
queer. You sure you ain't missing nuthin' else?"

"Nothing I can find. I reckon whoever it was just
wanted to do a little shopping for a few things. Hell, if
they didn't have no money, I'da give 'em credit for that
much—I'da heap rather give it to 'em then have 'em
bust up my door."

Blanton nodded, understanding. "You ought to
make you a solid door like the one I got out back. That
one'll stand up to about anything short of dynamite."
He paused while he poured Arvin a cup of coffee.
Then, grinning, he asked, "You gonna report the robbery to our acting sheriff?"

"A lot of good that would do," Arvin snorted. Then,
as a precaution, he looked over his shoulder to make
sure they were still alone. For such a huge man, Tobin
could move uncommonly quiet.

"It's all right," Blanton said, chuckling, "he's done
been here for his load of rations."

Even though he had remarked to Blanton that it
would do no good to report the break-in to their new
sheriff, Arvin still made it a point to be at the saloon
when Tobin ambled in for his evening meal. He waited
until the surly brute had finished his second plate of
side meat and beans before approaching him.

Tobin eyed the mayor with a glance that might have
been reserved for a cockroach. He harbored no toler-
ance for weakness of any kind, and he saw a weakness
in Arvin Gilbert that disgusted him. He made no efforts to disguise his contempt for all the citizens of

Medicine Creek, but Arvin was especially revolting to him. So, when the mayor stepped up to his table and paused, waiting to be acknowledged, Tobin simply leered up at him from under bushy black eyebrows. Arvin almost lost his courage and was about to turn around and leave the surly brute to scowl alone.

"What the hell do you want?" Tobin growled, his voice rumbling up from deep in his powerful chest. It stopped Arvin in his tracks.

"Why, nothing—that is, I was just going to pass the time of day," he lied. Summoning up his resolve, he blurted, "Well, there was something." He almost faltered when Tobin cocked an eyebrow at this, but figured he had gotten this far, so he spit it out. "Somebody broke into my store last night—busted the back door." When Tobin continued to glare at the little man, making no reply, Arvin began to sputter, already sorry he had even mentioned it. "Well, you know, you being sheriff and all—like you said—as long as you're using the jail." When his words were still met with silence, he made one more attempt to assert his authority. "As mayor, it is my responsibility to insist that the sheriff look into these matters."

Still Tobin did not respond. The only sign he showed that indicated he had even heard the mayor's timid protest was a darkening of his already stormy countenance. After a moment during which Arvin stood frozen, not knowing whether to say more or simply turn and remove himself, Tobin slowly rose from his chair. "I ain't got time to fool with your piddly little problems," he said gruffly as he brushed by the embarrassed little man and left the saloon.

Voices that had been low and subdued the entire time the baleful scout had sat at the back table noisily eating his supper, once again gained pitch and substance as the tension eased. Arvin turned around to find every eye in the place on him. *What do they expect?*

he thought. *I can't challenge the brute.* Looking toward the bar, he met the broad grin of Henry Blanton.

"We used to think Franklin Bowers was hard to get along with," Blanton said. "What are we gonna do about that devil?"

Arvin had no answer for him. He shook his head slowly, and shrugging his shoulders, abruptly turned and headed for the door. Feeling mortified to have been treated with such disrespect—and in front of a good number of his friends—Arvin simply wanted to go home and hope to forget about the incident.

It had been a typical spring season in the river valley and Medicine Creek had received a normal amount of rainfall. But during the last few days, as summer approached, it had been uncommonly dry. Even the ruts in the usually muddy street were beginning to dry out. Homesteaders were already complaining about their crops. With a stout breeze blowing from the south that rustled the leaves of the cottonwoods, conditions were prime for disaster.

Like a shooting star, the flaming arrow traced a brilliant arc across the dark moonless night and came to rest solidly in the dry shingles of the saloon roof. The solitary figure on the knoll behind the buildings paused to judge the effectiveness of his first arrow before preparing the second. Seeing that the kerosene-soaked cloth had effectively spread the flames to a sizable area of the dry shingles, he carefully ignited another arrow and launched it. Like the first, it spread rapidly across the dried-out roof, which had become like tinder over the last few rainless days.

After placing several more arrows at intervals along the roof line, he was confident that the kerosene rags had done their work. The townfolk of Medicine Creek had long since retired to their beds for the night, and by the time the building would be blazing hard

enough to waken the saloon keeper and his family in
their little house behind, it would be too late to extin-
guish it.

Little Wolf felt no compassion for the man who
owned the saloon. He wasn't certain Blanton was
among the burning and murdering riders who
stormed down on his little ranch. Even if Blanton
wasn't, he still supported the deed, even fed the half-
breed scout who held Rain Song captive. Little Wolf
was not concerned with individuals in his mission to
rescue his wife. From his point of view, there were only
two distinct personalities—the town of Medicine
Creek, and Tobin. They were both his mortal enemies.

Leading his horse in the dark, he made his way
along the base of the hills that guarded the eastern side
of the valley to a point opposite the jail and south of
the stables. Here, he tied his horse and sat down to
wait. From this vantage point, he could see the front
door of the jail.

The roof of the saloon burned for more than half an
hour before the interior structure caught fire and major
flames began to reach up into the nighttime sky. It
seemed like only seconds after this that the alarm went
out. The saloon keeper, a nightshirt tucked haphazardly into his trousers, ran hysterically back and forth
from the front of the burning building to the back.
After a moment, he ran into his house and emerged
seconds later with a shotgun, which he fired into the
air—three shots, which was the town's distress signal.
In a matter of minutes, people from several buildings
poured into the dusty street in response to the alarm.
A bucket brigade was hastily organized, but it proved
to be a fruitless effort. The river was too far away and
the buckets of water that were passed along were too
few to have any effect on the flames.

The one person Little Wolf was most concerned with
failed to respond to the town's emergency. Little Wolf

watched the door of the jail intensely, waiting for the burly scout to show himself and provide the opportunity Little Wolf waited for. Surely, Little Wolf thought, the town's sheriff would respond to the fire. Still, there was no reaction from Tobin, even when Blanton's son was sent down to the jail to fetch him. From a position closer now that would afford a clear shot at the door, Little Wolf watched as Blanton's boy banged on the solid door of the jail, yelling at the top of his lungs. In a very short time, the boy was silenced by a gruff voice from inside that obviously told the lad to button his lip and get the hell away from his door.

His plan had failed. Little Wolf now understood the singleness of purpose the big scout had. Tobin was totally unconcerned with Blanton's loss, and he was smart enough to realize that the fire was possibly set to lure him into the white Cheyenne's rifle sights. Little Wolf was disappointed, but not discouraged. How long, he wondered, would the people of the town tolerate their sheriff's reticence? With the patience that had come with many drawn-out battles with the army, Little Wolf resolved to test the will of Medicine Creek to demand action from Tobin.

Ike Frieze trudged wearily back to his stables. Near exhaustion, his face and arms were black with the soot and smoke from the saloon fire. With the other men of the town, he had tried to tote water from the river in an effort to keep the fire from spreading to the front of the building. When it became apparent that this was a useless effort, he, along with Blanton and his son, dashed into the raging building to carry out anything they could. When the whiskey barrels went up, they knew they were finished. There was nothing left but to stand by and watch it burn.

By his watch, it was two-thirty when Ike was awakened by Blanton's shotgun. He glanced at his timepiece as he approached the stables—it was almost five o'clock. It would soon be daylight. In about two and a half hours, Blanton had been wiped out. Ike shook his head sadly to think how devastating a similar disaster would be to him. Then, as if just noticing the grime on his hands, he walked around the building to the horse trough to wash his face and arms.

The water was cool and refreshing and he splashed it liberally on his face and neck. Realizing that his whiskers had been singed by the flames, he dunked his head in the water. The hand that clamped down on the back of his neck had the strength of a vise, and Ike was helpless to pull his head from the water. It had happened so suddenly that he had not had time to take a breath and he realized he was drowning. Even with his arms and legs flailing in an attempt to save himself, his desperation was not of sufficient strength to escape the trap he was in. He could hold his breath no longer.

A moment before sliding into unconsciousness, he was suddenly lifted out of the water trough and brought roughly to his feet, gasping for the cool morning air. At the very threshold of death moments before, he was concerned only with gulping great lungfuls of air. When he recovered his senses to a degree, the next sight that met his eyes almost sent his confused brain reeling. *It was him! Little Wolf!*

Ike had never seen the notorious Little Wolf, but he knew with certainty that this painted savage that stood towering over him in the gray predawn light could be no other. The sight was so terrifying to him that he could utter no sound except a feeble whine that seemed to simply ooze from his trembling lips. He knew he was about to meet death. Paralyzed by his fear, his body sagged and would have collapsed, had not the Cheyenne supported him with one hand around his throat.

"Stand up," Little Wolf commanded, his voice low and hard as iron. "I am not going to take your worthless life now. I have a purpose for you." Upon hearing the words that he was to be spared, the frightened little man summoned enough strength to support himself. Still holding him by the throat, Little Wolf backed him against the side of the barn. "The big scout is holding a Cheyenne woman in his jail. I will burn this town to the ground if she is not set free. You must tell the others this. Do you understand?"

Ike nodded his head up and down frantically, unable to find his voice. Barely able to believe he was still alive, he could not look into the eyes that bored into his face with determined intensity. Instead, he hung his head and continued to nod his understanding of Little Wolf's warning. When he was released, Ike slid down the wall of the barn to a sitting position and remained there long after Little Wolf walked to the corner of the corral and leaped onto his pony. The shaken little man was still sitting there when the tall Cheyenne rode unhurriedly into the hills behind the stable as the first rays of the morning sun filtered through the trees.

Tobin opened the door slowly, his eyes searching the hills behind the buildings across the street from the jail. He knew it would be one hell of a lucky shot if he got hit from that distance. But that didn't mean he'd count out the possibility. Stepping out on the wooden walk, he looked hard up and down the street before starting toward Blanton's.

When he walked up, Blanton, Arvin Gilbert, Ike Frieze, Morgan Sewell, and several men whose names he didn't know were standing by the still-smoking ruins that once were a saloon. Blanton had saved everything that could be salvaged, which amounted to very little. His face was a mask of dejection as he poked at a smoldering piece of timber with his toe.

"Well," he said when he saw the huge scout approaching, "here comes the sheriff."

Tobin ignored the hint of sarcasm in Blanton's tone. Instead, he glanced toward the house, now standing naked behind the blackened timbers of the saloon. Looking back at the gathering of men, he remarked, "Looks like you had a little fire." He said it as casually as if he'd said, Looks like you had a little rain.

Blanton looked dumbfounded, hardly believing the surly tracker's indifference to his tragedy. He opened his mouth to retort but Arvin quickly spoke. "Tell him, Ike. Tell him what that damn savage said."

When Arvin nudged him forward, Ike found himself standing almost toe to toe with the ominous scout, a position he was not especially comfortable with. It was the second time in the span of a few hours that he had looked directly into the eyes of death. Nevertheless, he pulled his shoulders back and stammered his message.

"He said you'd best let his squaw go. Said if you didn't, he's gonna burn the whole town to the ground." Having said his piece, he stepped back between Blanton and Morgan Sewell.

Tobin grinned. He didn't give a damn if Little Wolf burned down every building on the street. He knew there was one he wouldn't set fire to, not as long as his wife was in the jail. He also figured that, when he didn't budge, Little Wolf would become more and more frustrated, and get bolder and bolder until he got careless. That's when Tobin would get him. In the meantime, all Tobin had to do was sit cozy and wait him out.

The grin faded from his face when he looked back at the group of men before him. "I ain't got time to stand around here. Where's my breakfast?"

Blanton's mouth dropped open. He looked at Arvin, who appeared to be as shocked as he was. "Why, god-a'mighty, man—I've just been burned out!"

"I can see that, but the house is still standing. The damn kitchen's in the house, ain't it?"

As fearsome as the beast was, his callousness was too much for Arvin Gilbert to ignore. He stepped forward. "Now see here, Mr. Tobin, Henry's got more important things—"

That was as far as he got before the giant man struck out like a timber rattler, clutching Arvin by the throat. "Damn you, you little weasel! I've had about all I'm gonna take of your little mealy-mouth whining." He shoved Arvin back into the men standing behind him. "We made a bargain. I'd stay in the jail and you'd see to my grub. Now, I'm hungry and if you don't get that woman of yourn to cooking right now, I'm gonna visit her myself." He glared at Blanton. "By God, she'll cook then."

The men of Medicine Creek were stunned. They stood in shocked silence for a few moments before Blanton, his limbs trembling with rage, dutifully turned and went to the house to tell his wife to fix Tobin something to eat.

Tobin turned to leave. "Bring it down to the jail—and tell her to hurry up or I might help that damn Cheyenne burn this town down."

Arvin called after him. "What about what Ike said? That Indian means business. You're gonna have to let the woman go. It's not worth risking our homes and businesses for one woman."

There was no answer from the huge man. He considered cracking Arvin's skull, but he decided to ignore him this time. There would be time for that after the renegade Cheyenne was taken care of. But he made a mental note to skin the irritating little rodent before his business was done in Medicine Creek.

The group of stupefied men watched the departing bulk of their hostile sheriff in stunned silence. They made up the core of the Vigilance Committee, and if there had been any question before, there was no doubt now that theirs was a serious problem. Something was going to have to be done about it. When Tobin first rode into town and took over the jail, it was plain to see that he would be a difficult man to deal with. Now it was apparent that he could not be reasonably dealt with at all. He knew no law but his own selfish agenda, and he had not a care for right or decency. Arvin was right when he said the man was little more than an animal.

"What are we gonna do about that man?" It was Morgan Sewell who posed the question that was foremost in every man's mind.

A homesteader named Jake Bannister, who had witnessed the confrontation just taken place, spoke. "I know what you do when you got a mad dog roaming the streets. And I say we sure as hell got us a mad dog here in Medicine Creek."

Morgan turned to face him. "What are you saying, Jake? That we should just shoot him? In cold blood?"

Jake shrugged his shoulders as if hesitant to put it that bluntly. "All's I'm saying is, we got a committee to handle things like Injun trouble and other lawlessness. If the situation calls for drastic action, then so be it." He looked around for support. "We just do what we have to do."

There were a few nods of agreement but no one spoke out for a long moment. Arvin, feeling it his responsibility to lead, finally posed the question before them. "Are we talking about a firing squad? Or one man to do the job? I don't know if I like the idea of a planned murder. Maybe we should give him a strong warning from the committee—let him know we won't stand for any more of his behavior."

Blanton spoke up. "Are you crazy, Arvin? You can't give that murderer any warning. He'd kill us all!"

"Well, he's gonna kill us all anyway before it's over—either him or that damn Cheyenne he's trying to catch," Morgan replied. "I say we all get our guns and go down there and order him out of town. He ain't likely to stand up to all of us."

"What if he still won't go?" Arvin asked.

"Then shoot him down where he stands, same as you would any mad dog," Jake Bannister answered.

Arvin shook his head slowly. He was not comfortable with the way the discussion was headed. The impromptu meeting was interrupted for a few moments when Blanton's wife called for her son to come get Tobin's breakfast. They watched as the boy walked away, holding a tin plate piled high. Arvin's brow was furrowed with concern. "This is serious business we're talking about here. I think we better have another meeting to decide what action we're gonna take. I don't want us to go off half-cocked."

At least there was general agreement on that point. It was also decided that action would need to be taken soon, so a meeting was planned for that evening. Since their usual meeting place was now little more than a pile of ashes, it was decided to gather in Arvin Gilbert's general store.

The meeting got started a little sooner than usual due to the fact that Arvin could not provide the whiskey and beer that was normally consumed in Blanton's saloon. Though early in starting, the meeting went on later in the evening than most sessions of the vigilance committee. No one was anxious to confront the dark and fearful man holding the town hostage. But after much heated discussion for and against, there was general agreement that the town could not survive with Tobin ensconced as sheriff. The question to be debated and decided upon was exactly what ac-

tion the committee should take. Part of the group favored an execution-style ambush, giving the sinister
scout no chance to defend himself. Most of the debate
for this group was led by Jake Bannister. However, a
larger portion of the committee—influenced by the
passionate rhetoric of Reverend Norsworthy and the
pleading of Arvin Gilbert—voted to visit their unwelcome guest in sufficient number to guarantee no resistance. Half a dozen men, armed and determined,
should be enough to force the brute to leave town,
they reasoned.

As Arvin so eloquently phrased it, "It's our town.
We built it from the ground up with our own sweat
and muscle. We've banded together before in times of
trouble. If we stick together, no one can defy us, not
even an evil coyote like Tobin."

So it was decided. The meeting broke up around ten
o'clock, after a committee of six men were selected to
confront the surly half-breed early the following
morning. "Before breakfast," Blanton requested. "I
don't aim to feed that mean son of a bitch one more
time."

18

Under the cover of a thick clump of young willows close by the bank of the river, Little Wolf sat on his pony. He watched as the group of citizens that had assembled in the general store filed out of the building and went their separate ways into the night. He waited while the storekeeper doused the lamps and locked the door, then hurried the few hundred yards down the road to his house.

"I am returning the kerosene and cloth I borrowed from you," he murmured softly and nudged his horse forward. When he approached within seventy-five yards of the building, he reined his pony up and dismounted. Soon, a flaming arrow bored its way through the deep night sky and found its mark in the roof of the general store. More arrows followed. When he was satisfied that the fire was spreading, he unhurriedly climbed on his horse and rode back to the willows to watch.

For the second time in as many nights, the citizens of Medicine Creek were summoned from their beds to fight a fire—some after having barely settled in their blankets. As before, an attempt was made to hand water from the river, but the results were much the same as had befallen Blanton. Arvin managed to save some of his merchandise before the flames became too hot and drove him out. He was unable to rescue his little iron box under the back counter, the flames having caused burning beams to fall directly down from the roof at that point. Reluctant to tell his neighbors of his main concern, he could only hope that the metal of the box would protect its contents.

Little Wolf watched the chaotic scene from a safe point across the river, after having to leave the willows when the bucket brigade formed. He gazed impassionately at the frantic attempts of the men of Medicine Creek, intent upon assessing the effectiveness of his attack—although it was impossible not to be reminded of what Sleeps Standing and his wife had suffered at the hands of these same men. "Now we will see," he said softly and turned his pony toward the hills.

Sleep did not come easily for Little Wolf that night. He worried about Rain Song's safety, although his common sense told him the big tracker would be served best by keeping his hostage alive. It was no use telling himself that he must rest. There were deeper thoughts that troubled him. As he lay there, looking up into a black sky sprinkled with tiny points of light, he thought about the path he had traveled to come to this point in his life. His had been a life of war and violence, and always the threat of massacre rode with his people. Yet he did not regret having been found by Spotted Pony. Looking back, he would have chosen no other path.

Now his thoughts returned to the people of Medicine Creek and the crimes they had committed against his family and friends. It was time to make new medicine and call on the power and spirit of the grizzly again. He would rest now and prepare himself for battle.

Dawn found a troubled group of townfolk still milling around the burned-out shell of Arvin Gilbert's General Mercantile. There was no thought of sleep for the heartsick mayor of Medicine Creek. He had been effectively wiped out. He had managed to save the contents of his precious iron box from the ashes, but the gold there would not be enough to replace all of the stock he had lost. Morgan Sewell laid a hand on his shoulder in a gesture of sympathy, and Arvin just shook his head, fighting the urge to cry.

No one had even suggested sending for their sheriff this time. And no one was surprised that he again did not bother himself to offer assistance. As the sky began to brighten, Arvin became more and more angry. *Damn Sam Tolbert! Damn Lonnie Jacobs!* He wished with all his heart that the two had never stirred up the town over the discovery of the Cheyenne warrior. "He wasn't doing anybody any harm out there anyway." He didn't realize he had spoken the thought aloud until Sewell said, "What?"

"What?" Arvin echoed. Then, pulling his thoughts back to the group of men around him, he said, "We've got to get that bastard half-breed out of our town now! Let the damn woman go before that Injun burns us all out."

His words were met with unified accord. It was time for action, time to take their town back. All six of the selected Vigilance Committee were present and all were ready to get to their task. Jake Bannister stepped forward to check that every man was armed. Those who weren't borrowed a gun from one of the other men on the street. It resembled a lynch mob in preparation, causing Reverend Norsworthy to raise his hands in caution.

"We mustn't lose sight of the decision made last night, my friends. The purpose of the committee is to rid our town of this evil man. He must be allowed to get on his horse and go peacefully."

"The preacher's right," Arvin admitted reluctantly.

"We're not murderers here. We're just gonna run him out of town."

"But if he wants to put up a fight," Jake interrupted, "we'll by God give it to him."

Rain Song waited for the baleful Tobin to leave as he always did each morning. She did not understand why he lingered this morning. After stepping outside the jail door to urinate off the walkway, as was his custom, he stood there for a long time, watching the crowd of people at the far end of the street. She could not see them, but she had heard them mulling about in loud voices all during the night, and she knew that the crowd must still be in the street. After a few moments more, Tobin came back inside and picked up his rifle. Looking it over to make sure it was loaded, he propped it up by the door while he checked his pistol. She had no notion as to what was about to occur, but the usually dour giant of a man seemed to be amused by something he had seen in the street. He even paused to look into her cell, a hint of a grin on his face.

"Looks like you might have to go without your breakfast this morning," he said, chuckling to himself. Then he moved to the front door and cracked it enough to see the street outside.

The committee of six strode purposefully down the middle of the street, a cloud of dust kicking up from their boots. Leading them was Arvin Gilbert, Jake Bannister close at his elbow, the blacksmith, Jacob Schuyler, on the other side. Behind them, Blanton and two others followed. All were armed with pistols. At a safe distance, the rest of the crowd milled about in the dusty street, waiting to see the eviction.

Seeing no sign of the ominous half-breed but noticing the cracked door, Arvin halted his posse short of the step up to the walk. "Tobin," he called out, "step outside, we have something to say to you." He glanced quickly to his right and left to make sure the other five were still behind him.

Tobin did not answer at once, causing Arvin to call out again. Just before he called for a third time, Tobin spoke, his voice a low rumble from the dark interior of the jail. "Well now, ain't this a nice little visit? Which one of you is bringing my breakfast?"

"They ain't gonna be no more breakfasts," Blanton blurted, before Arvin held up his hand to silence him.

"Step outside please," Arvin said. "We're here representing the people of Medicine Creek and we've got something to say to you."

To a man, all six backed up a step when the door opened and Tobin came out, his rifle hanging down at his side. He smirked as his ominous gaze passed slowly from man to man, then came to rest on the mayor. "The people of Medicine Creek's got somethin' to say to you," he mocked. "Well, they damn sure better say it quick. I ain't got time to fool with the likes of you."

Arvin was shaken by the mere presence of the malefic brute, but, bolstered by the support he felt he had behind him, he was determined to issue his stern mandate. "It is my responsibility as mayor to inform you that you are no longer acting sheriff." When Tobin simply stared at him and made no reply, Arvin was encouraged to expound. "You've brought nothing but destruction to this town, and we're ordering you to vacate these premises at once." He paused, feeling the uneasy shuffling of the committee behind him. Still Tobin was silent. "And take that Injun woman with you." Satisfied that he had delivered his message with stern authority, he stood, feet shoulder-width apart, arms folded across his chest in a no-nonsense manner, and waited.

There was not a sound except that of a horsefly that had flitted over to investigate the confrontation. Tobin shifted his penetrating gaze to each man—measuring, evaluating.

Jake Bannister was at Arvin's ear. "I told you he ain't gonna listen," he whispered. "Tell him if he don't go peaceful, we're gonna run him out."

Tobin could not hear Jake's words, but he answered him anyway. "Well now . . . I reckon it'll be for me to say who leaves town and who don't. I don't plan to leave till I'm good and ready, so I reckon you boys is gonna have to kill me." He paused to let his words sink in. Pleased with the nervous shuffling they caused, he demanded, "Who's man enough to do the job?" He pointed his rifle at Arvin. "You? You little dried-up weasel. You?" he suddenly shifted his rifle to Blanton. He snapped his gaze back to Arvin. "Now I'll tell you something, Mr. Mayor. I'm telling *you* to get out of *my* town. If you ain't out of here by sundown, I'm gonna come looking for you. Is that clear?"

Arvin was frozen with the shock of Tobin's ultimatum. Blanton stood open-mouthed and confused. The three men behind Arvin stepped back nervously, unsure what to do. Of the six, Tobin had kept his eye on Jake Bannister. And, when Jake suddenly reached for his pistol, Tobin's rifle cut him down before he had a chance to level his arm.

In the chaos that followed in the next few minutes, things happened so fast that Arvin would find it impossible to recall exactly what had happened. All he could say for sure was that it sounded like a small war. Tobin did most of the shooting. When his rifle split the morning stillness, Jake Bannister went down, his pistol firing harmlessly into the dirt at his feet. Terrified, Blanton stepped backward and stumbled over Jake's body. This was all that saved the saloon keeper. Had he not gone over backward, Tobin's next two shots would have found their mark in his chest.

Cocking and firing as rapidly as he could, Tobin

could not be sure of the damage himself, holding his rifle hip high and pumping one bullet after another at the scattering committee. He turned back quickly, looking for Arvin, for he had an intense desire to do in the irritating little mayor. But Arvin was already down, lying beside Jake Bannister's body, so Tobin shifted his rifle back to bear on the others, now running frantically toward the cover of the buildings. Blanton, seeing his chance to escape, gave not a thought toward firing his weapon. Instead, he scrambled to his feet and ran between the buildings, not stopping until he reached the river. Out of the corner of his eye, Tobin detected Blanton's movements and whirled back around. Taking careful aim with the rifle, he pulled the trigger only to hear the metallic click of the firing pin on an empty chamber. Cursing, he dropped the rifle and pulled the pistol from his belt, but it was too late. His .45 slugs dug into the corner of the jail, ripping splinters out of the corner post.

Jacob Schuyler, who had fled as soon as the shooting started, peeked around the corner of the post office and fired a couple of wild shots at the enraged scout. Since Jacob was reluctant to expose much of his body, the shots landed harmlessly in the gable above the door of the jail. He received a .45 caliber slug in his shoulder for his trouble. Yelping in pain, he disappeared behind the building.

In a matter of minutes, it was over. Still impassioned to spill blood, Tobin strode after the fleeing vigilantes, throwing shots randomly at any piece of target he could spot. At the end of the street, near the still-smoldering ruins of the general store, the crowd of spectators dispersed like so many chickens at the sight of a fox. Soon, Tobin was alone in the street. He turned around in a circle, looking for a target. There was nothing more to shoot at, so he sent a couple of bullets through the window of the barbershop.

Satisfied that he quelled the attempted coup, he walked to Henry Blanton's little house and kicked the door open. There, huddled in a corner, he found Blanton's wife. Breakfast was still on the table untouched. Fixing Mrs. Blanton with a scorching gaze that dared her to make a sound, he scooped up the entire setting, using the tablecloth as a sack, and strode out the door with it over his shoulder.

Out in the street again, he started back toward the jail and the two bodies left lying in the street. As he approached, one of the bodies stirred. Tobin stopped and took a hard look. It was Arvin Gilbert. As he watched, Arvin suddenly scrambled to his feet and ran toward the stables at the end of the street.

"Why, that little skunk," Tobin mumbled and pulled his pistol once more. He fired three shots at the panic-stricken little mayor, but Arvin was too far away for Tobin's pistol to find the mark.

Tobin was sorely disappointed to see that the mayor was not dead. He remembered seeing him go down when he started spraying the street with rifle fire. In truth, the mayor was not wounded at all. Faint heart had saved his bacon that day—for Arvin had actually fainted when the shooting exploded around him. His explanation later that day, when the committee reconvened, was somewhat different, however, saying that he had dived for cover in an attempt to get off a shot.

Afraid and confused, Rain Song pressed her body as tightly as she could manage against the corner of her cell. She did not know what the shooting outside the jail meant, only that it was loud and accompanied by a great deal of shouting. She could not see outside since Tobin had blocked the window. Tobin had exchanged words with some men of the town just before the shooting started. She could not understand the words spoken, but she feared the gunfire might have involved Little Wolf. Now she ached for some word that he had not been part of the shooting. It hadn't lasted for very long. And soon after it stopped, Tobin came back.

"Looks like your man burned another building down last night," he said as he shoved the door shut and locked it.

He seemed to be in a good mood, pleased with himself. She had not seen him in such high spirits before. He carried a sack made of checkered cloth that he dumped in the middle of the floor, chuckling as he did so. She was surprised to see that it contained food— boiled meat and beans, plates and all, and panbread still in the skillet. His mood was such that he broke off a piece of the panbread and shoved it through the window in the heavy cell door. She scurried over at once and picked it up from the floor where it had fallen. She went back to her corner to eat. She could hear him chortle to himself in the other room and she knew for certain that he must be touched in the head. How long, she wondered, before he would take a notion to kill her?

On the south end of the settlement, close by the banks of the river, a gathering of some seven members of the Medicine Creek Vigilance Committee—all that could be found of the crowd that had gathered earlier—stood talking under the trees. In light of what had occurred earlier that day, it was not felt to be safe to hold a meeting in town. Not even the church was considered to be sanctuary from the evil presence in the jailhouse. All seven present lived in or close by the town, otherwise some of them might have scattered with the others to escape the wrath of Tobin.

It had been a dreadfully misfortunate day for the citizens of Medicine Creek. After Tobin's assault with his rifle, the toll was one dead and one badly wounded. And every man there marveled that the casualties had been that light.

"It's a wonder he didn't kill us all," Morgan Sewell said.

"He may yet," Blanton answered. "I know I thought I was dead meat. I heard two shots go right over my head. Damn!" He shook his head and looked at Arvin. "I thought you was dead, the way you was just laying there."

"I know, I know," Arvin quickly replied, avoiding Blanton's eyes. "I reckon I just outsmarted him. I do wish I could have gotten a clear shot at him though."

"A clear shot?" Morgan looked up surprised. "The man's as big as a barn and he was standing in the middle of the street!"

Arvin looked uncomfortable. "There was a lot of lead flying around out there. Anyway, that doesn't matter now. We've got to decide what we're gonna do."

"I'll tell you what we better do." This was Blanton. "The only thing we can do. We can't go up against that man—I reckon we damn sure proved that this morning. We better send somebody over to Lapwai and get some help from the army. Hell, that's what they're supposed to be here for."

This was met with immediate nods and grunts of approval. There were some disgruntled complaints that this idea was a mite late in coming. It should have been acted upon to begin with, when Tobin first took over their jail.

The question to be decided next was who should ride to the fort to seek help. Arvin immediately said it was his responsibility to go since he was mayor. When Blanton reminded him that Tobin had ordered him out of town before sundown, Arvin vehemently denied this had any influence upon his actions one way or the other.

"Well, it would mine," Morgan Sewell commented. "I ain't no damn hero. Arvin, you better go, all right.

And you'd best send your wife and boy over to my place."

"All right then, who's going to ride with me?" Arvin said. "I'd like two more men, so the army won't think it's just one man complaining." When there were no immediate volunteers, he turned to Blanton. "How about you, Henry?"

Blanton shook his head. "I reckon I'd best stay close to home. He's liable to come lookin' for his victuals, and I can't leave my wife alone to deal with him."

In the end, it was Arvin and two young single men who had no families to worry about. They saddled up and left immediately after their little meeting was over. Lapwai was little more than a half day's ride from Medicine Creek and, even though it was now afternoon, the days were long enough to allow them to reach the fort before nightfall if they didn't tarry.

19

Lieutenant Brice Paxton sat down on his cot and pulled his boots off. He stared accusingly at the rough stitching that pulled a hole together in the toe of his sock. There was an angry red welt directly under the stitching that would soon have become a blister had he walked much farther that day. The weather had been dry and the day had been hot, causing him to walk his horse often. He found it rather ironic that a cavalry man got blisters from walking. He would try the sock on the other foot tomorrow.

Paul Simmons pulled the tent flap aside and stuck his head in. "Knock, knock, are you decent?"

"No, but I'm dressed. Come on in."

Paul came in. He was carrying a bottle of whiskey in one hand and a cup in the other. "How about a little something to scrape some of the dust from your throat?" Seating himself on a small stool, he poured himself a drink and handed the bottle to Brice. "I'll furnish the liquor, but you'll have to use your own cup."

Without getting up, Brice reached over and picked up his canteen. He couldn't abide the fiery liquid straight like Paul could. He needed water to chase it. Paul laughed at the face Brice made when he tossed the whiskey down then hurriedly swigged down a huge gulp of water.

"Damned if I don't believe I'm wasting good whiskey on you."

Brice shook his head rapidly as if to clear away the flames. "You might be at that. I swear, I don't see how you can sit there and drink that stuff without a chaser."

Paul laughed and tossed the rest of his drink down, a slight grimace the only indication of the burning in his throat. Brice had noticed a sharp increase in Paul's drinking lately. It was a bad sign, and Brice knew it would only lead to trouble. But he didn't feel it was his place to say anything about it. A good majority of the men drank too much—it was the only way for most of them to escape the boredom of life in the field. He also knew Paul felt trapped at Lapwai. He didn't care for cavalry duty in the first place. He longed to be back East, in a desk job. But Brice knew, even though he genuinely liked the audacious young lieutenant, that Paul would never receive the appointment he so fervently desired. The army had already been reduced in regimental strength, and companies within regiments were seldom at full strength. He felt sorry for his friend, but that's the way things were.

"Damn, I'm tired," Paul said with a sigh, then shook his head as if baffled. "Tell me, just what was the purpose of that march up to Bugle Rock and back? I'd really like to know."

Brice shrugged, not really caring. "I don't know, just to keep the troops from sitting around getting bored, I guess." He yawned and stretched his arms out. "Besides, you've been in the army long enough to know that most everything we do is for no purpose at all."

"By God, I can't argue with that." He was about to say more when he was interrupted by Sergeant Baskin's voice outside the tent.

"Lieutenant Paxton, Sir. Are you in there?"

Brice didn't bother to get up from the cot. "Yeah, Baskin. What is it?"

Baskin stuck his head in. "Captain wants to see you."

"Now?"

"Yessir, now."

"Shit. What about?" Like Paul, Brice was tired and he had just gotten comfortable.

Baskin could not suppress a smile, seeing the lieutenant's reluctance to budge. "Three fellers from Medicine Creek just rode in. I ain't heard what it's about yet, but I reckon they've got some trouble."

"Damn, I just got my boots off," Brice complained.

"Shall I tell him you ain't coming?" Baskin couldn't resist baiting his lieutenant.

"Sergeant, you've got an ornery streak in you," Brice said while pulling his sock on. "Tell him I'm on my way." He glanced at a smiling Paul Simmons. "Did he tell you to fetch Lieutenant Simmons too?"

"He didn't say."

Paul laughed and playfully snapped a salute. "I'll remain at my post, guarding the whiskey bottle."

Brice was back in the saddle early the next morning, leading a detachment of twenty-two troopers, accompanied by Arvin Gilbert and two of his neighbors. The detail included no Indian scouts, as the purpose of their mission was clearly police work. Paul Simmons, aboard the ever-gentle Daisy, came along as second in command. With two riders out in front on the point, Brice and Paul rode side by side at the head of the column. Behind them, Arvin rode beside Sergeant Baskin. The other two civilians rode at the tail of the column.

"I swear, sometimes I think the colonel thinks there's only one company of cavalry on the post." Paul had not been in the saddle an hour before starting to complain. His mood was not particularly enhanced by the session he had had with the bottle the night before. "And Captain Malpas must think we're the only offi-

cers that don't have enough to do. Why in hell doesn't
H Company catch more of these details?"

Brice laughed, causing Paul's frown to deepen. He
knew H Company probably made the same complaints, thinking E Company didn't pull their share of
the almost daily patrols. "You need to work some of
that whiskey out of your system anyway. The captain's
doing you a favor."

"Dammit, Brice, do you always have to be so damn
cheerful about these details?" He rode along in silence
for a few minutes before mumbling, "This is a damn
fool trip today at any rate."

Brice didn't answer his friend's comment, but he
was thinking that Paul might be right in his assessment of their mission. He had only met Tobin once,
and that was when he rode into Lapwai with an air
about him like rules were for the other fellow. Brice
didn't like him from the start. Baskin had said there'd
be trouble anywhere that man showed up. And, if
Arvin Gilbert was to be believed, it sure looked as if
Baskin was right.

Maybe the situation with the renegade Cheyenne
had called for drastic action, and Colonel Wheaton
had a lot of faith in this man Tobin's abilities as a scout.
From what talk he had heard from Baskin and some of
the enlisted men who had ridden with him against
Joseph's Nez Perce, Tobin was unequaled as a
tracker—but he was also unequaled in pure meanness.
When Arvin related the events of the past week in
Medicine Creek, Baskin didn't doubt it one bit. Brice
wasn't sure whether he was being sent to save the
town from Little Wolf or Tobin. It appeared that both
were intent on destroying the settlement. He would
just have to see when he got there. The one order that
was crystal clear, however, was to advise Tobin that
the army wasn't paying him to lie around Medicine

Creek on his backside while Little Wolf was still at large.

The column struck the road to Medicine Creek at a point about three miles south of the settlement. By Brice's watch, it was half past one o'clock when his troopers filed past the charred remains of the general store. Morgan Sewell came out of the barbershop, followed by Jacob Schuyler—his arm in a sling—as the column came to a half. Seeing the column of soldiers, the Reverend Norsworthy scurried across the footbridge from the other side of the river. Within minutes, other frightened townsfolk emerged from the buildings where they had sought to avoid the ominous bully ensconced in their jail. Brice was struck by the small number of people that gathered. Medicine Creek looked for all the world to be a ghost town, a vast difference from the thriving little community he had observed the last time he was there. What Arvin had told him appeared to be true—the people were holed up like frightened rabbits.

"Want me to dismount 'em?" Sergeant Baskin asked.

"No," Brice quickly replied, "we're going straightaway to the jail, if Tobin is still there."

"Oh, he's there, all right," Morgan piped up. "He don't ever leave there except to look for something to eat."

"All right then, let's go talk to him."

"Talk to him?" Jacob Schuyler exclaimed. "You can't talk to him. Shoot the son of a bitch!"

Brice ignored the blacksmith's comments and signaled the column forward. He had his orders, but he also knew that he would evaluate the situation and carry them out as he saw fit. According to the information he had been given, Tobin was holding the entire town hostage. Brice found that hard to believe. The man was, after all, in the employment of the army. If he expected to be paid, he would follow the orders passed on to him from Colonel Wheaton. Of greater concern to Brice were the two fires in the community. There was little doubt who was responsible for them. His job, as he saw it, was to provide sentries to guard against any further attacks from the renegade, Little Wolf.

Looking as huge as a bull moose and wearing an amused smirk on his whiskered face, Tobin was standing outside to meet them when Brice halted the column of troopers in front of the jail. He watched unconcerned as Brice ordered the men to dismount and form a line while the handlers took the horses. Brice stepped up on the plank walkway.

"Well now, howdy-do," Tobin sneered, "looks like somebody went crying to the soldier-boys."

Ignoring the sneer, Brice said, "I've got orders from Colonel Wheaton to give you, Tobin. You're to leave Medicine Creek at once and proceed to go after the renegade. This was what you were hired to do. Furthermore, the people of Medicine Creek have requested the army's help in seeing that you leave."

"What about the matter of Jake Bannister's murder?" Arvin Gilbert stepped forward to express his concern. He stepped back immediately when the dangerous tracker snapped his head around to fix the little mayor with a stare that could almost cut glass.

"Shut your mouth, you little snot," he warned, then shifted his eyes back to Brice. "That was self-defense. Everybody saw it. The good citizens here tried to settle my gizzard, only they wasn't quite up to the job."

Unfortunately, this was the same accounting of the incident that Brice had been given, that Bannister went for his pistol and Tobin was quicker with his rifle. He had been ordered to rid the town of Tobin, not arrest him, although it would have given him pleasure to do it. To Tobin he said, "Get your tack together and be on your way. You were hired to do a job. Go do it, and leave these people alone. And, in case you get any contrary ideas, my orders are to bivouac my men here indefinitely. This town will be under military protection." Brice's orders were for fifteen days only, but he saw no need to spell that out for Tobin.

Tobin said nothing for a full minute. He just stood there defiantly, as if the lieutenant's words were bouncing harmlessly off his tremendous bulk. Inside, however, his liver was burning with the resentment he felt toward all army officers, and especially this young pup who had the gall to order him to do anything. When he spoke, it was a low, ominous rumble, making his words sound like a warning.

"I ain't ready to go just yet. I've got unfinished business here. You go on back and tell your daddy you brung the message, like you was told. I'll be along when I catch his white Cheyenne for him." He shifted his gaze toward Arvin Gilbert, singeing him with a fiery stare. "I was gittin' close to trappin' him, but he ain't likely to come if he sees all you soldier-boys in town."

"Maybe I didn't make myself clear. I'm ordering you to vacate this building and get your ass out of town."

Baskin could almost swear he saw sparks flash in the big tracker's eyes, and he was afraid Tobin was about to lash out at Brice. *He does and he's dead meat,* he thought. Without waiting for an order from Brice, he quietly turned and ordered the men to unsling their weapons. The move was not lost on Tobin.

Like a cornered panther, Tobin's eyes narrowed and he shifted his weight from one foot to the other, back and forth, wanting to strike out. But the line of troopers, their carbines at the ready, gave him pause. He strained to keep his temper from flaring. "Well, now," he said, "I call this kind of queer. I don't work for you anyway. Colonel Wheaton hired me." He began to feel his anger boiling up inside him. "And I'll tell you something else, sonny. He hired me because I get the job done, and I always do it *my* way." He was glaring directly into Brice's eyes now. "I'll decide who goes and who stays. I ain't in your damn army, so take your soldier-boys and get the hell out of my way, or I'll show you trouble your mama ain't never told you about." He started to turn back toward the door.

"Sergeant Baskin, if he goes through that door, shoot him."

"Yes, Sir. Be a pleasure, Sir."

Tobin was stopped dead in his tracks. He jerked his massive head around to fix his predatory stare on the young lieutenant. He didn't speak as he plumbed the depths of Brice Paxton's cold iron gaze, unblinking and determined. Tobin recognized a bluff when he saw one—he was a master of the bluff himself. But there was no bluff in the eyes of the young soldier. He shifted his gaze briefly to Sergeant Baskin. The sergeant appeared ready, even eager, to follow his lieutenant's order. Running roughshod over a half dozen nervous civilians was one thing. Calling a bluff in front of an army firing squad was another. Tobin was fearless, but he was not foolish.

"Goddam you, sonny. You got the drop on me this time, but you ain't heard the last of this."

Brice casually turned his head toward Baskin. "Sergeant, you and the men heard him threaten me." He turned back to Tobin. "They'll testify to a court martial in case you give me the slightest cause to shoot you. Now, let's go inside and get your things together. I want you out of here in fifteen minutes."

Tobin was smoldering. He could not remember wanting to kill a man more than he did at this moment. His fists clenched, the muscles in his neck standing out like knotted cords, he considered striking the young officer down and risking the firing squad. Only the leveled rifles of the line of troopers and the callous expression on Baskin's face held him in control of his emotions. After a long, tense moment, when both sides were a hair-trigger away from exploding, Tobin relaxed, conceding the contest. There would be other chances, he told himself. He would see to it.

Brice followed the huge man through the doorway, into the dark interior of the jail. He stood behind Tobin as the scout gathered up his rifle and saddlepack. Brice did not see the woman at first in the dim light of her cell. When he did, he was shocked.

"For the love of God . . ." he started, but was at a loss for words. It was the Cheyenne woman he had seen at Lapwai. But, in contrast to the hospital-like conditions she had been incarcerated in at the fort, her present conditions were appalling. She cowered in a corner of the tiny room, frightened and dirty. The stench of an unemptied slop bucket filled the cramped space with air that offended the nostrils. When she allowed herself to glance up, he noted a flicker of recognition in her almost glazed expression before dropping her eyes once more.

Seeing a key hanging on the opposite wall, Brice took it and opened the cell door. Still afraid to move, she remained where she was for some seconds, even though Brice motioned for her to come out. She did not move until he stepped back from the cell door, and even then it was with slow reluctant steps. Brice motioned for her to go on out the front door. She moved cautiously by him, like a frightened squirrel, her hand shading her eyes from the bright sunlight.

"I'm gonna be needin' her," Tobin said, his back to Brice as he picked up his rifle, his massive frame shielding his movements from Brice's eyes. The thought ran through his mind that he might win this little tussle yet. He could easily overpower the young officer while Brice was distracted by the woman.

Those thoughts were immediately quelled however, when he suddenly whirled around to find Brice's pistol aimed at his gut. "I still need that woman," Tobin repeated.

Brice was of a notion to have him shot anyway. "You don't need anything but to get your ass out of here, you filthy bastard. How can you treat a woman like that?"

Tobin looked surprised at the lieutenant's attitude, even slightly amused by his concern for an Indian woman. "She belongs to me and I aim to use her for bait. As long as I got that there woman, Little Wolf ain't gonna be far away." He thought it best to remind the lieutenant. "And that Cheyenne is sticking in your colonel's craw something fierce. He ain't gonna like it one bit if you go messing with my bait."

"Damn you, Tobin. You are one miserable excuse for a human being."

Outside now, Brice directed Baskin to detail two men to take Rain Song down to the river to let her clean herself. "I'll try to see if I can get you some fresh clothes," he said. She did not understand his words, but knew there was compassion in them. She nodded and went obediently with the two troopers Baskin called out.

Tobin stood fuming for a few seconds, watching the woman as she walked between her two guards, heading for the river some twenty-five yards back of the jailhouse. "She's my property. She can clean herself up, but I still need her. She goes with me."

"The hell she does," Brice shot back. "You're heading out of here alone."

Tobin didn't push it any further. He was too badly outnumbered. But he made himself a promise that sooner or later, he was going to look Brice up when he didn't have a column of troopers to protect him.

"What about my horse? Are you gonna put me afoot to boot?"

"No," Brice said.

"I'll be happy to fetch him for you, Lieutenant," Ike Frieze piped up, only too happy to be rid of the animal. He turned to leave, then paused. "I reckon the army'll be responsible for his feed bill."

"Maybe. I'll see," Brice replied and waved him on. He turned when Paul Simmons nudged his elbow.

"What are we going to do with the woman, Brice?"

"I don't know—take her back to the reservation at Lapwai, I guess. We can't just set her free."

All was quiet on the main street of Medicine Creek, except for a low buzzing of hushed conversation among the townspeople who had gathered to witness the eviction of Tobin. Tobin paced back and forth before the door of the jail like a caged lion, cursing softly to himself and leering at the solemn line of troopers in the dusty street, all waiting for Ike to return with Tobin's horse.

Private Otis Blankenship was not at all disappointed to be detailed, along with Private Bob Springer, to take the Indian woman down to the river. Under all that grime, she appeared to be a right handsome woman and might be something to see. He winked at Springer as they approached the willows near the water's edge. "Best take your frock off, little lady, so's you can get yourself cleaned up proper." He tried to make her understand with some rudimentary use of sign.

"Yessum," Springer chimed in, "you need to get your whole body clean." He took her by the arm and led her into the willows. "Get back of these bushes so nobody can look atcha. We'll watch out fer ya—won't we, Otis?"

Though the words were foreign to her, the leers of the two soldiers were not. Suddenly, she sensed that

she had more to fear than mere ogling by the two soldiers. While she stood there, unsure of what she
should do, Blankenship propped his carbine against a
large cottonwood near the willows and unbuckled his
belt. She started to run but was held fast by Springer.

"Now take it easy, honey. We ain't gonna do nothin'
that ain't been done before." He looked furtively over
his shoulder. "Make it quick, Otis. You ain't the only
one that's ruttin'."

"Dammit, Springer, hold her still. Clamp your other
hand over her mouth." Blankenship grabbed her legs
and forced them apart. "Hold her, dammit!" He fum-
bled with his trousers until he finally managed to get
them down around his knees while he fought to hold
on to her thrashing legs. "I got her now," he snorted
triumphantly, chuckling as he glanced up at Springer's
wide grin. "Look at what I got for you. Ain't that what
you squaws all want?"

Springer laughed. Then suddenly, his mouth fell
open as he gasped. His eyes bulged open as if glimps-
ing the doorway to hell as the knife blade sank deep
into his kidney, and he relaxed his hold on the woman.

"What the hell . . ." was all Otis was able to say before he was shocked speechless. As Springer slid to the
ground, Otis found himself looking into the face of
undiluted Cheyenne fury. Seeing that his death was at
hand, he released the girl and tried to run for his life,
only to be tripped up by the trousers around his knees.

Otis went down hard and, before he could scramble
up on his knees, he was driven down again, flattened
by the impact of Little Wolf's savage attack. The hap-
less trooper was mauled and battered as his body was
rolled over and over down the sandy riverbank, helpless to defend himself as Little Wolf rode him like a
mountain lion mauling a rabbit. When they splashed
into the water's edge, Otis struggled desperately to
free himself from the horror that had captured him.

Gagging and sputtering from the water he had swallowed, his eyes wide with terror, he managed one faint yell before his throat was crushed in the iron vise of Little Wolf's hand. The last vision of life Otis saw was the stern countenance of the white Cheyenne, his eyes locked on the fading trooper's. Slowly, the life was crushed out of his body until he finally went limp. Little Wolf picked him up, still holding him by the throat, then dropped his limp body in the shallow water.

It had all happened so quickly that Rain Song was fairly stunned for a few moments, the same few moments that seemed like an eternity to Otis Blankenship. Now Little Wolf stood up and turned to her. His face, still a mask of stern fury, softened instantly when his eyes met hers. He held out his arms to her. With her heart pounding in her bosom, she ran to him. He picked her up, cradling her gently against his chest. There were no words spoken—none were needed. She wound her arms tightly around his neck, her face pressed against his cheek while he carried her across the shallow river. As he lifted her up on his horse, he saw the tears that welled up in her dark eyes, and the feeling of love and compassion that flooded over him was overpowering.

"I was afraid he had killed you," she cried, the tears freely making their way down her cheeks. "He said he had shot you."

"It was no more than a scratch." He longed to comfort her, but knew there was no time. "We must hurry now, Little One," he said softly and climbed up in front of her. He turned the Appaloosa's head to the west, toward the hills, and with a light touch of his heels, the pony sprang away from the river and Medicine Creek.

Sergeant Baskin cocked his head around and listened. He wasn't sure, but he thought he might have heard someone call out—Blankenship or Springer—he couldn't tell which. But it sounded as if it came from the river. The two men had not been gone very long but still he decided to send another man to check on them. "Meadows, go down yonder and see what's holding them two up." He watched Meadows amble off toward the river then turned his attention back to the business at hand when Ike Frieze emerged from the stable, leading Tobin's horse.

Brice stepped back to let Tobin pass when Ike led the tan buckskin up to the hitching rail. The brooding scout scowled at him and then at the line of soldiers, their carbines still at the ready. He stepped down into the dust of the street and was about to mount when the cry of alarm came up from the river. All heads turned as one to see Meadows running as fast as his boots would permit in the sandy soil of the riverbank.

Meadows was yelling something but Brice couldn't catch it all. He thought he caught the word "murdering," but the rest was garbled.

Baskin yelled at him. "What is it, man? Slow down and talk plain."

Meadows stopped. They understood him then. "Springer and Blankenship—their bodies—murdered—dead," he blurted in breathless spurts.

Brice jumped off the wooden walkway in a flat-out run. No one gave any orders—the men just followed their lieutenant, running after him to the river. Tobin stepped up into the saddle and galloped after the troopers. He reached the riverbank at about the same time Brice did. The scene that greeted them didn't take a lot of scouting or brainwork to explain what had occurred. Springer was still alive, although just barely. He had bled a great deal and was mumbling incoherently. Blankenship's body was lying face down in the shallow water, his trousers down and twisted around his boots.

"Damn," Brice swore softly as he looked down at Blankenship's body. When Paul walked up beside him, he added in a low voice to keep the wounded man from hearing, "Two men, lost." For it was obvious that Springer was not going to make it.

"What the hell..." Paul was puzzling over Blankenship's trousers down around his boots. "What was he doing? Taking a dump when the renegade jumped him?"

Brice gave him a look, marveling at his friend's naivete. "He wasn't taking a dump. He was trying to rape the girl."

While Sergeant Baskin did his best to make Springer's last moments as comfortable as possible, Tobin looked briefly around the willows. He didn't need to take much time. It was pretty obvious what had happened, and he was furious. This event changed everything. No longer the lowly outcast, he was once again in charge of his personal manhunt. When Brice walked over to the willows, Tobin lit into him verbally.

"Goddam you and your little soldier-boys! He's got her now, 'cause of you and your interfering in something you don't know nuthin' about! I knowed he was close. Dammit, I could smell him! And I mighta had him too, if you'd just kept your nose out of it." He stepped up into the saddle again. "Now I'm gonna have to track him out in the open." He jerked the buckskin's head around and plunged into the river.

"Wait a minute!" Brice yelled after him but Tobin was already halfway across. "Dammit, Tobin, wait a minute!" He looked back at Baskin. "Sergeant, get the horses up here!"

Tobin called back when his horse scrambled up on the opposite bank, "You wanted me out of town. Well, I'm gittin'." He kicked his horse hard, following the obvious trail left by the Appaloosa.

"Damn you," Brice murmured. There was nothing he could do but wait for the horses to be brought up.

Paul Simmons was at his elbow. "You going after him?" When Brice didn't answer right away, he added, "Let the bastard go. Maybe he'll catch that renegade. He's supposed to be such a great tracker, let him track him. Our orders were to protect the town, not chase after that white Cheyenne anymore. That's Tobin's job."

Brice answered as if he hadn't heard a word Paul had said. "Damn right, I'm going after him. He killed two of my men."

Paul considered it for a moment before commenting. Looking back at the broken body now being carried from the stream, he said, "I wonder if you wouldn't have done the same, if it had been your wife."

Brice cocked his head sharply, his eyes narrowed slightly, reacting to what sounded like criticism from his fellow officer. Looking at Paul, his face wearing its usual blank facade, he concluded it was just Paul being himself—letting his thoughts tumble from his mouth. "What these men did was wrong. I don't deny that. But the fact is, he still killed two soldiers. I've got no choice but to bring him in for trial, which I aim to do. If Tobin catches them first, he'll kill Little Wolf and the woman too."

20

Rain Song's arms were locked around Little Wolf's waist, holding him tightly, not from a fear of falling off, for her body moved in rhythm with the Appaloosa's gait almost as well as her husband's. Rather, she held on to him desperately, as if something might snatch her away from him again. There had been little time for reunion except the short embrace at the river, for their pursuers were not far behind. She pressed her face against the bare muscular back of her husband as they moved together with the pony's steady pace. The only sound in her ears was the thundering of the horse's hooves as they pounded upon the grassy hills.

Little Wolf's first thought was to gain some distance between them and the soldiers, so he called on all the speed the Appaloosa could give him. The treeless hills that bordered the river offered little cover. He was intent upon reaching the slopes of the mountains where there were bands of pine and spruce. When he reached them, he would worry about hiding his trail. Now, it would be a waste of time. So he drove the Appaloosa on.

Upon reaching the slope of a mountain, he rode up a wooded draw and over the other side of a low ridge, still riding hard, in and out of the shadowy patches cast by the tall pines, until the forest closed in above them, leaving them in total shade. Not until then did he allow the Appaloosa to settle back to a slower pace as he weaved his way through the lodgepoles. Out of the trees and into the bright sunlight again for a short distance over a rocky flat, then back into the trees they rode. Below them, he spied a narrow stream that followed a ravine back down the slope. Holding to the slope, he reined his horse back to a walk, carefully picking his way through the deep pinestraw floor of the forest. When he intercepted the stream, he took great care as he entered it, leaving the loose stones and gravel undisturbed.

He stopped in the middle of the stream and listened. There were no sounds of pursuit, only the soft murmur of the wind in the pines high above them. Pausing a moment to let the horse drink, he then walked him downstream until he found a place where a flat rock protruded out over the water. Here he decided it safe to stop for a short while.

"You can rest here for a moment," he said, throwing one leg over the horse's neck and landing lightly on the boulder. He reached up and caught Rain Song in his arms, carrying her to the edge of the stream, where he placed her gently on her feet. She immediately stepped back into his arms and embraced him. After a moment, he kissed her tenderly on her forehead, then each cheek, before he held her at arm's length to look at her. "They have treated you badly," he said softly.

"It doesn't matter now," she whispered. Then remembering she dropped her chin, embarrassed. "How much time do we have? I must clean myself. You cannot look at me like this."

He shook his head sadly. It pained him to see the evidence of obvious abuse. "Don't say silly things." Then, "Are you hurt anywhere?"

"No," she quickly replied, "just dirty."

He smiled. "Hurry then. I think we have a little time until they pick up our trail."

"You were very careful. Maybe they won't follow us."

"The big one will come."

He went back up the ridge on foot to see if Tobin had found his trail. Looking back the way they had come through the pines, he could see no sign of anyone as yet. *The big one is good*, Little Wolf thought. *He will find our trail.* There had not been enough time to disguise his tracks completely. It might take him some time, but Little Wolf knew Tobin would eventually strike his trail.

He made his way carefully back down the slope to the stream, where Rain Song was trying to clean some of the grime away from her body. She looked up at him and smiled shyly, still embarrassed for her husband to see her in this state. It pained him to see the bruises on her arms and neck, evidence of the rough treatment she had suffered. He said nothing but the anger was rapidly beginning to boil within him, clouding his mind with thoughts of revenge. He was not aware that his face conveyed his bitter thoughts until he realized that she had paused in her bathing and stood looking at him.

"You are thinking of killing. I can see it in your face." A worried frown appeared on her face. "Do not think of revenge. They didn't hurt me. It's only a few bruises. Let's run from this land, go far away, maybe to King George's land to the north. There we can be free of the soldiers."

He heard her words but his mind was still churning with the anger he felt. "They should pay for what they have done to you." His dark eyes flashed with the spark of fury that was still welling up inside.

She was frightened. She had never seen him like this, his face a dark mask of anger. Before, when preparing to do battle, he had always maintained an air of quiet resolve, methodical and unemotional as he prepared his weapons, saving his rage for the actual combat. Now he was almost brooding, his muscles tense. She was afraid for him, afraid he was going back to meet the big tracker Tobin. She had waited so long for him to come for her, at times giving up hope that he ever would. Now they were together at last. She could not bear the thought of being separated from him again.

She waded out of the water and walked up to him. Putting her arms around his waist, she pressed her body close to his. "Please don't think about fighting. We are free now. I'm afraid something might happen to you." She looked up into his face. "Please. We want nothing more from these white people. Please . . . I'm afraid."

Slowly he relented to her pleas, unable to ignore the anguish in her face, until the faint hint of a smile tugged at the corners of his mouth. "All right, Little One, we'll head north."

She gave him a hard squeeze, then hurriedly climbed back into the soiled deerskin dress that had been her entire wardrobe for weeks. While she dressed, he went back up the ridge to take one more look. She was sitting on his horse when he came back down, anxious to start out for a new life in Canada.

Lieutenant Brice Paxton's column of troopers caught up with Tobin at a flat rock projecting out over a swiftly running stream. The big scout was dismounted, squatting on his heels, studying the hard ground around the rock. He turned to snarl at the approaching soldiers like a coyote over a fresh kill. He was plainly displeased to see the troopers, never planning for them to catch up to him in the first place. As far as he was concerned, the soldiers would just be in the way. It didn't take an Injun as slick as Little Wolf to see that mob of horses trailing him. Tobin was going to

have to move swiftly and cautiously to have even a
chance of surprising one as cunning as Little Wolf.
And he couldn't see that happening with some
twenty-odd blue-coated troopers in tow. Tobin silently
cursed the lieutenant and Little Wolf. If the renegade
hadn't been so effective in covering his trail, Tobin
wouldn't have had to spend that much time picking it
up again, and he would have been long gone before
the sassy young lieutenant and his soldier-boys got
there.

The brooding scout remained squatting as the detail
filed down through the trees of the slope. When Brice
pulled up beside the stream, Tobin spoke. "Ain't you
boys got nuthin' better to do than pester me? I thought
you was supposed to be back yonder, protecting the
good citizens of Medicine Creek."

Brice ignored the sarcasm. "Little Wolf is wanted by
the army so I thought we'd give you some support."
He didn't voice his real concern that Tobin was more
than likely planning to murder Little Wolf and the
woman with no regard for the colonel's orders to bring
the renegade back for trial.

"I don't need no damn support. Fact is, all this noisy
bunch'll do is scare him off."

Brice was unimpressed by the ominous scout's gruff
talk. "Well, I expect you'd best get used to this noisy
bunch because we're going with you. The colonel
wants that man brought back for trial and I intend to
see that the woman is returned to the reservation un-
harmed." He paused, fixing Tobin with a cold eye.
"That is, *if* you can track him."

"Huh!" Tobin snorted. "The man ain't born I can't
track. I'll track him, all right. If I don't, then you'll
know damn well he sprung wings and flew out of
these damn mountains."

"Good then. When you pick up the trail, we'll get
started."

*I wish it was just you and me without all them soldiers.
I'd dearly love to lift that fine scalp of yourn.* Tobin said
nothing for a long moment, studying the lieutenant's
face. He glanced over at a smirking Sergeant Baskin,
then back at Brice. "Well, keep them horses to hell over
on that side of the crick till I find a track." It was plain
to see that the army intended to dog him no matter
what he said, so he was going to have to play along for
a bit. Glancing at his own shadow stretching longer on
the rock, Tobin realized that it was getting along in the
afternoon. "It ain't much more till the sun gits behind
them mountains. This might take some time, tracking
this ol' boy. He ain't no ordinary Injun. This is as good
a place to set up camp for the night as any, so you
might as well settle your boys in. I'll scout up this
ravine a bit to see if I can set us a trail in the morning."

Brice was not to be bamboozled that easily. He
smiled and replied, "Good idea. I'll send a couple of
men with you to make sure you don't get ambushed."
Tobin's scowl deepened, but he didn't protest.

As it turned out, Tobin had not exaggerated when
he said it would be difficult to track Little Wolf. Studying the banks of the stream on both sides, Tobin
worked his way down the ravine and back again, for a
distance of a hundred yards or so. He didn't find anything, and was becoming more and more surly as the
afternoon ticked away. Sergeant Baskin had issued
specific instructions to the two troopers sent with the
scout to be on the lookout for foul play. So, with two
wary soldiers watching his every move, Tobin combed
the north and west side of the ravine that cradled the
stream. Just when he was beginning to think darkness
was going to overtake them, he found a partial print at
the edge of the trees.

He climbed upon a fallen tree trunk and looked out
across a low ridge. The print indicated that Little Wolf
had traversed the slope along the ridge instead of fol-

lowing the ravine. Tobin knew this country like the back of his hand, and he had a notion that it was new to the man he hunted. Little Wolf would be heading for Canada, he felt sure of that. Where else could he go to get away from the army? *So he'll be thinking to get through them mountains to the north and he's gonna find that there ain't but one pass through there.* Satisfied that he now knew where to find Little Wolf and Rain Song, he stepped back down from the dead tree.

He didn't reveal his find to the two soldiers accompanying him. To them, he announced, "Well, we come up dry for now. I suspect he rode yonder way, following the crick on down the slope. We'll pick his trail up in the morning." They all rode back to camp.

During the night, a light rain fell, causing sleepy, disgruntled troopers to search for cover anywhere they could. They had left Lapwai under light marching orders, so there were no tents for shelter. The best most of them could do was to seek refuge under the low hanging limbs of the larger spruce trees that covered the lower slopes. Even then, it proved to be a wet night's sleep for those who had not had the foresight to pack their ponchos or their rubber ground blankets. Those unfortunate enough to catch sentry duty could do little more than find a tree to stand under.

About an hour before daylight, the rain had slackened, and by the time the men began to stir from their soggy beds it had stopped completely. Sergeant Baskin made his rounds of the sentries who pulled the last tour of guard to see if there was anything unusual to report. There was not, so he assembled the detail to count heads. There were no formalities observed when in the field, especially when Brice Paxton was in command. So it was a quick muster and report to Brice confirming that everyone was accounted for.

"Cookfires, sir?" Baskin asked.

Brice didn't answer right away. He wasn't sure he could afford to take the time for a hot breakfast. The Cheyenne already had a fair head start on them, what with the time wasted the afternoon before. On the other hand, it might do a great deal for morale if the men could at least boil some coffee after the wet night they just endured. He was well aware of the complaining drifting back and forth between some of the members of his detail. When the column started out from Lapwai, the mission had been to bivouac near Medicine Creek on a guard detail. Standard rations of salt pork, hardtack, sugar, and coffee were issued each man. Before the store burned down the men would normally anticipate the opportunity to buy more palatable staples to add to their mess while camping in such close proximity to the town. He could understand their disappointment. The thought of a steaming hot cup of coffee certainly appealed to him at that moment. He reached down and pulled a soaked trouser leg away from his skin. As he did so, he looked at Baskin with a suspicious eye, wondering how the old campaigner managed to stay dry when he could not. The sergeant started to repeat his question when Brice interrupted. "Where's Tobin?"

The usually unflappable sergeant's face registered his discomfort in realizing he had not accounted for the surly tracker. "Why, I reckon he's still bedded down over yonder in that thicket."

"Well, you better go see," Brice said.

Baskin had reckoned wrong. Tobin had slipped out of the camp sometime during the night, probably while everyone else was busy trying to keep their backsides dry. The pine thicket he had chosen to bed down in was not shared by any of the men, since no one had any desire to sleep near the ominous hulk. So it was not difficult for Tobin to steal out of camp without being seen. The thing that irritated Brice was that he was able to lead his horse away unobserved. Of the sentries assigned to pull tours at horse guard during the night, none admitted to dozing. Yet none saw the huge scout quietly lead his horse out of camp. He could not come down too hard on the sentries, since Tobin's horse was not on the picket line with the army's horses. He should have suspected something when Tobin hobbled the big buckskin near the thicket, explaining that his horse wasn't sociable with other horses.

Brice was mad. He whirled on his sergeant. "That answers your question, Sergeant. No cookfires. Get the men mounted and ready to ride in five minutes."

"Yessir," Baskin replied and turned to carry out his orders. There was little need to repeat them, for all the men were within earshot. The little bivouac sprang alive with men grabbing their saddles and blanket-rolls. Some who had not waited for permission yanked tin cups from small, already blazing fires, and gulped down quick swigs of half-boiled coffee while kicking dirt over the flames. In a matter of minutes, the detachment was in the saddle.

"How the hell do we know which way to go?" Paul Simmons wanted to know.

"I don't know," Brice admitted.

"Tobin said last night that he figured Little Wolf followed the stream on down the mountain."

"I know," Brice answered, thinking hard on the matter. He didn't trust Tobin for a minute and the hostile bastard had been set on shaking the cavalry troop from the beginning. While the men waited for the order to move out, he rode across the stream and up the low bank on the other side. Looking out over the trees toward the mountains to the north, he thought for a moment and then wheeled around. "Sergeant Baskin."

"Yessir?"

"Where do you suppose Little Wolf would be heading, now that he's got his wife?"

"Why, Canada, I reckon."

Brice nodded his agreement. "That's what I reckon too. And, unless they moved it, Canada's that way." He pointed toward the mountains. With a hand signal to march, he led out across the ridge, confident that it was the same route Tobin took when he stole out of camp.

A fifty-dollar bonus when I bring your head to Lapwai. Tobin was pleased with the time he was certain he had gained on the white Cheyenne. Colonel Wheaton had promised him the bonus if he was successful in capturing—or killing, if unavoidable—the renegade. This was in addition to regular scout pay while he was hunting him. *Kill him if unavoidable,* Tobin thought to himself and laughed at the thought. *Oh, it's gonna be unavoidable all right, 'cause I'm gonna shoot him on sight.* The anticipation of it actually caused him to salivate.

He was confident he would overtake Little Wolf before he got to the Canadian border. It didn't make any difference to him if he had to cross the border after him—he didn't have to pay any attention to lines drawn on a piece of foolscap like the army did. But he was sure of his knowledge of the country and his ability to track better than any man alive, and sure enough to know he would run Little Wolf and the girl down before they made another thirty miles. He almost laughed out loud as he picked his way along the old game trail in the dark, ignoring the rain that ran off his buckskin warshirt. He had hunted this country for most of two years with ol' Kills Two Elks. He didn't need daylight to find his way through these mountains. *But Little Wolf does,* he thought. He kicked the buckskin sharply when the laboring horse sought to slow the pace.

The sun had been up for little more than an hour when he came upon their campsite of the previous night. He was reluctant to pause, but he knew he would be on foot soon if he didn't let the buckskin rest for a while. He cursed the nearly exhausted animal soundly as he led him to the tiny branch that trickled along the side of the trail. While the horse drank, he poked around in the ashes of the small fire that had been made up under a huge boulder. It had been a dry camp, out of the rain, he thought. *Ain't that sweet? They slept all cuddled up together.* The picture that formed in his mind brought him sudden pleasure. The prospect of the killing brought a warm glow to his brain.

Fresh tracks in the wet earth led out to the old trail. No attempt had been made to cover them. Little Wolf had found out by then that there was only one way through the mountains, so it was a waste of time to try to disguise his trail. He knew that it was now a race. What he didn't know—which tickled Tobin—was that his pursuer had made up a huge amount of ground on him during the night while he and Rain Song slept.

"Come on, you damned buzzard bait, I smell blood!" He jerked the reins, pulling the buckskin's head up sharply from the grass where the horse had been grazing. He knew the horse was tired, but he sensed the closeness of the Cheyenne and he could control his impatience no longer. He led the horse up from the stream and stepped up into the stirrup. Though still weary and hungry, the buckskin stood, with head down, obediently accepting his oversized burden. "You can rest while I'm drying that damn Cheyenne's scalp." With that, he kicked the horse hard into a gallop.

21

They had started that morning as soon as it was light enough to follow the trail. Little Wolf was worried by the frailness he saw in his wife. It had been more than two days since she'd had anything substantial to eat. Their supper the night before had been nothing more than some berries he had found near the trickle of water that was the stream they had camped beside. During the day, he had seen plenty of sign, but no game. Even had he seen a deer, he could not have taken the time to stalk it. He could not be sure how much lead he had over those who hunted him, so he had pushed the Appaloosa as hard as he dared. Now he was going to have to rest the horse. But, more important, he was going to have to find food for Rain Song. She rode behind him, never complaining. But he could feel the grip of her arms around his waist weakening.

He gazed up at the mountains on each side of him, towering, forbidding, with steep slopes that defied man or horse. They had been climbing steadily for the past two hours as the trail wound its way up between two mountains. With the crest of the ridge in sight, the trail steepened sharply for a hundred yards before descending again. To spare the horse, Little Wolf dismounted and led him. When Rain Song started to dismount as well, he stayed her with a hand on her arm. She did not protest.

At the top of the ridge, he stopped and looked over the trail beyond as it wormed its way down the other side. What he saw lifted his spirits considerably. The trail led down into a small valley split by a rushing stream that cascaded down from the mountain above. The floor of the valley was covered with grass as high as a horse's belly and interlaced with yellow and white flowers. He could not help but think of his valley near Medicine Creek, and he looked back at Rain Song to see if she had had the same thought. She did not respond but stared straight ahead with weary eyes. It hurt his heart to see her so tired.

He tried to comfort her. "It will still be early in the afternoon when we reach the valley, but we'll make camp anyway and I'll hunt. The horse needs rest and we must have food." He looked back the way they had come, searching the trail behind them. He could only guess whether the detachment of soldiers was still following. He knew for certain that the big scout was behind them somewhere, but looking back at the tall silent mountains, it seemed there was no one else on the earth but them. *If they follow, I would rather be strong and rested and ready to fight.* "We'll make camp in the valley," he repeated and smiled up at Rain Song. She acknowledged with a faint smile.

As the lush little valley first promised, game abounded. Little Wolf startled two young black-tailed deer as he led the Appaloosa down to the stream. There was no time to ready his bow. He quickly drew his rifle from the saddle sling and felled one of them, a doe, in midair as she leaped over the stream. Running quickly after her, he finished her with his knife. Rain Song would soon have the nourishment she needed.

Near the upper end of the valley, a group of cottonwoods framed the stream. They afforded the only cover in the grassy meadow that made up the valley floor, so Little Wolf made their camp there. If Tobin did overtake them before morning, he would have to cross the open valley. Little Wolf knew it was risky to camp so early but it was necessary to rest and eat, both for them and the horse.

The sight of fresh meat bolstered Rain Song's weary spirit and she was soon helping with the butchering. The sparkle returned to her eyes immediately as she joyously chewed the first strips of sizzling meat, pulled from the fire when barely done. By the time they had eaten their fill, daylight was fast fading from the little valley.

"This is a good place," she said and came to sit by him. She lifted his arm and laid it across her shoulder, snuggling her body close to his.

He smiled at her. "Yes it is a good place. I wish we could stay here, but we'll find a place as good as this in Canada." She felt good under his arm and he was relieved to see that her spirit had bounced back.

"Do you think the man, Tobin, still follows?" Her smile was replaced by a frown.

"I don't know. I don't think he will give up easily. But I hope he will tire of following us after a few more days."

She considered this for a few moments. "What about the soldiers?"

He shrugged. "I don't know. I think they will give up before the big one does."

She put her arms around his chest and held him tightly. "I knew you would come for me." She held him as if afraid he might be taken from her. "We must leave early in the morning. I'm afraid Tobin will catch us. I think he talks to the evil spirits."

He gave her a reassuring squeeze. "Don't worry, Little One, I'll protect you."

"I'm not worried for me," she said softly. She did not voice it, but she had seen what the evil tracker was capable of, and she did not want her husband to face him. They sat before the fire for a while longer, saying nothing. Then Rain Song looked up into Little Wolf's eyes and whispered, "I want you to make love to me tonight."

When the night had deepened and the moon appeared to rest for a moment on the high bluff to the east of their valley, he placed a few more pieces of wood on the fire and banked the ashes up around them. He had only a large elk hide to make a bed for them but the fur was soft and the ground smooth under the cottonwoods. When she had spoken of love earlier, he had been surprised. In their flight to escape from the soldiers and the big tracker, his mind had been on survival and in a state of constant alert, not concerned with thoughts of passion. He could not know that her need for him was not wholly spawned by her longing during the long weeks they had been apart. There was something more. She had seen the ferocious cruelty of the man Tobin, and she had known a foreboding feeling of tragedy, of coming danger for her and her husband. There was an invisible shroud of evil that cloaked the powerful half-breed, and she could not help but feel that their lives were doomed to cross his path in the end. Uncertain even of the morning sun, she longed to know Little Wolf's embrace at least for this night. So she came to him in the firelight, her tattered dress removed and folded neatly by the fire.

Rising to his knees, he placed his hands on her arms and held her there for a moment while he looked at her naked body. His heart was wounded when he saw the bruises, already fading to a yellow cast, that covered her arms and shoulders. With one finger, he tenderly traced a still healing gash across her wrist where a rawhide thong had cut her. She felt the muscles in his arms tense when he gazed at the angry scar in her left side where she had thrust Yellow Hand's knife. She moved closer to him and gently pulled his head against her bare stomach. They held each other tightly for a long moment, renewing the strength of their love and regaining the oneness that had been theirs.

After a while, they were ready. He picked her up and carried her to the elkskin. Laying her gently on the soft fur, he lay down next to her and pulled the elkskin over them. Their passion was gentle in the beginning, rising to a fury that only comes when desperate need is combined with genuine love that two people share. There were no thoughts beyond this moment. Later, when the passion was spent, he might berate himself for relaxing his alertness. But for now, he gave no thought to the danger they faced.

For that brief period, he had been able to forget the peril that had become his constant companion. Lying with Rain Song beside him, gazing up at the sea of stars above them, he felt as one with the earth. This was how man was intended to live—free with his wife beside him, at peace and naked before the Earth Mother. Then, for a few moments, he thought back over the events of his life, and all the people who had shaped it. Where would his path have led him if his blood father had not chosen to sell him to a drunken teamster bound for Oregon? If Spotted Pony had not found him, would he have grown up to be a soldier, like his brother, Tom?

The thought was immediately abhorrent to him, especially when he thought about his adopted family and the hours he had spent learning the lessons of the earth from Spotted Pony and his adopted mother, Buffalo Woman. The sickening thought arose of how his Indian parents died, massacred by soldiers of the 7th Cavalry. Other names flashed through his mind—Morning Sky, Black Feather, Sleeps Standing, Tom, Squint Peterson—names he had not thought about for some time.

Squint would tell him it was time to be a white man again, while he still could. But Little Wolf was not so sure that he still could. There had been too many war parties against the soldiers, too many scalps taken. Although his skin was white, he knew that every drop of blood in him was Cheyenne, and it would always be this way. There was no option now, anyway. He was being hunted, just as Crazy Horse, Sitting Bull, and the others were hunted. He had heard that they had fled to Canada, just as he was trying to do now. Would he and Rain Song find the freedom they sought there? He wondered.

Discouraged by the heavy thinking, he returned his thoughts to the moment at hand. He was tired, Rain Song was sleeping, his horse had been ridden too hard—all of them needed rest. He gently pulled Rain Song closer to him and watched her sleep in his arms. *We will see what the new day brings, Little One.* The thought came to his mind that this moment was the best of his life and, if their lives were to end now, he could not complain.

Tobin stopped in his tracks and listened, turning his ear toward the sound. His eyes moved rapidly from side to side beneath a brow furrowed in deep concentration. A single rifle shot, that was all. He waited and listened, but there was no second shot. Tobin smiled. It told him what he wanted to know. The white Cheyenne stopped to hunt, which meant he didn't know Tobin was this close. It also meant that Tobin could dispense with caution against ambush. He estimated the rifle to be no more than three or four miles away and he could make up that distance in short order. As an afterthought, he noted that there had been but the one shot, which indicated the Cheyenne had hit what he had aimed at.

Whipping the buckskin mercilessly, he galloped

recklessly along the old hunting trail. The horse endeavored to do his master's cruel bidding, but could not maintain the pace demanded. Finally, where the trail rose steeply toward the top of the ridge, the buckskin faltered, staggering under Tobin's massive weight. Cursing vehemently, Tobin stepped from the stirrup just in time to avoid going down with the horse. He beat the exhausted horse savagely, but to no avail. The animal was spent. Enraged, but realizing the animal could no longer carry him, Tobin pulled his rifle from the saddle boot and started up the incline on foot.

Cursing with almost every step, he pushed his massive body up the trail, walking so rapidly that he resembled a drunk staggering home from a night at the saloon, his boots sliding and rolling on the loose gravel and small rocks in his path. By the time he reached the top of the divide, his heart was pounding from the exertion and his breath labored in short gasps. At first glance, he was afraid his fears had been realized and Little Wolf had gotten away. But, upon a longer more concentrated look, his eyes caught the movement of a horse in a small stand of cottonwoods in the upper part of the valley.

His eyes locked on the trees and, while he did not sight Little Wolf or the woman, it was apparent the horse was hobbled or tied to a tree. The smile returned to his craggy features as he continued to pant for breath. He turned abruptly and squinted up at the sun—there were two, maybe three hours of daylight left. *He ain't planning to go nowhere before morning.* Tobin was sure of his quarry and would take advantage of his weakness. It was obvious that Little Wolf had stopped to hunt and take care of the woman. *That was a damn fool thing to do, Cheyenne. It's gonna cost you your scalp.*

He looked back the way he had come. Below him,

now standing by the side of the trail, his horse stood with its head down, not having taken a step. Satisfied that the animal wouldn't wander far, he faced the trail before him again and started down the slope toward the valley. It would not take him more than half of the remaining daylight hours to make it to the cotton-woods on foot. Recalling his only meeting with the tall white Cheyenne, he decided against jumping him immediately. No sense in taking a chance on getting shot. He would wait until darkness to make his move. In the meantime, he would make his way down to the lower end of the valley and find a place to get comfortable while he waited. *He ain't going noplace. He ain't gonna pick up and git this late in the day.*

"Scout up ahead," Sergeant Baskin called out.

Brice had already spotted the trooper waiting at the foot of a long narrow ravine for the column to catch up to him. Due to the steepness of the ridge they had just traversed, Brice had not sent flankers out. The column rode in single file behind him.

"What did you find, Morris?" Brice asked, when they were even with his scout.

"Looks like a trail through them mountains, proba-bly a hunting trail, used by the Injuns on their way to buffalo country." He dismounted and knelt close to the ground, tracing an imprint with his finger. "There's tracks here—two horses, neither one of 'em shod."

Brice looked at Baskin. The sergeant nodded his agreement and Brice sent the scout on ahead. "Stay about a quarter of a mile ahead, Morris. And watch yourself, dammit. I don't trust that damn Tobin any more than I do the renegade."

Brice had pushed the column pretty hard all morn-ing. He figured Tobin had three to four hours' start on them at the most, depending upon how much progress the half-breed made that night. There was bound to be some grumbling from his men, but he thought it imperative that they should not lose any more time. There was no pause for the noon meal.

The afternoon wore on as the troopers followed the old trail through the mountain pass. Approaching a sharp turn in the trail, Brice saw Morris waiting once again. He was holding the reins of Tobin's tan buckskin.

"Slap wore out," Morris announced as Brice and Baskin rode up. "I found him over yonder, pulling up grass." He pointed to a patch of tough bear grass.

"The son of a bitch is on foot," Baskin said, stating the obvious.

It was encouraging news for Brice. Tobin could not be far ahead of them now. His own horses were tired, but not to the point of exhaustion. He studied the sun for a moment. That was the problem immediately facing him. There was not much time left before it would be dark between these mountains. There was no sense in fretting over it. He had little choice—he could not lead his men stumbling through the mountains in the dark. They would make up as much time as possible before making camp. Maybe they would get lucky and overtake Tobin before then.

22

There was no moon, but enough starlight for a man to see his way, especially if that man was part panther. Tobin rose from the waist-high grass where he had rested while waiting for the cover of darkness. Looking around him in the deep, quiet night, he tasted the cool air and his nostrils flared as the excitement of the kill honed his senses. After a few moments, he checked his rifle and pistol to be certain they were ready. Then he set out for the stand of cottonwoods, making his way almost silently through the high grass.

Tobin's brain was barren soil for deep thinking, so thoughts of life's purpose never took seed there. He had set out to track and kill many times before, but he had never questioned his role as executioner. It bothered him not one bit whether his victims deserved killing. He only knew that it was the most enjoyable part of his job, a part he looked forward to, and one that brought a great measure of pleasure. Generally, he preferred a more open confrontation so he could enjoy the terror his victims knew before they died. With this white Cheyenne, however, he chose to forego that satisfaction and strike quickly, without warning.

He had little more than two hundred yards to cover before reaching the first trees that lined the shallow stream. Moving silently through the grass, placing each foot carefully, he in no way resembled the stumbling man who had recklessly ascended the steep trail

up the ridge earlier that day. One might grudgingly
admit to a savage grace in the way the huge man
stalked his prey.

His rifle cocked and ready, Tobin moved from tree to
tree until he spotted the red glow of dying coals in the
campfire. Under the shadow of the cottonwoods, he
had to pause and stare for a few moments longer before spying the sleeping bodies. *Ain't that dear,* he
thought, smiling to himself, *two little doves, all wrapped
up in a package.*

He was about to take another step when he was
halted by a low snort, and he abruptly jerked his head
to the side. The dark form of a horse stamped nervously under the trees. Tobin looked quickly back at
the sleeping lovers, ready to open fire. They didn't
move. He watched the bodies intently, looking for any
movement that would indicate they had heard. There
was none.

He stepped closer until he could clearly make out
the forms of the sleeping man and woman. Slowly, deliberately, he raised his rifle and took careful aim. In
the next instant, the quiet of the cottonwood grove was
shattered with the ear-splitting roar of the Winchester
as Tobin fired, cocked, and fired again, pumping bullets into the helpless bundle by the fire. He fired until
his rifle clicked on an empty chamber.

Cautious even after seeing every shot tear though
the tough elkhide, Tobin approached the riddled bed,
his eyes never leaving the hide. So that there would be
no question that the white Cheyenne was dead, he
would sever Little Wolf's head and present it to
Colonel Wheaton. The woman's fine black scalp
would be an excellent addition to his collection.

He stood over the bodies for a long moment, watching for any slight movement before pulling the wrap
of hide away. Convinced they were dead, he reached

down and lifted the elkskin and stood staring dumbfounded at two bullet-riddled cottonwood logs.

Like an animal caught in a trap, he realized at that
moment that he was doomed. Suddenly his veins were
filled with icewater and his spine became stiff as an
iron rod. Time seemed to pass in slow motion, allowing a thousand thoughts to flash across his stunned
brain. The thing that could never happen had happened. He had trapped a hundred men before this, re-
lying upon his cunning and superior strength. He
could not believe that he had been trapped this time.
He had walked right into it, outsmarted by the
Cheyenne for the second time.

In that frozen split-second, he steeled himself for the
impact of the bullet he knew was coming. When it did
not, he whirled around, angry at having been tricked,
his eyes searching desperately, straining to penetrate
the darkness. *I know you're here*, his instincts screamed
at him.

There was a faint sound to his left. He immediately
turned toward it, bringing his rifle up to fire—but it
had only been the soft popping from the glowing embers of the campfire. Then, when Tobin glanced up
from the fire, he saw him. The faint light afforded by
the flickering coals danced lightly across the phantom-
like features of the Cheyenne warrior, casting a shadowy veil about his naked shoulders. The warrior stood
there motionless, his arms down at his sides, a war axe
his only weapon, watching Tobin impassively.

Though puzzled by Little Wolf's defiant stance before him, Tobin did not hesitate to take his advantage.
He smiled and raised his rifle. "You shoulda kept on
running, renegade." With that, he pulled the trigger.
The metallic click reminded him that he had not re-
loaded the rifle. In angry disgust, he dropped the useless weapon and reached for the pistol in his belt. Less
than a second later, he heard himself yelp in pain as

the war axe struck his hand, sending the pistol flying across the campfire.

Both men sprang to retrieve it, but Little Wolf was quicker than his larger adversary. Diving across the fire, he rolled on the ground, snatched up the pistol and landed on his feet, facing Tobin. Tobin was stopped dead in his tracks by the sight of his own pistol, which was now leveled at his midsection. There followed a long eerie pause while the two faced each other. Tobin, again bracing for the bullet, was astonished when Little Wolf threw the pistol into the darkness behind him. The significance of the Cheyenne's action was not lost upon Tobin.

"So that's how it's gonna be." He could not repress the smile that spread across his face, for he knew the advantage had been returned to him. He drew the long skinning knife from his belt and lunged to meet the Cheyenne.

The impact of their bodies was like that of two bull elks, with Little Wolf recoiling backward a step from the superior weight of Tobin's body. Tobin grunted his satisfaction. No man had been able to stand up to him in hand-to-hand combat. With one huge hand, he held Little Wolf's wrist, nullifying the war axe. The other wrist was locked in Little Wolf's grip. They struggled against each other, their faces only inches apart. Tobin, confident in his overpowering strength, began to apply the pressure that would bend Little Wolf's back until it broke. After straining for several seconds, the sinister smile faded from Tobin's face. The Cheyenne would not bend. The veins stood out in the big tracker's neck as he summoned all the force he possessed. Yet it was to no avail. The tall Cheyenne warrior stood like a steel post, the hate and fury of years of pain and suffering flashing like sparks in his dark eyes. The moment of vengeance had at long last arrived.

Suddenly a cold chill ran the length of Tobin's spine, a feeling he had never experienced before. In a panic, he tore his wrist loose and stepped back. Little Wolf crouched and waited, his war axe ready. Desperate now, his swaggering confidence gone, Tobin feared for his life. In a sudden move, he lunged at Little Wolf with his knife. Little Wolf stepped deftly aside and brought the axe down in a crushing blow.

Tobin screamed in pain when the war axe came down on his forearm like a bolt of lightning out of the darkness. The sharp crack of the bone caused him to release his grip on the knife. Knowing he was fighting for his life, he tried to pick up the knife only to receive a second bone-smashing blow across his other forearm. He could not hold on to the weapon and it dropped to the ground. Terror like he had never tasted in his life before gripped Tobin's body as he staggered backward for a few steps, his useless arms dangling limply by his sides, still unable to clearly see his attacker in the dark shadows of the cottonwoods.

Cornered and knowing he was beaten, Tobin searched desperately from side to side, trying to see his executioner as Little Wolf circled him. He took another step backward, almost stumbling into the fire. Wanting to run but unsure of which direction to flee, he stepped around the softly glowing embers of the campfire, his fear overpowering the numbing pain in his arms. When he looked up again, he saw him.

Tobin gasped, unable to move. Facing him, Little Wolf stood tall and seemingly impassive, calmly watching the desperation of the helpless half-breed. Stunned and already dead in his mind, Tobin stood helpless, his eyes wide and unblinking. In the next instant, Little Wolf was suddenly upon him, before the huge man even knew he had moved. The war axe landed solidly in the side of Tobin's head and buried into the skull like a woodman's axe in a tree stump.

Little Wolf stepped back as the giant body slumped to the ground. He stared down at the lifeless mound for a few moments, his sober countenance disguising the fury that raced through his veins. "You will cause no more fear in this world," he pronounced softly, then took the half-breed's scalp. "You can now wander with no scalp in the spirit world."

Brice Paxton came up out of his blanket, awakened from a sound sleep by the series of rifle shots. He looked toward the fire where he could see others stirring also, and knew that it had not been a dream. It could only mean one thing—Tobin had found Little Wolf. *Maybe finishing him off,* he thought.

His immediate reaction was one of anger. He had hoped to prevent the savage Tobin from performing the cold-blooded execution he knew the baleful tracker planned. It appeared he might be too late. He wondered about the woman. "Sergeant!" he yelled at Baskin, who was already out of his blanket and coming to get his orders. "Saddle up! I want to find that bloodthirsty son of a bitch."

Baskin did as he was told and roused the men from their beds, knowing all the time that it was a useless exercise. That fact soon became painfully clear to his young lieutenant when he realized it was so dark in the narrow valley they camped in, that it was difficult to even find the picket line where the horses had been tied.

Conferring with his sentries, Brice found agreement as to the general direction the firing came from, but uncertainty as to how far away it might have been. Sergeant Baskin advised him that the men were ready to ride but he wasn't sure there was enough light to follow the trail.

Paul walked up to the fire leading Daisy. "Brice, have you taken leave of your senses? Are you really planning to head out in these mountains in this dark? You're liable to lead the whole detail off a cliff."

Brice made no reply. He stood there looking in one direction then another, as if seeking some sign of daybreak. He bent close to the fire and looked at his watch. There would be no daylight for at least two hours. He at once realized how impulsive he had been and felt a strong wave of embarrassment at having routed his sleeping troopers prematurely. Baskin and Paul stood there, waiting for him to make a decision.

"My mistake, Sergeant. I guess Lieutenant Simmons is right, we can't go stumbling around these bluffs in the dark. Have the men stand down. Leave the horses saddled. We'll ride at first light."

"Yessir." Baskin disappeared into the darkness, shaking his head.

When Baskin had left, Paul laughingly complained, "Dammit all, Brice, I just got to sleep about an hour ago."

"I'm sorry, Paul. I feel like a damn fool. I just want to get to that son of a bitch Tobin before he rides off and disappears in these mountains." He laughed at his own embarrassment. "I guess this is just one more thing Baskin can talk about with the other NCO's back at Lapwai."

23

Stingy fingers of dawn crept over the mountaintops and lit the tips of the tallest pines covering the slope where Little Wolf had made their camp. Below him, in the little valley, he could just begin to make out the separate forms of the cottonwoods that guarded the stream. He could not see Tobin's body yet, but he felt peace knowing it was there. The thought caused him to turn his head to gaze down at Rain Song, who was still sleeping. As if she felt his thoughts, she opened her eyes and gazed up at him. A smile immediately began to spread when she awakened to see her husband.

"Are you going to sleep all day?" He attempted to make a stern face for her but was unable to keep the smile from his face. "I was about to leave you here and go to King George's land alone."

"Do not tease." She got to her feet and came to him. Putting her arms around him, she held him tightly. "Never, *never* leave me again," she said, sighing.

He gave her shoulder an affectionate squeeze. "We must go now. The soldiers may be here soon, looking for the big one."

From shades of gray, the valley accepted the daily ritual of sunup and soon it was light enough to clearly see the grove of cottonwoods. Leading his horse, they made their way down to the valley once more to re-cover the elk robe they had made a bed with. Rain

Song shook her head and sighed as she held it up to examine the pattern of bulletholes, bullets that had been meant for them. They had very few supplies, so the robe would have to do until they found a place that was safe for them. Then Little Wolf would provide her with as many hides as she wanted.

Little Wolf retrieved Tobin's weapons and stripped his body of any items that might prove useful to them. He loaded them, along with the elk hide, onto his horse. "We need another horse," he said as he helped Rain Song up into the saddle. He climbed up behind her and turned the Appaloosa toward the north and a new life.

Walking the horse through the high grass of the valley floor, they were within a hundred yards of the tree-covered slopes again when they heard the short snap of a lead slug just over their heads, followed almost immediately by the report of the rifle. Looking back, he saw the advanced scout of the cavalry as he prepared to shoot again. This time, the shot was to the right of them. Behind the scout, galloping from the south end of the valley, he saw the column of troopers coming on fast.

He gave the Appaloosa his heels and the horse responded immediately, thrashing through the grass that whipped against his chest and forelegs. The soldiers were closer than he had suspected, and now they were going to have to run for it. The trees were not far and he made for them immediately. But he knew that his horse was carrying too great a load to attempt to outrun the soldiers. If he could gain just a little more time, he was confident he could lose them in the mountains.

They galloped into the trees with the troopers no more than two hundred yards behind. As soon as they entered the pines, Little Wolf leaped from the horse and quickly gave Rain Song instructions. "Go as fast as you can. Follow the slope up toward the ridge to your right. I'll hold the soldiers off until you are well away. I'll come after you as soon as I can."

"Little Wolf, no!" she started but he silenced her protests.

"Go!" he said sternly. "It's our only chance. I'll find you." He slapped the Appaloosa on the rump and the horse bolted away. Taking both his and Tobin's rifles, he ran to a position behind a fallen tree and prepared to stop the soldier's advance.

"He's gone to ground!" an excited trooper shouted. "We got him now!"

"Hold your fire!" Brice ordered and halted the column. He reined up beside the forward scout and dismounted, his eyes searching the trees for sight of the Cheyenne.

"He's holed up behind that big log yonder," the trooper said, pointing toward the fallen tree.

Baskin moved up to join Brice. "He's looking to pin us down out here in the grass while his woman gets away."

"Looks like," Brice answered. "Hold your fire," he repeated the order. "Where the hell is Tobin? Any sign of him?" he asked.

"No telling where that coyote is." Baskin began to get a little nervous when Brice gave no further orders for a few moments. "This here grass ain't the best cover for a skirmish line, Lieutenant."

Brice didn't answer him. Instead he continued to stare at the tree trunk where Little Wolf waited. *Exactly what is your crime? Protecting your wife, avenging your friends, protecting yourself from those who have hunted you. You have killed soldiers, but what could we expect, since you were raised a Cheyenne. Many of the men in my own company were once my enemies during the rebellion. They were given their freedom. Why not you? All you want is to be left alone.* He might be court martialed for doing it, but Brice knew what he must do.

"Brice, goddam, let's *do* something."

Brice looked quickly at Paul. "All right." Then he turned to Sergeant Baskin. "Sergeant, have the men fall back out of rifle range." He looked behind them. "Back to the edge of those cottonwoods by the stream."

Baskin didn't understand. "Fall back? Ain't we gonna go after that bastard? Hell, we've finally got him treed."

Brice shook his head. "No, we can't chase him anymore, and if we stay out here, he's gonna start picking us off one by one."

"Can't chase him anymore?" Baskin was thoroughly confused. "Why not?"

Brice looked at the sergeant with a cold eye. "Because he's in Canada. We can't legally follow him into Canada. Looks like he got away."

Baskin couldn't believe his ears. "Canada? Oh, nossir, we're a hundred miles from Canada, and, even if he was—"

Brice cut him off. "I believe you're confused, Sergeant. That's Canada." He turned to Paul. "Doesn't that look like Canada to you, Paul?"

Paul was mystified for a second, then he smiled broadly. "Why, yes it does. I believe you're right." In respect for his own hide, and the possibility of this conversation being recalled in a court martial at some future date, he thought to himself that he had only said that the country *looked* like Canada.

Baskin, slow in perceiving but eventually getting the message, finally realized what Brice was doing. *I reckon the poor bastard has had a pretty rough row to hoe with that damn Tobin riding his tail.* It really didn't matter one way or the other to him. If the lieutenant was

that soft in the heart, then so be it. He ordered his men
to fall back to the cottonwoods.

Puzzled by the soldiers' curious behavior, Little
Wolf held his fire and watched as the troopers withdrew to the grove of the trees where he had killed
Tobin. Certain that they had surrendered the advantage they had surely held, he did not stay to question
their judgment. With his two rifles in his hands, he left
the cover of the log and disappeared into the thick forest behind him.

Halfway up the ridge, he encountered Rain Song
waiting for him. "You did not run very far," he scolded
as he trotted up to her.

Her face reflected the joy she felt upon seeing her
husband again. Her cheeks streaked with tears, she
cried out, "I could not leave you again. If they kill you,
then they must kill me too!" When he was beside the
horse, she fell into his arms, almost causing him to lose
his balance. With her arms locked tightly around his
neck, she began to cry again. "I was afraid. I didn't
hear any shooting. I was afraid you had let them capture you so I could get away."

"Come," he said and, taking the horse's bridle in
hand, he started out along the ridge on foot. Rain Song
followed closely behind. When he reached a small
clearing that afforded an unrestricted view of the valley below them, he tied the horse in the trees and
moved to a position where he could watch the soldiers' activity. When Rain Song wondered why they
were not hurrying to escape the troopers, he explained
that he wanted to make sure they had given up the
chase. In reality, his curiosity was what held him there.
Why would more than twenty soldiers decide to quit
the chase against one man and one woman? He
glanced back at Rain Song and repeated a statement he
had made earlier. "We need another horse."

*   *   *

Back in the stand of cottonwoods, Tobin's body had been discovered. Brice and Paul stood over the lifeless form, staring down at the grotesque features of the ominous scout. With the absence of his scalp, the skin of his face seemed to droop into his beard, making him appear dark and even more sinister in death.

"Ain't that a pretty sight?" Sergeant Baskin joined them. "It's the best I've ever seen him. The country around here must suit him." The sergeant saw no need to speak reverently of the dead. To him it was no different than seeing a rattlesnake slain. "I reckon he finally met up with somebody who didn't back down to him."

Brice bent down to take a closer look. "Looks like Little Wolf killed him with an axe, the way his head's bashed in on this side." He glanced up at Baskin. "Wonder what all the shooting was we heard before daylight."

"From the looks of the way them logs is splintered and chewed up, I'd say ol' Tobin here was the one done the shooting. Thought he was murdering 'em in their sleep. He done a good job. Them logs shore look like they're dead right enough."

Brice didn't laugh at Baskin's rather macabre brand of humor, but he, like his sergeant, felt the world was now a wee bit better with Tobin's departure. Standing erect once more, he sighed, "Well, better get him in the ground."

Baskin assigned a detail to dig a hole to inter the oversized corpse with instructions, "Don't bury him too deep. We don't wanna cheat the buzzards out of a good meal."

Since Brice felt no urgency to return to Lapwai, he allowed his men to take a long break for the midday meal. Grateful for the opportunity to make a hot meal, the troopers soon had several small fires going and be-

fore long, the salt pork was frying. High above them
on the ridge, the aroma of the cooking meat drifted on
the wind to the man and woman watching them from
above.

"How long are you going to stay here?" Rain Song
asked impatiently.

"A while yet," was the answer.

It was past the middle of the afternoon when Brice
decided to have the troop mount and decamp, planning to make their evening camp in the same place
they had camped the night before. Rain Song and Little Wolf watched the soldiers file out of the cottonwoods, going back the way they had come that
morning.

Rain Song got to her feet. "We go now." It was not a
question.

Little Wolf did not move for a few moments. Then
he got up and stretched. "We will follow them for a
while."

"Why?" She could not understand.

"We need another horse," was the simple answer.

Brice Paxton threw his blanket aside and pulled his
boots on. The aroma of boiling coffee reached his nostrils, triggering an immediate need for the hot black
liquid. Looking around him, he saw his men stirring
from their beds. The night air had been chilly there in
the deep mountain pass, and some of the men had
used their saddle blankets in addition to the one each
usually carried. Brice felt good for no apparent reason.
His boots on, he got up and stretched long and hard
before going over to the fire Sergeant Baskin had
going.

Every man carried a tin cup to boil his coffee in, after
smashing the green coffee beans with a rock. Most of
the men wrapped the beans in a cloth of some kind to
do the grinding. Since it was an individual chore, some

less fastidious, used a sock. Baskin carried a coffeepot when in the field, so Brice and Paul usually shared the brew with the sergeant. Brice was blowing on his first cup of the steaming liquid when a trooper came up to inform him that they were missing a horse.

When Brice and Baskin went down to check on it, they found all the horses tied to the picket line, or so they thought. But a quick count assured them that they were one short.

"Hell, I counted 'em and there's a horse for every man," Baskin said.

"You're forgetting. We picked up Tobin's horse. We should have one extra."

"Damn, you're right, we should have an extra horse," Baskin said. "I'll have somebody scout around, see if it got loose somehow."

Brice and Paul stood by the fire and finished breakfast while some of the men searched for the missing mount. After a half hour, Baskin came back to tell them the search was in vain. The horse had obviously been stolen and there was little doubt as to who the thief was.

"It was Daisy," Baskin said, attempting unsuccessfully to keep from smiling—his eyes glued to Paul Simmons's face in gleeful anticipation of the outburst that was sure to come. He was not to be disappointed.

"What?" Paul exploded. "Daisy! Are you sure?"

"Yessir," Baskin tried to deadpan, but the smile spread across his weathered features.

"Oh, no—oh, shit," Paul groaned. "That whole picket line of horses, and he took the only one in the entire army that doesn't hate me." He turned to Brice for help. The desperation in his eyes caused Brice to smile broadly. "Oh, it's funny all right." Brice and Baskin broke into laughter but Paul could not appreciate the irony. "What the hell am I gonna do?"

"Don't worry, Paul. You won't have to walk back.

You can ride that big buckskin of Tobin's. He looks gentle enough."

More than twelve miles to the north, Rain Song swayed in rhythm with the gentle motion of the docile mare as she followed Little Wolf's Appaloosa down a wooded hillside. Before them, the snow-capped mountains in the distance stood tall like silent sentinels, promising protection in their vast wilderness. This time she knew they would find their place. She could feel it in her bones.

Little Wolf looked back at his wife and smiled when her eyes brightened in response. Like her, he had a feeling deep inside that this new land would bring them the peace they had sought for so many years. While he felt at peace with himself now, there was also a feeling of sadness in his heart. For his mind journeyed back to the early years and the many souls who had died along the way—friends who had ridden the warpath with him, loved ones who had been sacrificed for the white man's Manifest Destiny. But it was a white man who filled most of his thoughts, more so than even his brother, Tom—Squint Peterson, the old scout who longed most for the peace Little Wolf and Rain Song were now in search of. He missed Squint—he would always miss him—the huge grizzly bear of a man who never gave up in his efforts to persuade Little Wolf to return to the white man's world. Looking back at Rain Song again, he knew one thing to be true, *I am Cheyenne. I can never be anything else.*

He turned his face toward the north once more, and with his wife behind him, Little Wolf, Cheyenne, son of Spotted Pony, rode down into a green valley that would lead them to a land of shining mountains and lakes shimmering in the morning sun, of mighty rivers and rushing streams, a land where a weary warrior might rest.